A SENSIBLE WOMAN

Also by Fiona Cameron

White Cranes Dancing
Containment
The Swan Widow
By Heart

A SENSIBLE WOMAN

Fiona Cameron

Flying Swan Press

www.flyingswanpress.com

This edition first published in the UK 2016 by
Flying Swan Press
123 Irish Street
Dumfries DG1 2PE

ISBN   978-0-9933314-1-1 (e-book)
ISBN 978-0-9933314-2-8 (paperback)

CHAPTER ONE

'Rock bottom's not the worst place to start, Archie; the only way out is up.'

Mabel Mountjoy's pug gazed up at her and wagged his ridiculous curl of a tail half-heartedly. The pronouncements he liked best from his mistress included the words 'good boy', 'walk' or 'dinner'.

They stood side by side at the back door, looking down the long, lushly-planted garden towards the cottage. Mabel sighed. It was a chill, glittering forenoon at the end of January and she'd had an epiphany: she was living the wrong life.

She felt an uncharacteristic cold sweat of panic. Forty-five next birthday. An anniversary which the Oxford English Dictionary defined as the start of middle age. Had she wasted the best years of her life, with looking after Father, and sticking with Roddy for a decade too long? When Father was alive, her existence had been like a nostalgic and dated afternoon play on Radio Four; something with a title along the lines of 'The Daughter of the Retired Colonel'. She'd always thought there would be more *time*.

A fresh start, that's what she needed. Free of Roddy, free of Roddy's paintings. Free of the false hope of a megabucks sale for Roddy's damn *Miró*. She could sell up. Travel the world, alone; wake up in places where the police sirens sounded different (not that you heard those frequently in Kirkcudbright; a siren signified an *event*). Not quite alone: she'd only travel to countries where small pugs were welcome.

Mabel wasn't given to feeling sorry for herself, and she was normally skilful at concealing her moods. Most of her acquaintances would have agreed. 'Always looking on the bright side, our Mabs,' they'd say. 'A glass-half-full gal. And wise enough never to have got herself tied to a man. Such a sensible woman.' And they'd narrow their eyes in envy. Last Hogmanay, she had overheard Briony Hall, the woman she counted as her best friend describe her as 'a nippy sweetie'. She swept the memory from her mind; after all, she'd always known that Briony was jealous of her.

She should try to open her gallery earlier than usual this year, in an effort to boost her bank account. But what was the point? There were no tourists around so early in the season, and a handful of sales before Christmas was usually as good as it got for local trade. December had been a good month. She'd shifted more stock than normal – even if it had all been prints – and filled a plethora of framing orders: photos of people's children and grandchildren; paintings brought triumphantly home from primary school. She did all her own framing these days; she hadn't been able to justify keeping on the girl she used to employ. Single-handedly, she'd been responsible for cutting employment in Kirkcudbright by two, because she'd had to let her cleaning woman go too, more than a year ago.

January was always a dead month in business, as well as in the garden. Perhaps February would bring a further sprinkling of bread-and-butter jobs, but they would barely cover the cost of heating the gallery. She'd open in March, as usual.

In the early years, Roddy's work had earned enough to keep them in some style. The fact that Father had drawn a healthy pension hadn't hurt either. Over and over during the past year, Roddy had promised he'd cough up what he owed in rent and keep – as well as what he'd borrowed from her – when his Miró was authenticated and sold.

'The last auction, one of his went for seven million,' he'd say, rubbing his hands together. 'We'll be minted, old girl. Our ship will come in, you'll see.'

Our ship. *Our* ship?

'I suppose I'd better see if the bear still has a sore head,' she told the pug. 'You can't come with me, because he won't let you in. Stay, Archie. Good boy.'

Mabel headed down the garden towards the cottage where her tenant and one-time lover, the Roddy McCulloch formerly known as an artist, lived. She stopped in passing to bury her nose in the soft pink flowers of a viburnum that had been in bloom since November; an oasis of fragrance and delicate colour amid the desert of a Scottish garden in winter. She noticed the snowdrops nestling among the feet of the shrubbery, and smiled grimly: they were a little late this year. Picking her way across a strip of chilly earth, she laid her hand on the reassuring bulk of the stone wall that bounded the garden. It always seemed much older than the house, as if it had been there forever. Touching it brought both comfort and courage.

Time to have it out with Roddy, once and for all. She'd asked him twice already to find another place to live, but he showed no signs of packing up his possessions. To sweeten the pill, she intended to offer to cook a meal for him once more. In December, for the first time she could remember, Mabel hadn't decorated the house for Christmas. There didn't seem any *point*. She'd invited Roddy to dinner, then chucked him out soon afterwards, so she could go to bed with a book. She'd presented him with a bottle of malt to get rid of him.

She braced herself for the culmination of a quarrel that had been brewing for weeks; the type of fracas she knew the neighbours could overhear.

With those flapping ears in mind, she kept her temper for the first five minutes, while she explained that she couldn't afford to keep a man any longer, since she'd got a dog. She asked Roddy if he'd made a conscious decision never to dry out between binges, and he replied that there was nothing to sober up for. 'I'm not feeling the love,' he added.

'Love?' she yelled in exasperation. 'You've had nothing but love from me for the past two decades. Why else would I keep you?'

All her resolve scattered to the four winds when he chortled, 'Temper, temper, Mabs', because it combined the nickname she suddenly loathed, and the memory of her father's critical voice. Those three words marked the defeat of her effort to control the red mist rising before her eyes.

'Everything you are, you owe to me,' she yelled, her

cheeks turning a most unflattering shade of rose madder. 'I *made* you, you drunken lout.'

Roddy McCulloch regarded her coolly – or as coolly as a man with a quart-sized hangover could manage. 'What have we here? Ah, Miss Mabs Mountjoy. A woman of substance. A patron of the arse.' He drew himself up to his full height of five foot six and farted loudly and odiferously. 'Ex-squeeze me. Better out than in.'

Mabel screwed up her nose. How in God's name could she ever have slept with *that*? She slewed her eyes away from his dull, bloodshot ones. *Like the eyes of a dead trout.* Not that she had ever inspected a dead trout too closely.

'You are disgusting. Is this my reward for supporting you all these years, for using my gallery to sell no one's work but yours – in the days when it did sell, when you were still sober enough to hold a brush straight?' *And for allowing you into my bed for much of that time.* 'Have you looked at yourself in the mirror recently? Why have you let yourself go to such an extent?'

She felt a pang of pity and remorse amidst the anger. *Am I the one who's transformed him into this?* But that was ridiculous. He had free will, like all men. He'd achieved it by himself. She dug her nails into her palms.

'Sophie doesn't find me disgusting,' said Roddy smugly.

'Sophie Dempster's a scrubber.' Mabel felt a fresh stab of guilt. Sophie was just a kid. It was the concupiscence of men that had made her what she was.

He hooted with laughter again. 'It's her ma that's the scrubber. She scrubbed your fucking floors because you were too far up your own backside to do them for yourself.

Just as well you have to do your own cleaning now, Mabs. Shift some of the lard off you.'

'You pervert. The girl's hardly out of her teens.'

' "The girl" is serving her apprenticeship in the oldest profession, I'd say. Down the harbour every night, that one, looking for sailors fresh off the fishing boats while they've still some cash in their pouches.' The artist wriggled his shoulders and rubbed his bearded chin. 'You should try taking a long, hard look at yourself, Mabs. That's how you like it, isn't it – long and hard? You were keen enough to have me in your bed when you were getting what you wanted most nights. Why do you think I can't get it up any longer for you?'

'Advanced alcoholism,' said Mabel.

But the answer lay deeper. When they were both younger, the fact that he was fifteen years older than her had been thrilling. Nowadays it wasn't. End of story.

'You don't love me, Mabs. You never did. You don't know what love is,' said Roddy.

And in that moment, she was willing to believe it was true, because her heart was bubbling over with an emotion as far removed from love as possible.

'You've turned into a pernickety old maid,' he added. 'Better get shot of that mangy cur and get yourself a cat. You think a screeching harridan's attractive to a man?'

She headed for the door. Enough of this nonsense; it was damaging for the nerves. 'A man! Is that what you call yourself?'

'Slag!' he bawled after her.

How *dare* he call Archie a mangy cur? His coat had the

opulent texture of the most expensive plush, and he was a far more faithful and rewarding companion than Roddy had turned out to be. Many's the peaceful evening she had spent listening to Charles Aznavour CDs with no one but that sweet, quiet little animal for company. Not that Archie was particularly quiet. She'd hankered after a pug since she was a teenager, but Father hadn't tolerated dogs any more than he had cats. Her first act on the day after he was buried was to contact every Kennel Club registered pug breeder in Scotland. In the end, she hadn't needed to wait long for Archie, and had to travel no further than Ayrshire.

Sometimes, as she listened to the little dog puffing and snuffling, she wondered if she'd been wrong to fall in love with his adorable button nose and squashed face. After all, it merely encouraged the breeders, and perpetuated the fate of generations of pugs who wheezed. But no: love like this could never be wrong, because it was so assuredly mutual.

Mabel marched back through the main house, stopping to lift the mail from the mat, selecting the only item she didn't recognise. A handwritten envelope pushed through the letterbox, addressed simply to 'Miss Mountjoy'. The words withered her like an early frost. When Father was still alive, the tradesmen would have called her 'Mabel', or even 'Mabs'. It was the written estimate from the builder for a thorough overhaul of the roof. Without opening the envelope, she knew it would be a figure she couldn't afford. She'd known that since the day when Davie Ford had crawled all over the slates, come back down sucking his teeth, and told her that no more patch-up jobs were possible. If he'd been about to mention a more reasonable price, he would have told her to her face. A written estimate was always bad news. No point in trying to get other local firms to quote either; they wouldn't bid against one another.

The only other mail, apart from a phone bill, was a flier from the DVD shop in Newton Stewart. *The Forty Year Old Virgin*. It caught her eye. She glanced at the potted reviews. *Funniest film this decade*. Och, it was about a *man*. What else had she expected? If it had been about a woman, it wouldn't have been billed as a comedy.

She swallowed hard, ripped open Davie's envelope and glanced at the figure. Then she tossed it aside, collected a hat and jacket from the hall-stand and put Archie on his lead.

She headed briskly along the pastel-painted High Street of Kirkcudbright, the little dog trotting to keep up. The sunlight held no warmth. She'd attended a talk on climate change in the Millennium year: some specialist waxing eloquent about the prospects of vineyards clothing the slopes of Criffel by 2040. Fat chance. Last year, she hadn't even been able to ripen the tomatoes in her greenhouse.

She walked the length of the High Street, towards the harbour with its rusty blue-and-white scallop boats dancing on the incoming tide.

'A rising tide lifts all boats.' Where had she heard that? Didn't matter. Some were past being lifted. Some were useless hulks, suitable for nothing beyond the breaker's yard.

When she'd come home in 1986 after the brief and dispiriting experiment of teaching in Glasgow, her city friends had asked her how she could bear to bury herself in the South-West, where time had ground to a halt in the 1950s. But she loved it. She loved Ashers, the large family house where she'd lived all her life, and above all she adored her garden. *Rus in urbe*, wasn't that the term? It was safe for Archie, and not overlooked, though in the heart of town.

Ashers' roof leaked, the central heating had a mind of its own, and the place was far too big for one person. In the Russian revolution, it would have been commandeered and used to house half a dozen families. But it had been in the Mountjoy family for generations. She couldn't be the one to let it go – although one must face facts: she had no one to pass it on to. Father's only sister had never married. The Mountjoy twig on the family tree was grown exceeding thin. Mabel had long since accepted that she'd never have children of her own. She'd go, and leave not a trace on the world, not the tiniest footprint; a barren stock, like Good Queen Bess. Maybe she should start a women's housing co-operative? There had been an article about those in the *Guardian* the previous week.

In the cold, scarred light of a winter's day, Kirkcudbright was a stifling place; almost oppressive. If you scratched your backside as you got out of bed, everyone knew about it before lunchtime. And yet, and yet – there was an element of satisfaction and comfort in being the big hen in a small henhouse. If she was honest with herself, there were ample grounds for self-blame: she'd relished looking after Father all these years, able to please herself, the chatelaine without the hassle of a husband, running her own business, a stalwart of the Townswomen's Guild

(though she'd never made it to President; Briony Hall had hogged the position for herself these past four years. As bad as a Middle Eastern despot.)

Perhaps she'd end up like Miss Haversham. All of a sudden, the gap between forty-five and eighty-five seemed terrifyingly narrow. Any day now, she'd be putting in her order at the newsagents for *The People's Friend* instead of *Vogue*.

Friends. That was the answer. All the magazines were full of it: the importance of a substantial and substantive circle of friends for the modern, independent woman. She'd allowed herself to become too dependent on the company of two needy elderly men.

Mabel didn't receive many visitors. Since Father died (and for many years before) she'd not been one for having dinner guests. She'd always found the Continental idea of dining out with friends much more civilised and congenial than the stressful business of entertaining them at home. Cooking wasn't something she positively enjoyed – though she was a more than competent baker. In any case, the range of ready meals for one you could find these days was most appealing, and who was to know? Who could judge her, as long as she travelled to Dumfries to buy them in Marks & Spencer's Food Hall? And after she'd eaten her solitary meal in the kitchen, with no more judgemental companion than Archie, there was always the comforting thought that there would be another human being nearby, once the pubs closed and Roddy was safely back in the cottage for the night. She'd watch from behind the kitchen blind, to see his light go on.

Not that she was one of those ridiculous women who're afraid of things that go 'eek' in the night. Ashers was an old house. Its nocturnal rumblings and creakings as it settled to sleep after the boiler juddered to a halt were not for the faint-hearted. Strong. She'd always been strong. It was a matter of necessity.

Mabel thrust the parlous condition of the heating system to the back of her mind. Father had never been one to spend money on fripperies like a modern boiler, but it hadn't seemed to matter while he was alive, and the gas bills weren't a problem. What she had closed her mind to was the inevitability that his pension would die with him. So unfair. If she'd been his wife – the same fickle one who'd betrayed him all those years ago – she'd have been entitled to a substantial income in her own right. But she was merely his daughter.

She'd been coasting, ever since the funeral; that was the truth of the matter. She resisted the urge to pick up a reconstituted stone urn sitting on a doorstep and hurl it through the nearest window, to feel she'd made something *happen*.

She wanted to *live*. Yet she didn't want to leave the town. It had represented home all her life, even during the years when she was away at university. She craved the financial independence to travel a little, to rebuild her business, to refurbish her home. She also wanted a man in her life, but she was a pragmatist: the chances of a woman over forty meeting a suitable man in the Stewartry of Kirkcudbright in 2007 were nil. All the good ones were already spoken for, and the typical widower was over eighty.

As for a retread (that's how she thought of divorced men, with their inevitable burdens of school fees and alimony) – no thank *you*. She'd tried that once. Once was enough.

She turned the corner past the handsome war memorial, onto Castle Street, heading for Penelope's, the dress shop run by her friend, Sylvia Clearthorn. That was normally the best way to lift her spirits: buy herself a little something.

One of the perks of living in Kirkcudbright was more than one place to buy pretty, stylish clothes. No shoe shop, but having to drive to Lockerbie and take the train to Edinburgh for the delights of shops like Rogersons was a small price to pay. On her last sortie, she'd found delectable, elegant high-heeled shoes made in Spain (of all places), priced so as not to give her indigestion, and moulded so as not to pinch the joints of her big toes. She sighed to herself. She'd never thought twice about what she was putting on her feet until her last birthday. Feet weren't something you *noticed*. Ever since she'd turned forty-four, they'd been making their presence felt: a twinge in a toe one day, a discomfort under the arch the next. She had to face it: perhaps her days for stylish shoes were over, except on special occasions. Sensible ones it would be, from now on. Irritating, because her pretty legs and neat ankles were among her best features, and she suited high heels.

She sighed again. All downhill from here. Once the signs of ageing crept into your consciousness, there was no dismissing them. She'd felt so *young* at the Millennium, so full of hope and possibility; Father was the only one who'd been downhearted, mourning the death of the old century.

'The end of the era when we *cared* about one another,' he'd murmured, a sob in his voice. 'It's that creature Blair who's killed all decency.' (He'd smiled sardonically at the revellers who danced in the streets after the 1997 General Election; one of the few men who'd not been surprised by the speed thereafter with which we found ourselves embroiled in the Iraq war).

A short seven years on, and she was officially middle-aged. Instead of promising roads to the future, she seemed to be stuck in a cul-de-sac, and the Middle East was in a worse state than ever, now that Saddam Hussein was dead.

She passed the corner newsagents, and glanced at its billboard. *Rod Stewart to marry again.* He'd fathered another child a couple of years before, hadn't he, although he was well over sixty?

The situation for women was both ironic and unfair. As you reached the age where you no longer had to worry about the consequences of sex, you ceased to be of interest to men.

Even the terminology was chauvinistic and ill balanced. A man of a certain age who'd retained one iota of attractiveness was a silver fox – a creature both beautiful and desirable. What did they call women in their middle years who lusted after younger men? Cougars. Mabel racked her brains to visualise a cougar. It certainly didn't sound attractive. Ugly and predatory. Probably smelly. Or was that civet cats? Something foul-breathed and with mange is what the word conjured up for her. She'd die before she'd ever be a cougar. In any case, to be the type to attract younger men (other than weirdos) you needed to be rich or famous or both, and Mabel was facing one fact as fast as she could bear: she was anything but wealthy, these days.

She squared her shoulders, straightened her back, and gave herself a mental whack. You must never allow the black dog to creep up on you unawares. Never be needy, or pathetic, or tearful, or self-pitying, or impotent. Never be like Annette Gibbons who'd lived at the head of the close when Mabel was at school: after her husband had decamped with a twenty-year-old, she'd phone people (including Father) at four in the morning, weeping. *Oh God, don't let me turn into that. I'd rather be dead – are you listening?*

She swung briskly into the doorway of Penelope's, and decided that it was too cold to leave the pug tied to the lamppost outside. The shop was empty anyway.

As she ran her hands over a lacy cashmere scarf in subtly graduated tones of catkin green and pale flame, her friend emerged from the back shop, drying her hands.

'Haven't seen you for days – are you OK Mabel? You're looking rather flushed.'

'It's freezing out there. You don't mind Archie? He's sitting down, good as gold.'

Sylvia glared at the dog.

'You don't really want me to put him outside, do you?'

'I suppose he doesn't do any harm. At least he doesn't smell.'

'How much is this?' said Mabel, trying to mollify her friend with the prospect of a sale. She turned over the price ticket and glanced at it. She blinked and re-read the hand-written figure.

'Best hand-spun cashmere, and a hundred per cent

pure,' said Sylvia. 'It's from organic goats. I could do you a wee bit off since my January sale's newly finished – say fifteen per cent?'

Mabel released the scarf gently and reluctantly. What on God's good earth were organic goats? 'I mustn't. I haven't sold a single painting since Christmas. Not a sausage.'

'Roddy's work still not finding buyers?'

She wasn't sure that Sylvia's sympathy was genuine. She'd had a notion of Roddy herself when he first arrived in Kirkcudbright almost two decades before. Mind you, all the women had fancied him then, even the married ones, because in those days he was trim and muscular, his lush, curly hair and neat beard were still black as a raven's back, and his eyes were clear. Nowadays, their startling blue – the blue of the Adriatic in June – was scarcely noticeable, so bloodshot were the whites.

'Roddy's work hasn't been finding buyers for years. I even tried shifting some through McTears auction in Glasgow. Not one met the reserve. Yet look at the prices some artists are fetching these days. I saw a print of Ian Hamilton Finlay's *Rock Rose* sold for more than two thousand recently.'

'It's because he's died,' said Sylvia. 'As soon as artists die, the value of their work goes up astronomically.'

Mabel made a sound that might have been a chortle or a sob. 'What would you recommend – hitting him on the head? A pillow over the face? Or something in his whisky, that'd be the thing. Arsenic.'

Sylvia glowered at her. 'Where would you be able to get

arsenic in Kirkcudbright? You shouldn't joke about it. Poor Roddy.'

Mabel stooped to caress Archie's ears. Hadn't she read an article somewhere about a Victorian murderess who soaked fly-papers in water to extract the arsenic? No signature required in the poisons book. *Can you still buy fly-papers?* Roddy had a disgusting habit of licking and nibbling the ends of his paintbrushes. They all had marks in them from his small, sharp ferret's teeth. Maybe if she dabbed a tiny amount on each... *Stop it, Mabel! What a ridiculous idea. As if anyone poisons her lover nowadays.*

' "Poor Roddy"? He's been trying to kill himself with drink these past ten years.'

Didn't seem to have worked though. Because she'd always nursed him, kept him warm, looked after him, fed him to get his strength back, poured away the bottles of rot-gut whisky he turned to when he ran out of money for his favourite tipple, hidden his fags, tried to interest him in a healthy diet and pursuits.

Sylvia was shrugging impatiently. 'Kick him out then. His work, I mean. Clear the walls for other artists' work, before this year's busy season. Do you want this scarf or not?' She held the sumptuous gossamer against Mabel's neck. 'It suits you. Brings out the colour in your hair.'

She mustn't. Not even with bank interest above five per cent, because there was so little in the damn bank in the first place...

'How would you ever wash it without spoiling the lace effect?'

Sylvia tutted again. 'You can wash cashmere.'

'I know that, but…'

'How often do you have to wash a scarf, Mabs? Are you taking it then?'

'No. Och, yes. I like it.'

She knew she deserved a treat. What the hell. The cost of the scarf was a mere bagatelle compared to what Davie was asking to overhaul the roof; the buckets collecting drips in the attic would have to stay in place meantime. Twenty-two thousand. Where was she supposed to find twenty-two thousand?

She'd get a job, that was the solution. She smirked to herself as she punched in her credit card pin number. A job? What jobs were there in Kirkcudbright, or even in Dumfries? Barmaid? Women over forty found it difficult to get decent jobs at the best of times. Time to dispose of one of the Vettrianos Roddy had persuaded her to buy in 1988, with her inheritance from her aunt.

As she walked briskly home, the pug under her arm to save his little legs, she gave herself another mental clout. She'd hang onto her personal art collection meantime. It was always important to keep ones investments intact, against a rainy day. Thus far, it was merely drizzling.

Tomorrow, she'd do whatever was necessary to sell one of Roddy's over-busy daubings to pay for her little treat. If she lowered the reserve far enough, surely the auctioneers could shift at least a couple? Then she'd carry out the threat she'd made countless times before. She'd evict him from her cottage, and redouble her efforts to get shot of all his work, clear the decks. She'd go on a diet – not that she needed to lose *much*; she'd never get back to being a size ten with her build, but a twelve would be nice. She'd build a new life, with a watertight roof.

Tomorrow and tomorrow and tomorrow.

It all sounded so exhausting. If only something would *happen* so that the value of his work went through the ceiling, like Ian Hamilton Finlay's. Not a pillow or arsenic; that was too silly for words. Spontaneous combustion. Lightning strike. *Nonsense*! No matter how he tried her patience, she wouldn't wish anything *bad* on him. After all, she had spent the greater part of her adult life as good as married to him.

As she turned into the close, Mabel basked in a glow of pride when she saw her home. Sanctuary. The most important thing in her world, bar Archie.

The morning's clear sky had clouded over. Mabel prepared for another trip to the attic, to make sure the array of pans and buckets was still containing the influx.

CHAPTER TWO

Mabel managed to avoid Roddy for most of the following day, while she deliberated how best to tackle him. But she couldn't put it off forever. Time to act decisively. After she finished her afternoon tea (alone; she'd made sure the back door had remained locked), she wound her new scarf round her neck (so cosy, yet it weighed no more than a swan feather!) and headed down the garden in the gathering dusk. She could hear he was at home. His ghastly music was blaring through the open front door. Stuff suitable for teenagers, not a man in his sixties. No smoke from the chimney. He'd let the stove go out again, despite the fact she gave him free firewood as well as a free house. The man didn't seem to feel the cold – another effect of the sauce, no doubt.

He was through in the end of the cottage he used as a studio, standing in front of an unfinished canvas in the mirk, brush in hand. When had he last completed a single painting, far less one that was saleable?

She was assailed by a pang of regret. In the old days, she'd help him when he got stuck. Maybe she didn't have the skill of laying colour on canvas, but she had a good eye. Once upon a time, he'd respected her judgement, and hadn't resented advice.

Long, long ago.

'Why do you do that?' She tried unsuccessfully to keep the irritation out of her voice. 'Paint on when it's almost dark.' She switched on the light. 'Is that not better?'

Roddy didn't move away from the easel. 'Can't see with artificial light. It kills the colours. Murders them.'

Infuriating man! He wouldn't turn the light on to paint, but he'd go out and leave everything else switched on. The greedy electric radiator in the bedroom; his damn CD player; his TV set. Even on one occasion, Mabel's iron. It had burnt a hole right through the end of her only ironing board – and since when did Roddy ever iron anything for himself anyway?

She could smell the booze on his breath from across the room.

'We need to talk,' she said.

He turned, none too steady on his feet, and grinned at her. Amazing, the way he'd kept his teeth so white, despite his lifestyle.

'I thought you might be coming to suggest we need some rumpy-pumpy,' he said. 'You know I didn't mean what I said yesterday, you randy old thing. You're not a slag. I still have feelings for you. I'd manage to get in the mood if you let me into that nice, warm bed of yours again.'

'I want you off my property.'

'It'll be a different story when my Miró sells.'

'You can stick your Miró where the sun don't shine. It's a fake anyway. The Rodriguez man's taking you for a ride – I assume he's not doing all this "research" on your behalf for free? Who's paying for that?'

Roddy shrugged in the maddening way he had.

'I'll need to get another wee sub from you. But it'll be worth it. We're on the last lap now. Would you let me into your bed for a couple of million, Mabs?'

'The lab report said the paint proves nothing, one way or the other.'

'Ah, but it doesn't *dis*prove anything either. Come on, honeybee, give me a wee cuddle. Look how hard I've been working.'

She glanced with curled lip at the almost-virgin canvas on the easel, then at the other half-completed ones stacked higgledy-piggledy against the walls.

'Working! You haven't finished a single piece of work in the last year.'

'Bugger me, Mabs. You're forever telling me no one wants to buy the fucking things anyway. All they want nowadays is giclée prints of Jolomo.'

He looked so desolate that for a nano-second she pitied him.

'That's why I've been trying to persuade you to try something new. Artists do that. They don't paint the same damn thing all their lives.'

Though of course, some do. Some hit the winning streak and churn out pot-boilers decade upon decade. If it ain't broke, don't fix it. But Roddy *was* broken. He'd lost whatever it was he had in the glory days. The critics didn't mention him, never mind criticise him.

Mabel glared once more at the pathetic object on the easel. She could do better herself. *I wouldn't buy his bloody work: why should anyone else?*

'Put that fucking light off again. It's hurting my eyes.'

She flicked the switch so viciously, she felt it begin to separate from the wall.

'Time after time, I've begged you to pull yourself together. Stop drinking. Stop… whatever else it is you're on. Get well again. But you won't make the least effort. So I want you out of here. Now.'

Out of my house. Out of my life. Out of my heart.

'Ooooh!' Roddy walked towards her, swaying on his feet, the paint-laden brush still clutched in his hand. 'Can't you wait? Come here and give me a kiss then, see if we can't get things stirring in the trouser department.'

Disgusted, she pushed him away, and he snatched at her clothing. A smear of black oil paint fouled the new scarf from her shoulder to the tip.

'You clumsy bastard, now look what you've done.'

She slapped him across the face, with all the strength she could muster. He almost lost his balance, but Mabel had already turned on her heel. Not a chance she was going to give him the satisfaction of seeing her in tears (of rage as well as disappointment; she could be honest with herself in the darkness).

Mabel entered her own house, fed Archie and fondled his ears for a moment, drank a glass of water to stop her hands shaking, dried her eyes, then fetched her bag and car-keys, tossed the ruined scarf onto the chair by the door, and drove towards Newton Stewart. Just beyond Creetown, she pulled over and phoned her friend Nancy McGillivray, the poet, inviting her to have dinner at the Creebridge Hotel. Not that she saw her above once a year, but she didn't know anyone else in that neck of the woods, and she felt the need for both company and distance between herself and Kirkcudbright. She'd use up the hour until half-five doing a little shopping in Sainsbury's.

Nancy seemed both pleased and surprised to have been invited, and Mabel made a mental note to be more attentive to her – after all, her friend didn't drive, while *she* had the luxury of not only her own home but her own transport. She had also resolved not to use the evening as an excuse to vent her anger against Roddy. However, she found herself pouring out her heart to Nancy: not only about her former lover, but about her life in general, including the loneliness she often felt.

Her friend sat back in amazement. 'But Mabs, you're one of the most popular women I know. You have so many friends! I envy you that.'

Mabel wanted to say that she'd realised over the past few weeks that she had plenty of *acquaintances*…but that would have seemed mean-spirited and self-pitying, so she merely muttered something about counting her blessings, smiled brightly and ordered another glass of J20 (she had always observed drink driving rules as scrupulously as any Scandinavian).

'It's great that you're getting rid of Roddy at last,' added Nancy. 'You know what I've always told you about attracting abundance. You have to clear out the old to make room for the new. It's the same with men.' She grinned broadly, and winked.

Mabel fairly howled with laughter at the very idea (not that she'd ever put Nancy's advice on clearing out old clothes into practice either). 'You'll be telling me to try speed dating next.'

Her friend looked flabbergasted. 'No I won't. It sounds ghastly. Quite wrong for women like us.'

'So what's "right" for us then? An ad in the Times?'

They spent a merry half-hour composing suitable wording, with increasingly improbable acronyms, on the back of a napkin.

'What's GHANA?' asked Mabel.

'Glaswegian ham-artists needn't apply.'

'And MHOT?'

'Must have own teeth.'

'And GFMTOAN?'

'Good for more than once a night.'

'Nancy!'

By the time they parted, Mabel had a stitch in her side from laughing. She could face Roddy without a qualm. She'd just keep thinking about Ghana.

When she got home it was almost midnight; the cottage was in darkness.

'Of course there are no lights,' she told herself. 'He'll be lying dead drunk; likely as not he's pissed in his bed yet again. He's not my responsibility in any case.'

She stood at the back door, watching the little pug snuffle through last autumn's dead leaves, then called him in.

'Tomorrow,' she told herself. 'Tomorrow morning, I'll

knock on the door, see if Roddy's started packing up.'

By then possibly he'd have dried out a little, in every way.

When she'd let him back into her bed that disastrous night almost eighteen months ago, she'd realised what it felt like to share a duvet with a man you really didn't want to sleep with. To feel the nausea rise in your throat at the thought you'd *ever* wanted to sleep with him. Some couples lived like that for years; she knew from articles she'd read in magazines. Not her. Not ever. One night of it was one night too many.

She sensed something was amiss the moment she entered the cottage next morning. It was eerily silent.

Mabel stood still, staring around the empty room. She laid her hand on the wood stove: cold as the grave. She sniffed. Even above the usual aroma of turps and cigarette smoke, there was *something*. She looked down at the rug at her feet, then bent to feel it, snatching her hand back in disgust, and stepping across to the sink to rinse it under the tap.

The man was worse than a warthog these days, fouling himself where he stood. He'd apparently thrown up as well as wet himself. The rug would have to go to the dump – just as well it was an old one. Searching for a hand-towel, she rejected the grubby one hanging there in favour of a clean rag from the pile beside Roddy's easel. The one thing he always had a supply of; he'd tour the charity shops and buy up old sheets and lint-free cotton clothing, which he cut into neat, precise rectangles.

On the corner of the granite kerb around the wood-stove, there was a long smudge of dried red paint. Her mind elsewhere, Mabel seized a fresh paint-rag and a bottle of white spirit, and got down on her knees at the hearth to scrub the stonework clean. She stared at the rag. That hadn't been red paint at all. And there was a minute clump of hair attached to it. Roddy's hair, without a doubt.

She scrubbed harder, to remove all trace. Once she was satisfied that it was eliminated, she tossed the rag into the stove, and felt on the mantelpiece for matches. The cloth blazed up the moment the flame touched it.

She stepped gingerly through to the curtained-off sleeping area, expecting to find him spread-eagled across the bed in a drunken stupor, the way she'd found him so many times before.

The room was empty. It smelt of Roddy: the scent of strong tobacco that followed him wherever he went. That and stale sweat, and… other body fluids. She looked in the wardrobe. All his clothes appeared to be there – there were no noticeable gaps, no empty hangers. All of the jackets and overcoats she remembered were in their places. For a man with so little in the way of sartorial ambition in the last few years, he had a surprising quantity of clothing.

She'd quarrelled with him about that too, more than once, the way he'd dress in the same few threadbare items, as bad as a tramp, while he had a closet full of perfectly respectable garments.

'At least you'll have a brand new corduroy suit to be

buried in, like the poser you are,' she'd screamed at him the previous week.

Feeling a fresh sting of guilt, she drew back the sheets and inspected the mattress. Ah well, it could go out with the rug. No way she could manhandle that to the dump at Castle Douglas; she'd need to pay the Council for a special collection.

She opened the drawer of the bedside table. His collection of keys rattled around the bottom of it. One of his obsessions: he'd happily admit he had never thrown a key away. He'd hoarded the ones for every flat, padlock and suitcase he'd ever owned, right back to childhood. He maintained it was because his parents hadn't allowed him his own set of house keys, even when he reached university age. The only ones that appeared to be missing were the ones for the cottage and Mabel's house.

His wallet was gone too. So he'd left right enough, but without putting on a warm jacket? Silly! He must have popped out to the shop in his shirtsleeves. Or the pub? She wasn't even certain whether it was open at that time of day.

The front door had been unlocked when she arrived, but that gave no sort of clue, because he routinely left it open, even when he knew she was out. Careless! She'd not worried about it too much since the key for the back gate to the lane had gone missing, because it wasn't as if anyone could get *in*, without coming through the garage, or the bolted picket gate at the front. The eleven-foot-high stone walls around the garden were an effective deterrent to intruders.

Cruising on autopilot, she replaced caps on tubes of

paint, and carefully cleaned all the brushes, before heading back to her house.

She was uneasy as she ate her lunch. She'd already tried phoning Roddy, but it went straight to his silly Indian Love Call voicemail message each time. 'Where are you?' she'd texted. No reply. She had even sauntered past his drinking den of choice and stuck her head round the door. Not a sign; the place was empty.

As it began to get dark, she grew more troubled. Should she tell someone? Who? The police? And what would she tell them? She'd call Alison, Roddy's sister; that was most sensible. Not that the siblings had ever been close, but a sister was still a sister, presumably?

Ali merely sounded surprised. No she hadn't seen him for a couple of weeks, and she hadn't heard from him.

'I imagine he's got fed up with how you were treating him, Mabs,' she said, triumph in her voice. 'He's left you. Should have done it years ago.'

'How I was *treating* him?'

'Keeping him in a place that's no better than a dog-kennel. In fact, you wouldn't keep your precious damn dog there, would you? After all he's done for you, you owe Roddy a wee bit more than that.'

'I owe him nothing,' said Mabel, trying to hold her voice steady. 'I've kept him in food and clothing and painting materials for years, since his efforts stopped selling.'

Not to mention tobacco and booze, and home comforts, until he became too rank and feral to be kept in the house. She was lost in thought, remembering the Roddy who had lived there before the black dog settled on *his* shoulders. Before the collectors stopped buying his work, and the critics dismissed him as a trivial copier of more competent men's styles.

'Ah,' said Ali. 'His paintings – I think there are still a few in your shop?'

Bitch. It was a *gallery*. Ali was the shopkeeper.

'A *few?*'

'They're not yours. If Roddy's taken himself off to find a more congenial billet, remember the paintings are his, not yours. In fact, until he gets in touch, you'd better not sell any of them.'

'Sell? You could hardly give them away. Alison, when he gets in touch with you, can you tell him I need to speak to him, please? All his stuff's still in my cottage. Do you think I should go to the police and report him missing?'

'Please yourself.'

'You should do it. It's better coming from a relative.'

'But I've no reason to think anything's happened to him. What have you *done* to my brother, Mabs?'

'Absolutely nothing, bar telling him to sling his hook.'

'Why would the fuzz be interested? A grown man who's nobody's responsibility except his own has decided to leave the mistress who put him out to live in an unheated bothy in winter. Hardly a police matter.'

'He's taken none of his clothes, as far as I can see.'

' "As far as I can see",' Ali mimicked her. 'Since when did you take any interest in the poor man's clothes? Dressed in rags he was, half the time.'

'Was?'

'Is, I mean. Unless you know more about this than you're letting on?'

Mabel wakened in the middle of the night, and went downstairs for a drink of water. She glanced out of the kitchen window, and caught her breath. The lights were on in the cottage.

Well, she'd known Roddy was thoughtless, but honestly, to have come home in the middle of the night without ringing her first! And how had he got in anyway? Probably she'd forgotten to re-bolt the front picket gate. She often forgot, when it was bin day. That'd be what had wakened her, the sound of the gate being opened.

She debated with herself. Would she go and have it out with him now? Or would she wait until morning? She consulted her watch. Half past three. Damn, it wouldn't wait. She knew she'd get no more sleep anyway, because sleep and anger aren't good bedfellows.

As she got halfway down the garden, the cottage windows were plunged into darkness. Double damn. She hadn't brought a torch, and she hadn't left her own back door light on. She tiptoed cagily along the rest of the path. The door was unlocked, as she'd anticipated.

'Roddy?'

She switched on the light.

'Roddy?' she called again, pulling aside the curtain that served to give some privacy to the bedroom. No one there. He must be in the bathroom then. With the light off? She tapped on the door, then opened it; the room was empty.

Mabel, who prided herself on being afraid of nothing and no man, found herself suddenly terrified. She ran out of the cottage, and didn't stop until she had reached the safety of her own back porch, and locked the door.

By the time she'd made a pot of tea, she'd convinced herself it must have been a trick of the light. Possibly the moon, reflected in the cottage windows? That would be it. And it had disappeared behind a cloud as she started down the path. In spite of herself, she fetched her diary. The new moon was due in two days.

She didn't go back to bed that night.

Next morning, she called Ali again. 'Did Roddy mention anything to you about coming back here?'

'When hell freezes over, or maybe a week or two after that. Why would he come back to you?'

'He was in the cottage last night. There was a light on.'

'You were probably dreaming. Guilty conscience.'

'I have absolutely nothing to feel guilty about. I haven't seen him since Wednesday. Are you going to go to the police?'

'No. I'll leave that for you to do. After all, the man was practically your husband, until you decided he was surplus to requirements.' Alison slammed down the phone.

Over the next thirty-six hours, Mabel busied herself with anything and everything to take her mind off what she should do about finding Roddy. She took Archie to his

favourite beach, even although it was too cold for more
than a brisk walk. She checked the buckets in the attic twice
a day. She opened her wardrobe to make a start on Nancy's
favoured space-clearing tactics, then closed it again. When
she heard the letterbox clatter, she fairly raced downstairs.

Mabel turned the letter over and over in her hands,
undecided. It was thoroughly bad form to read someone
else's mail, but she could see from the postmark and the
return address that it was from Brian Rodriguez, the art
authentication expert who'd been advising Roddy on the
Miró painting he was sure he'd found. She should do
whatever it took to get word to him if there had been A
Development.

She gritted her teeth and tore the envelope open.

> Dear Roddy
>
> Bad news, I'm afraid. The ADOM has, as I
> warned you was likely, rejected the
> authenticity of your painting.

In other words, the Miró Committee says it's a fake. Mabel
groaned.

> Worst of all, they have demanded that it
> should be destroyed, and since it is still
> in the possession of Dr Carnon in Paris, I
> am very doubtful that we can secure its
> return. There are apparently precedents,
> and in those cases action in the French
> courts to prevent destruction was
> unsuccessful, but extremely costly for
> the owners.
>
> I have asked a French colleague if he can

recommend a solicitor who could advise you on the niceties of the legal situation, but I am not optimistic.

I understand that Dr Carnon has approached the Miró Committee on an informal basis, to enquire if they would consider returning the painting to you if we agree to an indelible stamp being placed on the reverse, refuting its authenticity, but they have declined to consider this. We could always try a more formal approach along those lines, but I'm not hopeful that they would arrive at a different decision.

I'm absolutely devastated on your behalf, because we were so certain that such provenance as we had been able to assemble would satisfy the Committee, even though the scientific tests were so disappointingly inconclusive.

However, it is imperative that you let me know as soon as possible how you wish to proceed, because it is my understanding that the Committee will instruct the seizure and destruction of your painting within the next month.

Yours aye

Brian

Mabel phoned Ali once more.

'I have an important letter for Roddy. Can you please

ask him to contact me? I've left seven messages on his mobile since this morning, but he hasn't responded. It's absolutely essential that he sees this within the next day or two.'

'If he hasn't got back to you, he clearly doesn't want to.'

'Then give me an address where I can forward this to him.'

'You can send it here.'

As if she'd trust Ali with a confidential letter. 'I want to make sure he gets it.'

Ali snorted.

'If you let me know when you're likely to be seeing him, I'll bring the letter. I'll just hand it to him, you can tell him that.'

'He doesn't want anything to do with you.'

'I want to see him. I want to be sure he's all right.'

Ali hooted with laughter. 'Pity you didn't think about that before the poor man had to leave, to get away from you.'

'Are you sure he *is* all right? Have you seen him?'

'I haven't seen him, no.'

'You've heard from him?'

'Why are you bothered about it?'

'Because as far as I can tell, he left without anything more than the clothes he stood up in, four days ago.'

'Bring the letter over to me. I'll make sure he gets it.'

Mabel sighed, and said she'd be there in forty minutes. She decided not to take Archie with her, as Roddy's sister loathed dogs as much as he did; they were banned from her premises, unless they were guide dogs. She felt as uneasy as she always did on entering Alison McCulloch's shop. It was one of those businesses that lacked focus. It also smelt of joss sticks, which for some reason she found disturbing.

Ali looked as weird as ever. She was wearing a tweed skirt and a jumper of an indistinct khaki shade. Mabel couldn't help thinking she'd have looked better in motorbike leathers, with that wrestler's build.

'So, where is he, your errant brother?'

'Around somewhere.'

'When will you see him?'

Ali shrugged. 'Soon.' She held out her hand for the letter, which Mabel handed over reluctantly. 'You'll make sure he gets it? He must reply – it's very urgent. Look, unless you can tell me exactly where he is, I think I will go to the police to report him missing, if you don't want to do it.'

Ali's tone was smug. 'You do that. I'm surprised you haven't already. Shows how much *you* care.'

'Of course I care, Alison. I care very much for Roddy.'

Mabel knew she wasn't likely to be offered a cup of tea, so she left as quickly as was possible without being rude, after buying a 'Blank inside for your own message' card depicting a leaping hare.

She went straight to the nearest police station where she expected to find anyone on duty. Mabel was sure the bored officer who took down the details was laughing at her. She didn't recognise him. Not that she'd ever had anything to do with the police in Castle Douglas, but the office in Kirkcudbright was hardly ever manned these days.

No doubt as soon as she'd left he'd be guffawing with his cronies in the back office, over a box of doughnuts. 'Silly old bat wants us to find her fancy man and bring him home. Should have asked if she'd had him microchipped. Haw, haw, haw.' Things hadn't half gone downhill since Sergeant Thompson retired.

'If he'd had an accident and been taken to hospital, someone would have been informed, wouldn't they?'

'His next of kin would have been. Are you a relative?"

'No. A friend. I was his landlady.' She wanted to tell him to stop smirking. 'So his sister would have heard, if anything had happened to him?'

'I should think so, if she's next of kin.' He consulted a computer screen. 'Has she reported him missing?'

'I don't believe she has. She doesn't seem to think there's a problem.'

The officer glared at her. 'Then why do you think there is – has he done a moonlight flit owing you rent or something?'

'He did owe me rent, as a matter of fact, but that's not why I'm concerned about him.'

'Is he a vulnerable person?'

'Well… '

He tutted impatiently. 'I mean, does he have a chronic illness for which he requires medication, or mental health issues? Is there a reason why you imagine he may have harmed himself, or come to harm?'

'Not specially. He drank too much. But he wasn't ill. He left without any of his clothes.'

'What – he was naked?'

'No! I mean, he didn't take a jacket with him.'

The officer closed his notebook, and told her rather sniffily that if she was seeking to pursue Roddy for unpaid rent or damage to her property, that was a civil matter.

Two uniformed officers turned up at Ashers the next day. They had a good nosey round the cottage, then asked if they could look in the house.

'But I know he's not here!'

'Just a formality. You mentioned that he had occasional access.'

They opened the door of every room. She could also hear them opening cupboards and wardrobes. They asked where the pole for the attic hatch was, and she heard one of them stomping about up there.

'Can you please be careful not to move any of the buckets and pans on the floor?' she called.

'Is there a cellar?' asked the other officer.

She showed him the cellar door, and switched on the light for him. 'Be careful on the steps. They're a bit worn.'

Mabel stifled a giggle. She should have said 'Mind the cobwebs,' because that's all he'd find in the racks down there: cobwebs and mouse-droppings. When the Scouts had come looking for donations for their Christmas bottle stall, she'd given them two bottles of rather expensive shampoo, and one of the cheeky wee devils piped up, 'Is this all? Everyone says you've a huge cellar full of wine.'

Within half an hour the officers were on their way, presumably confident that she wasn't secreting the artist in her wardrobe or her knicker drawer or her cellar. They'd borrowed the only good recent photo she had of Roddy on his own.

After the house was empty and silent once more, she allowed herself to admit how much she missed him, or missed knowing that he was there, at the bottom of her garden, like an evil elf. She missed him in much the same way she'd missed Father during the first few months; a nostalgia mitigated by relief at being unburdened; an emotion that relied more on revisiting old memories than dwelling on recent ones. It wasn't the recent Roddy she missed – the animalistic one – but the old one, who'd died years ago. She missed his laughter, his talent, his wit, the way his own creativity struck sparks off hers. The way he could charm the butterflies off the buddleias; the way he could talk confidently to anyone, from a dustman to a duchess. She missed his slight, taut body beside her in bed; not a comforting presence, but enervating.

Exhilarating. That's what life with the old Roddy had been. Oh, how she missed that.

Mabel dialled the number for her friend's hotel. Briony answered.

'Mabs! Haven't seen you for an age.'

'Is it my imagination, or did you once mention you'd heard of someone who works as a private detective, tracing missing people?'

'He's a pal of someone my cousin works beside at Albion TV. Why do you want to know?'

'Just out of interest. Do you know how to get in touch with him?'

'I can find out, if you want.'

'Thanks Briony. That'd be very useful. You're a pal.'

'Come round just now for a coffee.'

But the scene playing out inside Mabel's head was last year's election for the presidency of the Townswomen's Guild, and Briony's gloating smile. 'I'm terribly busy. I'll see you soon.'

Mabel was aware that she should nurture the friendship more. Briony was ten years older than her, a childless widow who'd shown no signs of wanting to remarry. Her parents, who actually owned the hotel, were both elderly and infirm.

'I shouldn't begrudge her the damn Guild. It means more to her than it would to me,' she told herself sternly. So easy to think, so hard to *believe*!

She thanked Briony again, promised to see her soon, and hung up.

CHAPTER THREE

Mabel recognised the man on her doorstep two days later. She'd seen him standing outside Roddy's favourite pub with the other smokers, his cigarette turned into his palm against the wind, spitting on the pavement like a tramp.

She wished she'd kept the chain on the door. Mind you, he was a little weed. What Mrs Dempster would have called a 'wee bachle'. She'd be the stronger any day.

'Yes?'

'I'm looking for Roddy. My pal. Haven't seen him for more than a week.'

Mabel bit her lip. 'He's gone.'

'Gone where?'

'I haven't a clue. Gone owing me rent.'

The obnoxious gnome guffawed. 'Rent! From what I hear, he didn't pay you rent, missus. You got your payment in kind.'

'I have no idea what you mean.'

He chortled again, and made an obscene gesture with his left hand on the inside of his right forearm. Mabel felt herself blush.

'I think it'd be better if we discussed this inside,' said the weed. 'Your neighbours might be listening.'

And right enough, she could see the woman from halfway down the close pretending to water her plant-pots. In the first week of February?

'Come in then,' she said frostily, standing aside to let him pass.

He started towards the sitting room.

'I think the hall will do for the very short discussion we're going to have, Mr –?'

'Just call me Ron. What have you done with him then? Poor man, he used to be fair exhausted with servicing you all night.'

'I think it's best you leave now.'

'I want to see my friend.'

'And I've told you, he's gone. He did not leave a forwarding address. If you're such a friend of his, I'm sure you know how to contact his sister.'

'Ali? I know how to contact her OK. But she doesna have much use for men, does she? Not like Miss Mabel Mountjoy. I hear you like it rough.'

'Get out of my house.'

He turned back to the door, laughing.

'Hoity-toity. Ah well, maybe I'll need to ask around a bit more widely. Maybe when some of your pals in the Townswomen's Guild hear about what you like to do in bed, you'll mind on where Roddy's gone. I'll be back in a day or two, in case your memory's improved.'

'If you think you're going to get money out of me, you've another think coming.'

'Money! Now there's an idea. We haven't even got to that bit yet, Mabs.'

'Don't you dare call me Mabs. And don't come back

here, if you know what's good for you.'

'You must be saving a good bit, now you're not giving Roddy any cash to snort up his nose. Must be some to spare for an old friend?'

'I haven't the faintest idea what you're talking about.'

'Oh, I think you do.'

As if he could read her mind. But she'd never *known*, only suspected.

He turned at the bottom of the steps, made the same lewd gesture, and headed down the close, cackling to himself.

Mabel was feeling almost calm by the time she reached home next day. A trip to the M&S Food Hall in Dumfries was never quite so exciting as it promised to be, but at least she had also taken the opportunity to buy herself a new blouse, and had splashed out on a bunch of pink Asiatic lilies. So important to have fresh flowers occasionally in the dank days when there was no colour in the garden. She recognised with a pang that the only person who had ever bought flowers for Mabel was: Mabel. At least the next time she visited, the shops would surely have cleared away their displays of mawkish cards and heart-shaped balloons, to make way for the Easter eggs.

She shook herself free of her raincoat, hung it up, squared her shoulders and headed for the kitchen with her shopping bags. Onwards and upwards, Mabs. Self-pity is not an attractive feature in the middle-aged woman. She suppressed another shudder.

Then she noticed what was on the kitchen table. She knew at once what it was; what it was *called*.

Leaving her lilies in their plastic wrapper, and her groceries still packed, she put Archie on his lead and walked up to the Roseberry Arms. Briony was, uncharacteristically, behind the bar.

'Did you get the details of that man who can trace missing people?'

'I did. Fergus Learmonth. Why?'

'I think I must do something proactive about finding Roddy.'

Briony rolled her eyes. 'Proactive! I'd say you're well rid of him Mabs.' She tore off a sheet from the order pad and jotted down a phone number and email address. 'This is the people-finder. You know my cousin's a receptionist at Albion TV? He used to work there. He's famous. *Learmonth on the Lookout?*'

Mabel shook her head vaguely.

'When are you going to join us in the twenty-first century, Mabs?'

'Do you know what he charges?'

'Not a clue. Small fortune probably. He's a widower, by the way, according to my cousin.'

Her slightly bulging eyes sparkled. 'Maybe a sugar daddy for you, Mabs.'

Mabel stifled the desire to tell her friend that if people grow to look like their pets, Briony was the one who should have a pug, instead of a Siamese cat. But that'd be cruel. The hotel-owner was one of her few friends, and her heart was probably in the right place, even if she was set on bed-blocking the presidency of the Townswomen's Guild.

'Here,' said Briony suddenly, handing Mabel a bag containing several heart-shaped chocolates wrapped in bright red foil. 'You're missing out on our Valentine's Day dinner again. I'm always hoping on your behalf, Mabs. Maybe next year… you know, you can afford to be choosy.'

'What do you mean?'

'Well, look at you. Owner of a positively fabulous house and your own business, no one to tie you down, so you can please yourself. In your prime. You could take your pick.'

'Of the men here?'

Briony blushed slightly. 'Perhaps cast your net a little wider.'

'If I want to cast it at all.'

'But you *like* men. I'm only trying to be helpful. We all worry about you.'

Mabel thanked her for the sweets and fled. When she got home, she steeled her nerve, donned her gardening clothes, armed herself with storage boxes, and set about clearing out the cottage. It didn't take as long as she'd feared. She realised with a pang how little Roddy had to show for a lifetime of work. Once his possessions were boxed, the rubbish bagged and the half-finished canvases stacked in her kitchen, she mopped the floors. She kept her eyes and her mind averted from the granite kerb where she'd found the bloodstain. Surely it couldn't have signified anything other than a minor accident? It had been so tiny. But then there had been *hair*. Her own hair prickled. She should have told the police about it – only they'd have asked searching questions about why she hadn't reported it the moment she found it, and try as she might, Mabel couldn't find a sensible answer to that.

She washed her hands carefully once more, went through to her father's study and composed an email to Fergus Learmonth.

DI Tom Ellis was bored. It was a long time since Dumfries and Galloway had coughed up the sort of crime he liked to get his teeth into. He asked himself for the third time that day – as he did on most days – how he had ended up stuck here, rather than in one of the metropolitan forces, where there was excitement and faster promotion to be had. Not necessarily the Met. Strathclyde would have done. Even Edinburgh or Manchester. Anywhere but here, within thirty miles of where he'd been born.

Jackie's mother, that was the reason. He'd known when they got married that she was under the manipulative maternal thumb, but it was only when the kids came along he realised how firmly he was trapped, like a wasp in jam. Still, there was one perk from being based in an HQ that was larger than required for the number of staff these days: he had his own office – the only DI to have such a luxury. He enjoyed the degree of privacy it gave him.

He sighed and picked up a slim file from the stack beside him. Computers were all very well, but there was still a hell of a lot of paper to deal with. The DCI had dropped the file on his desk earlier, saying casually that he knew Kirkcudbright was Tom's old stamping ground, so could he have a dekko, see if the people involved rang any bells.

A missing person follow-up. As he started to glance through it, he thumped his feet down from the desk and whistled softly. Mabel Mountjoy! It gave him a jolt to read her name. He hadn't seen her for years, though he still thought about her with troubling regularity.

The man she'd reported missing was the sleekit wee gutter-rat she'd shacked up with a mere couple of years after deciding *he* wasn't good enough for her. A so-called artist. That's the sort of object Mabs had preferred to the lad she'd sat beside in primary school, and who'd been well on the way to passing his sergeant's exams by the day he proposed to her.

Damn it, no way he was wasting his time on this. He opened his office door and beckoned to Rachel Field, the DC who was the new kid on the block.

'This guy was reported missing five days ago, by his par... his landlady. Sixty-odds and a known drinker. The local troops had a squizz round the place he'd been living, and spoke to his sister – she didn't seem convinced there was anything untoward. His phone's still live, though he hasn't responded to our calls. Check if he's shown up, could you?'

He sat at his desk, head in hands, remembering the precise shade of ripe conker Mabel Mountjoy's hair had been when she was twenty-three, and the way the soft skin of her neck always seemed to be fragrant with a perfume that hadn't come out of a bottle.

As soon as he saw Rachel come back into the outer office three hours later, he was on his feet. 'Well, any news?'

'I didn't see him, if that's what you mean. The sister doesn't seem unduly worried. And his mobile's still live right enough – she showed me a text he sent her a couple of days ago. I'd say it's just a case of a man taking himself off from a relationship that'd gone sour.'

And indeed, the smile Tom Ellis gave in reply was a little sour, as well as triumphant.

Archie never barked. More than once, Mabel's pals had teased her about it. 'Why keep a dog and bark yourself?' Ho ho ho. But he growled. And Archie's growl was the most menacing sound she knew.

As quietly as she could, she slid out of bed and stood listening. She heard a faint sound from downstairs – so faint she could have been imagining it. No; there it was again. She put on her dressing gown, closed the bedroom door silently on her dog, and crept to the top of the stair.

'Roddy?'

No answer.

'Will you stop doing this? I have all your clobber in the attic. Come back in daylight and you're welcome to take the lot. Take your damn paintings too. Only stop harassing me. Roddy? I know it's you, and if you think I'm frightened by your antics, you've another think coming.'

She listened again. There was a grating sound. Someone had turned the key in the back door; she'd been meaning to oil the lock for months. The hair on her arms prickled. What if it wasn't Roddy? It could be a burglar, or a crazed rapist. She retreated to her bedroom again, and closed the door softly, scooping the quivering pug under her arm and locking both of them into the en suite. After what felt like hours – she hadn't thought to collect either her watch or her phone – Mabel opened the door and tiptoed back to the landing. Complete silence.

This time, she went all the way downstairs, and flung on the kitchen light. No sign of any intruder. She tried the door. Locked, and the key in its usual place, on a string beside the window. Nothing seemed to be missing. No drawers had been left open, or cupboards ransacked.

By morning, she was ready to believe she'd dreamt it all, except for the fact that Archie spent a quarter of an hour sniffing all around the kitchen, his tail stiffly uncurled and the hairs on his scruff bristling.

CHAPTER FOUR

Fergus Learmonth was in contemplative mood as he walked slowly down Kirkcudbright's High Street after parking outside the Roseberry Arms, where he was staying that night. Pretty little town, with its pastel-coloured houses and fine old structures like the Tolbooth, all sparkling in the pallid winter sunshine. The pervading scent of wood-smoke heightened the sensation of stepping back in time. There was a stillness about the place that was soothing rather than stagnant.

There were few people around in the street. The natives seemed friendly, although he hadn't seen any flashes of recognition. He'd grown accustomed to the puzzled gaze of strangers tracking him, wondering where they knew him from. With every month that passed, that happened less frequently anyway. Thank God he'd got out of the world of TV in time, rather than hanging on past his sell-by date, like Bruce Forsyth. Amazing how quickly people forget; nothing he had achieved would be remembered beyond the end of last year's TV schedules. Amazing and hurtful.

He was surprised he hadn't visited Kirkcudbright before. A Georgian planned village, by the looks of it. It had an opinion of itself too. He'd noticed the signs as he drove in. 'The Artists' Town'. The type of place Serena would have revelled in.

He closed his eyes for a heartbeat and sighed as he thought – for the umpteenth time since he'd wakened that morning, as almost every other morning – about his wife; the day took on a more sombre hue. He remembered how she had loved making small gardens in enclosed spaces. Many of the houses he was passing had such features; not exactly the intimate patio of a house in Córdoba, or a Moroccan riad, but inward-looking, secretive patches of ground all the same. Closes lined with plant-pots. Window boxes and planters which no doubt overflowed with geraniums and trailing lobelia in summer. Oh, she'd have been in her element here. Fergus forced his face into a smile. Think happy thoughts. Serena always preferred him when he was in good form. He had a vague recollection that her aunt, the redoubtable Peigi MacKenzie, had a friend who lived in this part of the world, but no anticipation at all of running into her. The request for his services had come via a colleague of Anita Forrest, the head of station at Albion TV's Edinburgh headquarters. He doubted if a friend of the MacKenzies moved in the same circles. How much more he could have done for Serena and her career, if only she hadn't acted so foolishly and precipitately…

It was only a few days since the anniversary of the last time he'd seen her alive. That was the principal reason why he'd been determined to visit somewhere new, mingle with people whom he'd never met before.

What was he doing with his life, when it came down to it? He'd burnt his boats with what he did best, abandoning the work that had served him well since he was in his twenties, and had made him a household name.

And nothing, *nothing* he could do would bring Serena back. He'd told himself the fresh direction to his career would numb the pain. All it seemed to have done was numb every other part of his brain as well as the rest of his anatomy. He still thought about her every hour of every day. Sometimes, he imagined he'd prefer it if he could be dead too. When he tried to peer into the future, it was like a faulty TV screen: a haze of white noise.

He gave himself a shake. Didn't do to fall into the slough of despond when he was on the cusp of a new assignment. His hair and beard might be well-peppered with silver these days, but there was plenty of life in the old dog yet. A clock close by chimed the half-hour and Fergus hastened his steps. His tactic was to arrive precisely twenty-five minutes early for a first appointment. This was the Learmonth technique: a good aid to assessing the mental state of prospective clients, he'd always found.

He was looking for Mabel Mountjoy's house. Since he'd started his consultancy work (as he liked to call it) the previous year, he hadn't constructed a table of fees. So this was how he operated: he scoped out the client's house first, and dreamed up a figure based on his assessment of value. It worked well. Fergus gave himself a mental pat on the back. Onwards and upwards. It's what Serena would have wanted.

A middle-aged woman, this prospective client, trying to trace a man who had disappeared. He'd been asked to deal with this sort of scenario before: the toy boy who'd thought better of it one morning when he beheld the wrinkles in full daylight, or when the cash started to run out, and had fled to find another gullible older woman. Wouldn't touch it with a thirty-foot pole. Thus far, he'd managed to avoid the more sordid end of the market. And a woman of a certain age trying to trace a man: that was almost always sleazy. He'd only travelled as far as Kirkcudbright because he didn't want to say no to Anita's colleague. Well, that plus the fact he'd never visited the area before. Another one ticked off the bucket list.

Ah, this was the address. Crosskeys Close. One of the quaint, cobbled closes off the High Street, with a Virginia creeper trained against the wall. Unprepossessing enough houses on either side, though. Then he lifted his gaze. Facing him was a substantial tree in a stone-bordered circular island among the cobbles, and beyond that – behind a set of elegant iron railings flanking three stone steps up to the colonnaded front door – was a classical Scottish town house of the late eighteenth century. He could read the discreet brass nameplate from where he stood: 'Ashers.' Nothing wrong with his long-distance eyesight at any rate.

A beautifully-proportioned house, with fine architectural details. Large enough to be imposing, not so large as to be impractical. Dressed ashlar margins around the windows, under-stated Doric columns at the doorway, rough stone walls painted a warm and well-mannered shade of poached salmon – although he noted that it was some time since the paint had been refreshed. At either side, he could spy tree-tops, indicating a substantial garden behind.

Pound signs flashed in Fergus's imagination. The relative of Anita's pal had mentioned that the owner was the only daughter of a man who'd been the area's most prominent solicitor. There was old money here. Modest Scottish prosperity.

Not that Fergus had taken up this work for the money; in the past twelve months, he'd earned roughly a third of what Albion had been paying him, but at least it didn't leave him so much time to brood. He didn't have to cope with imagining Serena sitting there every time he entered the newsroom or a studio. And it brought him some satisfaction that she'd been the one to give him the idea for his new career. 'You're so good at finding out things, and people,' she'd said. One of the last conversations they'd had before she…

He dabbed his eyes discreetly and refolded his linen hankie in his breast pocket. As he climbed the steps to Mabel Mountjoy's front door, he checked in his right-hand pocket for his silver business card case – not that he'd ever present his card at the door, like a double-glazing salesman. But useful to be able to leave one with a prospective client. His cards carried his name, business mobile number and email address. Nothing so vulgar as 'Private Investigator', because that had connotations that didn't describe his work anyway. No chance he was ever going to get himself involved in the distasteful detail of hanging about outside cheap hotels, and so on.

He raised the polished brass knocker and rapped smartly three times. After precisely thirty seconds, he repeated the exercise. He thought the woman who opened the door looked a tad hostile. Presumably the lady herself; damn few could afford servants nowadays. An uncalled-for attitude; she'd asked to see him, after all.

The frown was surely not her habitual expression, since she lacked the vertical lines between the brows that characterise the habitual frowner. Interesting; she was assuredly upset about something.

'Ms Mountjoy? Fergus Learmonth. I'm afraid I'm a few moments early,' he said, extending a hand. He knew his hands were always beautifully warm. Most women seemed to find that reassuring.

'You're twenty-five minutes early,' she said, waspishly. 'And it's "Miss".'

A warning shot, Fergus. Women can be excessively touchy about these things. 'Sorry – *Miss* Mountjoy. I overestimated how long it would take me to find you.'

She touched the proffered hand with her fingertips. 'I suppose you'd best come in anyway.'

'Now, that's lovely!' he added placatingly, as she stepped back to allow him to enter the hall. 'Bokhara? I'd say that's a genuine Afghan one too, not your average modern tat from Pakistan?'

'What?' she snapped.

An extremely strange reaction.

'The rug. I'm assuming you're a fan of oriental rugs? That's a beauty.'

'Oh, I see. Yes. It's old. My father had something of a collection.'

'My wife was keen on oriental rugs too. Quite an expert.' He smiled fondly. 'She loved the way you can get lost in the pattern. There's always an idiosyncrasy, a small disharmony - not a *mistake* you know, because the weavers did it deliberately. They believed only God could make perfection.'

Mabel Mountjoy tossed her hair back and led the way into a handsome room with panelled walls and an ornate plasterwork ceiling, crisp and white as icing on a wedding-cake. The tall, astragalled window to the front overlooked the close, giving a neatly-framed vista through to the High Street that would be lost once the tree in front had its leaves. The rear window showed a garden, at least twice as long as it was wide – a typical town rig – burgeoning with shrubs: mostly roses, he'd guess. The stone walls at its sides were easily eleven feet high, and seemed to have fruit cordons trained against them. It appeared to be bounded by the ends of other gardens; very private.

The air in the room smelt of lavender furniture polish. His type of house, and no mistake.

He'd felt reassured as soon as he heard Mabel Mountjoy's accent. It was the type that denotes Scottish upper middle class: comfortably off, never had to wear shoes with a hole in them in her life, fee-paying school, university whether she was clever enough or not; almost the twin of his own accent. This might yet shape up to be an agreeable assignment. Because Fergus had recognised a significant fact by the time he reached the sitting room: this was an agitated woman. And he felt she wasn't accustomed to letting anything rattle her cage. *Crank the pressure down, Fergus. Small talk, until she's reassured.*

'I see you've always had careful decorators here. The

plaster detail's not clogged with paint,' he added, gesticulating.

It had cost him the thick end of two grand to have a tradesman painstakingly howk out the gunge from his own ceiling cornices in Edinburgh.

'Mmmm,' she replied.

'In the family a long time?'

'Seven generations, including me.'

'Ah, that's what makes the difference.'

A small dog ran up to him and began sniffing suspiciously around his ankles.

'You don't mind Archie?' asked Mabel. Her tone implied that if he did, then he could bugger off.

Fergus assumed his most benign expression. 'Of course not. I love animals. He probably smells my cat.'

The pug's ears pricked up at the word.

'He's just a baby,' said Mabel defensively, as if she could read Fergus's mind. 'He's not quite three.'

The sitting room furniture was mainly dark mahogany, and fussily old-fashioned. The seating provision consisted of four tall wing-back chairs upholstered in faded oxblood leather: a triumph of practicality over comfort. Invited to sit, Fergus selected the chair facing the garden window, beside the white marble fireplace. A fire had been laid, but not lit; the room was chilly. That was the worst of those lovely original windows, of course: single-glazed.

Another Bokhara rug here – a larger one – and a very fine small Heriz before the hearth.

The big surprise was the paintings. They were all at least two centuries younger than the house, and they were mostly very much to Fergus's taste. Since he'd lost Serena, he'd come late to an appreciation of twentieth century art.

He patted his pocket. 'Do you mind if I smoke? Just a cigar.'

'I most certainly do mind. I've only newly managed to get the smell out of this room since… since anyone was allowed to smoke tobacco of any kind here.' She seemed more agitated than ever.

'It's just that I noticed you have a rather fine antique pipe rack – German, I'd say? Black Forest?'

She glared at him. 'I have no idea. It was my father's. I'm sure he wouldn't have had a *German* one. Freud killed himself smoking cigars, you know.'

'No, I didn't know.'

'Cancer of the mouth. Ghastly.'

Time for another change of subject, to calm her a little more. Fergus remembered something he'd been meaning to ask. 'What's the tree outside – the one at the end of the close?'

'A golden chain tree; laburnum.'

'Must be a very old one?'

'I believe so. I've read they don't live longer than thirty years, but I can't remember that one not being there. It's glorious when it's in flower.'

'Helps to shield the house from any nosey people who wander in off the street too, I'd think?'

'Quite. It's a nuisance though. I have to pick up every single pod as they fall, in case some child poisons itself.'

❖

Mabel was still flustered from having been caught unawares. She'd hardly had time to shove last night's forgotten sherry-glass behind an ornament on the mantelpiece, pat her hair straight and compose her features before the second round of peremptory raps of the front door knocker. She had often toyed with the idea of getting one of those new-fangled wire-free bells, but almost all of her friends who had installed one had experienced trouble with it, and they seemed to play such very *vulgar* tunes. The brass knocker that had served six earlier generations of Mountjoys would see her out. So very, very rude to turn up almost half an hour ahead of the appointed time. Extremely unprofessional.

She'd meant to prepare more fully for this first meeting. Make sure her hair looked immaculate. Put on some lipstick and blusher. She was aware that she'd surveyed the barrel-chested individual on the doorstep with some distaste, even as he apologised for being ridiculously early. He was clearly not going to offer to leave and come back. She'd stood aside, with an ill grace, and told him he'd better come in, since he was there. All the same, she shouldn't have snapped at him. *Manners, Mabel.*

The truth of the matter was that on first sight of him, she'd had the strangest sensation that something *significant* was about to happen.

And now here he was, settled confidently in Father's armchair, his long legs stretched out, as if the place belonged to him. She rather liked the suit he was wearing, all the same. A light grey tweed with the slightest hint of lovat in it, a white shirt with broad stripes in subtly varied shades of purple, and a tie that echoed the silvery tone of the tweed. The overall effect was pleasing, redolent of a Scottish moor in autumn. The sort of rig-out Father would have recognised as denoting the 'right' class. What let the ensemble down a little was the fact that he needed a haircut. *His beard could use a trim too.*

'Now, Mrs Mountjoy…'

'Miss.'

'I beg your pardon. *Miss* Mountjoy.'

His mouth worked a little. Oh bloody Nora, surely he wasn't going to come out with some rubbish about how could a lovely woman like her, et cetera? *Unclaimed treasure,* as Father used to say. No, the damn man was struggling not to *laugh* at her.

'I understand from Mrs Hall that you are keen to find a missing person?' continued Fergus.

Exactly how many beans had Briony spilled? Though probably her friend had been trying to help, by preparing him for the encounter.

'I am. I've been told this is the sort of work you do nowadays?'

'Indeed.'

Fergus's expression was completely bland. A good poker player, no doubt.

'As I'm sure Mrs Hall told you, I am an art dealer. Roddy McCulloch, one of my most prominent exhibitors, has disappeared. I need to find him, so that I can pay him for any paintings I sell. He was also my tenant.'

'And he has been missing for how long?'

'A little under three weeks.'

'That's not very long at all. Perhaps he has simply taken a holiday.'

'I doubt it. I'm worried that something's happened to him.'

'I assume you've reported your concerns to the police?'

Mabel shifted uncomfortably in her chair and smoothed her skirt for the umpteenth time. She found the steadiness of his gaze disconcerting.

'Och, they know me and they know him. I imagine they know him quite well. They seem to think there's nothing at all to suggest he hasn't left of his own free will.'

'So why don't you believe that's what has happened?'

'It's not like him to simply vanish.'

Fergus stood up, and began pacing the room. Mabel felt her blood pressure rising. How rude, to stride about a stranger's sitting room, as if you owned it.

'This is a lovely piece too,' he said, picking up the pipe-rest that always used to sit beside her father's chair (in spite of that, there were still a few burn marks on the leather arm at the right-hand side). It was a carved ebony fox, with a hollowed-out bowl to hold the pipe where the animal's back would be. She knew how tactile and pleasing it was to hold. She'd often pick it up and run her fingers into its comforting smoothness when she was feeling discomfited or dispirited.

'I take it your father eschewed cigarettes in favour of the tobacco pipe?' he added.

She pushed away an urge to say that no, he had smoked a hookah.

'Indeed,' she replied.

'You've lived here a long time?'

'I have never lived anywhere else.'

Presumably Briony had filled him in with these details anyway. She had always been impressed by the fact that Mabel owned what was probably the most desirable house in the town.

'It's a most splendid building. Quite unexpectedly grand, in a close like this.'

'It was apparently built in 1784 by a wealthy merchant, William Asher – not a direct ancestor of my father. I like having the privacy of the close. Most of the other larger houses in town open directly onto the main street.'

Her visitor strode to the rear window and looked out. 'I see you have a fine garden too. Surely you don't have to keep all of that up by yourself?'

'I do nowadays, yes.'

When Father was alive, they'd been able to afford a man who came in three times a week. Awfully handy, because he didn't mind chopping firewood for Roddy's log stove.

Fergus Learmonth waved his hand towards the end of the garden. 'And that's the cottage where McCulloch lived?'

'Yes. It doubles as a studio.'

Fergus Learmonth sat down again.

'I can see why you'd never want to leave here.'

'Leave?' She couldn't keep the alarm out of her voice. 'I have no intention of leaving.'

'All I meant was that a house this size must be very expensive to keep up. When you're…'

On your own. Go on, say it. I'm sure everyone else does, behind my back.

'So, this artist,' said Fergus, running his left hand insouciantly through his hair (rather nice hair; thick and prettily peppered with silver among the dark brown even if it did need a trim). 'Sorry, what's his full name?'

'Roderick Hector McDonald McCulloch.'

He claimed to be descended from Horatio McCulloch, the landscape painter. Idiot.

'This Roddy – you last had contact with him exactly when?'

Mabel contemplated what 'contact' meant. When she last saw him? When she last spoke to him on the phone? When he last rose from her bed? When he last penetrated her body with his? When she walked out of her cottage, leaving him staggering around like the drunken idiot he was? Her eyes welled up. She turned away, pretending to attend to Archie, who was pawing at her knee.

'I last saw him on the thirty-first of January. I have had no contact whatsoever from him since. I've tried phoning and texting him. He doesn't answer.' Her voice faltered a little. She cleared her throat.

'You're genuinely concerned about him, aren't you?' said Fergus, much more gently.

'I'm worried that he might be ill or hurt. He'd drunk heavily for most of his life. But I suppose he's all right, because I think possibly he's broken into the house a couple of times.'

'Broken in? Now that *is* a matter for the police, no question.'

'It's not the right term. He had keys to this house at one stage. I daresay he kept a set.'

'What makes you think he's been here recently?'

'I heard him in the kitchen.'

He was looking at her as if she were mad.

'I mean, I heard someone; I think it was him,' she added. 'I believe he's trying to wind me up. That's the sort of sense of humour he has. And last week, after I came home from being out on business, he'd left something on the kitchen table.'

'Something?'

Fergus Learmonth was looking alarmed.

'Not anything scatological, the way you read about in the papers. This.'

She rose and fetched it from the sideboard. She held it out for him to take.

'It's quite clean,' she added.

Fergus turned it over in his hands, and looked up at her questioningly.

'Slag?' he said.

'Exactly.'

'What makes you think McCulloch would have left this?'

She felt her face becoming hot. Damn. She'd always blushed too easily.

'Because of something he said to me one of the last times we spoke.'

'And this was left while there was no one in the house? But it was fully locked up – even the windows?'

'Even the windows. I'm particularly careful about that sort of thing.'

'So you believe he has keys, and he came in while you

were out, left this and locked up again when he left?'

She nodded.

'Then he's not missing, is he?'

Mabel didn't reply.

'You parted on bad terms?' Fergus continued.

'Very bad. I'd ordered him to leave as soon as possible.'

Fergus frowned. 'I don't understand. If you asked him to leave, and he's left, why are you worried about him?'

Because he didn't say goodbye. Or thanks. And there was that mark, the hairs…

'He didn't take any of his possessions. Not even a jacket, as far as I know. I'd been asking him to move out for ages. He'd never shown any signs of preparing to leave, so to go from doing nothing about it to leaving at night, in winter, without so much as a coat – of course I'm worried.'

'Have you spoken to anyone else who has seen him since?'

She cleared her throat again. Maybe she was getting a cold.

'His sister claims to be able to contact him, though I don't know that she's seen him.'

'Claims? It sounds as if you don't believe her?'

It took a moment for Mabel to find her voice. 'I find it very worrying that he hasn't responded to any of my phone messages. The police didn't seem to take it very seriously.'

'I doubt he'd be classified as anything more than a low risk case, unless he's shown suicidal tendencies in the past. Has he?'

'Never.'

Fergus was watching her with that disturbing level of

intensity again. 'I need more information about this chap before I can get an idea of whether I can do anything to help you. Do you know his date of birth?'

'July the fifth 1946,' she replied. *Damn! Should have pretended to think about that. Need to stop sounding like a lovesick schoolgirl.*

'So he's what – sixty-one this summer?'

Mabel nodded impatiently. 'I need someone who can find out conclusively where he is, and that he's not had an accident, to set my mind at rest.'

'You said you have a number of his paintings in your gallery?'

'Indeed. I was the only gallerist who supported him during the past ten years. I have almost all his extant work either on display or in storage.'

'And who owns them if he doesn't turn up?'

She looked up at him in alarm.

'He must turn up, surely? Anyway, I suppose I own them. That was one of the terms on which we dealt. I took – take – an extremely modest commission on sales, in exchange for which the ownership of the unsold works reverts to me in the event of his... anything happening to him.'

'Now, now, let's not fear the worst. "Extremely modest". What sort of figure are we speaking about, if I may ask?'

'You may not, because it's not germane to the problem.'

'I understand that around forty per cent is the norm,' he continued, unfazed. 'I assume we are speaking about a much lower figure?'

'Much lower.'

'So in some ways you would profit if he *was* dead?'

Mabel lowered her gaze. What very piercing eyes Fergus had, despite his general appearance of a middle-aged roué. A most distinctive blue. Not unlike Roddy's, when he was still young and fit, but the colour of the sea on a dull day, not a sunny one.

'I say – you haven't bumped him off have you?' he added.

She was unable to prevent the scarlet flush running from her neck to her face. She bit her lip. Was that the impression she gave to strangers: a sort of latter-day Madeleine Smith, who'd think nothing of murdering an inconvenient lover?

He gave her a most endearing smile. 'Sorry. Just joking.'

'I don't think I share your sense of humour, in that case.'

'You're not giving me much to go on. Is he unmarried then?' asked Fergus. 'I mean – was he ever married, is he still married, widowed, divorced?'

'I believe he'd been married when he was very young. His sister told me. He never mentioned it. I assume if it's true then he was divorced in short order. There were no children at any rate. He couldn't have any.'

Too much information, Mabel. She felt the colour rise in her face again as she recalled an early remark of Roddy's: 'Not to worry, Mabs, pet. I'm not myrtle,' and how amused he'd been by her puzzlement over this particular use of rhyming slang. 'A Jaffa orange. Seedless. I only fire blanks,' he'd added. 'Bad case of mumps when I was eighteen.' Difficult to believe that conversation had taken place a quarter of a century ago…

Fergus had produced a notebook, and was scribbling.

'Ah ha, a sister. Does she live locally?'

'In Port Alexander, further west along the coast. She owns a shop. Craft work and cards, that sort of thing.'

'Name?'

'Of the sister or the shop?'

'Both, please.'

'She's Alison McCulloch. She prefers to be called Ali. Her shop's called Frogs and Princesses.'

'You don't get on?'

'I didn't say that!'

'Can I have your full name, and date of birth?'

'Why on earth do you need to know that?'

He shrugged. 'For the client record.'

'Mabel Rose Mountjoy.'

'Date of birth?'

God. She hated the finality of it. Just over five years, and she'd be sweet fifty.

'May the eighth, 1962.'

There was a slight flicker of surprise. Had he thought she was older? Younger?

'You don't have any idea of the wife's name?'

'Wife?'

'Roderick McCulloch's wife.'

'Not a clue. Sorry.'

'Background?'

'What?'

'His background. What sort of home was McCulloch from.'

'His father was a sheriff in Lanarkshire, so he'd had a comfortable upbringing. Glasgow Academy and all that, then a degree course at the Mac – the Glasgow School of…'

'I know what the Mac is!'

'He was the black sheep of the family, I'd say. Wasted his talent through drink right from the start.'

Worse than that too, but she'd always steered her mind away from the subject. It had been relatively innocuous substances in the early days of their affair. If only she'd been wise enough to perceive clearly at twenty what had become glaringly obvious later. The addictive personality. Enough books had been written about it to fill many shelves.

'So, place of birth, Glasgow? You said you don't believe he's simply gone on holiday; can you tell me in more detail *why*?'

Mabel shrugged. 'Intuition. I've known him for a very long time.'

'He'd lived here with you? In this house?' he added when she hesitated. 'That's why he had keys?'

She blushed again. *Damn.*

'Not in recent years. I'd found his drinking bouts too distressing. That's why I asked him to move to the cottage.'

'Forgive me pursuing this, but if I'm to help you, I need to fully understand the situation – I assume you were in an intimate relationship with McCulloch?'

Oh God.

'At one stage,' she croaked. 'But I had ended it some time ago.'

She fell into a reverie. When had the handsome, amusing, confident, talented young lion of the Glasgow art scene who had arrived in Kirkcudbright all those years ago transmogrified to a dishevelled, ill-smelling, drunken, lecherous sponger?

'Ah.'

Fergus eyed the lump of slag, which he had placed carefully on the fireside table.

'An acrimonious ending to the relationship?'

'You could say that.'

'But he stayed on in your cottage?'

'He had nowhere else to go.'

'His sister?'

Mabel chortled miserably. 'She'd never have given him a home. I'd say it was either me or the Salvation Army.'

Fergus raised his eyebrows. 'Really – that bad?'

'That bad.'

'Do you have a photograph of him by any chance?'

Damn! She should have thought of that. She racked her brains; was there another more or less recent photo of Roddy on his own?

'Just a moment.'

She ran upstairs and rootled in the middle drawer of her bedside cabinet. She found one from around five years before – but not before her eyes had flickered over the older ones, where she and Roddy were a couple, and she was a woman in love.

'Would this do?' she held out the print to Fergus.

'When was this taken?'

'Recently enough. He still looks like that.'

He studied it closely. 'I'd say he was a good-looking man in his youth?'

'Very.'

'Can I hang onto it meantime?'

'Of course.'

He placed the photo carefully inside his briefcase, rose to his feet, and walked to the rear window again. Mabel moved to stand beside him.

'Could I have a look at the cottage?'

'That's it.' She pointed down the garden.

'I mean, can I see inside it?'

'There's little to see. I've packed up all his stuff. I wanted to be able to register it as empty, so that I'd save a little on Council Tax. I might try to let it this summer.'

'All the same, I'd find it helpful to inspect it.'

She fetched a key; with what she knew seemed like an ill grace, she led Fergus to the back door, and down the path to the stone building at the garden's westernmost edge. She unlocked the door and stood aside.

'If you don't mind, I won't come in. I'll go back to the house and make a pot of tea. Or would you prefer coffee?'

He looked horrified. 'Good God, no. Tea every time. Do you happen to have Lapsang Souchong? I take it we're not talking tea-bags?'

'No to the first question, yes to the second. We are not talking tea-bags. I have Assam or Darjeeling or Blue Lady.'

'Assam then, please.'

Lapsang Souchong indeed. She loathed the taste. It was

to tea as Glen Fruig, the uber-smoky Hebridean malt Roddy favoured, was to other malt whiskies. But it was so unusual to find a kindred spirit – someone who cared about the finer detail – that she looked out the silver teapot, even gave it a quick buff-up while the kettle boiled.

He was back within a quarter of an hour. She had laid out her best teacups and saucers, ready to carry them through, but Fergus settled himself at the kitchen table. She sighed a little. It was all right. Somehow, she felt less nervous in her own kitchen since Fergus had arrived, even though she'd managed to scald herself because she wasn't paying attention.

'What have you done to your finger?' he said.

'It's nothing.'

Fergus took her hand gently in his and examined it. He tutted. 'Haven't you got any burn dressings?'

'Not worth the bother. There's some Savlon in the drawer.'

He watched while she dabbed the scald with ointment.

'I assume as well as tidying the cottage you've given it a damn good clean since McCulloch left?'

Mabel bridled. 'Of course. Have you ever lived with a drinker, Mr Learmonth?'

'I have not. But I can imagine they're not particularly house-proud.'

'It was filthy. I'm very angry that he took so little care of it.'

'I assume you didn't charge him a high rent?'

'High! I charged him nothing at all.'

'And when you tidied, you found no clues as to where

he might have gone?'

Mabel shook her head.

He set down his cup. 'Could I possibly see the items you've packed up?'

'Do you need to? There's absolutely nothing of interest. Just clothes and so on.'

'It's more any paperwork I'd be interested in. Any bank statements for instance? Diaries?'

'Roddy didn't know what day it was in the last year or two, far less keep a diary. He didn't hold with any sort of paperwork. He was the limit. You've no idea how many times the power or the phone here was nearly cut off because Roddy had put the bill in the fire.'

Fergus nodded. 'Perhaps I could take a quick look tomorrow then?'

'I really don't see any point. There were no diaries, or anything of the sort. I'm not certain that I want to hire you. I'll need to think it over.'

He looked a little taken aback. *One-nil to you, Mabel, old girl.* He brushed his hands together, and stood up. Hoity-toity. He didn't like that did he, someone daring to fail to take the bait on the first cast?

'Well, if you could let me know,' he said crisply. 'I mean to stay in Kirkcudbright overnight, and I'll probably head home tomorrow, so I'd be grateful if you could perhaps let me have your decision by then.'

'What are your fees?' She knew as she asked that she wanted him to stay, and to find Roddy.

'Three hundred a day, plus out of pocket expenses from when you sign a contract with me. I assure you, I normally get results very quickly; often within twenty-four hours.'

Mabel swallowed hard. 'I'd like you to work for me,' she said quickly. 'I need to find out what's happened to Roddy. The paintings are the least of it. I've known him a long time.'

Fergus sat down again, and gave her a smile of surprising sweetness. 'Forgive me, Miss Mountjoy, but I may need to ask you some more rather personal questions before we get much further.'

'I understand. And please, call me Mabel. Miss Mountjoy sounds terribly formal.'

Fergus cleared his throat. 'Then you must call me Fergus. I take it you and Roddy had been living together as partners for a considerable time?'

She nodded, studying the pattern on her cup. 'Until a year or two ago.'

'Ah. You met when you were a student in Glasgow?'

'We did.'

'The age-difference must have been rather noticeable at that point? You were one of *his* students?'

Mabel tried unsuccessfully to keep her tone nonchalant. 'Yes. No, not in the way you mean. I was only an evening class student at the Mac. I was an adult in any case.'

'Hmm. And you had been a couple ever since, until recently?'

'More or less. Roddy was away for a few years after I graduated. Then he moved here.'

As an excuse to escape that shrewd gaze, Mabel carried the teapot to the sink and began tipping the dregs into a sieve. She could still feel him watching her closely, and that was unsettling.

'I put them on the rose-beds,' she explained. 'The tealeaves.'

Fergus beamed. 'My mother used to do exactly the same. I imagine we had a very similar upbringing, you and I. That always makes it easier. So many things don't need to be spelled out. Could I trouble you for a glass of water.'

As she turned on the tap he added, 'I don't suppose you have any mineral water?'

'Of course not. The tap water's perfectly pure here.'

He pulled a face. 'I've got out of the way of it. Living in London – even in Edinburgh these days – you can taste the chemicals. I only drink Evian.'

'Well, I don't have any.'

'I'll pass then.'

She fumed silently for a moment. 'Was the tea up to scratch, or could you taste chemicals in that too?'

'It's all right once it's boiled.'

Ridiculous man. It was almost as if he'd expected her to say she'd run to the shop for some. Evian indeed. Probably you couldn't even buy that in Kirkcudbright's tiny Tesco. As for the Co-op…

By the time he left, she was emotionally drained. It had taken her by surprise when he asked to see the cottage. Thank God she'd cleaned it so thoroughly. And thank God he hadn't insisted on seeing her attic, where several boxes, neatly stacked beside the pile of unfinished paintings, held all of Roderick McCulloch's worldly goods.

Not that it wasn't immaculately tidy. She was up there

every second day, with her gallon can and filler funnel, emptying the various receptacles that caught the drips. In fact, when she'd been stowing Roddy's gear there she'd discovered another leak. She didn't want a stranger seeing that she couldn't afford to maintain her home.

However, the prospect of meeting Fergus Learmonth again was not unappealing. Although she recognised an arrogant bastard when she saw one, she could admit to herself it was a characteristic she secretly admired. He was what her father would have labelled 'a fine figure of a man'. Could probably stand losing a stone or so, but he had the height to carry it off. He reminded her of some breed of dog she couldn't pin down. Large and shaggy and willing to please. A good protector.

She shook herself. 'Stop it, you ridiculous woman.'

She poured a glass of tap water, then wrinkled her nose before she started to drink. Perhaps there *was* a hint of chemicals?

How had she and Roddy McCulloch met, Fergus had asked. How indeed? She'd gone to evening classes at the Mac while she was doing her degree, suddenly aflame with the idea that she was an artist manquée, wasting her time studying Fine Art instead of practising it. A couple of weeks at the classes soon disabused her of that notion. It wasn't that she was less competent than any of the others; she simply recognised that she'd never be a *great* artist. It was only common sense and good manners to acknowledge the fact.

Their lecturer went off sick at Christmas and was replaced by another. The very first class in January, he had spent almost the entire two hours eyeing up the talent. Not the quality of the students' work: eighty per cent of the evening class students were female; seventy-five per cent of them were under twenty-one. Towards the end of the class, Mabel had become conscious of him standing at her shoulder. She was wearing flat shoes, so he was exactly her height. He was so close that she could feel his warm breath on her neck even before he spoke. When he did speak, it wasn't to offer constructive criticism of her work. It was to say, 'I'd like you to sit for me some time, Miss Mabel Mountjoy, with your swan's neck and Pre-Raphaelite hair.'

She'd turned and taken in the outfit and the man. Roddy McCulloch; a tad under thirty-five, a cross between a Victorian dandy and a teddy boy in his chocolate brown corduroy suit and red Paisley-pattern silk cravat; the luxuriant mane of coal-black hair, the neat wee goatee, the sea blue eyes (roving eyes even then; she'd known from the start he'd break her heart).

So she'd tossed her hair back and said she'd think about it, and Roddy had laughed and laid his warm hand possessively on her shoulder.

Afterwards, she'd gone straight to the library and pored over Julia Margaret Cameron's photographs of the Beautiful People of the Pre-Raphaelite diaspora. When she left, she felt differently and walked differently. Homely, ginger-haired Mabs, the tim'rous beastie from provincial Scotland, was suddenly up there with Lizzie Siddal and Jane Morris and Fanny Cornforth. She straightened her shoulders and held her swan's neck more proudly. Her fate was sealed.

The first time her lecturer asked her out for a meal,

she'd known perfectly well how the evening would end. Dinner with Roddy meant dessert between the sheets. By the time she'd graduated, she was already living in his glamorous Bohemian flat in Hyndland, rolling in his warm bed every night, and modelling for him without clothes.

But she'd have been mortified to let Fergus Learmonth – or anyone else – know that even after his fall from grace she'd allowed Roddy back into her own bed, if only for one night, as recently as eighteen months ago. It had been an unrewarding experience from every point of view.

When she'd first been led into Roddy's elegant home in 1982, Mabel had assumed he owned it. Only after she'd moved in with him did she realise it was rented. She'd loved it all the same: three-metre ceilings with plain egg-and-dart mouldings at the cornice, instead of the more flamboyant styles; tall windows that flooded the rooms with light, even on dreich days.

There was normally little food in the fridge, but always an abundant supply of wine and whisky, and more exotic tipples. It was there that she'd first tasted 'the green fairy', as Roddy liked to call it, long before the days when you could buy absinthe quite openly in the larger supermarkets. She loathed the taste, although she'd wanted to like it, since it brought a frisson of near-illegality. Drink had been where it began and ended. She'd always been too much of a coward to try anything more adventurous. Roddy would tease her about being Daddy's good little girl, a charming provincial wuss. 'Pussy-wussy,' he'd say, tickling her under the chin. Most of the time, she overcame the urge to slap him.

She and Roddy would hold court, like Arthur and Guinevere (bit of an age-difference there too, she'd read). She basked in reflected glory to keep herself warm. Indeed, there had been an occasion when one of his weirdo friends had produced a crown for her, a tawdry object, papier-mâché and paste; most probably acquired from the bin outside a theatrical costumiers. She'd had enough to drink to feel pleased with herself as he placed it on her head.

Her cheeks grew hot with shame at this memory. What a shallow creature the twenty-year-old Mabel Mountjoy had been.

Father was self-sufficient in those days, still running his practice effectively and profitably, although he was over official retirement age. Amazing how suddenly an elderly parent and a former lover can become needy and clinging.

CHAPTER FIVE

Fergus was pensive as he made his way back to the hotel. Possibly he should have told Mabel Mountjoy he couldn't help, and scarpered back to Edinburgh post haste.

He persuaded himself it was the house that had swayed him, because it conjured up such strong memories of the single period in his life when he'd been truly happy. The one time he'd been truly loved. He gave himself a shake. No point in descending into self-pity. An act as lonely as onanism.

If he was honest with himself, he'd also been influenced by Mabel's frank and troubled amber-coloured eyes, and her luxuriant auburn hair. A million miles away from the species of high-maintenance brunette he'd always thought of as 'his type', but an extremely attractive woman. Capable too, he imagined. His grandmother would have approved of her.

In any case, the only person waiting for him in Edinburgh was his cat; Gorby would be happy enough for another three days with the sitter. Fergus paid her to come in twice a day, and spend time with the animal.

He'd treat this as a little holiday. The Roseberry Arms was more congenial than he'd expected, and after working so assiduously to get the book finished on time, he had earned a break. If he could track down Mabel Mountjoy's irritating friend within two days, well and good. It'd be something to keep his mind off life in general. And it'd be a small salve to his pride.

Inside Mabel's garden cottage the atmosphere had been cold, dank and unwelcoming. Apart from a lingering smell of turpentine and strong tobacco, it was tremendously clean and tidy, and soul-less.

A few aspects of her behaviour troubled him. Some of her remarks had been oddly phrased – such as saying that William Asher wasn't an ancestor of her *father*.

There was something peculiar about her level of concern over the artist too, and she'd become very flustered when he'd cracked a silly joke about her doing away with him… She was holding back on something, and clearly obfuscating about the reason for her disquiet over McCulloch's disappearance. His guess would be that she'd lent the man a substantial amount of money, and was ashamed to admit she'd been so gullible. It wouldn't be the first time he'd run into that flavour of set-up! Perhaps she was merely bonkers. You'd be able to hide it rather well in a place like this: charming eccentricity. All the same, her conviction that the disappearance was more sinister than it seemed worried him.

Mabel didn't strike him as the type of person who'd commit a violent act, and if there was one thing he was confident of, it was his ability to judge character. At this point, his mind swivelled once more to Serena; ah well, that had been his *one* slip-up. Possibly his first two marriages as well. In fact, no 'possibly' about it in the case of the second.

'Get a grip, Fergus,' he told himself. 'Clearly you're no better at judging women's characters than you are at skateboarding.'

Once she'd got over her initial jitteriness, Mabel Mountjoy had turned out to be one of those people who can worm your life history out of you on short acquaintance. He'd even found himself showing her the photo of Serena he carried in his wallet.

Mabel felt more settled by the time Fergus Learmonth left. She also found she was glad he was coming back. Despite the sticky outset, she'd liked him. He was solid and respectable. Nice teeth too – unusual in a smoker. Possibly he was as vain about that as Roddy, and forever getting them whitened. Mabel studied her own teeth in the hall mirror, and frowned.

If only he wouldn't talk about his dead wife all the time, although having been shown the photo that Fergus carried in his wallet she could see why he hadn't got over her. Serena. The most stunningly beautiful woman she could recall seeing, with her black hair, skin so supernaturally white it was almost transparent, and superb cheekbones. The type of face men start wars for. The type of face that led to the downfall of Troy. The type of face that would have Roddy's trousers around his ankles in a twinkling, superficial old lecher that he was.

The wound still seemed very raw. She felt a twinge of wistfulness. Oh, to be loved like that! But the woman had been so exquisite that Mabel knew she couldn't begin to feel remotely jealous. Totally out of her league – quite apart from the fact that Serena had presumably been in her twenties when the photo was taken.

Father would have approved of Fergus, she felt: the sort of man he would have picked for her if he could. They'd have sat in their armchairs, one either side of the fire, wrapped in a cloud of fragrant Virginia tobacco smoke, discussing cricket and music and Oriental rugs.

It wasn't that Father and Roddy hadn't got on. More that her parent had been unable to speak to her about the fact he must have known damn well that the artist spent his nights in her bed (her lover had been vocal in his pleasures when he was a younger man).

The other men she'd met over his lifetime had never quite measured up to Father. Ne'er do wells, in his estimation. The posh boys from good schools and good homes always seemed to pick anorexic bimbos, not a strong-boned girl like her.

If her mother had hung around to see her grown, life could have been very different; she'd have had someone to counsel her, someone to confide in – as well as someone to temper Father's attitude to suitors. Although she'd never been fashionably sylph-like, even as a teenager, Mabel had always been considered a handsome woman.

After she graduated, she hadn't seen Roddy for five years, because he'd taken off, without warning, for New York. He hadn't invited her to go with him. She'd managed to stick with the teacher-training course at Jordanhill – just – and realised after a year or two of working in a school that she hated and feared teenage children above all other creatures. Their painted nails and knowing gaze and sarcastic whispers filled her with dread. With the younger ones, she always felt she lacked the knack of knowing how to talk to them. So she'd crawled back home with her tail between her legs. After she gave up on teaching, she had acted as her father's housekeeper, sometimes his secretary (she laughed when she saw adverts for highly-qualified legal secretaries; what qualifications did you need for *that*, beyond tact and common sense?), never his confidante. On her twenty-fifth birthday, once Father had realised that she didn't plan to abandon him to forge a career with her Fine Art degree from the University of Glasgow, he had presented her with the keys of the building that was now her gallery, and told her she had a good business head on her shoulders, she should get on with it.

And that was that. The years slid past, until McCulloch turned up again towards the end of 1988, at the official opening of the revamped Waterside Gallery, a rucksack on his back and his easel under his arm. He looked exactly as he did when she'd last seen him. 'Remember me?' he asked, kissing her as if they'd parted only the day before. 'I've decided to live in Kirkcudbright.'

She'd tried hard to present a chilly front, but the spark was still there. All it needed was a small breath of air to jink it back to a flame, and it's always breezy at the coast…

She'd not been without suitors before or after he decamped, and had in fact lost her virginity to a promising young medical student of good family at Glasgow University when she was nineteen. The affair hadn't lasted.

She had discovered the hard way that she wasn't the only girl to be sharing his bed.

There had been no local hopefuls apart from the boy who'd sat next to her in primary school, and had never left Kirkcudbright. He was the only one who wasn't fazed by her father's glaring disapproval. He'd proposed to her, but she turned him down. *Such an opinion of yourself you had at twenty-three, Mabel.* All the other Stewartry lads were terrified of Father. Apart from that librarian chap the year before Roddy came back. But he'd been on the weedy side, with an Essex accent and a face badly-pockmarked from teenage acne. And of course his name had been *Nigel.* She could not have spent her life with a Nigel, or a Norman, or a Geoffrey.

Within months of Roddy reappearing, he had more or less moved into the main house; Father had dealt with the matter very tactfully, pretending to believe that the artist still slept in the cottage where he worked.

Once they'd been together for several years, and he'd become something of a fixture in the town, Roddy had started dealing in nineteenth-century Scottish paintings. He specialised in turning on the charm for elderly women and separating them from their artistic inheritance for disconcertingly low prices. That was how he'd come by three of the paintings Mabel still had in the gallery. It was a worry. The last thing she wanted was to be associated with ripping off women older than she was. The ones he reckoned would do well, he'd taken up to McTears in Glasgow. Or rather, she had, because Roddy had opted never to drive. Why bother, when he'd always been assured of a willing female chauffeur? On very rare occasions, he'd even haul a canvas down to London, as long as it wasn't too large to take on the train (Mabel baulked at driving *that* distance); as often as not he'd come home having bought something even better. It was thus that he'd come by the putative Miró, the previous year.

And that had been the long and short of it; a quick slide into relatively contented domesticity. Latterly, Mabel had felt it was the best of a bad job, because she'd observed that once you hit thirty, the majority of unattached men are taking their second ride on the merry-go-round, and tend to have children in tow, even if only weekend ones. She'd never been good with children. She found their shrill voices, their noisy music, their constant demands for attention, exhausting. And she'd observed, from the experience of friends, that the children of broken marriages always seemed to be particularly whiny and obtrusive.

There had been a Peter a year or so before, not long after she put Roddy out of the house. Another friend of Sylvia's. But he had the care of his twin girls every weekend, and they seemed to regard Mabel's intrusion on their time with him as an excuse for behaviour that went beyond all the bounds of what she could tolerate. The final straw was when one of them hurled her dinner (and one of Mabel's precious Mason's Ironstone *Indian Tree* dinner plates) onto the dining room floor.

So Peter had to be given the heave-ho within two months. She could hardly have demanded that he choose between her and his children. In any case, all the time he was there, Mabel had been heart-wrenchingly aware of

Roddy McCulloch in his lonely single bed, a short garden-length away.

A pity, because not only was Peter an Eng Lit graduate from her own university, he was reasonably good-looking, and financially independent. Plus, he was tall and well-built enough to make her feel petite. *Always the pragmatist, Mabs.*

Poor Fergus Learmonth was the opposite of a pragmatist. He had lost a wife he clearly doted on. All Mabel had lost was a handful of unsuitable suitors, and a drunk with a flaccid penis and halitosis. Well, perhaps not all: she'd also lost the best years of her life. She sighed deeply, putting up a quick and indeterminate prayer (she believed neither in God nor in guardian angels) that Roddy had simply abandoned her for a fresh billet and a new life, because perhaps if she was the one who had turned him into what he'd become, someone more caring could mend the damage. A love with no strings attached. She shook back her hair and set about pruning her indoor fig almost viciously. It *wasn't* her fault. She hadn't fallen out of love with Roddy: he'd fallen out of being a man anyone could love – even a sister, by the sound of it. By the time the plant was looking like a bonsai and she had made herself a fresh pot of tea, she had shoehorned her thoughts away from Roddy and towards Fergus Learmonth.

She spent the next hour reading everything she could find about Fergus on the Internet. More famous than she had appreciated. He had specialised in what she supposed one would call investigative journalism. His entire career seemed to have been in television, first as a news journalist with the BBC, then with Albion, where he'd proceeded to get his own programme series by 1991, eventually working out of London for Albion's parent company. She wasn't sure Father would have approved of such a frivolous metier.

She found she was positively looking forward to Fergus's return the next day. That night, she took a long, hot bath and used the last of her Jo Malone *Red Roses* bath oil. She washed her hair with more attention than usual, then spent two hours laying out most of her dresses and skirts on the bed to see which made her look slimmest.

CHAPTER SIX

The following morning, she had to force herself not to stand in the hall waiting to fling open the door the moment Fergus knocked. *Foolish woman. Anyone would think you were a teenager waiting for your first date to show up. Keep your mind on why he's here.* She disciplined herself to stay in the kitchen, having run a duster quickly over the polished surfaces in the sitting room. She made a fresh pot of coffee, and sat with her hands wrapped round the warmth of her favourite earthenware mug, while she closed her eyes and pictured Fergus taking a leisurely breakfast in the Roseberry Arms' dining room. A Full English fan, or coffee and croissants? Although hadn't he said he never drank coffee? Mabel tipped the last of her drink into the sink, and rinsed everything thoroughly, so that not one vestige of coffee aroma lingered. She lit the sitting room fire, remembering how chilly it had been the day before.

Wrestling with the cellophane on a fresh packet of Lapsang Souchong from the deli, she cut her finger.

When she heard the knocker applied to the brass plate, at exactly the appointed hour this time, she made herself stop and count to ten before she answered. She patted her hair and smoothed her skirt over her hips.

As soon as she opened the door, and saw him smiling

at her, she felt a fresh pang of jealousy over the dead wife. What a waste, to have netted a man like Fergus Learmonth and then had the bad taste to expire. At least he'd had the sense to put on a waterproof jacket today, even for the short walk from the hotel. She hung it on the hallstand, and smiled to herself.

'I'm sorry I was waspish when you arrived yesterday,' she said. 'Some of the things that have happened recently have left me a bit jittery.'

'Quite understandable. It was inconsiderate of me to turn up far too early.' He gave a most reassuring smile.

'What first?' she asked. 'Tea?'

'I've newly had breakfast,' said Fergus. 'Perhaps in a little while. Have you hurt yourself again?' He gestured to the sticking plaster on her finger.

'It's nothing.'

He asked if he could see over the house, so Mabel gave him a guided tour of the public rooms.

He came to an abrupt halt in the dining room, studying two canvases each depicting a woman alone at a table. 'Are these Vettrianos?'

'They are. *Café Nights* and *Moon River.* Early work.'

'Not the ones I've heard described as soft porn either. These are tasteful.' Fergus whistled through his teeth. 'His *Singing Butler* sold for more than three-quarters of a million a couple of years ago, didn't it? A good investment.'

'I suppose you turn up your nose at his work? Almost everyone who fancies himself as a connoisseur seems to. I like them very much, as a matter of fact. I love the way they tell a story. A friend recommended buying them when they were first exhibited, in the eighties. I hope they've appreciated some since then. In fact, I'm thinking of selling one. I have some repairs to make to the house…'

'It's always sad to part with a painting, but you're right. Needs must, sometimes. My grandparents had a Turner. One of his Heidelberg scenes – a small example. I sold it when I moved to London, because the cash came in handy and I'd probably have had to keep it in the bank anyway. So much art theft nowadays, particularly in the south east.'

He'd tried to put the cash towards buying back his grandparents' home in Inveresk, but the family who owned it by then flatly refused to sell.

Fergus sighed, and continued to inspect the artwork on the sitting room walls. There was a Jolomo, from his earliest period, before he was slinging out dozens a month and you found prints of his work everywhere you looked. A Steven Campbell, dark and brooding. Two others which he felt he should have recognised. He peered at the signatures.

'Bellany,' said Mabel. 'And these landscapes are Bet Low.'

'You're a big fan of modern Scottish art!'

'I am. Roddy McCulloch knew a lot of these artists from the Mac.'

'What was here before? On the walls before you started collecting,' he added, in response to her puzzled look. 'Family portraits?'

'None of those. Just dull Victorian watercolours.

Heather-and-dead-stag and variations thereon. Nothing valuable. Not in the same league as a Turner anyway! I have no idea what the earlier generations hung there. I sold them on to people who like that sort of thing. Or rather, Roddy did.'

Mabel was relieved that the inspection of her art collection stopped short at what was downstairs. Family portraits indeed! The painting which was possibly her favourite in the world hung in her bedroom – for no ones eyes except her own: a red-haired nude stretched on a couch, her legs bent a little so as to conceal her pubis, her head turned away from the viewer ever so slightly. Roddy had often painted her naked in the early days. This one was the best, the most flattering. The most *like* her, he'd said, more than once...

He'd painted it in 1983, when she was on the point of graduating. Not long before they split up for the first time.

'You're not an artist yourself?' asked Fergus, startling her.

'No! I used to dabble. It helped me appreciate art more, so it wasn't a complete waste of time.'

'So what are your hobbies then – are you a golfer?' he asked.

'I am *not*. Are you?'

He shook his head. 'I can't abide games that involve anything smaller than a rugby ball.'

'I had you down as a cricket man.'

Fergus guffawed. 'Cricket? Never. I played rugger when I was at school and university, and boxed a bit.'

'Which school did you go to?'

'Fettes. I know – snobs' paradise.

'Same as the sainted Tony.'

He pulled a face. 'Don't even begin to compare me! Where were you educated then – local comp?'

She laughed aloud in her turn. 'St Leonard's. Presumably Father assumed it offered the best opportunity for running into any stray royals who'd ended up at St Andrews University. A few decades too early, as it turned out.'

They sniggered together.

Fergus fought a sudden impulse to lay his arm around Mabel's comfortable shoulders. He switched his mind to the artwork hanging on his own walls. Although from a century earlier than these, his collection would look good in this room; even better than in his flat in Edinburgh's West End.

'Magnificent house,' he said wistfully. 'I envy you. My grandparents lived in one very similar to this, at Inveresk, on the outskirts of Edinburgh. My mother's parents. I've always regretted that it was lost out of our family. I don't suppose you know the name of the architect of this one?'

'I'm afraid not.'

'I suppose there was a plethora of good, provincial Scottish architects in those days. Handsome, solid houses.

Nothing so good since. It's amazing – even the joiner-work of the doors and skirting boards here is the same as Inveresk.'

'Why on earth did your family let it go then?'

'Death duties when the grandparents died.'

Well, she knew all about that. It had seemed so unfair. All these years caring for Father, and yet when he died she had to pay inheritance tax on her home and furniture as if she'd never lived there. Fergus had looked intensely sad when he spoke about his grandparents' home. Not so hardboiled as he liked to think, then?

'I've always regretted that I never managed to buy it back,' Fergus was saying. 'The same family who bought it in 1979 still own it. You inherited this house alone – no siblings?'

Mabel shook her head. 'I'm an only child, and I came back here in my mid-twenties, to keep house for Father.'

How parochial it made her sound. She had always tried to avoid thinking of her life that way, but was suddenly struck by the fact that she'd barely been out of Kirkcudbright for more than a few weeks at a time for over twenty years. The world had changed so fast during her lifetime. After all, it was only in the year she'd gone up to university that the Glasgow University Union voted to admit women.

'You lost your mother early on?'

Mabel wriggled her shoulders uncomfortably. 'When I

was a month or so under four. I barely remember her.'

Vague Proustian memories of perfume – Chanel No5, she thought – and pretty clothes and a body that was soft and rounded, the antithesis of Father's awkward, angular frame.

'Your father didn't remarry?'

'I think she put him off other women for life. I don't even remember him going on dates with anyone else.'

Or if he did, he'd been damn discreet about it, and waited until she'd been shipped off to boarding school. She pinched herself furtively. It didn't do to let a stranger see how badly her mother's desertion had hurt her.

Fergus looked faintly puzzled. 'And you've never married?'

'Too choosy.' She flashed him a brittle smile. 'I'm not the marrying kind. I value my independence too much.'

She'd thought possibly he was an intelligent man, but he seemed to suffer the same delusion as the rest of his sex: a woman of substance and reasonable looks who hadn't netted a man and reproduced by the time she was forty had failed in a God-given task.

'Probably wise,' said Fergus calmly. 'I was married and divorced twice before I met Serena. It's easy to make the wrong choice, specially when you're young.'

Married three times? Jesus! 'So I've heard, from friends.'

'You lost your father recently?'

'It'll be three years this July. He was ninety-two.'

'You must have been a very late baby!'

'Mphm.'

'You had to nurse him for a long time?'

'No, thank God. He was blessed with singularly good health. Came through the war unscathed too. He died shortly after having a major stroke.'

She fell into reverie, remembering the morning she'd heard a dull thump from the bathroom, and rushed breathless up the stairs, to linger on the landing and listen to the silence behind the locked door. She'd had to get Roddy to help her kick it in (she was still surprised that he'd had the physical strength to accomplish the task: *in vino est fortitudo*). Father on the floor, his face the colour of putty, dribble running from the corner of his mouth. Less than two weeks later, he was dead. A mercy, really. Oblivion. Briony and a couple of her other friends were caught up in the interminable trauma of dealing with parents who'd lost their minds along with their physical mobility, and no longer recognised their own reflections in the mirror.

She'd looked after him faithfully until the end. Who would do that for her? She'd end up having to bribe someone who was still young and fit enough to take her to Switzerland as soon as she felt incapacity coming on. Fat chance; what warning had Father got? At least she'd never be a burden to anyone, other than the hired hands in some cold, linoleum-floored nursing home. No one whose future *she'd* blight. No one she'd lay a guilt trip on.

'I don't imagine I'd be a good nurse,' she said briskly, smoothing down her skirt. 'Haven't the patience. Are your parents still alive?'

Fergus pulled a face. 'No. My mother died at eighty-five, eighteen months ago. Sounds as if we're alike in that too – both from long-lived families.'

'Mmm,' said Mabel, clearing her throat. 'You lost your father earlier?'

'My father was killed in the Korean war.'

'Really?' She was immediately interested. 'I don't think I've ever known of anyone who died in that war. Were you close to your mother then? I suppose you would have been, same as Father and me?'

'I didn't live with her after I went to University. But we'd see each other often.'

Fergus had often kicked himself for not hanging onto his mother's house, if only for its garden and the memories it held, even though it was in Lauder rather than Edinburgh. Not so handsome as this one – a rather dour Victorian pile, truth to tell; and at least he'd got an excellent price for it.

He'd been able to visit his mother more often after Serena died, of course. Sad that the two women who had meant most to him in his life, whose love he'd craved most, had detested each other.

His mind swivelled involuntarily to an incident when he and Serena had been driving back from his mother's house to Stockbridge one winter night. There had been a car parked in a lay-by outside Lauder, and when their headlights swept across it, he'd seen clearly what the couple in the front seat were doing: the woman was sitting astride, and the man was clearly at the point of no return. Fergus had pulled in, to watch. Although Serena had tried to turn off the headlights, he'd kept his hand over the switch. He'd been so desperate with lust by the time they got home that he didn't even let her get upstairs to the bedroom before he... Afterwards, she had looked at him with an expression of utter contempt. The memory made his eyes sting. He *must* get more control over his thoughts.

'Are you all right?' said Mabel. She was watching him with concern. 'You've turned quite flushed. Do you want a glass of water? I got in some bottled stuff. Sorry – I know how it feels, suddenly remembering someone who's dead.'

He gave himself a mental and physical shake. 'I'm fine. It's a little warm in here. Think I'll take a turn in the garden, maybe have a smoke.'

Fergus strolled among Mabel's shrubs, rattled by having let his guard slip before such an attractive woman. Almost forty-five? Well-preserved for her age. No wrinkles, no eye-bags. Shapely women aged so much better than skinny ones. He permitted himself sixty seconds of wondering how Serena would have aged. Not well, he suspected. She'd have been haggard, like those models you'd see in magazines. Although, perhaps she'd filled out a bit after having children. What sort of mother would she have made? He simply couldn't imagine her with kids; always too wrapped up in herself. He found himself wondering where they were now. They'd be at school. The boy must be, what, seven, eight? He used to wish he had a photo of them. Serena would have been forty this year. He wasn't sure how she'd have coped with that either. He gave himself another mental shake. *Don't think ill of the dead.*

When he went back in, he settled more comfortably into the armchair Mabel said had been her father's, and held out his hands to the fire. He hoped that if he was to spend any time at all in this house, she would relent over the cigars.

'You'd have got on well with some of the previous occupants,' said Mabel.

'Your father you mean?'

'Earlier than that. Apparently the first owner and his sons weren't above a bit of smuggling. I presume they smuggled tobacco and spirits as well as salt, although I've heard salt was one of the more important items of trade. Imagine. Nowadays, we're all being told not to put any on our food.'

'Does the house have secret hidey-holes then?'

He felt the look she gave him was rather startled.

'There's a cellar,' she said. 'No secret tunnels.'

'That you know of!'

'That I know of,' she agreed.

'Mabel,' he said suddenly. 'I've never known a Mabel. It's a lovely old-fashioned name.'

'I've always loathed it. I'll tell you a secret. I was christened Maybelle.' She spelled it out for him. 'Have you ever heard the like? I changed the spelling when I went to secondary school. Father called me Mabs.'

'But you don't like that either? You have a middle name: Rose, isn't it?'

'I wouldn't want to be called Rose,' she replied too quickly. 'It was my mother's name.'

He was about to say she didn't look like a rose, but stopped himself short. Because that was exactly what she *did* remind him of, with her rich, delicate colouring – plus the fact that, even on slender acquaintance, he recognised that there were a good few thorns.

He formed a mental picture of the roses that had climbed against either side of the door of the summer-house at Lauder. Sumptuous and subtle peachy lemon, pink-flushed, blowsy blooms. He couldn't remember the name of the variety. His mother had praised it to the skies: a strong grower, disease-resistant, prolific in its flowering. What he remembered best was that not only did the blooms avoid assailing the eye with their colour, even the scent was reticent and good-mannered. You'd to bury your nose in its heart to appreciate how lovely it was. A secretive rose; shy.

'Belle. That could be short for Maybelle,' said Fergus.

' "Belle Mountjoy"? Sounds like a prostitute. The kind you have to phone for an appointment.'

Fergus was startled by the simile. Then, composure regained, he said, 'I don't think it sounds like that at all! You look like a Belle. It suits you. It suits your colouring – does that sound daft?'

'Very.' But she couldn't help smiling.

'Then may I try calling you Belle?'

'I suppose. I'll let you know if I think I could get used to it.'

This was shaping up as a most odd business arrangement. Moving far too quickly. Mabel stroked the pug's ears, revelling in how lovely it was to have someone to *talk* to, someone who heard what she was saying. Someone who understood her life. It was too many years since Roddy had been like that. And of course, Father…

She smiled to herself, remembering how Fergus had almost jumped out of his skin when she'd uttered the word 'prostitute'. That pleased her. Didn't do to be too easy to read.

'It'd be handy if we could drive round the area, so that you can point out to me the places McCulloch frequented,' announced Fergus.

She was glad he'd stopped referring to Roddy by his first name. Almost as if he'd been placed at a safe distance. McCulloch. That sounded like a stranger.

'We'll go in my car,' added Fergus, 'so that people don't notice you. I assume your car's well-known, around the town at any rate?'

'I'd say so. It's pretty distinctive.'

'Oh?'

He perked up, and Mabel laughed. 'If you're picturing a bright red sports car, you're in for a disappointment.'

'What do you drive then?'

She supposed he was now envisaging something along the lines of a navy blue Corsa.

'Come and see. You haven't been inside the garage anyway. Maybe there are some clues there, though I doubt it. Roddy never went in.'

She led the way down the garden.

'He didn't drive, you said?'

'Lost his licence years ago, long before I knew him, and never bothered to get it back.' She tugged open the wooden door leading from the garden. 'Anyway, this is my transport, so you see why I agreed that it's a tad conspicuous.'

'Jesus!' muttered Fergus under his breath.

'It's eminently practical. There's a huge amount of space in the back. I can get very large canvases in, if I pack them diagonally.'

She loved the Land Rover Defender, even although it was far from young and far from unsullied. A safe vehicle. That's what mattered. In any case, it suited her temperament. Anyone who thought Mabel Mountjoy was the fluffy type – a 'little woman' – was barking up the wrong eucalyptus.

They drove sedately around Kirkcudbright in Fergus's well-mannered Volvo estate. At the corner of the main street and the town car park, he had to stand on the brakes, as a grossly overweight teenage girl wheeled a pram directly into their path, without looking.

'Holy fuck!' Fergus appeared to register Mabel's startled expression. 'Sorry! That's what comes of a lifetime spent with journalists. I don't like to swear in front of women.'

'How quaintly chauvinist.'

He grinned at her. 'This place has more than its fair share of traffic hazards. I already encountered a kamikaze mobility scooter when I first drove in.'

Mabel giggled. 'At this corner, yes, you often meet one.'

'Does no one pay attention to the traffic?'

'You get used to watching out.'

'Forewarned is forearmed, I suppose. There are definitely some people in this country who shouldn't be allowed to breed.'

'You can't say things like that!'

'To you I can, and I can think them. Don't tell me that kid was old enough to look after a child of her own properly. You've only to look at the NHS and all the public services. The same handful of feckless people are using up all their time and resources.'

'You'd just leave people to die if they're poor, or ill?'

'I'm not saying that. But a lot of them are poor and ill because they have no self-discipline. Look at all these junkies! Costing the state a fortune. Lifestyle choices, Belle.'

'You smoke. Smokers cost the NHS a fortune.'

'But I at least pay my way. It's the ones who put nothing back that'll sink the ship.'

'You're a fascist!'

'I'm a pragmatist.'

She shifted uncomfortably in her seat.

'I was wondering – since you're a smoker, how do you keep your teeth so white?'

'Chemicals! I'm vain enough to have them done every year or so.'

As bad as Roddy.

'Where's your gallery then?' Fergus asked.

'Just round here, at the back of the castle. You must admit, it gives the place a certain something? Quite French, the chateau plumb in the centre of town.'

He nodded. 'Pity it's a ruin.'

Mabel pointed to a long, low white building. 'That's it. The Waterside Gallery.' Damn! Yet another thing to be seen to before the start of the busy season. No way she was paying an extortionate price to have it done. Slinging on a fresh coat of whitewash couldn't be all that difficult; she'd do it herself.

Fergus drew into the parking space. She watched his expression carefully.

'Pleasing building. I'd say there's good light inside?'

'There is. I'd show you, only I don't have the keys with me. I'm getting it repainted in the next week or two. You'd wonder at how quickly it weathers, with the pure air we have here.'

'It's the salt,' he said.

They drove on past the harbour and turned back towards the main shopping street.

Mabel pointed to a pub which hadn't seen a coat of paint for many a year. 'Roddy often drank there. Most of the time, in fact.'

'A man of some discernment then. Fresh sawdust on the floor most weeks, I wouldn't be surprised?' He became flustered. 'Sorry. I seem to be doing nothing except apologising. I don't mean to imply that I find your home town lacking. Most of it's lovely. But that place isn't.'

'Kirkcudbright's better than a lot of small towns. But I don't wear rose-tinted specs.'

'The Port in a Storm? What a ridiculous name.'

'The locals just call it The Port.'

'It's nowhere near the port.'

'I think it used to be. Where the car park is now was an old dock, I believe. They filled it in.'

'Shame. The village would look much more attractive with a waterfront in the centre.'

Mabel giggled. 'Don't let anyone hear you calling it a

village. It's very definitely a town.'

'I suppose it is. The whole county's named after it. The Stewartry of Kirkcudbright, isn't it? Typical though.' He waved his hand towards the ugly car park. 'The lack of foresight of Scottish town councils in the 1970s. Leith avoided a similar fate by the narrowest of margins.'

'This part was filled long before the 1970s.'

'Look at it now though – posh restaurants end to end. Leith,' he added, in response to Mabel's raised eyebrows. 'I always regret that I didn't snap up a couple of sea-view properties there when they were going for silly prices. Cheap as pommes frites.'

'This will never be like Leith. There's not the catchment area, or the money.'

Mabel fell silent, thinking of how vibrant the town must have been once upon a time, when it was the haunt of the Glasgow Boys and their coterie. Jessie M King and her husband. Hornel. Even Roddy, in his younger days; that had been one of the first things they'd laughed about together. When he'd moved in with her and Father, she'd dreamed of recreating the vibe there must have been in Kirkcudbright right up until the 1930s. A community of artists, rivalling one another in terms of creativity, the whole greater than the sum of its parts. A constellation with Roddy and her at the centre. That dream had lasted half a dozen years.

'Still, there are probably more artists and craftspeople in Kirkcudbright than in most small Scottish towns,' she added, defensively. 'There's a creative buzz here, specially in the spring and summer with all the studios open to the public.'

Fergus gave her a sideways glance. 'But perhaps an oversupply of galleries?'

'Perhaps. One or two have closed in the last few years.'

She sank back in her seat again. He'd touched a raw nerve.

'Hideous!' he said suddenly.

'What now?'

'The way these fine old buildings have been ruined by modern shop-fronts. It's the same all over Scotland, even in conservation areas. As a nation, we seem to have a death-wish as far as aesthetics are concerned.'

'It's the same everywhere, not only Scotland.'

'You don't see such crassness in the prettier villages in Cornwall or the Cotswolds.'

Mabel shrugged. This time, she let the 'village' pass.

Fergus parked opposite the Port in a Storm. He reached across to the back seat and lifted a camera. 'I'll grab a quick snapshot of every place he went regularly, as an aide memoire.'

Mabel cowered down a little in her seat, trying not to look as if she were hiding. She wanted to tell him about the visit from Roddy's drinking buddy, but she didn't know how to broach it without sounding like a hysterical fool.

'Right – where to next?' asked Fergus briskly. 'Other pubs?'

She pointed out a couple more, including one within a few hundred yards of Ashers.

'He wouldn't have gone there very often,' she said. 'He claimed it was too posh for him. Mostly The Port.'

Fergus peered at her shrewdly. 'Where did he get the

money to booze all the time if he wasn't selling any of his work?'

'I've no idea. I assume he had some of his inheritance left.'

'So he could buy alcohol and tobacco, but he couldn't pay you rent? Sorry, for the third time. It's none of my business.'

She didn't reply.

'Where else did he go then – did *he* play golf? Was he a keen walker?'

'No to both.'

'Hobbies, clubs, anything of that sort?'

She shrugged. 'He wasn't the joining type.'

'Any close friends in the town?'

'Just his drinking buddies. And he didn't bring them home, so I can't say I know them. He's a bit of a loner.'

She dismissed the pang of pity she felt. Roddy had brought it on himself.

'Sailing,' she added. 'He and his sister are boat crazy. They used to have a yacht and kept it moored at Kirkcudbright. But a couple of years back, Ali was moaning about the high cost of moorings here, so I'm not sure if she sold it or moved it elsewhere. They have small boats too though: sea kayaks, and a rowing boat big enough to take an outboard motor. The pair of them went over to the Isle of Man in it a couple of times. Madness.'

Fergus was thoughtful. He was pondering how another person would answer these questions about *him*. He wasn't much of a joiner-in either. Did he have close friends? Or would people say of him, 'Ah yes, Fergus Learmonth: the cat who walks by himself'?

Suddenly, the world seemed to take on a bleaker hue. He released an involuntary sigh.

'Sorry,' said Mabel. 'I'm not being much help I'm afraid.

He smiled, to reassure her. 'It's not that. I was just thinking.'

About the dead wife, no doubt.

'Did your wife die recently?'

He looked taken aback. 'I wasn't thinking about my wife. No, it'll be five years this summer.'

How he must have loved her, to be so distraught after all that time. Mabel wasn't sure what to say. What sprang to mind was, 'Get over it. Life goes on', but you can't say that to a stranger. Inappropriate. She had a moment of deep sadness, recognising that no man would ever miss her so deeply. *Change of subject required, Mabs.*

'Is this the main type of work you do, tracing missing people?'

'It is. Since the married-for-life nuclear family has broken down in the west, you'd be surprised how many people are trying to trace lost relatives: siblings, half-siblings, even parents.'

'How do you start on a case where there are no clues?'

'There are always clues. There's a lot you can find out

from public records, such as where and when someone married, and their spouse's name. Then you can usually trace the spouse, unless you end up with a tremendously common first name and surname. But mind you, a paper-trail's not much use in such a very recent disappearance.'

'And when the paper trail runs out?'

'You need to be like the python-hunters in Florida. Get into the zone. Get inside the mindset of your quarry. You need to figure out where they'd go – their preferred habitats – and who they'd go with, how they'd react to certain events. It's basically the same technique I used to track down cowboy builders and the like, who'd done a bunk. You said there are lots of caravan sites around this area?'

'It's awash with them. Why?'

'They're notorious as bolt-holes for people who don't want to be found.'

'You reckon Roddy's hiding in plain sight?'

'It can be the most effective tactic.'

'But he'd need to come out to do his shopping?'

'Unless someone's helping him.'

Mabel raised her eyebrows.

'His sister. Drinking pals.'

She shrugged, but didn't share the fear that had taken root in her mind.

CHAPTER SEVEN

Mabel had resolved to offer Fergus dinner; after all, if she fed him, it could hardly be set down as an out-of-pocket expense? She was a little taken aback by the alacrity with which he'd accepted.

When he turned up that evening at seven precisely, as invited, he'd obviously taken some care over his appearance. She didn't think he'd had a haircut, but he'd done something to make it look tidier, and he had most definitely trimmed his beard. He presented her with a bouquet of flowers that must have come from the town's only florist, rather than a supermarket. That'd have cost a pretty penny. Mabel grinned to herself – maybe it would appear on the bill, concealed as something else. God! What a shrew she was becoming. A harridan, Roddy had called her. Possibly he was right.

She was glad she'd called upon all her cooking skills, as well as dressing extra-carefully and spending half an hour on her face.

She'd opted for a casserole rather than roast meat; less risk of producing a burnt offering. She'd been profligate with the wine she used in it; the cellar was empty, but she'd been able to pick up a couple of decent bottles on offer in Tesco. The apples for a tarte Tatin were already caramelised; it only remained to pop the pastry lid on and put it in the oven as they sat down to eat. A slightly superior bottle of Rioja Reserva was out on the table, in the silver holder.

Fergus sniffed his glass appreciatively. 'I see you have excellent taste in wine.'

'Father was something of a connoisseur, so I had a good teacher.'

The meal was an unqualified success, even though Archie did his best to spoil the effect by scratching at the door and whimpering while they ate, giving the lie to Mabel's assertion that he was never allowed into the dining room. As soon as they'd adjourned to the fireside, the pug heaved his solid little body onto her lap, snagging her tights.

'As bad as a cat,' said Fergus benevolently. 'I'm afraid I'm not having much luck with tracing your friend. But I shan't charge you for today, because I've been doing some sightseeing too.'

'How long do you think it *will* take to find him – assuming his sister's correct and he's not dead?' she asked.

Fergus gave her a long, level look. 'Dead? Why on earth would you think that?'

She turned scarlet. She'd merely voiced a thought she'd had earlier, when she was daydreaming about a sudden and buoyant market for Roddy's work.

'I don't know why I said it. Of course he isn't.'

'Was he in poor health?'

'No more than any other alcoholic.'

'It depends if he wants to be found. I'm not getting any sort of steer on where he might be. What are you looking to do when I manage to find him?'

She hadn't thought of that. 'I need to speak to him. I'd like you to get him to agree to a meeting with me. A purely business meeting, to discuss our arrangement for sale of his paintings.'

'You could presumably discuss this by letter or email or telephone, in the event he doesn't want to meet?'

Mabel looked doubtful. 'I suppose so.' What was he thinking – that she was desperate to lure Roddy back into her bed?

'I've done a little preliminary work. His wife was Gillian Reid. They were divorced in 1986, she remarried the following year, and she hasn't heard from him since.'

'1986?' *The bastard.* When he'd seduced her in 1982, he'd sworn blind he was unattached and fancy-free. 'You've spoken to her?'

'By telephone, yes. She knows the woman he went to America with, but doubts he'd still be in touch with her…'

'He went to New York on his own.'

Fergus studied his glass. 'Ah. She must have got it wrong then.'

'What was the name of this woman?'

'I don't think she told me that.'

'Of course she did. What was it?'

He pursed his lips and took a notebook from his pocket. 'Fenella Green.'

Mabel gave such a start that Archie jumped off her knee, scraping the leather of the armchair on his way down. Fenella Green had been another of Roddy's students. She'd probably made polite conversation with her in his house.

Damn, damn, damn. The utter, unreconstituted, shameless, two-timing low-life. All her pity for Roddy began to slide away. Hell mend him. She'd spent the past weeks wondering what she'd do if her former lover turned up, clean and sober and cured – *would* she take him back? Now she didn't care if she never set eyes on him again.

'He hadn't married her too, while they were in America?' she asked hoarsely.

'Definitely not.'

Mabel relaxed a little. 'Naughty dog, Archie,' she said, stroking the pug's ears.

'I meant to visit the sister this afternoon,' added Fergus, 'but I didn't get round to it. I'll maybe try speaking to her by phone tomorrow morning. Assuming she can give no leads as to his whereabouts, I'll probably have to stay here another day.'

'You did say you charge expenses on top of your fee?'

'I have to.'

Mabel threw caution to the winds. 'How about if you stayed here, in the cottage? It's very comfortable, once the log burner's lit. I suppose you're stuck with the Roseberry Arms for tonight, but if I light the stove first thing tomorrow, and fill the firewood basket, it'd be cosy enough.' Damn! She'd forgotten about the mattress. The one in the best spare bedroom should be all right; it had scarcely been slept upon. But she could hardly invite him to help carry out his own bed. She would manage to drag it downstairs by herself. If she put a sheet of plastic underneath, it should be possible to get it to the cottage unscathed... 'There's a kitchen area, quite well equipped, plus a bedroom and bathroom. If you stay there rent-free, would that work?'

'Is there a good Internet connection?'

'You could use your computer here, in Father's old study. There's an enormous desk – a traditional partners' desk.'

'Actually, it might suit me very well to stay here for a couple of weeks, if the cottage is available. An ideal place to work. Quaint and quiet, no distractions. I'd pay you rent of course.'

Quaint and quiet! Probably how he perceives me. If only he knew.

'I wouldn't think of charging rent. Tell you what – we could set it against the bill.'

He turned that delicious smile on her again. 'I was teasing you about not charging for today. I don't imagine I'll be presenting a bill, Belle. And I wouldn't be working on finding your artist friend for more than a small part of the time. I'm trying to get going with writing a book.'

She was immediately interested. 'What sort of book? I have a friend who's a poet.'

'Nothing so glamorous as poetry, I'm afraid. I'm transforming my PhD thesis into a book, and EUP's interested. *James Gillespie Graham and the Urban Scottish Landscape.*'

Can you have an urban landscape?

'How exciting. So you're actually Dr Learmonth?'

He coloured up a little, and nodded. 'I'd never dream of calling myself that.'

'Why ever not?'

'When I first started in the media, it would have been a downright liability. And once I'd carved myself a niche catching out villains, even worse.'

'So you did this PhD years ago?'

'Finished when I was twenty-four. But the thesis is still relevant; no one else has covered the same ground. Since I've put in more than a quarter of a century as a journalist, I'm a much better writer now too. It'll be a textbook, but hopefully not a dry-as-dust one. My first book's actually coming out very soon. Rather different style.'

'What's it about?'

'How to avoid hiring cowboys. Not only builders; all tradesmen.'

She recalled Briony saying that's what he was famous for: a long series of TV programmes where he helped people who'd been ripped off find the culprits and confront them. It wasn't the sort of thing Father would have watched. She herself had never been one for television. The last few years of his life, she'd park Father in front of the set, the way she'd heard mothers of young children did, only instead of Disney films she'd find programmes about angling, or a cricket match, and he'd be contented as a calf in clover, for hours on end.

Nothing for it but to admit she'd never watched *Learmonth on the Lookout*. She'd quizzed Briony about it, and felt a twinge of regret over not watching – her friend said it had been an excellent programme. 'I don't know how he did it,' she'd added. 'I'd have been terrified. He'd go after these guys single-handed, and most of them were not nice people.'

'I hear your TV programme was very popular,' said Mabel.

He looked at her sideways. 'I take it you weren't a fan?' Then he laughed. 'Don't feel you need to pretend. I know it wasn't everyone's cup of tea. It wasn't mine either, towards the end.'

'I'm afraid I didn't ever see your programme, but my friends were keen on it. Why builders, in particular?'

Because of people like Davie Ford, who just think of a number. She felt a surge of indignation.

'Because people have such an emotional investment in their homes,' said Fergus. 'Not that the ones I focused on were places of any pretension. If you live in a fine house, you don't normally hire fly-by-nights with no fixed office address to begin with.'

'I heard some of the people you tracked down were thugs of the worst sort. Weren't you afraid, facing up to people like that on your own?'

'There would normally be a cameraman and a sound guy with me, who could have been witnesses, at the end of the day. I always felt I could look after myself.'

'That's lunacy! These days, thugs are as likely as not to have a knife, or a gun.' She found herself breaking into a cold sweat at the thought of Fergus being stabbed or shot. She clutched her hands instinctively over her chest.

He merely grinned at her again and shrugged.

'But if it was successful, why did you give it up?' she asked.

'Because I was disillusioned. Cowboy builders make people's lives a misery. They make away with their life savings, and leave them without a roof that's watertight. But you could number them in the hundreds. Maybe even the dozens. I'd come to the conclusion I was wasting my time on trivia, in the greater scheme of things. I wanted to expose organised crime in our towns, corrupt pharmaceutical companies, corrupt charities, corrupt cops, corrupt public bodies like health boards. The ones who bury their mistakes. Then I realised I was too old and tired.'

'You don't get involved in anything *illegal*, doing this work to trace people?'

He gave her another searching look. 'What – phone-hacking and so on? No, I don't. I'm not in that league, I assure you. Why, do you?'

She felt the blood drain from her face.

'Only joking,' he added, a small concern in his voice. 'No fake Hornels in the gallery, I hope?'

Mabel shuddered. 'I loathe Hornel's work. All those young girls; distinctly odd.'

'No one thought anything of it in those days. Same as Lewis Carroll.'

'Exactly.'

Fergus laughed. 'I didn't have you down as one of the PC brigade.'

'I find that man's paintings distasteful. I'm sure it *was* all quite innocent, but the children look too much like the drawings that were popular in the seventies – Moppets. Do you remember?'

He nodded. 'His house is open to the public isn't it?'

Mabel busied herself with removing some invisible dust from the mantelpiece. 'Not until Easter. You'll need to come back then if you want to see it. I've always found the garden more interesting than the house.'

He smiled at her. She snuggled into that smile. She found the idea of Fergus coming back at Easter pleasing. It was early that year: Easter Sunday was the eighth of April…

After he took his leave to go back to the Roseberry Arms for his last night there, Mabel wandered round the house, glass of red in hand (what the hell? When it's gone, it's gone), the pug under her other arm, trying to look at her home through Fergus's appreciative eyes. Seeing it properly for the first time in years: the heart-achingly perfect curve of the turning stair, with its tall window inundating the hallway with light on a sunny day, and the silken smoothness of its handrail, polished by more than two hundred years-worth of hands. The crisp white plasterwork, the well-mannered, muted colours of the rugs, the dull gleam of well-patinated floorboards. She must dig out the quartet of Georgian silver candlesticks that used to stand on the hall table and the one upstairs on the landing. It'd mean polishing them, but it'd be worth the effort.

How could she ever think of leaving this place? Although she couldn't claim the credit for acquiring it, or even furnishing it, apart from most of the paintings, it had been left in her stewardship.

She'd ensure that Roddy was found, whatever it took, and insist he sold all his damn paintings for what he could get, so he could pay what he owed her. It *must* be possible, because if she had to sell Ashers, she couldn't bear to live in another house within a hundred miles of it. There had to be a way of staying put in her home with her ambitions to be

Kirkcudbright's alpha female intact.

Fergus had been permitted to smoke a cigar in the comfort of the sitting room after dinner. She could still smell the fragrance of tobacco hours later. It gave her a strange little skip of the heartbeat to realise she enjoyed it.

When she heard a knock at eight-thirty the next morning, Mabel thought, for one giddy moment, that Fergus had decided to decamp early. Perhaps he was as eager to see her again as she was to see him?

But when she opened the door, she was amazed to find Sophie Dempster on the top step, dressed as usual in clothing infinitely too skimpy for a Scottish February. Her first thought was that the girl was looking for work, but she could no more afford to pay her than she could her mother. Sophie had been a pretty wee thing when she was at school, but as soon as she'd turned sixteen, she'd started dressing in a most inappropriate way. She wore skirts so short you could see her knickers. Mabel used to tell herself over and over that she'd never let a daughter of hers go out looking like that, but the mother seemed to have no control over her.

'What can I do for you, Sophie? I hope your mother's well?'

'I was looking for Roddy.'

Well, of all the cheek.

In the past, Sophie would sometimes accompany her mother to the house when there was heavy work to be done: turning mattresses, or taking the big downstairs rugs outdoors in spring to beat the winter's sourness out of them.

Mabel hadn't twigged that Roddy had asked the girl to model for him until she'd seen her vanishing into the studio one day when Mrs Dempster wasn't there. She'd had a bad feeling about the whole set-up from the start.

'Och, she's just sitting for me,' Roddy replied casually when she'd tackled him about it.

Mabel had tried to sound light-hearted. Roddy still lived in the house with her at the time. 'Fully clothed, I hope?'

'Of course. You think I want to end up in the clink?'

And indeed, the first canvases featuring the girl's pinched, moppet's face and dank blonde hair had shown her very fully covered – as often as not in her school uniform.

Then the sittings had started to take place behind closed doors, and Mabel would hear loud music and raucous laughter from the cottage. She'd remonstrated with Roddy about it, but he'd merely laughed and said the girl had turned sixteen, she wasn't a child, and in any case, he wasn't painting her in the nude. 'She has no tits to speak of anyway,' he'd added.

'And you know this how, exactly?'

'Because I'm observant. Nine points of the law, in being an artist.'

The debacle came when she'd blundered into the cottage one day the previous autumn, to find Sophie on her knees in front of Roddy, on the cold, stone-flagged floor.

He'd spun round when he heard Mabel's footsteps. His flies were undone.

She should, of course, have walked straight out again, but it was like a slap from a wet haddock that he should want a child like that after having had *her*.

Instead, she had yelled at the girl to get out, and Sophie had grabbed her fake sheepskin coat and fled, doe-eyed and scarlet-cheeked. Roddy, meanwhile, had adjusted his clothing and was laughing quite openly.

'We were only fooling around,' he said.

'You think you can use my house to have sex with a teenager?'

'No way! You think I'd dip my wick in a lassie like that? Her name's a by-word in the town.'

'You needn't think you're staying on my premises one more night, if you've been screwing her.'

'Temper, temper!' Roddy had chortled. 'You've frightened the poor lass out of her wits. She was looking to see if she could sew on a button for me.'

'Don't even try lying, McCulloch. I know exactly what she was doing, and it had damn all to do with needlework. Why do men have nothing in their brains except sex?'

'Come on, Mabs,' he'd cooed, trying to put his arm round her. 'You know what Clinton said, and he got away with it. "I did not have sex with that woman." '

'Woman? She's easily young enough to be your granddaughter.'

'I fear you have a dirty mind, Ms Mountjoy.'

'And you have dirty habits.

'Bollocks.'

'Have you no pride, even if she hasn't? To want to do *that* with a girl who's hardly out of school.'

Mabel had rushed back into the house, locked all the doors, and stood for half an hour in a shower that was too hot for comfort, scrubbing herself with a loofah, to kill the sensation of ants crawling over her skin. It was more than a year since she'd lain in a bed beside Roddy McCulloch, but she felt soiled. That was the only word for it.

'Roddy's moved away,' she told Sophie, frosty-voiced and pink-faced. 'I have no idea where he's gone, or if he's coming back.'

'He's not answering his phone. He never said anything about moving.'

'I can't help that. He couldn't pay his way, so he's gone. In fact, if you find him, you can let me know. He owes me a year's rent.'

The girl regarded her pityingly.

'Can I look in the cottage, in case he's left me a note?'

'He has left nothing, I can assure you.'

Sophie glowered and left reluctantly.

When she'd gone, Mabel found she was sweating so much she had to run upstairs and change her blouse before Fergus was due.

Fergus looked a little abashed when he arrived. Her heart sank. He'd thought better of it...

'I should have said yesterday: I'm happy to rent the cottage from you, and continue trying to find your friend.

But there's a condition – I must be able to bring my cat.'

'I didn't know you had a cat.' She knew she sounded hesitant.

'I have, and I'm not willing to leave him in the sitter's tender care for more than a few days at a time. He's only thirteen, so he's not one of these cats who sleep all day.'

Mabel gave an involuntary start. 'I didn't think cats lived so long?'

'They do if they're well looked after. Much longer, if they're in good health. They can live into their twenties. He was my wife's cat, and I'm particularly attached to him. I take it you're not a cat person?'

She considered that for a moment. She wasn't sure of the correct answer.

'I've never had one. The single thing Father and Roddy had in common was that they both detested dogs and were allergic to cats.' No, not the single thing. They'd also shared the belief that she'd been put on earth to be their servant and loyal companion.

'This could be a major snag, if you're allergic too – although I'd keep him in the cottage. He's an indoor cat. He's an exceptionally clean animal, and he has an excellent litter-tray I imported especially from Canada. No mess, no smell.'

'Briony Hall has a cat, and that's never caused me any problems. I look after it for her when she's away. I'm sure it'll be fine. How is he with dogs?'

'He's never met a dog. Why – does your pug chase cats?'

'He's never met a cat. He'll have seen them from afar

on his walks, but none come into the garden.'

'In that case, as long as I can have Gorby in the cottage with me, I accept your terms.'

'Gorby? What a peculiar name.'

Perhaps it's from one of those Harry Potter books everyone's kids read?

'Gorbachev. My wife named him. It's very apt. He's white, with an orange splodge on his head. If it's OK with you, I'll drive up to town tomorrow and collect more of my things, and Gorby, and all his kit. It'll only take me about seven hours all-in, I'd say. I won't charge you for the day.'

He grinned at her discomfiture. 'I'm teasing you.'

He let his hand rest on her shoulder for the briefest of moments as he was leaving.

Gorbachev seemed delighted to welcome Fergus home. He wasn't prone to taking the huff when he'd been left, the way his mother's cat used to do: a highly-pedigreed Abyssinian, too arrogant for its own good. Gorby had been the greatest constant in his life for the past decade. Perhaps the *only* constant in his life.

Fergus lingered in the hallway, the cat twining around his ankles, remembering the early days, when he'd first brought him home as a present for Serena; a tiny white kitten, in a wicker basket ten sizes too big for him. How they'd laughed together at his kitten antics, and exchanged anecdotes about his amazing prowess in learning to be a cat, like parents admiring their child's first steps, first attempt at reading, first day at school. What a short time that had lasted. When they'd divorced, the greatest wrangle of all was over who should get custody of the cat. He'd given way, but in the end he'd only been parted from Gorby for a few months. His ex-wife was as fickle in her attachment to the animal as she had been to him.

His heart wrenched with grief – although that had been happening less frequently over the past day or two and the pain, when it came, was less searing. Perhaps the change of location had helped after all?

He'd stayed on in London for more than two years after Serena died, but his heart hadn't been in it. He'd sold up, and returned to Edinburgh, where he could at least take a daily walk past the house he had shared so briefly with her. He hadn't been able to find a flat he liked so much as the one he'd sold when he'd moved south, but the one in Learmonth Terrace wasn't too far from Stockbridge. It had seemed appropriate too, the name. Gave the sort of address that made postmen do a double-take.

He'd returned to work at Albion's Scottish studios, but after a few months he handed in his notice. Serena was everywhere he looked, and although he knew she meant well, Anita Forrest, the studio boss, showered him with such solicitude that he felt as if he were being suffocated.

He packed enough clothes to last him for a month or so, and a couple of boxes of books and CDs. Once all Gorby's accoutrements, including the roomy wicker carrying basket, were added, there was no room for more.

Even in the space of considerably less than a week, he felt comfortable with Mabel Mountjoy. She understood the important things in life, such as using good quality loose-leaf tea instead of the ghastly tea-bags Serena had insisted were easier. Belle even understood that not all single malt whiskies taste the same.

On an impulse, he crammed the rest of his CD collection into the car, as well as the Linn Klimax music system. There was a reasonably up-market hi-fi unit at Ashers, but nothing of this quality. Belle appeared to share his tastes in music, catholic as they were. He meant to set up this kit in the main house, for the good acoustics, and they could look forward to companionable evenings in front of the fire, listening to Mahler and Schumann and Courtney Pine. And Jussi Björling, his favourite.

He pictured the two of them, sitting side by side on a huge, squidgy sofa. But there was no such item of furniture in Ashers. He decided he'd make that his contribution to the household. At the earliest opportunity, he'd insist they drove into Dumfries together to choose a sofa.

He inspected the cabinet where he kept the good crockery and crystal, wondering idly if any of the glasses he and Serena had got as wedding presents had survived, and if so, where they were now. Thank God he'd rescued his grandparents' Royal Doulton dinner service, one of Frank Brangwyn's designs from the 1930s. Not to everyone's taste, but he was fond of it. It was the sort of thing Belle would appreciate. He'd never let Serena lay hands on it, once he realised that when her dander was up she'd fling plates at the wall as enthusiastically as the customers of any Greek taverna.

On the way back to Kirkcudbright, he suddenly

remembered the name of the roses he'd so admired in his mother's garden: Peace. That was the rose Belle reminded him of. Peace. A quality he found he craved from life these days, every whit as passionately as he had once craved excitement and change and danger and stimulation.

In many ways, she resembled the friends' granddaughters his grandmother would produce like rabbits out of a hat when he was in his early twenties: eager, scrubbed-cheeked, wholesome girls who had shiny hair and sturdy thighs, and owned ponies.

Grannie knew him best after all.

He must ask Belle if she'd ever had a pony. He chuckled to himself. Best not. She'd look at him with the same worried expression she had when he'd enquired for Lapsang Souchong.

'A *pony*? No, sorry. Why?'

He recalled with a pang that he and Gorby wouldn't be living *in* Ashers. The cottage was their domain.

'We need to play our cards right old chap,' he told the cat. 'You'll like her, and she'll like you. Just don't take your claws to her dog, and everything will be fine.'

CHAPTER EIGHT

The first full day back was the most traumatic. The moment Fergus opened the door that morning, Archie, who had been patrolling the garden anxiously, scenting the air, shot into the cottage. The pug ran out again less than a minute later, his face streaming with blood. Then his owner appeared, her face like thunder. It was almost a matter of everything having to be repacked for a tactical withdrawal to Edinburgh

Fergus grew impatient. 'Jesus Christ, Belle, the fuss you're making you'd think the dog had been mauled by a tiger. It's no more than a tiny scratch on his nose. The cat reacted quite naturally to being frightened. Hopefully Archie's learned not to breenge at him like that,' he added. By then, he'd produced his animal first-aid kit and soothed the pug's wound with a liberal smear of green Vetzyme ointment. 'That'll heal in no time. There won't even be a mark.'

In the blink of an eye, Mabel had gone from fury to laughing at him for being such an old woman, carrying veterinary products around in an immaculate plastic case, ordering special litter trays; he'd always found it better to be safe than sorry where animals were concerned. In any case, wanting to laugh was preferable to wanting to brain him or ostracise Gorby.

And sure enough, Archie seemed to have learned the most important lesson: the cat was boss. By the time he'd been in residence for a few days, Gorby had made himself quite at home, and peace reigned not only with Archie, but with his owner.

'You're honoured,' said Fergus. 'I've never known him jump on anyone's lap, except mine and Serena's.' Mabel was sitting on the tatty chaise longue in the cottage. Fergus was wondering if it was too soon to broach the subject of a sofa for the sitting room.

Mabel stroked the cat, a little tentatively at first, then more enthusiastically, as the animal settled and purred contentedly.

Fergus tried to push away the stab of jealousy.

'You've owned him since he was a kitten?' she asked.

He nodded. 'I bought him for Serena when we'd been married a few months. I thought she was feeling broody. Though we didn't want children, either of us, by the time she was heading for thirty, well, you know, hormones and biological clocks, and all that.'

'Women's biological clocks don't run down at thirty!' The cat jumped off her knee, startled by her raised voice.

Fergus blushed a little. 'Maybe I don't know much about these things.'

'You never, ever wanted children, either of you?'

He sighed heavily. He'd known from the day he met Serena that she wasn't the type of woman who'd want sprogs. In fact, it had been one of the main attractions about her, at first. That and her icy, unapproachable, surreal beauty. He'd been so *sure* about it. And he'd been right, hadn't he? If only she'd been content with Gorby as a child-substitute.

'No,' he said, noticing the expression of concern that flitted across Belle's face; he knew it was because he hadn't managed to eradicate enough of the sadness from his voice. 'How about you?'

'It wasn't a conscious decision. It didn't happen for me. I don't regret it.'

Her voice carried a message that was diametrically opposite.

'We're the ones who should have bred, when you think of it,' he said.

'Why?'

'Because we're literate and cultured. We're responsible citizens. If people like us don't reproduce, the country will be over-run by the uneducated unwashed.'

'Fergus! I don't know what the opposite of politically correct is, but you're it, in spades.'

'Honest,' he said. 'That's what the opposite of PC is. If more people were willing to say what they feel rather than what they think is acceptable, society would be in a more stable and sustainable state. Can't stand the mealy-mouthed brigade. In animals, the fittest breed, and the less fit don't. The red deer and the black grouse have got it right.'

'Which will be why the black grouse is now a Red List species? You realise you're talking absolute nonsense? And you're confusing physical strength with intelligence. In my experience, there's no guarantee that the two go together.'

Fergus looked embarrassed. 'Sorry. I just feel very

strongly about the state of the world's population.'

Mabel's expression softened. 'You mustn't ever say these things in public. You're an intelligent man – you wouldn't want people to think you're an idiot.'

'I certainly don't want you to think I'm an idiot.'

He nudged her with his elbow and gestured to where Gorby and Archie had settled amicably only a metre apart on the floor in front of the log burner. The pug's head was nodding in sleep, and the cat had his paws tucked comfortably under his chest.

'They've got more sense than we have,' said Fergus.

Really, the cat was no trouble at all, apart from the fact that the special low-dust litter for his special litter-tray apparently had to be ordered online. However, Mabel felt she had a duty to make it clear she felt sorry for Gorby, never being in the fresh air.

'Can we not let him out? He'd be safe in the garden here – he'd surely not be able to get over these walls?'

'I'd perhaps need to put some wire netting above the cordon apple-trees.'

'We'll easily do that.'

With a single trip to the garden centre, this was accomplished.

The weeks that Fergus had promised to stay turned into months. Time seemed to fly past. It was already almost the end of March, and Mabel hadn't got round to whitewashing the gallery walls. Perhaps it could wait until summer was well and truly in. She was somewhat taken aback when Fergus expressed an interest in seeing Roddy's work. He still hadn't set foot inside her business premises.

'It'd be useful,' he said. 'Help me get more of a handle on the type of person I'm looking for.'

'It may not be to your taste.' Mabel was still mulling over what it would feel like to have owned a Turner, even briefly. 'Come with me when I go down there this morning then. We'll take Archie, and you can bring him back.'

As soon as she flung open the double doors, she felt the same surge of pride as always. The interior of the Waterside Gallery was a superlatively pleasing space. Daylight poured in from a row of roof-lights facing north-west, and she had planned the artificial lighting of individual exhibits with great care.

There were fourteen of Roddy's paintings on display. It represented all of his extant work that was complete and fit for sale. Two of the canvases dated from well before the Millennium. Fergus made straight for the first of them, an almost impressionist still life.

'I like this very much! He has real talent.'

'He had when he was younger.'

'This too.' He paused in front of the second early McCulloch: a subtly abstract landscape which Roddy had painted *en plein air* at Carrick Shore. It was large – more than a metre and a half square – and he'd made full use of every nuance of blue and green and gold on his palette. 'You say no one wants to buy these?'

Mabel pretended to concentrate on adjusting the hang of another frame. 'I've possibly priced them rather high.'

She wasn't about to admit that she'd never wanted to let them go.

Fergus peered at the printed cards beside each. 'Six thousand? I'd have thought that's a reasonable gallery price for good quality work these days.'

'People might have paid that for a Roddy McCulloch once upon a time. Not in recent years.'

'I'll buy this one.' He laid his hand on the frame of the landscape. 'It'd look magnificent on the wall of my hallway, so that it's the first thing you see on entering the flat.'

'You can't possibly make a snap decision on spending so much!'

'Of course I can. I don't expect a discount, by the way.' He grinned at her. 'Don't you want to sell it to me?'

'Gladly, if you're serious.'

'I'm serious.'

He strode around the rest of the gallery, not stopping for long in front of any of the other paintings. He barely glanced at the wall where she displayed the prints that constituted her staple trade.

'I can see why some of his others are harder to shift, but these two are superb. I'm tempted to buy both.'

Mabel tried to smile. 'I'd have to give you a discount then!'

It'd amount to more than half of what she needed for the roof repairs. How comforting it must be to be able to contemplate spending twelve grand on a whim. For a moment, she almost resented Fergus. But that wasn't fair; he'd brought her good luck, it seemed. Sales at the gallery were picking up already; there seemed to be fresh optimism in the air, and people were parting with cash. Quite apart from that, when he'd accompanied her to the supermarket over the past weeks, Fergus had paid before she could get her credit card out...

He was studying her, head on one side. 'You don't want to let them go, do you?'

Don't blush, Mabel you idiot. Fight it. 'I'm not sure I can sell any of Roddy's work until I get hold of him.'

'But you won't sell them to anyone else – I get first refusal?'

In the end, he stayed with her until lunchtime, and they walked back to Ashers side by side, like old friends, the pug trotting between them.

Fergus was diffident about putting his CDs in Mabel's player in the sitting room. The Linn system was still in the cottage. *Softly, softly, catchee monkey.* He'd heard her listening to pop music on the kitchen radio when she thought he wasn't in the house. He'd even spied her pirouetting cheek to cheek with a bundle of bath towels still warm from the drier, but hadn't wanted to discompose her by wading in (as he'd longed to) and asking: 'Ya dancin?'

He decided to try her with Bach. 'Glenn Gould,' he said as the glorious music started. 'Tragic that he died so young.'

'Ah,' she said, 'The Goldberg Variations. The Aria.'

He couldn't hide his surprise. Then he noticed the tears in her eyes. Sometimes it got him that way too, though he'd never admit it. No: she was genuinely distressed, not merely moved.

'What's wrong?'

'Roddy used to play. Rather well, in fact. This was one of his party pieces. Then he gave up, the same way he gave up on painting.'

Fergus was stung by jealousy. He'd formed a picture of McCulloch as an uncultured lout, even although he was an artist. Now he had to cope with a mental image of cosy evenings round the piano, Belle smiling as she turned the pages for Roddy, like a role-reversal version of a costume drama. What would she do if the prodigal turned up again, a reformed character: welcome him back?

'I should have been able to do something about it,' added Mabel. 'I should have got him into a treatment programme.'

'That only works on willing participants. You can't take responsibility for another person's self-destructive behaviour.'

She shook herself. 'I know that in my head. Do you play?'

'Very badly. Compulsory tuition as a child was as far as I ever got. You?'

'Same. I still have a piano, if you ever feel so inclined.'

'I'm far too rusty.'

'I bet you're not. I bet you can play more than competently. Renaissance man.'

Fergus looked up at her sharply, to see if she was teasing him. She was. He loved the way she could throw off a sombre mood so quickly, through willpower. A strong woman, like his grandmother. He'd also been surprised to find how he enjoyed being teased. That's what had been wrong, those past few years. Everyone had taken him far too seriously, ever since he'd had his little... incident at Serena's funeral.

'Which came first, I wonder,' said Mabel, 'music or architecture?'

He was profoundly relieved that her mind had moved away from McCulloch. 'What a strange question. I love the way your mind works. Music, surely?'

'I'm sure people sang. I suppose what I mean is instrumental music.'

He wanted to tell her they could figure that one out when they visited the world's great cathedrals together. Having ascertained that Mabel had never visited Andalusia, he'd determined that they'd start with Seville and Granada and Córdoba (though the latter always left him feeling squeamish on behalf of all of Western Christendom; the sheer vandalism of what had been done to the Mesquita: that ghastly excrescence bursting through its roof like a chancre, over-gilded paintings of saints invading the serene order of the columns...). But there was time enough to get to know her better before sharing those particular plans.

It hadn't taken Fergus long to find ways to charm the local shopkeepers. He had turned out to be a competent and inventive cook. He'd been insulted when Mabel expressed surprise.

'Of course I can cook, woman! I've lived on my own most of my life.'

And he'd realised with a pang how true that was. As an adult he, Fergus, the one Anita Forrest had teased about needing to be married, had never lived with a woman for more than two years at a time.

There were two good butchers in the town, and another half-dozen in the neighbouring settlements. He soon ascertained that they knew how to produce a properly-hung prime steak. But it was the local delicatessen that benefitted most from his custom. They'd never found any cause to stock Pommery Moutarde Royale, but once they got some in for Fergus, it simply flew off the shelves. The same with the Vignotte cheese he demanded they source.

'You're keeping them in business,' Mabel teased him. 'At least it means you don't keep having to flee back to the capital to pig out at Valvona and Crolla!'

He was startled, because she'd read his mind. Even after a few weeks' absence, he was hankering for Edinburgh and all its amenities, both gastronomic and cultural.

They had decided on a sortie into Dumfries, to explore the area's larger supermarkets. Mabel had already toured the town without him a handful of times, on the pretext of buying picture-framing supplies, and giving her non-driving friend Nancy a day out, but Fergus knew that at least part of the reason for these trips lay in her hope of catching sight of the missing artist among the crowds on the High Street. There were pubs and to spare in the Queen of the South, and probably a surplus of gullible middle-aged women too. But there had been no sign of Roddy; she'd surely have told him, wouldn't she?

'Turn left here,' she said as they travelled along Kirkcudbright's main street. 'It's the road over the bridge.'

Fergus looked at her out of the corner of his eye. 'That's not the route I usually take.'

'I know, but this is quicker.'

'How can it possibly be quicker? It brings you onto the A75 a good distance west of where the other one comes out.'

'It's not so far to get onto the better road, so it's quicker.'

'You'd call the A75 a good road? It's no quicker at all, just longer.'

Mabel sighed and studied her hands.

'I hate the other road. Never use it.'

'Why ever not?'

'Because Father had a bad crash there a few years back. I was with him, so I don't like using it now.'

Fergus was immediately concerned. 'Your father was driving?'

She nodded, hunting for a hankie in her bag. Clearly, even thinking about it still got to her.

'Were you hurt?'

'Neither of us was badly hurt, thank God. The car was a write-off. Father stopped driving after that.'

'It was his fault?'

'Not at all. It was a lorry coming far too fast the other way, at the Tongland Bridge.'

'A lorry! You're bloody lucky you weren't injured then.'

'It was a very sturdy car: an ancient Bentley. It was

beautiful, and it had to be scrapped.'

'Is that when you bought the Defender?'

She blushed a little. 'It was the only thing I thought I'd feel safe in.'

'I won't tease you about it any more then. And we'll always take this road.' He squeezed her hand briefly.

By mid-April, Fergus had made a further flying visit to his flat to fetch another batch of clothes, plus more books, plus Gorby's SmartCat scratching post. He had found he could work more productively in old Mr Mountjoy's study than he ever had in his own flat. It was peaceful, and he was conscious of having Mabel there – not always in the house with him, now that the gallery was open five days a week, but in the same space on the Earth's face. It produced a sense of tranquillity that was most conducive to writing. He knew he should turn his full attention to Gillespie Graham. But not quite yet…

An additional expedition was made to Dumfries, and a sofa was purchased.

April had brought fine weather. Most evenings, Fergus and Mabel would stroll out of town, on one of the routes bordering the estuary of the Dee. They walked side by side along roads unseasonably fragrant with wild garlic and bright with early-flowering red campion and buttercups. As often as not, they'd take Archie with them, although any extended outing meant carrying him for a good deal of the return journey.

Fergus became childishly excited by the fact that you could see the Isle of Man from the coast. He didn't believe it until he saw it for himself, looming out of the sea mist like the Isle of Avalon, and used a compass alongside a map, to reassure himself that it wasn't a mirage.

One particularly fine Sunday afternoon, they'd gone as far as the small beach at Nun's Mill, where they could look west to see Ross Island floating as if suspended between an apricot sky and a peach, shot-silk sea.

'You see why I love it here?' said Mabel.

'Look at this though,' said Fergus, gesticulating towards the garlanding of discarded blue nylon rope and assorted plastic flotsam at the high-water mark. 'As bad as the Firth of Forth. We used to depend on the sea to clean up all our dirt.'

'It's returning the compliment.'

Mabel had been reading – belatedly – James Lovelock's book about Gaia. 'Perhaps Lovelock was right,' she said. 'Perhaps the earth is a living organism, and the sea its digestive system, spewing back what we try to hide in it.'

That was one of the things he liked best about Belle. She thought about the world; she took a responsible attitude.

They sat side by side on a tartan-fleece-covered groundsheet laid over springy beach-top grass that was still in its winter brown, eating their cheese and plum chutney sandwiches, and drinking bottled water. Fergus thought he'd never tasted food so delicious.

Afterwards, all three lay flat, the sun on their faces, the first sun of the year that had real warmth. Fergus reached for Mabel's hand; she didn't draw away, but returned the clasp of his fingers. They lay for an hour, not talking, or needing to talk. Then they walked onto the beach, removed their shoes, rolled up their trouser-legs and paddled in the freezing water, shrieking like badly-brought-up toddlers, much to Archie's alarm.

Fergus was elated. Probably the last time he'd immersed any part of his body in the bracing chill of Scottish sea water was when he was thirteen or so, staying at his grandparents' house, and on an outing to the beach at Joppa.

Although they'd been very comfortably off, his grandparents hadn't held with foreign travel. '*Plenty of delights to visit in our own country, Fergus.*' He'd been taken to places like the Isle of Arran for holidays. Perhaps that's why they'd harboured such bitterness against his father, forever off in far-flung and dangerous destinations?

He told Mabel this and she laughed. 'You make your grandmother sound like Miss Jean Brodie.'

'She was a bit Brodie-esque. But comforting with it.'

That's it, Fergus told himself as they headed for home, still giggling. What he appreciated most about Belle was the way she made him feel young again.

When they reached Ashers, he almost wanted to demand cocoa for supper, and a teddy bear to take to bed. He felt a fresh sting of regret that the bed he had to go to was in the cottage at the bottom of the garden, not the same one Belle slept in.

That evening, he did what he'd been longing to do ever since the second or third time he'd been inside Ashers: he opened the glass-fronted bookcase, to nose around among her reading material. Quite a mixture: dusty, leather-bound legal tomes that had presumably belonged to her father, alongside assorted paperbacks; some modern, some classics. *The Wild Sargasso Sea. Sunset Song. The Living Mountain. Miss Garnett's Angel.* Then an entire two shelves of crime fiction. Jo Nesbø: *The Devil's Star.* Henning Mankell: all eight Wallander volumes that had appeared in translation. Karin Fossum. Arnaldur Indriðason.

Mabel arrived in the room suddenly and caught him peering at the titles.

He grinned at her. 'I had you down as more of a litfic type. I read crime fiction too. Especially Scandi-noir. I don't know Karin Fossum – can I borrow *Calling Out for You?* I like to read in bed.'

'So do I.' They glanced at each other shyly and obliquely. 'Help yourself. I wouldn't have thought my reading habits come up to your exacting intellectual standards.'

'Bollocks.' Fergus pointed at the Sally Vickers title. 'I've seen that in the bookshops.'

'It's newly-published.'

He flicked through it. 'Can I borrow this too? I assume it's not actually about angels?'

'I'm not sure that it's a man's book. It's about a woman – an older woman – who goes to Venice. '

'Venice! Have you been?'

'I have, but I hated it.'

'How on earth could you hate Venice?'

'For the same reason I hated Florence. It's so crowded, you can't move. I get claustrophobia in crowds. I panic.'

Her skin still crept at the memory of the herds of tourists, charging like wildebeest, so that she was carried along by the stream, propelled against her will, until they stopped to graze on the next morsel of antiquity and she could elbow her way to the outer perimeter and escape.

'Then we must go in winter when it's quieter. As long as you wrap up well, it's still very pleasant.'

'Oh must "we"?'

He blushed a little.

'I've been thinking, we should go on holiday together. We'd be ideal travelling companions, because we both like the same things, and we've been brought up in very similar ways. We could almost be siblings.'

'I suppose you're right,' said Mabel. 'Maybe a holiday would be a good idea.'

The last time she'd been abroad with a man was one of the trips to Rome with her former lover. 'Before I even think about that, I really should concentrate on making the police look harder for Roddy. Ali's obviously not shaking their tree hard enough. They always pay more attention to a relative too. You'd think she doesn't care about what's happened to him.'

❖

Fergus was kicking himself; he certainly didn't think of Mabel as a *sister*. 'I wish you'd stop worrying about him. If Ali's not bothered, and the police think it's all kosher, there's clearly nothing wrong with the man.'

He'd been about to add that perhaps Roddy had needed a holiday too, but bit his tongue. *A bloody long one, I hope, if that's the case. A permanent one.* In fact, he didn't give a damn if Roddy McCulloch had vanished from the face of the earth.

CHAPTER NINE

Mabel cursed inwardly when she recognised the man who was at the door. She'd almost forgotten about him.

'I told you not to come here again. I still haven't the least idea where your pal Roddy is.'

He peered past her towards the hall, where Fergus was lingering.

'I see you've got in another man already. Fair play to ye, missus. That's what Roddy always said, mind you. Can't do without it for two nights in a row. Randy as a rabbit.'

She pushed him backwards, and slammed the door. She could hear him laughing as he walked down the steps.

Fergus was gazing at her with incredulity. 'Who the hell was that?'

'A drinking pal of Roddy McCulloch's.'

'He's been here before?'

'He has. He says he's looking for Roddy. I suspect he has a wider agenda than that. I think he wants money, or he's going to spread vile rumours about me.'

'Rumours?'

She felt her face and neck turn scarlet. 'You heard him, I imagine?'

Before she realised what was happening, Fergus had thrown open the front door and sprinted up the close. In a few moments, he returned, propelling Ron in front of him. He pushed him into the hallway.

'If I ever hear of you spreading one single word of tittle-tattle about Miss Mountjoy's relationship with McCulloch, or see you in the vicinity of this house again, you'll be in court before your feet can touch the ground.'

'And who the fuck are you?'

'I'm Miss Mountjoy's legal adviser.'

'Legal adviser is it? You're no' one of the solicitors from these parts.' Ron had got his courage back. 'No law against saying what's true.'

'I understand you've been harassing Miss Mountjoy and threatening to spread allegations based entirely on hearsay. I think you know what that's called, my friend. That's slander. That means we see you in the Court of Session.'

'I never asked her for money. All I said is straight from the horse's mouth. A horse that was a coke-head, by the way. Did she tell you she paid for his drugs?'

'I think you'll find repeating the spiteful ravings of an embittered drunk with a score to settle is a very flimsy defence against being sued for defamation. Your pal was pissed off because his work wasn't selling any more, and Miss Mountjoy was a convenient person to blame. Now, fuck off.'

Fergus opened the door, and shoved the man out.

He placed his hand under Mabel's elbow and steered her into the sitting room. He poured her a large measure of brandy. 'This decanter could do with a refill. Remind me when we go shopping. And promise to tell me if that creature ever troubles you again.' He sat down at her side, and laid his fingers over hers. 'You're still shaking. Was McCulloch using drugs in your house?'

She shrugged. 'I don't know. I didn't want to know.'

'Did you clear out the cottage thoroughly?'

'I binned a lot that had been his. If there was anything I wasn't sure about, I binned it.'

Fergus shook his head at her, then giggled. 'You were lucky then, if you dumped half a kilo of coke in the wheelie bin and no one noticed. There's nowhere in this house he could have hidden a stash?'

'No. I'm sure of that.'

'In that case, relax. It's over. I'll deal with that spiv if he comes back again.'

'Why did you say you were my legal adviser?'

'Because I am. I was very careful not to say I was your solicitor. I'm advising you on a few points of law on which I'm an expert. So I'm your legal adviser.'

'He'll be back. His kind always are.'

'Then we'll deal with it. Damn it, he can't be allowed to threaten you.'

'He'll go on spreading rumours about me.'

'Who'll believe him? You're a respected citizen, and he's a drunken sot.'

Fergus saw that Mabel was lost in thought. If that vile man was correct, it went a long way to explaining why Roddy had turned from what sounded like a perfectly pleasant and talented man into a coarse animal during the past seven or eight years. She'd mentioned that her former lover had smoked pot at every opportunity, and Fergus knew it was far from impossible for a man of that age to suddenly discover hard drugs. The rest of the bar-fly's accusation was more worrying, because he knew that's what had got under Mabel's skin.

'Belle?' he said. He heard the note of uncertainty in his own voice. He cleared his throat. 'I realise that wee turd was talking nonsense. I know you're not that sort of woman.' He flexed his hands, made them into fists again. 'I wanted to kill the little rat. Punch his lights out.'

'Just as well you didn't. He'd be after both of us then.'

'That's better. I thought I saw a smile there?' He laid his arm around her shoulders and gave them a squeeze. 'Don't worry. If he sets foot near the place again, I'll see to him. Just don't face up to him by yourself. Has he ever approached you outside the house?'

She shook her head.

'That's OK then. I won't leave you alone again till we've got this whole business sorted out. If I have to go away overnight at any point, you'll come with me.'

'Who'd look after the animals?'

'We need to find a sitter for Gorby. We can always take Archie with us.'

'I think there are catteries.'

Fergus was horrified. 'Gorby doesn't do catteries. How would you like to be locked in a tiny cage among strangers? There must be reliable cat sitters in this area.'

❖

Fergus lost patience with the fact that the only exit to the rear lane was via the garage, since the key to the back gate had been lost long before he arrived. He drove to the ironmongers in Castle Douglas and came home with a substantial brass lock, which he proceeded to fit to the gate, after complaining bitterly about the shortage and poor condition of woodworking tools in the house. Mabel asked him if she looked like the sort of woman who can do carpentry, and he replied that truthfully, yes she did, and dodged her when she mock-attacked him.

'There,' he said with some satisfaction, standing back to admire his handiwork. 'Now you can park in the lane and not have so far to carry things.'

Mabel was impressed. 'I didn't realise you were handy.'

'There's a lot you don't realise about me.' He slid his arm companionably round her waist as they walked back up the garden. She didn't resist. 'As long as we're careful to check all the doors and windows at night, and keep the gate locked, no one can get in unless it's a ghost. So we can sleep peacefully, and we have a lock-up-and-leave house.'

'But I don't want to lock it up and leave it.'

'For when you come to Edinburgh with me.'

She made a huffing sound. 'Maybe, once I close the gallery for the winter, I could come for a visit.'

Mabel sat up and clapped her hand to her chest, as if that could quieten the thudding of her heart. She'd been wakened by Archie's growling. Making as little noise as possible, she slid out of bed, and crept towards the stairway.

She closed the door carefully on her little dog.

No sign of light. She listened: complete silence. But in the air there still hung the aroma that had caused the palpitations to start. There was no mistaking the stench of strong tobacco. She had never met anyone other than Roddy who'd even pretend to smoke Camels. You couldn't buy them locally, she was sure.

She crept down, pausing for a moment on each step to listen. When she reached the hall, she registered the fact that the front door was locked and bolted as usual. She followed the scent-trail into the sitting room, and sat down heavily in her father's chair. The blue Swedish glass ashtray was on the side-table, a single butt-end in it. She held her hand close to it, tentatively. She could feel, even without directly touching it, that it was still warm. Then she spotted the empty tumbler. She sniffed it. Glen Fruig. Tar and dirty socks; as immediately recognisable as the best French perfumes. Fergus wouldn't touch the stuff. His preferred dram was a Campbeltown malt, Springbank. There was no similarity whatsoever in the aroma.

A faint sound from the kitchen brought her to her feet again. She seized the stout brass poker from the hearth, and stole towards the doorway, as quietly as she could. No light, no further sound. Perhaps the window was open, and Fergus's cat had managed to get in? That was ridiculous. Gorby could never jump that height. Besides, she knew Fergus wouldn't let him out at night. 'Fergus?' she called softly. No reply. She moved cautiously to the window – securely closed, as she'd known it would be – and peered down the length of the moonlit garden. The cottage was in darkness. No sign of anyone or anything. It was a remarkably still night for Kirkcudbright. Just a slight breeze rustling the camellia leaves.

She tried the back door. Locked, and the key swinging on its string at the side, as she left it every night, because she was paranoid about being trapped if there was a fire. She began to tremble again. Whoever it was must have been in the house already when she locked the door. He could have come to her room while she was asleep. He might still be there. He could have killed her. He could have...

She should call Fergus on his mobile. As she lifted the handset on the kitchen phone, she realised it was a pointless exercise. You could barely get two bars of signal even in the back garden. Inside the cottage: forget it.

Mabel fitted the key in the lock, turned it as quietly as possible and fled down the path. Even as she was pounding on the cottage door, she began to feel unutterably ridiculous. She was on the point of running back to the house, when the light was switched on and a bleary-eyed Fergus appeared in the doorway, wearing a stylish dark silver dressing-gown in material that had a sheen to it, with lighter grey cuffs and revers.

'What's wrong? Come inside – it's freezing.'

She followed him in.

'I'm sorry. I'm probably being silly, but I think someone's in the house.'

'A burglar? Have you phoned the police?'

'No, because I can't see any sign of a break-in. Fergus – I left Archie shut in my room.' She burst into tears.

'Wait here.' He laid his hand on her shoulder. 'Good

God, woman, you're in your bare feet.' He snatched up a fake fur throw from the day bed and wrapped it around her, then lifted the sand-filled dimple whisky-bottle that served as a doorstop and strode out of the cottage, closing the door softly behind him.

He was back within a quarter of an hour. He dropped her sheepskin moccasins at her feet and the pug in her lap and regarded her quizzically.

'There was a drawer open in the dining room sideboard, but no sign of anything else being disturbed, as far as I can see. Except – the poker was in the kitchen.'

'I left it there. Did you not see the empty whisky glass in the sitting room?'

'I did. I assumed you'd had a night-cap and been too tired to clear up.'

'In other words, you think I'm boozed-up and had a bad dream?'

'I suggested no such thing.'

'Did you smell the glass?'

Fergus shook his head, still gazing at her in concern.

'Glen Fruig,' she said curtly. 'Some detective you are. You know I won't touch the stuff, any more than you will. I don't believe there's a drop of it in the house. And you think I've taken to smoking Camels as well?'

'Now, that I *did* notice.'

'The cigarette-end?'

'The smell. I wondered about that.'

'You *wondered*? It was still warm when I felt it,' said Mabel.

'That's not a burglar. That's someone trying to spook you. What wakened you?'

'Archie growling. I'm a light sleeper. Once I was awake, I could smell the cigarette smoke. At first I thought you must have come over to the house for some reason, and you were being quiet, trying not to wake me. Then I realised it wasn't the sort of tobacco you'd smoke, not in a million years. So I reckoned maybe a window had been left open, and someone had been standing outside having a ciggie. But when I got up the courage to go down, I saw that all the windows were fastened as usual. That's when I went into the sitting room.'

He sat forward in his chair and took both her hands between his. 'You're still cold. Were you terribly afraid?'

'Of course I was.'

'Would you like me to come back to the house with you for the rest of the night?'

'Yes please.'

Fergus stood up, and drew Mabel to her feet. 'Come on then. I assume there's a spare bed somewhere?'

'Father's room. There's even a brand new duvet there. It never got used. What about Gorby?'

'He's asleep on my bed. He'll be fine until morning.'

He draped his warmest jacket around her, locked the cottage door behind him, and followed Mabel along the path. She was cuddling the pug to her chest. When he was a younger man, he'd have been able to sweep both up in his arms and carry them. He sighed briefly.

Once they were inside Ashers, he locked the back door,

checked all the downstairs windows – even the small cloakroom off the hall – and followed Mabel into the sitting room.

'Look,' she said, indicating the ashtray and tumbler.

'Hmmm,' said Fergus. He produced a roll of plastic bags from his dressing-gown pocket, and using one of them as a glove, he bagged up both items. Mabel raised her eyebrows.

'Did you touch either of them?' he asked.

'I held my hand close to the cigarette end. I didn't touch it.'

'Or the glass?'

'I picked it up to smell it.'

He grunted. 'We should call the cops anyway.'

She was very pale. 'I was so sure it was Roddy. I could *see* him. Maybe it means he's dead?'

'You don't believe in ghosts do you?' he asked.

'Of course not.'

'I didn't think you're the type.'

He followed her towards the stairs, rattling the lock of the front door on the way past. 'You don't keep the key beside this one?'

'I read somewhere that they have devices they can use to hook it through the letterbox. I take it out and put it on the table.'

'And you always fasten the bolt?'

'I sometimes forget. Not tonight though. Look – it's fully across.'

'Whoever it was must have got out through the back door when you came to the cottage then. But how would he get out of the garden without a ladder?'

'The picket gate at the front. It bolts from the inside.'

Fergus tutted. 'We'll do something tomorrow about padlocking that.'

He followed her upstairs.

'This is Father's room,' said Mabel, opening the door and standing back. 'There's none of his stuff left, by the way, in case you'd find that creepy. One of the things I did get around to doing over the last couple of years. Goodnight then. I'm sorry to have disturbed you for so little.'

'It's not *little*. You were quite right to come and fetch me. Do you think you can sleep now?'

'I'll try.'

'Leave your door ajar, and I'll do the same.'

She turned back. 'There's no cover on the duvet. Hang on and I'll fetch one. And a sheet.'

'Never mind. I'll just lie down under it. Goodnight, Belle. Try and get some sleep.'

Mabel dropped out of sleep with a start, conscious of the figure beside her bed.

Then she was wide awake. 'What's wrong?'

'Nothing. I've brought you a cup of tea.'

'God! Some hostess I am. What time is it?'

'Bit after ten.'

'*Ten*? In the morning?'

'You obviously needed a good long rest. You're in a

state of shock.'

'I haven't been sleeping well since... since Roddy went.'

'But you said he'd not been living with you, in this house I mean, for more than a year?'

'He hadn't. I mean since he vanished.'

'I'm glad you managed to sleep a little anyway, after all the kerfuffle. Maybe you need a guard dog.'

'I have a guard dog.'

'I meant one who barks. Something from the terrier side of the spectrum.'

'Were you comfortable enough in Father's room?'

'I was. It's a much better bed than the one in the cottage.'

She bit her lip. Go for it, Mabel. 'You could move into the main house full time. I'd rather have you than a guard dog.'

He laughed and coloured up a little. She could see he was discomfited.

'Serena used to say "Fergus" was a name only suitable for a West Highland terrier.'

Now it was her turn to blush. 'I didn't mean...'

'I know you didn't. I'd be very glad to stay in the house. But what will your friends say?'

'They don't need to know.'

'Right.'

Was she imagining it, or did he sound a little disappointed? He was correct of course. It would be all round the town within twenty-four hours. Mabel smiled secretly, hiding behind her hair.

'You must fetch your clothes then, and Gorby's kit. You're both very welcome, since he and Archie get on so well now. If we make sure the front porch door's always kept closed, there's no risk he'll get out into the street.'

The living arrangements proved very successful. Fergus spent every afternoon in Mabel's father's old study, typing as if possessed. Normally, she brought him some sort of refreshment at around five, when she came home from the gallery.

Right on cue, she put her head round the door to ask if he wanted tea. 'You look like Hemingway,' she said, standing close to his shoulder.

He regarded her quizzically over the top of his reading glasses. 'No I don't. He was too vain to wear his specs, though I'm sure I've read somewhere that he needed them.'

He folded his arms, resisting a sudden impulse to reach out, embrace her curvaceous hips and draw her close. *Down boy*!

'I still think you look like him. In a good way,' she added, laughing. 'How's the book coming along anyway?'

'Quite well, as a matter of fact.' He realised that it looked as if he was trying to hide the screen from her. Silly! He felt like a schoolboy who'd been caught with a dirty magazine tucked inside his Latin primer.

'James Gillespie what's-his-name. Did he live an exciting life?'

Fergus grinned. 'I think you've guessed I'm not

working on James just now.'

She leaned over to peer at what he'd been typing.

'It's a detective novel,' he said, reddening. 'I thought I'd try my hand at it. It was after we were discussing what we like to read. I thought, "why not give it a shot".'

'So you're going to give Ian Rankin a run for his money?'

'I think it might be a bit darker than Rebus. The bookshops are awash with detectives who have a drink problem and a poor track record with women.'

'But they need a character flaw. What one does your hero have? What's his name anyway?'

'I haven't finally decided. I need a name that's unusual but not improbable. He's on his own with an autistic child after his wife committed suicide.'

'And he doesn't drink?'

'He uses other methods to numb his mind.'

'Sounds bleak.'

'It is. I think it'll work though.'

'Set in Edinburgh?'

'Set in rural Scotland. There's too much that focuses on Edinburgh or London or Manchester. You get crime in rural areas too. The Scandinavian writers have a good handle on that one.'

'Kirkcudbright, for instance? Dorothy L Sayers set one of her Lord Peter Wimsey novels here. *Five Red Herrings*?'

Fergus grunted. 'Can't get into her work. Too anodyne. The only one I've read is *Gaudy Night*.'

'Can I read some of your book?'

'Not yet. It's a very early draft.'

She laid her hand fleetingly on his shoulder. 'Don't tell me any more then. I've heard that you can run out of steam if you talk about it too soon. I won't keep you from your work. I'll give you a shout when dinner's ready,' she called over her shoulder as she headed for the kitchen.

He heard her singing to herself a few moments later. He slid his fingers over the spot where hers had rested. He could still feel the glow.

Mabel had almost forgotten what day it was, until she heard a soft knock, and Fergus elbowed his way carefully around her bedroom door, carrying a breakfast tray complete with a single red rose.

'Happy Birthday!' He leaned in and gave her a peck on the cheek.

There was a wrapped package lying under the rose. Mabel seized it.

'Eat up first, or it'll get cold.'

'What about you?'

'I had some while I was making yours. I'll have a cup of tea with you though. You'll have to do without coffee this morning.'

She shuffled aside, to make room for him to sit alongside her.

'What do you want to do today?' he asked. 'I'm taking you out for dinner, but we need to think of something special until then.'

Sunshine was flooding the room. 'We could go to

Logan Gardens. Their rhododendrons will be out. Or is that too far?'

He smiled at her indulgently. 'Nowhere is too far. It's your special day.'

And it was a special day. The best birthday she could remember since she was in her twenties. A new Jo Nesbø book – *The Redbreast* – a healthy walk among gloriously flowering plants, and a delicious dinner in Portpatrick.

It was after eleven when they got home, and Mabel announced that she was so tired she was going straight to bed.

'Good night then, birthday girl. I'll lock up.'

He kissed her lightly on the lips.

She'd felt exhausted, but she lay awake for a long time, savouring that kiss. After twenty minutes of tossing and turning, she had to throw off the covers, because she couldn't stop herself wondering how it would feel to sleep beside the strong, confident man lying in bed not ten metres away from her. How different would her life have been if she'd met Fergus when she was twenty? If he'd been the first man she'd slept with? For the first time in thirty-six years she thought about Gareth.

Gareth McMenamin Calder. Date of birth: tenth of May 1961. Place of birth: Invergordon. Eyes: grey, hair: dark brown, weight: 160 pounds, height: six foot one, occupation: theology student. He was handsome and he was always laughing. He had an alcohol dependency at twenty.

They'd got stuck in a lift together in the university library tower at Gilmorehill. Much later, she learned he'd been on his way to meet another girl from her reading session, and that his pals called him Shag-a-Polo.

Not that she'd lost her virginity in a lift, although that would have been Gareth's style. No, she'd lost it on the none-too-clean sheets of his room in a tacky student crash-pad. He'd gone into the bathroom and produced a grubby towel for her to lie on. 'Saves washing the sheet. Now, relax. You'll enjoy it. It doesn't hurt.'

It damn well did. Maybe initiation rites have to, or they don't work. It hurt, and she'd felt nothing, nothing except relief when it was over.

He'd laughed ruefully. 'Sorry. I can usually last longer than that even the first time. But you're so lovely and tight, like one of these Egyptian girls that's been sewn up. God! There's blood everywhere.'

She'd thought that made her his. She'd believed the duty of love was born of the fact her blood was on his thighs as well as her own. She wasn't so naïve as to fail to recognise him as a selfish bastard. The sort of man who'd be in another town and another woman when she was having his child, then arrive late having weaved round closed snow-gates, bearing filling-station flowers for her and chocolates for the midwife. And she'd have been sitting up in bed trying to look cheerful, with her hair fixed and her make-up done. It'd all start over. He'd probably have given the nurse one in the sluice-room on the way out.

Where the naiveté showed was in the belief she could change him. That illusion lasted six weeks and five days, until the afternoon she came home early to find him in her flat. She had lent him a key so he could do his washing.

That was OK. She had the key to his flat too, though God alone knows what she was supposed to find there of any use to her.

They didn't leap apart when she blundered into her room. They were locked together like randy dogs, on the new primrose yellow sheets she'd bought for his sake. Gareth slowed on his stroke, turning his head to grin at her. 'Coitus interruptus!' he said affably. 'Coming in beside us? No? Well, shut the door behind you, there's a good girl.'

She'd gone calmly back to the kitchen, forced open the door of the washing machine with a screwdriver and thrown his clothes into the muddy back court. Even the radio on maximum volume didn't drown out their noise. She'd wanted to kill him.

In the end, she'd got her punishment anyway. After she'd turned Gareth and his floozie out of her bed, she'd burned the sheets, and regretted it later, because they'd been expensive. But the old woman downstairs complained to the landlord that she was chucking rubbish out of the window and lighting bonfires. She'd been evicted, and she had to pay for a repair to the washing machine too.

She shepherded her thoughts back to Fergus, drew the quilt over herself again, and fell asleep.

Mabel sat bolt upright. There it was again, and she knew this time she wasn't dreaming. The wind chimes in front of the kitchen window were tinkling. And the only way that could happen was if either the window or the door had been opened, or someone had run their hand across the spiral cascade of bronze owls.

It'd be Fergus. He'd gone down to fetch a glass of water.

She got up and walked softly across the room, not stopping to put on her slippers. She listened again, then stuck her head round the door. No lights on anywhere.

'Fergus?'

'Are you OK?' asked a sleepy voice from Father's room.

'There's someone down there again.'

She carried on downstairs. The kitchen door was open, and she was sure she saw the silhouette of a figure move to the side of the window. Fury overcame her fear, plus the discomfort of standing barefoot on freezing flagstones.

'Roddy? What the hell are you playing at? Why are you doing this to me?'

She switched on the light.

The room was empty. The wind chimes sounded again, quite distinctly. The window was wide open.

'Roddy?' she called again. 'Will you bloody well stop this? If you think it's funny, think again. I'm going to call the police, right this moment.'

A futile move. Probably the nearest bobby at that time of night was in Dumfries or Stranraer.

'You have no right to be in my house,' she shouted. 'Breaking and entering, that's what it is. No better than a common thief. Here I go, I'm lifting the phone now.'

Fergus appeared at her side, on silent feet – amazingly silent, for such a big man.

'What's wrong?'

'He was here.'

'You saw him?'

'I saw *someone*. Who else could it be?'

Fergus crossed the room and closed the window firmly.

'I was certain we'd checked this?' he said. 'I made sure that the snib was over the bottom sash.'

'I remember. It was.'

'So it could only have been opened from the inside?'

She nodded. He was watching her carefully, his head on one side.

'Look.' He pointed to where the back door key was lying on the draining board. 'Did you take it off the string?'

'Of course not. I always leave it there, in case there's a fire.'

'If it was Roddy, where is he now – did you see him leave?' Fergus tried the door. 'Fuck it – it's not locked.'

Mabel felt giddy, and sat down suddenly on one of her elm chairs.

'I saw a figure beside the window. But I didn't see the door open. There's a moon. If someone had opened it, they'd have been quite visible against the moonlight. I didn't hear the door open or close either. Oh God, Fergus – that means he's still in the house? What if it *is* a burglar?'

'Wait here.' He lifted her ten-inch Sabatier knife from the rack. 'Keep this beside you, in case he manages to sneak past me.'

'I want to come with you,' she said, following him into the hall.

He shook his head. He opened the door of the cloakroom and switched on the light.

'Stay in here, and lock the door behind you. Where's the dog?'

'Shut in my bedroom. I don't want to stay here.'

'Do what you're told.'

She went reluctantly into the room and sat down on the wooden seat cover.

'Lock the door now, and keep calm. You're shivering. Here.'

He took off his dressing gown, to reveal smart plaid pyjamas. He drew the woollen robe round her, still warm from his body. Then he lifted a dry towel from the shelf and wrapped it around her bare feet. 'You'll catch pneumonia! Sit tight. I'll only be a few moments.'

'Be careful then.'

'I've dealt with my fair share of villains. Don't worry.'

She was still trembling with cold and fear when he knocked at the door.

'You were ages.'

'I was precisely ten minutes. There's no one in the house. I've checked all the other doors and windows. Come on back through to the kitchen.' He released the knife gently from her fingers, which were still welded around it. 'I've put the kettle on. You're certain you saw someone?'

'Pretty certain.'

She perched on a kitchen chair, still wearing Fergus's dressing gown. She snuggled her hands into the sleeves. He regarded her calmly, head on one side. 'I don't suppose you sleepwalk?'

'Never in my life. I don't suppose *you* do?'

He smiled. 'Touché. Well, if it wasn't either of us, who

was it? No one could have come in at the front door because it's bolted. I suppose someone could have got in at the back though. Who could have keys, apart from you and Roddy?'

'The cleaning lady used to; I suppose she could have had a copy cut. But it's him. I know it is. He's doing this to punish me.'

'What would he punish you for?' Fergus's eyes flashed particularly blue.

Mabel returned his gaze calmly. 'For putting him out.'

He sighed and drew the snib fully across the matching brass plate on the lower sash of the kitchen window. He relocked the door.

'There. Every possible means of entry thoroughly closed and bolted. Do you want a cup of tea before you go back upstairs?'

Mabel shook her head. 'Do you?'

'I'll have water.' He drained the current bottle of Evian. 'Come on then, let's get back to bed. And Belle, in the morning you report this to the police. You *have* to.' As they climbed the stair side by side, he took her hand. 'You're still freezing.' On the landing, he hesitated, then wound his arm around her, and drew her close. She didn't resist. He tipped her face up to his, and kissed her. A long, deep kiss this time. She didn't resist that either.

'Your place or mine, kid?' he said huskily.

'What?'

'Do you want to come in with me, if you're frightened?'

The world spun faster on its axis for a moment. But, good God – in bed with a man in Father's room? It would be positively indecent. Her beautifully crisp white Egyptian cotton sheets seemed a better prospect.

'We'd be more comfortable if you come in with me. I have a bigger bed. Queen-size.'

Fergus was grinning at her. 'So we can have a side each?'

Easily. And room for one more in between.

'Quite,' she said.

The mattress on her bed was under two years old, firm and well-sprung. So it would be eminently feasible to have a side each, because it didn't dip even a smidgin in the middle, the way a mattress which has supported two bodies for many nights spread over two decades does: the type where, even if you're not speaking when you go to bed, you end up in a huddle in the centre by morning.

That had been the last straw as far as having Roddy in the house was concerned. On the occasion she'd taken pity on him one night when he was so drunk he couldn't stand up, and was fifty shades of maudlin and a hundred shades of contrite, he'd rewarded her by wetting the bed.

Suddenly, Fergus laughed. 'Get on with you,' he said, and he smacked her roundly on the bottom.

She couldn't remember anyone doing that to her since she was a child. She wasn't sure whether she was going to laugh or cry.

'I'm sorry,' she said frostily. 'I didn't realise you were just making a fool of me.'

'I'm not,' he said, full of wounded innocence. 'Come on woman, it's cold out here. Are you inviting me into your queen-sized bed or not? Separate sides be damned,' he added once they were under the covers. 'We're both cold, and you're scared out of your pretty little wits. Cuddle up.'

CHAPTER TEN

Fergus was disoriented when he wakened during the night. He was sure he'd gone to bed wearing a full set of pyjamas, but now he appeared to be naked. He was aware that he had an urgent need to pee. Then he realised he was in Mabel Mountjoy's bed, and hers was the comfortable waist his arm was twined around. She appeared to be naked too. Ah yes. Now he remembered!

He began to extricate himself as gently as possible; not an easy manoeuvre, because the pug had joined them at some point during the night, and was lying stolid and immovable in the crook of his knees. Mabel stirred.

'What's wrong?'

'I didn't mean to wake you. Need to visit the bathroom.'

'It's OK, I'm a light sleeper. Put the lamp on so you can see where you're going.'

As he switched on the light, Mabel rolled over to face him. This was a dilemma. How many years was it since a woman he wanted to impress had seen him in the buff? More than he cared to remember. He was sure his last ex-wife had always shut her eyes tightly. And how did Belle feel about hirsute men? Serena used to call him The Ape. His body-hair was still dark, although his head and beard were salt and pepper. He slid over the edge, pulling in his stomach as much as one can with a full bladder. He headed towards the bedroom door.

'Use my bathroom,' said Mabel, a smile in her voice. 'You and your Evian water!'

When he got into bed again, she had turned over, away from the light. He settled at her back, and slid his arm around her, a little tentatively – after all, last night was last night, and sometimes women regret actions born of the heat of passion. But she nestled against him with no hesitation. He kissed her shoulder blade, then lay in the dark (and how dark it was, at the back of the house, despite the street-lamps in the town), trying to analyse the tidal wave of emotion that seemed set to drown him. He felt wonderful. Utter contentment, only marred by a small fear that such comfort was too good to last. He'd lain down beside Belle the previous night overwhelmed by an irresistible desire to soothe her and warm her and make her feel safe. Then, when he drew her into his arms to stop her shivering, and it had become clear that she didn't mean to repel his advances, he'd been overwhelmed by another urgent desire, even stronger than the impulse to play the knight in shining armour.

It had been as exhilarating and refreshing as waking to sunshine after a long, drear winter. He revelled in the euphoria of snuggling close to a woman who *desired* him. He blinked away a tear. Fulfilled. That was the correct word. But you never heard men use it of themselves. Only women.

He cuddled Belle Mountjoy close and fell into another deep, contented sleep.

Mabel woke gradually. Normally, she slept so badly that the least thing roused her. Normally, she was cold when she woke, despite the 15 tog goose-down duvet. This morning, she appeared to be covered by nothing more than a sheet, yet she was gloriously warm. As warm as the body snuggled against hers. Ah yes. Fergus. She smiled into her pillow, revisiting what had happened the previous night. He'd been so gentle and kind, polite even, enquiring solicitously whether he wasn't too heavy (and she had murmured 'Not at all', and wanted to purr like a cat, because the sheer solidity of the man was so comforting; Roddy had been a lightweight, in every sense of the word. Fergus made her feel cherished, and safe).

She reached her right arm back to stroke his leg, amazed at her own boldness. He stirred and stretched.

'Good morning.'

'Good morning to you too. I didn't mean to wake you.'

'I was awake anyway. I can't remember when I've slept so well.'

'Me too.' She heard the smile in her own voice.

Was this love, this warm, fuzzy feeling? Mabel was confused. But she also recognised that she felt more contented than she could remember. An old Ella Fitzgerald song that Father used to like was running in her head: 'Someone to Watch Over Me'

'I hope I didn't snore?' asked Fergus.

'A teensy bit, when you were dropping off to sleep. I jabbed you with my elbow and you stopped.'

He reached an arm above his head and ran his fingers over the headboard.

'This is gorgeous.'

She'd had it specially made, in the days when Roddy's paintings sold like warm fudge at a fair, and she made a modest profit on each.

'Isn't it? It's sycamore. I love the colour, and the way he managed to use the natural markings as a design.'

'You have such superlative taste in everything. I used to do a bit of woodwork,' he added ruefully. 'Enjoyed it, but I haven't done any for years. I assume that portrait of you on the opposite wall is a McCulloch, by the way? It's stunning. *You're* stunning.'

Mabel wrinkled her nose. 'I was young then.'

'What age – about twenty?'

'Twenty-one.'

'You still have the same lovely body.' Fergus yawned and stretched. 'I suppose I'd better get myself dressed and make Gorby his breakfast.'

'He'll hardly starve. Where is he anyway?'

'On my bed, I daresay. In the other room, I mean. Shift, dog. I'll feed you too. How does he manage to get up here? I didn't think something with such short legs could jump so high?'

Mabel giggled. 'He has a special step at my side. What time is it?'

Fergus rolled over and groped automatically on the

bedside table. 'Haven't a clue. My watch is in the other room.'

'Och well, it's not as if we've anything pressing to do. It's Sunday, isn't it?'

Right on cue, a church bell started ringing. Mabel giggled. 'It must be quite late.'

She leapt out of bed, snatched her dressing gown from the back of the door and pulled it around her, in one elegant movement. She vanished into the bathroom. When she got back, hair brushed, skin glowing, Fergus had retrieved his pyjamas.

'You should stay put while I make breakfast,' Mabel said. 'You're the guest. I'll give the animals a snack too.'

'Nonsense. We'll make breakfast together.'

'Which do you prefer first thing – tea or coffee?'

Fergus stifled a grin. 'Tea,' he said. 'Get it into your head, woman: never coffee, at any time of the day!'

As they sat companionably at the kitchen table in their dressing gowns, at eleven o'clock in the morning, Mabel half-wished that Briony would happen by. That'd give her something to tell the Townswomen's Guild.

Then, all of a sudden they were each a little unsure of the other.

Fergus cleared his throat. 'I don't want to make any false assumptions.'

'Neither do I,' said Mabel, her mouth full of toast.

'I thought I was the only one at risk of that. What assumptions can you possibly be afraid of?'

'That this isn't going on the bill.'

They both laughed until they could barely catch their breath.

'Belle, you are the most amazing woman in the world.'

'Surely not! In Kirkcudbright, maybe. So what false assumption are *you* worried about making?'

'That you won't put my rent up.'

They giggled afresh.

'Seriously though,' said Fergus. 'Will you want me to go back to sleeping in the other room? Or even in the cottage?'

'Why would I want that? Do *you* want to?' *Oh, you're a brazen hussy, Mabel Mountjoy.*

'I'd rather not,' he said, almost too quickly. 'But it's your call, my dear.'

She replied briskly, almost managing not to blush. 'Then it seems silly to have to make two beds when we only need one.' This conversation was turning out to be infinitely more embarrassing than their nocturnal embraces.

He took her hand across the table. 'I'm glad. I'm very happy here with you. I haven't been so happy in years.'

She hadn't been so happy in her entire life. That only went to prove what a shallow, unfeeling person she was; the last man she'd shared her bed with hadn't been seen for more than three months, as far as she knew. God knows what could have happened to him, and here she was, giggling like an adolescent. Then she remembered Fenella Green.

'I'm happy too,' she announced decisively.

'I think we're a particularly well-suited couple,' added Fergus. 'We're from the same type of background, and we share the same tastes in the things that matter, like tea and fine wine and music.'

And sex. But she was going to have to do something

about his belief that all she ever listened to was Bach and Mozart. One of these fine days, he'd catch her in the kitchen listening to Radio One and dancing as if no one was watching (because, indeed, no one *was* watching). Perhaps he'd condemn her for being as much of a philistine as any teenager.

'And in bed, I think,' he was saying.

'What?'

'I enjoy making love. I fancy you do too? Do you have any idea how pretty you are when you blush?'

She'd have preferred him to say he loved her, but maybe that's what he meant anyway. A well-suited couple: love must come into that equation somewhere?

'Once you're ready, you can put your clothes in my wardrobe – there's tons of room,' she said.

She sprinted upstairs, humming to herself, and eventually found her nightie in the far corner of the bedroom, behind a chair. She must fairly have hurled it when she'd helped Fergus remove it the previous night. *Oh, Mabel, Mabel!* She'd need to stop thinking of it as her bedroom. *Their* bedroom. Regarding it with an impartial eye, she decided that at least two items had to be relocated. Roddy's portrait of her, for a start. There was something almost indecent about being in bed with another man while the nude twenty-one-year-old Mabel watched from behind that curtain of auburn hair, because somehow it meant that the artist was also spying on them. And he was the last person she'd been thinking of the previous night.

She'd move her doll's house too. What adult woman had a doll's house in her bedroom? Her friends would have howled with laughter, telling her it should either be on display in the sitting room (it was a most sumptuous and well-appointed house; Father had spared no expense), or else given away to someone who had a granddaughter of an age to play with dolls. She hadn't the faintest idea why she had kept it anyway, and wouldn't have shared the secret with another human being that she frequently opened it to rearrange the furniture, or move the dolls to another room.

'What on earth are you doing?' Fergus had arrived in the doorway without her noticing. 'Here. Let me help you. It looks heavy.'

It was. Roddy had tensioned the canvas using heavy-duty stretchers, and the frame he'd chosen for it was wide and wooden and substantial.

'I want to move it.'

'You're not thinking of getting rid of it? It's gorgeous.'

'I thought it might be better in another room.'

Fergus didn't comment further. He understood. She *knew* he understood.

'Hang it in the study,' he said suddenly.

'In Father's study? God forbid.'

'You father's not here any more, Belle. I'd like to be able to look at it every day, and you've mentioned before you don't want to display it in any of the public rooms, so the study's ideal.'

He carried it carefully downstairs, fetched a duster and removed the cobwebs from the back, then helped Mabel rehang it, double-hooked rather than on a cord, as it had always been.

They stood back, side by side and looked at it.

'I want you to be able to hang onto the good memories. I can tell that Roddy loved you very much, and you loved him,' said Fergus.

Her eyes brimmed over. 'Not any more. But I'm *worried* about him.'

'I'll try harder than ever to track him down. I'm sure he's safe and sound.'

The doll's house could stay put in their bedroom meantime, until she figured out a better solution.

Fergus sang to himself as he hung his shirts in the far side of Mabel's wardrobe. He'd seen a totally different side of her the previous night. An extremely passionate woman. Who'd have thought it? Mind you, it sounded as if she'd had a more active sex life than he had over the past few years. He'd lost interest, to a great extent, after Serena died… There had been the brief and unsatisfactory attempt to rekindle the old flame with Anita Forrest while she nursed him back to health after his breakdown. Not a lot else.

Although he'd managed to acquire the reputation of being a rabid womaniser, he'd been involved with surprisingly few women, apart from his three wives. In truth, he had run away from that sort of involvement more often than he'd sought it. This realisation surprised and depressed him. He had often thought he'd have preferred to live in the age of the troubadours and courtly love. If he was honest with himself, he was slightly in awe of women:

their changeable emotions and sudden hatreds, their irrational volte faces.

When he still worked in TV, women threw themselves at him — attractive, successful women too — but it had seldom led to anything beyond one-night stands. What relationships he'd had were hollow and unsatisfying. He'd certainly not have said Belle had thrown herself at him, but neither had she gone in for silly games of playing hard to get. Her arousal had matched his. He smiled to himself at the memory of her wholesome, honest pleasure in their lovemaking.

And where was the harm? They were adults, both free of other entanglements. They weren't cheating on anyone else, and there were no kids to get in the way.

Serena had been wrong for him in every way: intellectually, emotionally and physically. He'd almost realised that on the very day when he first met her, an apparently weeping figure huddled against the parapet of North Bridge in a pre-Christmas gale. He had stopped to see if he could help, and when he saw her face, the alabaster skin with just the faintest flush of pink to the cheeks, contrasting so dramatically with the luxuriant swart hair, his first thought had been that she'd be a superb model for the black and white portrait photography with which he'd become fixated. An Art Nouveau Celtic goddess. Then she raised her eyes to his face (or rather, her left eye, because it turned out that the cause of her distress was a lump of sharp Edinburgh grit in the right one). Oh, the colour of that eye; somewhere between cornflowers and the inner part of a gas flame and the most expensive sapphires! His fate had been sealed.

Yes, she'd been exceptionally beautiful, and he'd found that beauty utterly seductive, but she'd been incapable of loving the way a real woman should. She had led him on, got him worked up, then cried off. She never made love with him the way Belle had. She never welcomed him. She had left him frustrated rather than satisfied. He'd been afraid, every time (and in something under two years together, there had been surprisingly few times), that he'd crush her body beneath him like a small bird. There was a passage in Gabriel García Márquez's *One Hundred Years of Solitude* that reminded him of that image…

He shuddered, shook himself, and exorcised the image of his ex-wife as a quartered sparrow.

Belle Mountjoy was the diametric opposite. A fastidious woman, but not an ounce of prudishness in her. Lovely and loving, as well as sensible. No one who cared about animals so much could possibly be a bad person.

He studied his reflection in the wardrobe mirror, trying to draw in his paunch. If he lost a little weight and got a decent haircut, he'd be quite presentable. 'I reckon you put up a more than adequate performance last night, considering your age and everything else,' he told himself. 'All parts in first-class working order.' They made a handsome couple, he and Belle, in this beautiful house.

Mabel turned on the radio as she prepared to ransack the freezer for the makings of an extra-special dinner. Best avoid Radio One today. She'd need to break Fergus into that gently.

'You were right,' she said when he poked his head round the door. 'I need to tell the cops about the intruder.'

Not that they seemed terribly bothered. A bored young PC arrived, ascertained that nothing appeared to have been stolen, or broken, and indeed that whoever had got in hadn't forced entry, and prepared to leave again in short order. 'I'll mention it to DI Ellis,' he said casually as he left. 'He takes a special interest in this part of the area.'

Mabel clutched at her throat. All these years, and she'd hardly thought about him once.

'Is that Tom Ellis?' she asked huskily.

'It is indeed.'

'Hang on,' said Fergus. 'I've thought of something that could be useful.'

Mabel heard him sprint upstairs. He was back in moments.

He held out a plastic-bag-covered whisky tumbler to the constable. 'Could be worth dusting this for prints, because I suspect that the intruder's touched it. Miss Mountjoy's prints will be on it too, but I'm sure that's easily dealt with.'

The young man laughed uneasily. 'There's no way that could be used in evidence. An officer would need to have collected it. We need a chain of custody.'

'I know that! But wouldn't it be useful to see if there are prints you have on your database?'

'No point, sir. Our fingerprinting people are overworked as it is.'

Fergus swore under his breath as the PC left.

'You know this Ellis guy?'

Mabel shrugged, in an attempt at insouciance. 'He's from Kirkcudbright. I was at primary school with him.'

Next morning, Mabel got a call from the police HQ in Dumfries, asking if she had heard from Roddy McCulloch in any way, shape or form since she reported him missing. Fergus noted how pale she became, how her hand flew to her heart when she heard the artist's name. He experienced another sharp pang of jealousy – an emotion he had always prided himself on being immune to.

'I think I'd better visit Alison again,' Mabel said as she hung up the phone. 'I'm sure she knows damn fine where her brother is. I'm sick of their little games. Do you want to come with me?'

Fergus was taken aback. He didn't want to foul up his plan before it was even under way. 'Certainly not!'

Mabel pursed her lips.

'It's better she doesn't see me at present,' he added.

'I see.'

'I don't think you do. It's not that I don't want to keep you company. But if I have to make a couple of trips there to check things out, she'd recognise me. Or someone would. You said Port Alexander's even smaller than Kirkcudbright?'

'Sorry, I'm being obtuse.'

'You're not. But you're not a devious person either.

You said she was unhelpful before; let me go and have a shuftie. This could be a particularly opportune time, if the cops have been in touch with her too.'

'That'd be best. I'm sure they must have spoken to Ali, even before they contacted me.'

He kissed her on the nose before leaving the house, alone.

Fergus parked at the main square in Port Alexander.

'Another pretty, sleepy little town!' he murmured to himself, as he strolled up the main street, taking in the picturesque harbour and the fact that there were at least two decent-looking restaurants.

He wondered, as he had in Kirkcudbright, how many Scots were unaware of these provincial architectural gems in their midst? Wonderful for a quiet, bracing holiday or for retirement, but not a permanent base for the likes of him. Not for another couple of decades at any rate.

It was easy to find Alison McCulloch's shop. Its frontage was painted a sickly lime-green, with an impressionistic trim of painted elves and fairies. Presumably she'd drawn them herself? From what little he'd seen of her brother's work, he was the more competent draughtsman.

Mabel had said that Ali lived above the shop. He slowed his pace, and took in the building's details, then crossed the square to examine it from the far side. It was a typical early nineteenth-century house, the shop frontage probably added in the 1930s. It was two storeys tall, with additional dormers in the attic; the small windows looked filthy. He concluded that the owner didn't use the top floor. A chimney-stack at either end; as far as he could judge, all the chimney-pots were capped. That didn't preclude a stove-pipe at the back of the building – but it was possibly a fair enough bet that the proprietrix of Frogs and Princesses didn't go in for open fires.

Fergus made another circuit of the town, looking for any sign of bins out. It was Thursday. When he'd asked, Mabel had looked puzzled and said she thought the rural collection was usually made on a Friday.

He selected a pleasant, old-fashioned café diagonally opposite Ali's shop, and ordered a pot of tea and a scone. Turning on the Learmonth charm, it didn't take him long to get into conversation with the waitress.

'Such an attractive town,' he said. 'I noticed that the streets aren't marred by the usual array of plastic refuse-bins either. I take it this isn't bin day?'

'No,' she said. 'That's a Monday morning.'

'Only one collection a week? That must make it difficult for businesses like this – or is there another for commercial waste?'

'No, we get by with the one.'

He finished his tea, which tasted even better now, thanked her, left a generous tip and went on his way.

The following Sunday, he told Mabel he'd be out briefly, very late on.

'Leave the back gate unlocked,' he said. 'I'll see to it when I come in. I'll have something to unload from the car.'

'Would it not be easier to bring it in through the close?'

'It's something I want to put in the cottage.'

'What?'

'Wait and see.'

'What's "late"?' she asked. 'Tennish?'

'Much later than that. Maybe even around one in the morning. So I suppose technically it'll be Monday, not Sunday.'

'What on earth are you doing at that time?'

'Work,' he said, tapping the side of his nose.

'Can I not come too? You said I could help with your next assignment.'

'Not this time. You can help me once I get back if you're so inclined.'

They spent Monday forenoon sitting on the floor of the cottage. Fergus had produced a plastic sheet from somewhere. He insisted that Mabel wore rubber gloves. He announced that they were going to sort through all the items from Alison McCulloch's bin.

'Every bag?' she said, screwing up her nose. 'What are we looking for?'

'Paperwork of any description. Put everything like that in a pile at one side.'

'All I'm finding here is supermarket receipts.'

'Put those in the pile.'

'What on earth are you going to learn from what she buys in Sainsbury's?'

'Does she smoke?'

'I've no idea. I suppose she might. Not heavily, I'd say.'

'A boozer like her brother?'

'She's not tee-total, but no, not like Roddy.'

'Then I'm interested in what she's buying.'

Mabel sighed. 'You want me to look at them as I go along?'

'Just pile them up for me,' said Fergus distractedly, skimming over all the shopping receipts.

Mabel had turned her attention to the empty bottles. 'Two bottles of the calibre of wine I'd use for cooking. No whisky or brandy or port. She doesn't exactly live high on the hog.'

'No sign of her stocking up on ciggies either,' said Fergus. 'I wouldn't say her brother's living there in that case.'

'I've never believed he would be. It'd be weird if they were suddenly thick as thieves. What on earth are we going to do with this once we've sorted through it? Some of it will go in my bin, but not all. How can one woman produce so much rubbish?'

'She doesn't seem to have a separate one for the shop. We can burn all the paper in the stove here.'

'Even so.'

'Then we'll need to take the rest to the dump ourselves.'

'You do this often, for work?'

'From time to time. It can be an easy way to get a lot of information.'

'Look,' said Mabel. She proffered a bundle of cards. 'She obviously cleared these out in the past week – old birthday cards to her, all from Roddy. You'd think you'd keep that sort of thing, wouldn't you, if it was from your brother who'd gone missing?'

They stared at each other helplessly, realising that neither had the faintest idea how it felt to have a brother, missing or otherwise.

'What do we actually know about this woman?'

'Ali?' Mabel shrugged. 'She loves boats. They both do. It's the one thing they have in common.'

Latterly, she'd contemplated the possibility that this was the main reason Roddy had decided to stay in Kirkcudbright all those years ago.

'Did she live in this area before he moved here?'

'I'm not sure. I think so. Maybe there's a family connection. To tell you the truth, I didn't always pay much attention to what she was saying.'

It took a further midnight trip to the deserted streets of Port Alexander before Fergus found what he was looking for.

He patted the pile of papers he'd sorted out from the fresh haul of bin-bags, grunting with satisfaction. 'Gold-dust!'

Mabel looked at him with raised eyebrows.

'The last half dozen bank statements for a certain Roderick McCulloch.'

She practically tore the pages from his hand.

'How did she get her mitts on these?'

'They're addressed to him at her house. Maybe that's why you never noticed any while he was living here. Careful!' He reached over to take them back from her.

'Well, damn him. Did you see the balance on this account?'

'I did.'

'And he sponged off me for nearly twenty years. You think he's living with Ali after all?'

Fergus shrugged. 'Keeping himself well-hidden, if that's the case. Never more than one light going on upstairs at night. Unless, you don't think...?'

'Yuck,' said Mabel. 'No, I *don't* think. Look – his account's not been used since January.'

'Do you know his pin number? Is he the type to share information like that?'

She coloured up. 'Of course not. I've never known that, any more than he knew mine. Why?'

Fergus felt triumphant. 'That's what whoever's coming in here is looking for then. How quickly did you move his stuff out of the cottage?'

'I don't remember. A week, maybe?'

'But you said his wallet was missing – I'm assuming his bank card was in that?'

'I suppose so.'

'I bet he kept his pin number in a diary or address book.'

'I'm sure he didn't possess either.'

'Most people have something. You'd be surprised. Did you get the impression that he'd inherited a lot of money?'

'The parents were pretty well-off, I think. I suppose the inheritance would have been split between him and Ali. I never heard of any other siblings. But no, I don't think there was any sort of enormous family fortune.'

'Maybe Roddy's money came from another source, and she was in on it too?'

'What other source? I know for certain he hadn't sold one of his own paintings in years. And he wasn't dealing in antique ones to *that* extent. He was pinning all his hopes on the one that turned out to be a fake. Poor Roddy. His precious Miró will be a pile of ashes by now.'

'Remember what his drinking buddy said about his habits? I wonder if he'd been engaging in a bit of private enterprise?'

The significance of what Fergus was saying seemed to dawn on Mabel.

'Surely not. There can't be a great market for anything stronger than cannabis in a place like this?'

Fergus rolled his eyes. 'Heroin and coke and worse are ubiquitous nowadays. This place will be awash with them, like every other town.'

'But I'd have *noticed*, wouldn't I? You see it on TV, all sort of shady characters turning up at dead of night in hooded tops.'

'He'd have been cute enough not to deal from here.'

'But he never *went* anywhere. I can count on the fingers of one hand the times he was out of Kirkcudbright in the last ten years. How could he be getting supplies?'

'These local beaches you took me to – places like Brighouse Bay and Carrick Shore. You can get a fair-sized yacht close in. And remember that evening we remarked on the number of kayaks and rowing boats sailing around the ones that were moored offshore? You told me this area was notorious for smuggling in the past.'

Mabel looked thoughtful. 'There are better places than those too. More secluded.'

'If anyone imagined he had a stash of drugs here, that'd also explain the attempted break-ins.'

'Fergus – if he was mixed up with people like that, *anything* could have happened to him. Should we tell the police what we suspect?'

'Not much point at the moment. We've no evidence. Belle, cheer up. Roddy's gone, and hopefully all his gear with him. Look out all the cleaning materials you've got. We're going to give this cottage another thorough going-over. And I want to look through every last item of his you've got in the attic. Just in case.'

'What are you looking for?'

'Older bank statements. That sort of thing.'

Mabel fetched pails, mops, a vacuum cleaner and assorted bottles of cleaning fluid. Together, they spent the next four hours hoovering, dusting, scrubbing and polishing the garden cottage to the point of borderline OCD. Fergus demanded a stepladder and checked all of the roof-beams. He took a long-handled duster and produced a cluster of spiders' webs from behind the wood-burner. Finally, he was satisfied that the place was clear.

'I'll tackle the stuff from your attic tomorrow,' he said.

He gripped her hand firmly as they walked towards the main house.

'You don't feel frightened any more?' he asked, and she

replied that she felt safe as houses; in fact, a good deal safer than houses appeared to be.

'You should sell off every last one of that sponger's paintings,' he added. 'Get back a little of what you're owed.'

The next day, Fergus brought all the storage boxes down from the attic. He carried them into the study, and dumped them on a clean plastic sheet. He drew a pair of thin blue latex gloves from his pocket and tossed them to Mabel, before taking out another pair and smoothing them onto his own hands.

'What do we need these for?'

'Always safest to avoid fingerprints, or touching something that might damage you.'

'You carry a supply of these around with you?'

'I do. Best to be prepared.'

'Were you a boy scout?' She conjured up a mental picture of an adorable child in shorts.

'I was *not*. Right – one pile for any paperwork. We can repack.'

Before long, Fergus had assembled a stack of Roddy McCulloch's old bank statements, plus assorted receipts. The most recent among them was from around fourteen months before. Large sums had been paid in at regular intervals.

Fergus set them aside without showing them to Mabel, then sat back on his heels, studying a single sheet. 'Do you know what he paid for his so-called Miró?'

'A couple of thousand, he said.'

Fergus whistled under his breath, and held out a sheet of paper.

'You're out by a factor of around fifty,' he said.

'Let me see. Where did he get that sort of money?'

'A hundred grand – and look at what he paid the dealer as commission on top of that. What's 'Pearlies', by the way?' Fergus was studying another invoice.

'Some fancy dentist he went to in Dumfries. He was always incredibly vain about his teeth; even worse than you. Forever getting them whitened.'

'He must have been getting more than that done! Unless the guys here are charging ten times what I was paying in London, and that I doubt.'

He held out the invoice for her to see.

'Three *thousand*? That's unbelievable.' Mabel swallowed down hard on the bolt of sheer fury in her throat.

'There's more than one payment to the same place. He's been having some sort of cosmetic dentistry. Probably veneers, to run up bills like that.' Fergus was pensive for several minutes. 'You're absolutely certain there's nowhere else in this house where he could have concealed anything – how about the cellar?'

'The cops had a good root around there. I'm sure if there was anything to find they'd have found it and I'd be in the clink by now for drug-running.'

Fergus was pensive. 'And you're certain there was nothing in the cottage?'

'I told you before. Anything I couldn't identify, I got rid of.'

She stared out of the window at the garden, trying to banish the mental picture of that small tuft of hair, glued together with blood...

CHAPTER ELEVEN

'You realise that there isn't a decent bottle of wine to be had in Kirkcudbright?' announced Fergus.

He'd been as enthusiastic as a small boy finding a train set when he discovered that Ashers had a proper cellar, complete with oak racking and cool slate floor.

'We'll fill this gradually,' he'd announced. 'That's always been the problem in my flat, having a place to store it. We'll bring a case or two back when we go up to town. Meantime, let's see what we can find online.'

They spent a long, happy evening at the computer, and by the end of it Fergus had spent more than a thousand pounds.

'You must let me pay half when the bill comes due,' said Mabel.

'Nonsense.'

'But you've been buying all the food too. You've been far too generous.'

'And you've been providing the accommodation. We're quits.'

'I've been thinking: I'll get a locksmith to call. I've been careless. Over the years, I've lost control of who has keys.'

'I imagine there are few locksmiths here?'

She looked surprised. 'I'm sure there must be at least

one locally.'

'That's what I mean. This is a very small pond. I think it's preferable that as few people as possible stick their noses in your business. Let's go into Dumfries – there must be a larger ironmongers there?'

'There's Homebase,' she said doubtfully.'

'They'll have locks. I'll do it myself, then no one need be any the wiser.'

'You know how to change locks? Proper door ones, I mean?'

'Of course I do, woman. Your newly-usable back gate stands testimony.'

She smiled to herself. 'Is that right, Dr Learmonth?'

He looked up at her in surprise.

'I've decided to call you that when I'm annoyed with you. The equivalent of the naughty step.'

'Do I annoy you, Belle?'

'Only when you call me "woman".'

By that evening, the front and back door locks had both been replaced. As they headed up to bed, Mabel seemed much calmer. Fergus bolted the front door firmly, all the same.

Mabel woke first, but the moment she sat up, Fergus was awake too.

He leapt out of bed. 'What the fuck was that?'

'Breaking glass.'

He already had his dressing gown around him. As he

opened the bedroom door, she could hear movement downstairs.

'Don't go down,' she hissed at him.

He laid his finger to his lips, and pushed the door silently closed again.

'Grab some clothes and lock yourself and Archie in the bathroom,' he said softly.

'No. I'm coming with you.'

'Do what you're told. Now, Belle.'

She headed reluctantly for the en-suite.

'Not that one; there's no window.'

'So what?'

'I'd like you to be in a place where you had an alternative way out. Hush. And stay calm,' he added, leading her onto the landing, the pug under her arm. Fergus handed her his mobile. 'Dial 999,' he mouthed.

'But...'

'*Now.*'

'What are you going to do?'

'Wheesht! I'm going to see what's what. Will you please phone. Lock the door behind you.'

She saw him lift one of the heavy silver candlesticks from the landing table. Still reluctant, she went into the bathroom, locked the door, and phoned the police. They seemed to be able to hear her, despite the fact she only had two bars of signal. The call made, she couldn't bear the suspense. She opened the door a crack, and listened. Not a sound. Hands shaking, she crept onto the landing and looked over the banister. Nothing to be seen. Suppose Fergus was lying injured? Straightening her shoulders, she decanted Archie back into the bedroom, picked up the other candlestick and began to tiptoe downstairs, taking care to avoid the step that creaked.

She shrieked as a hand was laid on her shoulder.

'I thought I told you to stay upstairs? Have you phoned?'

'They're on their way. But it could be ages. I suppose there's no one nearby at this time of night. Did you see anyone?'

'Only a glimpse. He got out the back door as I went into the kitchen.'

'Definitely a man?'

'Quite tall. I didn't get a good look at him.'

'What got broken?'

'The small window beside the door. It was someone who's familiar with this house. He knew where the key's kept.'

'Roddy's not tall. Not compared to you.'

'This person was five-ten at least, I'd say. Where's Archie, by the way?'

'I shut him and Gorby in the bedroom.'

'Some guard dog he is!'

'I'm glad he didn't go downstairs. The burglar might have knifed him. He might have knifed *you*.'

'Well, he didn't.'

He slid his arm round her. 'No harm done. Only a broken window. I'll try to board that up, but we'll need to wait until the police have been.'

'I keep thinking about what could have happened if we hadn't wakened.'

'We did. That's what counts. We're all safe. I shouldn't think that he got away with anything. He was in the hall when I went down, but I'm pretty sure he'd newly come from the kitchen. He turned tail whenever he realised I was there.'

They sat close together on the sofa, a fur rug round them, until they heard a knock at the front door, and saw a torch being shone through the window beside it. It was a constable whom Mabel didn't recognise. She thought he looked too young to have left school.

'He must have been close,' she murmured to Fergus. 'You never get a policeman out so quickly at this time of night.'

The officer padded gingerly around the area below the broken window.

'I've asked the SOCO to come,' he said. 'I'm pretty sure there are foot marks. That could be helpful. Make sure you don't walk anywhere near there until they've been. I'll put some tape around it.'

'Can we not board up the window?' asked Fergus.

'If you must, sir. But it would be better if you didn't. There may be finger marks.'

'He was wearing gloves. Black leather ones by the look of it. I saw them quite distinctly as he was heading off.'

'Ah.'

'I think perhaps we have something equally useful.'

Fergus opened the front door and gestured at the laburnum tree. 'We put a security camera there. I don't have it wired up to a computer in the house, but there's a motion sensor. You can take the tape out.'

That was easily accomplished, using Mabel's kitchen steps.

'Any idea when your forensics people will come?'

The officer shrugged.

'I suppose a break-in while people are asleep isn't a priority for you lot. We could have been murdered in our beds. I can't even begin to think what could have happened if Miss Mountjoy had been here on her own.'

'I'll do what I can to get them to attend as soon as possible, sir.'

Fergus walked with him as far as the roadway. Mabel pulled her dressing gown tightly around her and glared at the shattered glass on the floor. She went out to see what was keeping Fergus. Damn! The nosey woman from next door was standing beside the laburnum.

Mrs Alexander caught sight of her. 'Are you all right, Miss Mountjoy?'

'Fine. Someone tried to break in. The police have been. Everything's secure now, thanks.'

'Do you want to come into mine for a cup of tea?'

'That's kind of you, but we've got it under control. I'll see you in the morning.'

'When did you put that camera up?' she asked Fergus, as soon as he arrived back at her side.

'Weeks ago. You've had too much on your mind to notice.'

'Why didn't you tell me?'

'Didn't want to worry you.'

❖

Fergus laid his arm around Mabel's shoulders, and led her back upstairs. He was amazed by how calm he felt, and how much he relished having someone to care for. He felt more married than he ever had after going through the palaver of church ceremonies. This is what it was *meant* to be about: companionship during the day, trading pleasures of the body in the dark (and occasionally in daylight). Mutual support.

The scenes of crime officer arrived next morning. They both watched anxiously as he carefully dusted the window frame, inside and out. 'Try the door key,' Fergus said. 'I couldn't swear to it, but I think he may have taken off a glove to get the key off the string where we keep it.'

There was nothing.

By lunchtime, the local joiner had repaired the window. The entire episode felt like a bad dream. The young constable from the previous night was back not long after four. He had a laptop with him.

'Do you recognise this person, by any chance?'

He ran the video from the tree-camera. A hooded figure crossed the screen. Tall, as Fergus had said, and heavily-built.

'That's certainly not Roddy,' murmured Mabel.

The officer looked up, surprised. 'You thought you might know who'd done it?'

'I've suspected that Roddy McCulloch, who used to rent my garden cottage, might have been trying to get in. He'd have known where the back door key's kept. But that's not him.'

'I believe you reported him missing earlier this year?'

Mabel seemed taken aback. Computerised records have a lot to answer for, thought Fergus.

'I did.'

'But you've seen him since that time?'

'I've caught glimpses of someone I thought was Roddy. But the person on that video definitely isn't him.'

DI Tom Ellis glowered at his computer screen, and swore. Mabel Mountjoy again! It seemed like fate, that she should cross his path twice in a matter of weeks, after all this time. He stuck his head round the door and beckoned to Rachel Field.

'Another break-in at a house in Kirkcudbright. This is the third or fourth one, according to the owner. We turned out for the last one, found nothing, but this sounds more serious. I'm going to pay a visit. You can come with me.'

By eleven that morning, they were standing outside Ashers. It raised the hairs on the back of Ellis's neck to be back at this house, more than twenty years after he'd last set foot inside it. He experienced an ache of mingled fury and agony. How dare she, how *dare* she go on living here, Lady Muck in her fancy mansion, as if nothing had happened?

'Aye, Mabs,' Tom said cheerfully as she opened the door. It gave him a start to see her again. Really, she had aged very gracefully. No wrinkles. No kids either, of course. 'It's been a while. Still living in this old place then?'

'Where else would I live? How are you?' she added with an ill grace.

Ellis ignored the greeting. He'd caught sight of the burly, bearded man standing behind Mabel with a proprietorial air.

He was aware that he failed to hide the fact he was discombobulated by this individual's presence, and he noted that the stranger was equally surprised by the familiarity with which he and Mabel greeted each other, she with downcast glance, he with a searching gaze. Rachel Field merely fixed Beardie with googly eyes.

The quartet proceeded awkwardly into the hall. Tom sniffed. The house still had that distinctive aroma he could remember from years back: lavender furniture polish; flowers; freshness.

'Best sit in the kitchen,' said Mabel. 'Fergus, could you be a gem and make some coffee? There's instant in the cupboard.'

They smirked at each other, as if this were a private joke. *Fergus*? What sort of pretentious name was that? Ellis settled at the table. 'I've been looking through the files, and I see that in February you reported your former lodger missing? Yet you seem to think the person who broke in last night was this man?'

'No, we *don't* think that,' said Fergus.

'And you are…?' Ellis asked.

'Sorry – I should have introduced you. This is my friend Fergus Learmonth,' said Mabel, holding Ellis's gaze. 'He's been a guest here for the past couple of months. Fergus, this is Tom Ellis.'

'Detective Inspector Tom Ellis. And this is my colleague, DC Rachel Field.'

'You need to tell them everything,' said Fergus. 'Right back to the things that happened before I came to stay, and since.'

So she did, feeling more foolish with every sentence.

'I reported Roddy McCulloch missing, but your people didn't seem to have any luck tracing him. Well, ever since, he's been doing these things to annoy me. But this! This is well beyond the pale. And it wasn't him on that tape. He must have put someone else up to it. This is much more serious than the earlier times when it was just Roddy trying to wind me up.'

'You have actually seen Mr McCulloch in your house since you reported him missing?'

'I haven't *seen* him – but I know it's him. Well, I knew it was him the other times.'

'When did you last see him? A positive sighting, I mean.'

'I told you when I reported he was missing. The thirty-first of January, mid-afternoon.'

'It seems surprising to me that the police didn't make more of an effort to trace him at that time. I'm assuming you have reason to believe he's safe and well?' added Fergus.

Both officers glared at him, and Ellis cleared his throat. 'We can't comment on that.'

'But you reckon you know where he is? I'd say he has a few questions to answer.'

'Don't worry, we'll be dealing with that, sir.'

'You have an address for him then?'

'We'll be in touch with him.'

'When you are, tell him I want all his possessions removed from here too,' said Mabel.

'What I can't get my head round, Mabs, is why you believe the person who forced entry to your house was connected with McCulloch?' said Ellis.

'Who else would it be? I'm sure it wasn't a random burglar.'

'But you say that on previous occasions the person had gained entry to the house without breaking any windows?'

'Roddy McCulloch used to have keys for this house. He could easily have had copies made.'

'So why the forced entry this time?'

'I changed the locks after the last incident,' said Fergus.

'But didn't you tell my constable that the intruder clearly knew where to find the back door key?'

'We keep it in the same place the old one had been kept.'

'You thought Roddy McCulloch was trying to wind you up, as you put it, Mabel. Why would he do that?'

'Because I'd put him out.'

Ellis consulted his notebook. 'For non-payment of rent?'

'That's it.'

He noticed that Fergus had clasped Mabel's hand, under the shelter of the table.

'I think we should tell Inspector Ellis about the visits from McCulloch's drinking buddy.'

She shot him an apprehensive glance.

'Who was that?' asked Ellis.

'I only know him as Ron. He's called a couple of times.

The last time, Fergus was here and told him to clear off. He hasn't been back since.'

'What did he want?'

'He said he wanted to find Roddy. He didn't believe that I have no idea where he is.'

'But you think his visits were significant?' Ellis gazed at Fergus.

'He was trying to blackmail Miss Mountjoy.'

'*Blackmail* you?'

'He said he'd make me regret it if I didn't tell him where Roddy was.'

'Did he ask for money?'

'Not yet. But I know he was going to. He threatened to spread rumours about me.'

'Rumours?'

'About my relationship with Roddy.'

Ellis registered the flush that spread from Mabel's throat to her face.

'He strongly implied that McCulloch was a drug-user,' added Fergus quickly. 'He threatened to implicate Belle.'

Ellis was taken aback. 'Who's Belle?'

'It's Fergus's nickname for me.'

'I have wondered, since his last visit,' Fergus continued, 'if that has something to do with the attempted break-ins?'

'Were you aware of this, Mabs?'

'Aware that Roddy took drugs? I knew he used to smoke cannabis the odd time, when he first arrived here. But nothing more. As far as I know, the only substances he abuses are alcohol and tobacco.'

'The Ron character implied something stronger than

cannabis,' said Fergus calmly.

'McCulloch lived in your cottage?' asked Ellis.

'For the last two years he was here, yes.'

'And before that?'

'In the house. He rented the cottage when he first arrived, but after a time he moved into this house.'

Ellis's eyebrows shot up. 'While your father was still alive, Mabel?'

'Yes, of course.'

'When McCulloch was living in this house, was he using drugs?'

'I would never allow anything like that in my home.'

Ellis smiled grimly. 'And you don't know the full name of this Ron?'

'I have no idea. He hangs out at the Port in a Storm. I can give you a good description.'

Rachel was sniggering as they got back to the car. 'You've not the faintest idea who Fergus Learmonth is, have you?'

Ellis shook his head. 'I'll drive.'

'He's famous. He's on TV.'

'I've more to do with my life than watch crap on TV.' He crashed the gears as they pulled away.

'An Inspector Calls! I never in my life heard of anything above the rank of DS turning out for a mere breaking and entering,' said Fergus. 'In fact, you're usually lucky to get CID at all. Either you're a much more important citizen

than I'd appreciated or else you know the Ellis chap pretty
well?'

'For years and years. He proposed to me when I was
twenty-three.'

'My God! He had a nerve.'

'Why? He was a good-looking man. Still is.'

'Honestly, Belle! A village cop? I'd say he was pitching
far out of his league.'

'I turned him down anyway.'

'I assume he married someone else?'

'He did.'

'He still carries a torch for you though.'

'Nonsense.'

'I have eyes, woman. I've made a mental note never to
let you go off in a car alone with him. That's better. I'm
sure that was a smile I saw.'

CHAPTER TWELVE

Mabel stuck her head round the door of the study. She was wearing her dark green gardening apron and pink plastic clogs, and had tidied her hair back into a neat ponytail.

'You look like a delectable overgrown schoolgirl,' said Fergus.

'I'm going to get a move on with tidying the garden, since summer's here. I've been neglecting it. I wondered if you'd like to keep me company?'

He leapt up with alacrity and followed her out of doors, where she armed him with secateurs and a plastic sack. Although they were in the centre of town, the sounds of urban life were muted. Just birdsong.

'I did all the serious pruning in winter, but there's still plenty of tidying to be finished.' She proffered a pair of green suede gardening gloves.

'I don't need gloves.'

'There are thorns. Put them on. It's all right, they're new ones.'

'I haven't gardened since I was a teenager,' said Fergus happily.

Mabel ran her fingers over the glossy leaves of a low shrub near the back door. 'Look at my Daphne! Plenty of new growth coming. It has the most fabulous scent when it flowers in March.' She clucked in satisfaction.

Fergus turned his attention to a rather untidy tangle of branches. 'I take it roses are your favourite?'

'Adore them. This isn't the ideal climate, probably. Not enough heat and too much rain. I need to spray them relentlessly, although I hate using chemicals.'

'What's this one?'

' 'Buff Beauty'. And the one next to it is 'Cuisse de Nymphe'. Then there's a small clump of 'Penelope'. They'll all be in flower in a week or two. Late this year because we've had too little sun.'

Fergus smiled. 'I'm very ignorant. I hope they're scented ones? Never seen the point of the ones with thorns but no scent.'

'They all smell glorious. The downside of the old-fashioned varieties is a short flowering season.'

'Have you been to the Alhambra – well, the Generalife?'

'I haven't, but I've always meant to visit.'

'Lots of roses there. They're a fundamental part of Islamic gardens. And Persian carpet designs. You said there's a spring somewhere in the garden?'

'You and your Persian carpets! It's down to the left of the cottage. It's a perfect nuisance. Makes a boggy patch that never dries out.'

'We could open it up, and put in a fountain, to go with your rose-garden. That's the description of paradise in the Qur'an. "Gardens beneath which rivers flow".'

Oh could 'we? Mabel giggled. 'I thought paradise was supposed to be an endless supply of virgins? I suppose that's only for men. I wonder what women get?'

'Rosebushes to tend. What shade is this, by the way?' Fergus added, snipping off a stray last year's flower-head from a huge hydrangea.

'Blue. Quite a dark blue. It's rather lovely.'

'Do you bury bits of old iron around it to keep the colour?'

Mabel grinned. 'I do indeed.' *That's what I could do with Roddy's key collection!*

'My mother used to do the very same! I loved helping with her plants, but once I moved away – I haven't really had a garden since.'

Fergus fell silent. A sobering realisation had dawned. All too rarely had he worked alongside his mother, in her garden or anywhere else. The hydrangeas he'd been remembering were at Inveresk and the woman he'd helped to prune roses was his grandmother. Need to keep a watch on his tongue. Although it was possibly the greatest compliment he could pay any woman, best not drop a hint to Mabel that she reminded him of his grandmother.

'I always wished we had one of the houses with ground going right down to the estuary, like Hornel's place,' she said.

'This is better. Much more private.' To illustrate his point, he seized her round the waist and cuddled her.

He hadn't wanted to fall in love. It had always ended badly for him. After Serena, he'd vowed never to leave himself open to such hurt. But this affair with Belle carried an air of inevitability. Emotions he thought he'd conquered had flared up, like a poorly-tended heath fire. Tenderness, the longing to have someone – a woman – to cherish, and to cherish him. Anita Forrest used to tease him about it. 'Terribly unfashionable to be a uxorious man in this day and age,' she'd say, prodding his ribs with a sharp, friendly finger.

'You and Mother would have got on tremendously well,' he told Mabel.

She pushed him away gently, and turned back to her shrubs. A small cloud had blotted out the sun. Was that all there was to it, that she reminded him of his mother? Although perhaps that wasn't an entirely bad thing, and all one could expect at her age.

Fergus was on a roll now. She wanted to tell him to shut up. She held her tongue.

'My mother couldn't stand Serena,' he was saying. 'Wouldn't even turn up for the wedding.'

He seemed so miserable, it sounded as if *he* was the one who shouldn't have turned up for the wedding.

'But you and Serena were happy?'

Fergus bit his lip. 'It was a mistake from the start. She didn't want sex.'

Mabel was glad she could busy herself with the dead twig-ends on 'Penelope', and keep her face averted from his. She was in love, possibly for the first time. She'd never given much thought to Roddy's feelings. But then, Roddy had never seemed vulnerable. The confident, brash, burly man beside her was as tender as a hermit crab in transit between shells, if she was reading him right. Maybe that's why it had felt as if they were old friends, almost from the start. Two people who'd been sheltered by a distant but over-protective parent, then turfed out, unprepared, into the world of grown-up love, to get hurt.

'Oh, I see.' She tried unsuccessfully to keep the asperity out of her voice. 'That must have been extremely difficult for both of you. And you didn't discover this until after you'd married her?'

'She was skilled at disguising it as charming reticence. Put on a tremendous act as an ingénue. When we were first together, I told myself she didn't hold with sex before marriage because of her religious upbringing. When I realised she didn't want it after marriage either, it was more than any sane man could take. It's not as if she was a shy virgin when we met – though I cottoned on to that too late as well. She'd clearly been with other men. *You* don't find me repulsive, do you?'

'What a strange idea. You know I don't. There is nothing remotely repulsive about you. It must have been a mental block with her. Poor Fergus.'

His eyes brimmed.

'I'm sorry,' she added. 'I didn't mean to stir up unhappy memories.'

'It's not that. Put down those secateurs, woman.' He drew her into his arms again. 'You are the sweetest girl, Belle Mountjoy. No one ever saw the situation from my point of view. It was "Poor Serena", always.'

Fergus tangled his fingers in her hair, and blinked away tears. He seemed to be wrestling with conflicting emotions. 'Everyone was always so ready to blame me. Serena herself. Her friends. The sainted aunt, Peigi MacKenzie. Ursula, the busybody who lived downstairs from us in Stockbridge. Friends who knew both of us from work, until I filled them in with a little of the detail: the screaming and tears if I tried to touch her, her determination to sleep in a separate room.'

Mabel struggled to control her jealousy. Her first instinct had been to slap Fergus and tell him to stop telling her details she couldn't bear to hear. Then she'd wanted to run away. She did neither. 'I've never loved anyone the way you clearly loved her,' she said, mustering as much sympathy in her voice as was humanly possible.

'It wasn't love. It was lust. I've not been able to admit that to myself until now.'

'Can you have lust without love?'

Of course you can, Mabel. You never loved Roddy McCulloch. Probably. Not like this, at any rate.

'Of course you can. What you probably can't have is love without at least a smidgin of lust.'

He kissed her even more passionately.

'Stop it! People might see.' She still hadn't managed to get the green-eyed monster on a short enough leash for this sort of behaviour. *Honestly, men. Never met one with an emotional intelligence quotient into double figures...*

'What people? What if they do anyway? We're only having a snog, not committing lewd and libidinous acts. Though I have every intention of taking you indoors shortly.'

'We have the roses to finish.'

'Bugger the roses. They can wait till tomorrow. The Spaniards have the right idea. A wee siesta in the afternoon.'

'I bet they don't do *that*. It's too hot.

'Look!' She held up a white feather, hoping to change the subject and lighten the mood. 'An angel's been here. Either that or a seagull. Sorry,' she added, her voice full of consternation. 'I shouldn't mock. I didn't think you were the type to believe in angels.'

Fergus hadn't realised he had so little control over his expression. He'd been beating himself up mentally for spewing out far too much information about his relationship with his ex-wife, and he didn't know how to explain to Mabel that now she'd triggered a memory of the time Serena found a black feather (from a blackbird rather than a crow, he seemed to recall) on the doorstep, and had become hysterical. She'd refused to go out, so he'd had to spend the entire day at work remembering to go along with the excuse that she was ill. That bastard Nick what's-his-name, who fancied his chances as a news anchor, had even made some crude jokes about 'an interesting condition', and kept asking Fergus if he had any good news to share.

Serena and her bloody fantasies. She'd been so unreasonably agitated about so many random things, it was hard to distinguish between genuine premonition and a childish desire to make a scene, be the centre of attention.

Belle was the diametric opposite. Solid, sensible, down-to-earth. And earthy. A copper-coloured beech leaf from last autumn was caught in her hair, and she had a tiny smudge of dried mud on her nose. He leaned in and kissed it away. He plucked the feather from her fingers and threw it into the bushes.

'I don't believe in angels,' he said, 'and I sure as hell don't believe in signs and omens. But I most certainly believe in the wisdom of the Spaniards.'

He grasped her hand, and led her indoors.

As they lay in each other's arms an hour later, Fergus sighed with contentment.

'You are the most amazing woman. You're clever and talented and beautiful, and yet you seem to find me as desirable as I find you. I feel like a king.'

Mabel didn't reply; she stroked his chest softly.

'Serena never wanted me, ever,' he added.

'Could we perhaps not talk about her when we're in bed together?' she said. 'I find it rather difficult to deal with in these circumstances.'

'Sorry. I knew I'd said too much. The last thing I want to do is hurt you.'

'Why always her anyway? You never talk about your first two wives.' She sounded more waspish than he reckoned she'd intended. He experienced a fresh twinge of guilt.

'Not a lot to say. I was always a sucker for a pretty face in those days.'

'I see.'

'Belle! That was before I was grown-up enough to twig

that you need to look for the attractive personality first.'

'Slow developer, eh?'

Hell, hell, hell. Why was he being so clumsy?

'I am. Was. Sweetheart, you're beautiful, but there's so much more to you than that! You make me complete. Real. Grounded. Serena certainly never made me feel like that. That's why I need to exorcise her.'

It seemed to Mabel that the procedure was more akin to lancing a boil than holding an exorcism. In her heart, she didn't mind. Mopping up the poison was a loving thing to do.

'I can see she hurt you badly. She must have been a cruel woman, and extremely selfish.'

'She was bonkers. Away with the fairies. Literally. She believed in them. And in ghosts and ghoulies and fucking Santa Claus. Highland, you know: from the Isle of Soma. The whole family was nuts. Except for her aunt; she was too sharp for her own good. She could have helped, but she wouldn't admit the girl needed treatment. There again, Serena was good at hiding it. I paid for psychiatric help for her, but she wasn't interested in getting better.'

Mabel knew it wasn't quite so simple. When she lived in Glasgow, she'd spent a small fortune on therapy to cure her phobia of crowds. No use whatsoever.

'The thing is,' continued Fergus, 'it was a contagious madness. She made me into a monster. I hated who I was with her.'

Mabel recognised that feeling. Increasingly, over the weeks since Roddy had gone, she had convinced herself that she had been the one to make him what he was latterly: a drink-sodden, burnt-out parasite.

'Being with you makes me a *better* person,' added Fergus. 'I swear I won't ever mention her again.'

'It's good for you to get it out of your system. But perhaps in other surroundings, if that's OK?'

He kissed her delicately on the nose. 'Stay put, gorgeous. I'll bring you a cup of tea – or a glass of wine. Which?'

'Tea,' she pronounced.

She lay grinning to herself, listening to Fergus singing as he clattered around in the kitchen. He had a most pleasing baritone. She stretched luxuriantly, thinking that if she were a cat she'd purr. She laughed aloud to think that a man she didn't know less than four months before was singing in her kitchen, wearing (to the best of her knowledge) nothing but a bathrobe and a smile. Archie arrived precipitately on the bed, and gazed into Mabel's face in alarm.

She slid from beneath the covers and began to retrieve items of her clothing from the parts of the bedroom floor where she had strewn them an hour before (oh Mabel, *Mabel*). She laid them neatly on a chair, brushed her hair and arranged herself in bed again, tastefully propped against two pillows.

She was sleepily aware of the phone ringing, then Fergus appeared beside her, holding out the kitchen handset.

'Call for you. It's a *man*.'

'Who is it?' she mouthed.

Fergus shrugged and rolled his eyes as he left the room. She was sure it was Roddy.

'Well, well. At last,' she snapped.

The person on the other end of the line seemed to have swallowed a frog. 'DI Ellis here,' he croaked.

The world stopped spinning for a moment.

'Tom? I thought you were someone else. You sound strange.'

'Bit of a throat thing. I just wanted to let you know – we're not a lot further forward with this business of someone entering your house illicitly.'

'I didn't expect it to be a priority, since nothing was taken.'

'We've spoken to all the neighbours. No one saw or heard anything out of the ordinary.'

Mabel grimaced. 'That doesn't surprise me. Have you found out anything more about Roddy McCulloch?'

'I had someone track down the friend of his you mentioned. He wasn't much help. I take it he hasn't been back to harass you – the friend, I mean?'

'He hasn't. And Roddy's sister – you've spoken to her?'

'She still doesn't seem particularly concerned.'

'Ah well.' Mabel felt suddenly embarrassed to be sitting up in bed without a stitch on, talking to Tom Ellis. She drew the sheet around her, and spent a moment wondering if Tom ever thought about the brief fling they'd had. Probably not. He'd married someone else shortly afterwards, and had a gaggle of kids. 'You'll let me know if you do hear anything?'

He promised he would, and rang off abruptly.

'Who was that?' asked Fergus, setting a tray carefully on the bedside table. She handed the phone back to him.

'Secret lover.'

'That's what I suspected.'

'It was the police, idiot.'

He put his head on one side. 'On a Sunday afternoon?'

'I suppose they work all hours.' Mabel was realising what had struck her as odd about the conversation with Tom – the usual background sounds you get from an office were missing.

'What did they want?'

'Just updating me on the fact they haven't the faintest idea who broke in. Typical.'

'No word on what's-his-name?'

She shook her head. A cloud had spread over her day. She was thinking again about that small smear of blood, and the hairs adhering to it. She flung back the bedclothes.

'I'm getting up. I'll drink my tea once I'm dressed.'

She fled into the bathroom.

Although he tried to hide it, Fergus knew Mabel had realised he found her home town dull. They had already ascertained that the only organisation Kirkcudbright could offer that was remotely likely to be congenial to him was the Rotary. Mabel had tried in vain to interest him in fishing, extolling the virtues of sea angling on the Solway coast, not to mention the salmon and sea trout rivers, but he'd laughed and asked if she wanted to get rid of him so badly.

'I don't suppose you play bridge?' he asked hopefully.

'I'm afraid not. I'm hopeless at all these things that are the root of polite society in small Scottish towns.'

'Bridge is entertaining.'

'There are dozens of people I know who play. I can introduce you to some.'

'I'd thought it might be something we could do together.'

'You need to make friends apart from me!'

'You wouldn't mind if I went out without you?' he asked.

'Not at all.'

He laughed and drew her onto his lap. 'We're like twin souls, you and I. Born outside our times, I think.'

'You're telling me I'm one of those folk that's born middle-aged?'

He bit his tongue in time to choke off the remark that Serena used to level the same accusation at him.

'We both are,' he said. 'That's why we get on so well. We understand each other completely.'

'I thought conventional wisdom says opposites attract?'

'Bullshit. Opposites never see eye to eye on anything.'

Mabel rested her cheek against his neck. 'I give in. You can teach me to play bridge.'

A nurturing woman. He'd waited half a century for his mother to love him (or even notice him), and suddenly here was this beautiful, warm woman who appeared to adore him, and to pay attention to everything he said.

That night, he dreamt he was walking in the Pentlands with his grandfather, hearing the gorse pods pop in the heat of a late August sun, sounding like footsteps following them. 'Don't be scared, laddie,' his grandfather said. 'It's the bushes spreading their seed, so that there'll be other generations of gorse and whin here.'

'Will there be other generations of Learmonths?'

Peter Fairbairn laughed sadly. 'That's up to you, Fergus. Of course there will.'

He woke full of nostalgia, and the feeling that he'd been given a commission to fulfil. Then he was drowning in regret that he hadn't met this woman twenty years before. She stirred beside him, and he voiced that thought.

'We should be glad we've met now.'

Dear Belle, so down to earth and sensible.

'What's wrong?' she added.

'I had a very vivid dream.'

'A bad dream?'

He shook his head. 'About when I was a child.'

So strange. In reality, he didn't remember his grandfather as the conveyor of deep messages, but his grand*mother*. In most of the life-situations he'd found himself in, particularly the contentious ones, the women seemed to have been vastly more influential than the men.

'Would you say Scotland's a matriarchal society?' he asked Mabel, over a breakfast of toast and boiled eggs (he resisted the impulse to cut his toast into soldiers).

She frowned at him, as if she suspected he might be coming down with a fever.

'I've never perceived it as that. Mind you, I haven't had the chance to observe many normal families. The kind with both parents, and grandparents and aunts and uncles, I mean.'

'What do we need to do to find a local cat sitter?' asked Fergus suddenly.

'I asked around. There's apparently a girl in the town. Isla something-or-other.'

'Recommended?'

'Briony says she's dependable and honest. I asked the vet about her too, and he says she's excellent with all types of animals.'

'Then call her and let's give her a try.'

'We're not going to be away anywhere.'

'We can't leave it to chance until we *are* going to be away. Call her, and we'll let Gorby meet her, and see what we think. She could come in a couple of times when we're not away overnight, as an experiment.'

Once Belle was satisfied that the animals would be well looked after in their absence, he could progress his plans to wean her away from small-town Scotland. He closed his eyes, and visualised leading her round the National Gallery of Modern Art, watching her face as she feasted on a smörgåsbord of the artworks she loved. He could picture her in his flat too, admiring the views, relishing the fact that you could buy every variety of cheese known to man within five minutes' walk…

After three trial sessions looking after the cat while Mabel showed Fergus more of the attractions of rural Galloway (he was amazed by how much more lush the Logan Gardens had become, in the space of a month), Isla was pronounced a success.

'A treasure,' pronounced Fergus. 'A reliable cat-sitter's worth more than… a reliable handyman.' He'd been going to say 'a reliable wife', but caught himself in time. He must stop generalising from his own experience.

Mabel had spent the forenoon with Briony Hall, catching up (reluctantly) on second-hand gossip about Fergus. Another of Briony's friends allegedly knew the aunt of Serena's whom he'd mentioned.

What she heard left Mabel feeling more than usually pensive. She tried not to show it, but Fergus seemed to catch her mood. He drank a little more than normal with dinner that evening. The bombshell: Fergus and Serena had been *divorced*. From what Briony had found out, Serena Learmonth – not that she'd called herself that; she'd kept her maiden name, MacKenzie – had a very successful media career in her own right, then married a prominent cancer consultant after she and Fergus split. *And* she'd had kids before the died.

Clearly, there was more poison to be cleaned out. Fergus had to be allowed – no, he had to be *encouraged* – to speak about it. She sat at his feet, on the big footstool in front of the fire. She laid her hand on his knee. She cleared her throat.

'Fergus, you must stop blaming yourself for what went wrong with your marriage. And for the fact that Serena died. She'd been someone else's wife for years by that stage, hadn't she?'

He looked at her in some confusion.

'A friend of Briony's knows her aunt,' she added.

'I should have realised. This is a very small town. Almost inevitable.'

'Why didn't you tell me?'

'Because I try not to think about it.'

'And Serena had children with the new man?'

Fergus raised tear-bleared eyes to hers.

'That's what killed her.'

'She died in childbirth?' Mabel was shocked. 'I didn't think that happened, in this day and age.'

'Her heart packed in. That pig was using her like a brood mare. I'm sorry. I shouldn't be laying all this grief on you.'

'I'm finding it difficult to understand why you couldn't accept she wasn't your wife any more. Did you hope she'd come back to you, even though she had someone else's children by then?'

'Have you never hoped someone would change?'

Of course she had. She had wasted years of miserable days and lonely nights hoping she could conjure up the old Roddy, by sheer force of will.

'It was the finality of it, I suppose,' added Fergus. 'The sense of failure.'

'Briony's friend mentioned that Serena went on holiday

and brought home an illegal immigrant, after you got divorced – a Russian, I think she said?'

Fergus made a non-committal noise.

'Why on earth would she have done that?' Mabel persisted.

'Search me. Maybe she wanted a sense of adventure. He was a reasonably talented musician, I understand. Cellist. That can't have been the attraction, because Serena's taste in music didn't extend to anything you'd hear on Radio Three.'

'And she lived with this man, this Russian?'

'She had him in the house. I don't know that she slept with him. Poor sod. I almost pitied him. Max, he was called. My grandmother's sister had a dachshund called Max. Yappy little brute.'

Mabel stroked his thigh. Fergus could be right. Bonkers

He'd been aware from almost the first week of their marriage that Serena treated strangers more kindly than she treated him. That curl of the lip: not even the filthiest tramp on the street would be shown that side of her. All reserved for Fergus.

'I heard you were apparently particularly upset at Serena's funeral,' said Mabel. 'Why did you even *go*?'

He shrugged miserably. He didn't want Belle to find out what had happened afterwards – although having a nervous breakdown when your wife died carried no stigma these days. He should drop Anita Forrest a line too. If it hadn't been for her, he could have ended up hospitalised, and who would have looked after Gorby then? Poor chap might have landed in some dreadful animal shelter. But Anita had looked after the cat as well as Fergus, feeding and grooming both of them, cleaning up after them, stroking them and allowing them to sleep in her bed at night.

They'd had a thing going in the '80s, long before he met Serena. In fact, Anita had been the rock upon which his first marriage foundered. They'd known even in those days that it wasn't a permanent solution: it had a best-before date, and little patches of rot on the side hidden from view, like supermarket peaches.

'It doesn't sound to me as if you failed her in any way,' said Mabel. 'None of it was your fault. You're a good man.'

He drew Mabel onto his lap. 'You are the most intelligent and intuitive woman I ever met.' He buried his face against her neck, savouring her solidity, the wholesome, warm, spicy fragrance of her. 'What scent are you wearing?'

'*Vol de Nuit.*'

'Guerlain.'

'How do you know that? Most men know nothing about perfume.'

He smiled to himself. He wasn't about to tell her it was the one his mother had used. The scent that had been familiar to him all his young life. The scent that had signalled unattainability. How amazing it would have been to have a mother like Belle.

'Someone I know used to wear it. Not Serena,' he added, seeing the cloud that passed across Mabel's face. 'It was my mother, in fact.'

It struck him that he had no recollection at all of which scent Serena had preferred. She was as much of a butterfly in that as in her affections. No loyalty, to perfume or to people. Or to cats. She had only tried to hang onto Gorby out of spite at the division of spoils following the divorce.

'You have the most exquisite taste in everything, from perfume to tea,' he murmured, his mouth still against Mabel's neck. 'You are, in fact, perfect.'

'We aim to please,' she said. 'You don't think I'm too plump?'

He was scandalised. 'You're comely, not plump! There's a world of difference.'

He wanted to explain further why he so valued her curvaceous, sturdy, healthy body, but he knew he had to choose both his words and his moment. He needed to conclusively banish the mental image of Serena's fragile, chicken-bone thin-ness.

They sat that evening, as on others when the weather was clement enough, on the companion seat Mabel had once occupied alone, each with a glass of wine and a book. Fergus reached across and squeezed her hand. 'Paradise indeed,' he said.

She closed her eyes and savoured the warmth of the westering sun on her face, the distant sound of the seagulls at the harbour, the muffled rumble of cars on the High Street. She didn't want the moment to end.

'If I died this very minute, if I had a massive heart attack like the ones you read about, or one of those brain haemorrhages that takes you unaware, I'd know I'd had at least a few weeks of being perfectly happy,' she told herself.

She thought about her friends. She was sure Briony had never been contented like this. Had her own parents, before she arrived in their lives? Had they sat close, here in this same garden, their hands touching from time to time, and breathed in happiness? She knew how lucky she was to have even one day of this. Bliss.

'Let's go out for a drink,' announced Fergus.

Mabel recoiled. 'Where?'

'There must be a couple of respectable pubs?'

'No way I'm going to sit in Briony Hall's bar. She'd ask far too many questions. There's the King's Arms,' said Mabel dubiously.

'A McCulloch watering-hole?'

'Occasionally. He always maintained it was too respectable.'

'Come on.' Fergus stood up and pulled Mabel to her feet. 'It's good to get out occasionally to see how the world's turning. If we're both to have a drink, it has to be somewhere local.'

Rather reluctantly, Mabel fetched a jacket. 'It's just round the corner. We can both get completely tiddly and still get home safely, I suppose.'

Although the bar was perfectly clean and well-decorated, as he peered in at its window Fergus seemed to have a moment of doubt. 'Maybe this is a mistake. I'd be surprised if the house wine's fit for anything more than stewing beef with.'

Mabel wrinkled her nose. 'Know what? I'd rather have a pint. Well – a half-pint. Need to maintain decorum. I don't want you getting the wrong idea of who I am. They usually have some decent beers here.'

'I'll find out what they have on tap.'

Settled in the lounge, they could overhear the conversation in the public bar: an informed and erudite discussion of whether Telford or Brunel was the better engineer. Opinion seemed to lean in favour of Telford, on the grounds that he came from a humble background, rather than getting a leg up.

'Only in parochial Scotland,' said Fergus, laughing. 'It can't be so different from the level of bar-room chat Burns was used to, once he was immured in deepest Dumfriesshire.' Then he sighed. 'Edinburgh's where the Bard flowered. This area's what killed him.'

Mabel sighed in her turn. She knew the way his mind was working. 'Are you terribly homesick?'

'I've been thinking – why don't we go up to town for a while? You'll love the flat, and there's so much to *do* there.'

'Maybe.' She tried not to sound too evasive. 'I already told you, this is the worst time of year for leaving the gallery. Anyway, I don't really feel I can go anywhere until Roddy's turned up. My round.' She stood up briskly and headed for the bar. By the time she carried the glasses back to their table, she felt Fergus looked more cheerful; almost contented again.

It was closing time before they headed home, arm-in-arm. Passers-by in the street greeted Mabel affectionately and respectfully. 'See?' she said. 'This place isn't so bad, if you give it a chance.'

Under the streetlight at the end of Castle Street, Fergus swung her round to face him and kissed her. 'You're an amazing collection of women, Belle Mountjoy. All equally seductive.'

Mabel was due to have lunch with Briony the next day. She was agog to know if any rumours had reached her friend yet. After all, two middle-aged people necking in the street like teenagers – that'd be round the town like wildfire if anyone had spotted them, since one of the people was Arthur Mountjoy's daughter.

But Briony said never a word about public canoodling. She launched straight into a story about having seen Alison McCulloch apparently having trouble with the cash machine at the Bank of Scotland, then heading into the Port in a Storm.

'What'd she have been doing through here, and in a place like that? I'm sure the Port must have been one of the last pubs in Scotland to let women through the door at all.'

'Not a clue,' said Mabel. 'Maybe she was on her way back from somewhere and fancied a drink. What do you mean, "having trouble" with the cash machine?'

'Och, you know, card in, press some buttons, card out, put it in and try again, looking agitated. I'd say it had told her she was out of funds.'

'And then she went into the pub?'

'She did.'

'Poor Ali! I don't suppose her business makes much money at this time of year.' Mabel basked momentarily in a warm glow of satisfaction. Waterside's early flurry of business was holding up.

Briony puffed out her cheeks. 'Huh. Poor Ali be damned.'

'Maybe she was just looking for Roddy's pals, to check if anyone's seen him?'

'You've heard nothing further from the police?'

'They don't tell me anything. I assume they keep in touch with Ali.' For some reason, she didn't want to mention the phone call from Tom Ellis.

'Cheer up. No news is good news.'

'I'm hoping it means he's found himself a job, maybe, and settled somewhere else.'

'A *job*? I can't imagine him wanting one of those.'

Mabel could only agree. She relayed the conversation to Fergus when she got home. He rolled his eyes.

Just before six that evening, Fergus stuck his head round the kitchen door.

'I'm going out for a while.'

'Don't you want any dinner?'

'I've made myself a sandwich. I'll grab something more substantial later, perhaps.'

'Where are you off to? You look as if you're going to rob a bank.'

Fergus started a little. 'Why do you say that?'

'You're dressed the way you'd be if you didn't want anyone to remember what you were wearing.'

Now he grinned. 'That's very perspicacious of you. Exactly the effect I was aiming for.'

'So where are you going?'

'Port Alexander. I want to see what our mutual friend does after she closes the shop.'

'Ali? I imagine she goes upstairs to the flat and sits in front of the TV all evening.'

'Then I shall spend a very boring few hours.'

He was back by eleven.

'Well?'

'You were right, more or less. Except that you didn't mention she cleans her car obsessively.'

'I can't visualise Ali cleaning anything obsessively.'

'She spent at least half an hour working on the carpets and upholstery, with what looked like one of these shampooing machines. Not the easiest thing to do without making yourself conspicuous. I don't suppose she has a garage?'

Mabel shook her head vaguely. 'She doesn't even have a lane behind the house to park in.'

'You'd think she'd just take it to a valet service.'

'Maybe she can't afford to.'

Fergus shrugged. 'After she'd finished that palaver, she popped across to the supermarket, then, as you predicted, seemed to spend the rest of the evening indoors. You can usually tell quite a lot from tailing someone. I'm positive she didn't know I was there, but I felt she was putting on an act, even to crossing the road to the Co-op in her slippers. That's a woman with something to hide. By the way – didn't you say McCulloch's not very tall?'

Mabel nodded.

'Not much of a family resemblance then. The sister's built like a prize fighter,' he added.

'That's what she has to hide. Until about ten years ago, she was Alistair.'

Fergus guffawed. 'That explains her reading choices then.'

Mabel raised her eyebrows.

'I popped into the local newsagents when I arrived, to pay the bill for my elderly auntie.'

'You don't have an elderly auntie.'

'They had a good hunt though. Gave me a chance to see what Alison McCulloch reads, because my aunt's name is McGinty.'

'So what *does* she read?'

'Ali? *Practical Boat Owner. Motor Boat and Yachting. Autocar.* No sign of *Good Housekeeping.*'

'What a sexist remark! How did you talk your way out of the aged aunt thing?'

'Just said she'd lost her marbles completely. Possibly she hasn't had anything on order there for several years.'

'What next then – on Ali, I mean? Will you try following her when she goes out.'

'Possibly. You can really only do that once, in an area like this. That's why I've been careful never to take on work that needs surveillance. It's practically impossible to do on your own. Any wide boy or girl with half decent eyesight is going to clock you PDQ, and once you're spotted, the game's up. You need a team of people and a fleet of cars, if you don't want to show out in the first half hour.'

'I'm sure someone could be following me, and I'd never notice. You see it all the time on TV shows though. Some people know at once.'

'If they're ordinary punters, it takes them a while to cotton on. The experienced criminals have tricks like doing several circuits of a roundabout, or slowing right down so you have to pass them. I suspect that Ms McCulloch would notice. Her behaviour was verging on furtive.'

He spent the next hour huddled over his computer. Mabel stayed in the sitting room, listening to a political discussion on TV with her eyes closed.

'Did you know that Alistair McCulloch has a criminal record?' Fergus's voice was triumphant.

'No, I didn't.'

'Convicted of GBH in 1978. Sentenced to ten months in Barlinnie, according to the *Herald*.'

Mabel sat up, hugging a cushion.

'Why on earth did you look that up?'

'Because I'm a nosey bastard.'

CHAPTER THIRTEEN

'What's wrong?' asked Mabel. Fergus had been driving her mad since dinner: pacing, the way Father used to do. It had completely eroded the euphoria she'd felt earlier in the day, making up the accounts for the gallery.

'I absolutely need to go home to Edinburgh for a bit,' said Fergus. 'Come with me, darling. You'll love the house there – it's your sort of place.'

'It's not a house. It's a flat. I got over any inclination I ever had to live in one of those in my early twenties. You learn more than you'd ever want to know about strangers, whether you want to or not. You can hear what other people do *in bed*. You told me you had no attachment to the place anyway. Even from a practical point of view, it's absolutely impossible. This is the busiest season for the gallery, as well as the garden.'

'Get someone in to mind both for you.'

'Don't be ridiculous. For the past year or two Waterside's barely been profitable, never mind paying someone to manage it. Business is good just now, but I can't assume it'll stay that way.'

'Then sell it.'

'Why should I? It's my livelihood.'

Fergus sighed. 'You're being contrary. How can it be

your livelihood if it doesn't make enough money?'

'Well, it is. That's that.'

'You could be an art dealer in Edinburgh, and use all your skills and knowledge to some avail.'

'My gallery's in Kirkcudbright. I thought you'd decided you enjoyed living here anyway?'

He sat down at last, and drew her onto his lap. 'I enjoy living with you, Belle. I'm deep in love. I know you don't want to leave here. But I desperately want you to come and live with me in town. I know you'll miss your garden, but I'm sure if you give Edinburgh a chance…'

'I already gave Glasgow a chance. I hate large cities. And I wouldn't dream of leaving my garden,' she said firmly. Besides which, she didn't feel she could leave the area while there was still a chance that Roddy would turn up again like a stray, homeless and miserable, looking for his clothes.

'I'll be honest. Charming though it is, I'll go stir crazy if I have to live in a small place like Kirkcudbright all year round. I'm too used to being in a city.'

'Oh.' Well, that was her told. Living with her was driving him crazy.

'It's too bland and safe here,' he continued. 'I need to feel there are dangerous places. Edgelands. That's why I love Edinburgh – it still has a dark underbelly. The gentrification of the Old Town has been dire, but it hasn't completely killed it. Kirkcudbright has no dark side.'

'You'd better pack ready to head off then. I have work to do, before the sun sets.' Mabel grabbed a pair of secateurs, swished them a few times to test the blades, and marched towards the garden.

The Bic pen that Tom Ellis was twirling between his fingers snapped into two pieces. He cursed, and threw the fragments into the bin. Really, he must stop thinking about Mabel Mountjoy. After all, he was fairly sure she rarely turned her mind to *him*.

Time to go home, because he'd put in so much overtime during the previous fortnight. He rose heavily and studied himself in the small mirror on the wall of his office (the one that made his colleagues smirk and tease him about vanity). He ran a hand through his hair. So much grey! He'd often observed that men seemed to age faster than women in this line of work.

He waved half-heartedly to the ones still hunched over their desks in the outer office. 'I'm off home.' But he didn't go straight home. Instead he turned west onto the A75 and drove back towards the town of his birth.

Tom strolled into the Roseberry Arms, as casually as someone who's known to be a cop can. Briony was busy in the restaurant, arranging flowers.

She greeted him with some surprise. He saw trepidation in her eyes too.

He was too stressed to waste time on small talk. 'This Roddy McCulloch guy – you obviously knew him. Should I be worried, even though his sister isn't?'

Briony guffawed, and her face relaxed. 'The only thing

I'd be worried about is if he comes back to batten onto
Mabel again for another decade or two. Good riddance, I'd
say. I'd offer you a drink, but I suppose you're on duty?'

'I'm not, as a matter of fact. Social call. I'll take a coke
– no, make it a diet coke.'

He sipped his drink morosely. 'Is Mabs OK?' he asked
at last, his voice husky.

'Of course she is.' Briony directed a mysterious smile
not at Tom but at the rose she was holding in her hand.
'This is a new beginning for her.'

'So you'd say this artist has merely toddled off?'

'For reasons known only to himself. Or perhaps he'd
had a falling-out with someone. From what I've heard, he
wasn't above borrowing cash right, left and centre. Never
from me, by the way. I have more sense.' Briony trimmed
the stem of a carnation almost viciously. 'He'll be lying low
until they've calmed down a bit.'

'And the Learmonth guy?'

'He's good for her. She's more cheerful than she's been
in years.'

Tom drained his glass and left abruptly.

Meantime Fergus was sitting glumly in the kitchen of
Ashers, his head in his hands. The conversation with Belle
hadn't gone at all as planned. Yet he meant what he'd said.
He needed his fix of town. Even the journey from his home
to Stockbridge hadn't completely lost its ability to create a
small *frisson*, although the area was fast being lost to the

moneyed set – as like as not non-Scots – who had moved in, tarted up the houses with AGAs and Ikea kitchens, and imported the rest of the paraphernalia of their preferred lifestyle: cheesemongers and pâtissiers instead of pawnbrokers and small, mean shops. Something had been lost. The interplay of dark and light that added texture to his beloved home city, the places where the veil was stretched thin.

He could admit it to himself now: life without any element of risk whatsoever was too insipid for his palate. Perhaps it was genetic; his father must have relished danger. All *he* had done to satisfy the urge was face up to a handful of thugs masquerading as builders, and marry dangerous women. And now he'd managed to upset the one woman he wanted to share Edinburgh with. He rose and followed Belle to the garden. He found her removing the last millimetres of dead twigs from the hydrangeas.

Mabel heard Fergus approaching, but kept her head bent over her work.

'I thought this might be a solution,' he said, trying to draw her round to face him. 'How about if I get rid of my flat, and buy a tiny place we can use as a pied à terre? It wouldn't be in such a smart area, with the way prices are there, but we'd find someplace reasonable.'

'And live in Kirkcudbright most of the time?' Mabel couldn't keep the hope out of her voice. She turned to him, slipping the secateurs into her apron pocket and drawing off her gardening gloves.

'*Some* of the time. We both want to travel, don't we? We could take a map of the world and close our eyes and stick a pin in it. Or spin a globe and stop it suddenly, and wherever your index finger is, that's where we go next. We could up sticks whenever we pleased. If we stayed around the south of Europe, we could even take the animals.'

'That's a ridiculous idea.'

'All right, so we can buy a holiday home, and be more settled and middle-aged.'

At first, she had imagined he was working up to proposing a more formal arrangement. Disappointment made her throat tight. *Pull yourself together, Mabel you idiot. This isn't a fairy tale.* She went back to her pruning and kept her head bowed until she was confident she had control of her features.

'I'd ask you to marry me, but I've made such a hash of it every time before,' he added. 'I'm frightened to suggest it. But if I thought you'd have me... would you marry me?'

'Of course not,' she replied brightly. 'It's an outmoded institution.' That's how she'd taught herself to think of marriage: akin to a madhouse or a prison. 'I'm not thrilled by the idea of becoming any man's chattel, and being expected to give up my own name and so on.'

'I'm happy to put anywhere we buy in joint names, so if something happens to me, you still have the second house. A bit of security.'

She studied his face. 'You're serious, aren't you?'

'Of course.' He sounded hurt.

'Any spare cash I have has to go into this house.

You've seen for yourself the state of the roof, and you're always complaining about the heating.'

'The roof will be seen to in late August.'

Mabel blanched. 'What do you mean?'

'I got another couple of quotes, because I know a fair few honest tradesmen around the country.'

'You managed to get another local firm to quote?'

'They're from Cheshire. I said they could camp out in the cottage while they work.'

'You did that without asking me?'

'I knew you'd only have worried about it.'

'I'll need to make arrangements with the bank, Fergus. You should have told me.'

'Let's just say it's in exchange for these paintings.'

'We'll say nothing of the sort. I've always paid my own way.'

Fergus sighed. 'I love Ashers too, and I appreciate how much it means to you, but I need more variety. We don't have to penny-pinch. We won't have a million in the bank, but we can be very comfortable.'

'I'm very comfortable here. All year round.'

'Come to bed,' Fergus said. 'It's getting late. I don't want us to quarrel.'

'Neither do I. You've been too generous to me; I'm used to being independent.'

'Which is no reason under the sun to fall out!'

But the quarrel hung in the air like poisonous gas. It was

still there next morning, after a night when both had pretended to fall asleep at once, but neither had slept.

As soon as breakfast was over, their voices were raised once more.

'I don't know how you stand it. How can I work here?'

'You said you were managing to get on with your new book faster than ever.'

'Can't live on thin air meantime. I need to get more consultancy work.'

'You told me you're not doing it for the money.'

'I'm not. But it's interesting. And it pays reasonably well.'

'You do it all by computer anyway. Well – nearly all.'

'I've got to be closer to civilisation to get commissions in the first place. You admit yourself that this is not exactly a densely-populated area.'

'Civilisation? Dirt and junkies and beggars on the street. High crime levels. That's what you call civilisation, is it? It's what the big towns are nowadays, even Edinburgh.'

'And what's Kirkcudbright? *The House with the Green Shutters* meets *Pride and Prejudice*!'

'Make up your damn mind. Yesterday you were telling me the problem is it has no dark side.'

'God knows, Edinburgh's hardly a metropolis, and it's far from perfect, but at least there's some life in it. There's a mix of people, not just the back-biting you get here.'

'Back-biting? There's none of that here. Neighbourliness, that's what there is. Folk looking out for you. If you'd rather live among people who don't know you, and care less, hell mend you.'

'Belle, you have to admit it's claustrophobic.'

'Claustrophobic? I'll tell you what that means. It means having to fight your way through swarms of people who won't get out of your way. It means having no personal space at all.'

'Edinburgh's not like that!'

'Och, Edinburgh, Edinburgh. So far up its own backside it can't see daylight. But it's all you ever think about isn't it? Well, go back to your precious Edinburgh. I won't be coming with you. I need to go to work soon. I have to open the gallery in less than two hours.'

We all have to make choices. If Fergus's choice was a grubby, grey town, however fashionable, rather than her, then he had to make that choice alone.

'Belle, there's not more than a handful of places you can even get a decent meal in this area, never mind the theatre or exhibitions. I love you, but I can't stand being stuck here.'

'Stuck is it? I've no idea what's sticking you. Not me, I can assure you.'

Fergus was still on a roll. 'I'm sure small-town Scotland has its place. But I can't live here. Not for three hundred and sixty-five days a year. It'd be like being buried alive.'

'A *year*? You've haven't even been here five months. I've lived here all of my adult life. It's never done me any harm. You've such an air of entitlement, just because you think you're some sort of media star. If my home town drives you crazy, that says more about your mental stability than it does about the town. Boredom is a sign of insufficiency of character. Bugger off back to your urban hell-hole then. Not a chance I'm leaving Kirkcudbright, no matter what you think of it.'

Rejection of her home felt like rejection of everything she stood for, because at heart Mabel was exceptionally fond of small towns. Indeed, she had often fantasised about living in one of the tiny, enclosed hilltop towns of Lazio if she ever had to leave Ashers. Someplace along the lines of Fiuggi Cittá, which she had visited when she accompanied Roddy on one of his frequent trips to Rome, the reason for which she'd never been able to fathom (they seemed to have little to do with art or culture). He'd always been too mean to shell out for a hotel in the Eternal City itself, so they'd fetched up in the Grand Palace Hotel in Fiuggi Fonte, where the general ambience was redolent of an Agatha Christie novel.

She'd been happy to be left behind on the many days when her companion disappeared into Rome on business. She'd travelled up the steep hill on the shoogly, hard-seated local bus, and wandered the labyrinth of tranquil medieval lanes and closes, where many of the more promising flights of steps ended in a blank wall, or someone's garden. She felt she could have been blissfully happy there, in a narrow-fronted house whose roof was canted with age, like all its neighbours, an air of genteel dilapidation, and a window-box of geraniums. No Roddy. No Father. No Townswomen's Guild.

Fergus's eyes blazed. 'I'm off then. It's clear you attach very little importance to anything between us. You are the most headstrong, stubborn woman I ever met, Belle Mountjoy. You want to know the truth, as I see it? You're obsessed with that creature who lived with you. Don't imagine I've been taken in by "I only want to know he's all right". You think of the man at least as often as you think of me. Well, I've no intention of spending one more day acting as a stand-in till he turns up.'

'That's nonsense, and you know it. You're the one who's obsessed. You've never got over your wife, although she's dead, and was another man's wife long before that anyway. It's un-natural. It's unhealthy. I bet half the reason for wanting to go back to your flat is that it's crammed full of *her* stuff. That's sick.'

'Sick, is it? When I have to look at a nude painting of you that creature made? At least any pictures I have of Serena, she has her clothes on.'

'You're always so sure you're right and everyone else is wrong. No wonder she left you.'

'I left her, as a matter of fact,' he said quietly.

Mabel stuck out her tongue at his retreating back, even as she held in the tears.

Within a couple of hours, he had packed most of his possessions into the Volvo. Gorby, incarcerated in the travelling basket he loathed, had already set up a persistent howl.

By digging her nails into her palms, Mabel managed to stay dry-eyed as she watched them drive away.

Mabel closed the gallery at lunchtime, leaving a note with her mobile number on the door. She couldn't bear being indoors, surrounded by Roddy McCulloch's paintings.

Once home, she headed for the garden. No point in wasting the whole of a sunny afternoon. She stood on the back step for a long moment, contemplating the shrubs and trees that had been there for all the time she could remember. Then she walked down to the long strip of lawn. How many days she had spent there, watching her mother pruning and weeding and digging. She closed her eyes. She could feel the rough, comforting wool of the well-washed tartan rug. She pictured a doll's tea set – whatever had become of that? There had been child's gardening tools too: a miniature watering-can, a fork and trowel. A more recent memory surfaced. She flung open the door of the stone lean-to that had been an outside toilet once upon a time, and rooted among the discarded flower-pots on a shelf. There it was! She carried her little watering-can out into the sunlight. Its ivory enamel surface was almost completely eaten away by rust.

'Like my life,' she said aloud, then sat on the step and sobbed silently.

As soon as he unlocked his front door, Fergus realised he had made a colossal mistake. He stood in his hallway, sighing. The flat smelt cold and sterile. It didn't smell of fresh-baked scones and Belle's perfume. He'd been crazy to set his need for Edinburgh's charms above his need for hers. If only she'd been more willing to *understand*, to meet him half-way. He longed to be able to take back what he'd said about her obsession with the artist, even though she'd given as good as she got.

It had been a strange journey. Driving into town when he'd been away usually gave him such a buzz of mingled excitement and comfort. This time, everything seemed two-dimensional and lacking in colour.

He shook his shoulders to get the stiffness out of them, took off his jacket and rolled up his sleeves. He'd burned an important bridge. Perhaps it could be mended, but first things first. Addressing the practicalities always helped; need to get the washing machine on. Gorby had, predictably, befouled the blankets in his basket. The cat was now hiding under the spare bed, sulking.

Belle was right. It wasn't as if he had any attachment to the flat itself. He'd bought it a couple of years previously – an investment as much as anything – when he found he couldn't hack it in London any longer (he'd tried there, God knows, but after Serena died, his heart wasn't in it. He'd relinquished the struggle, and begun to extricate himself from his shiny new life). Because the prices in the English capital had skyrocketed since 1998, he'd made enough profit in selling up to be mortgage-free in Edinburgh. When his mother died, he'd toyed with the idea of keeping her house in Lauder and commuting, but in the end he wanted to be in town, and he didn't have the same sort of affection for his maternal home as he'd had for his grandparents' house.

The sale had given him a reassuringly large nest egg all the same. He wasn't wealthy the way some in Edinburgh were these days, when houses in the most desirable areas were changing hands for over two million, but unless he was very indiscriminate in his spending, he shouldn't have to worry about money. One less thing!

He knew what was wrong. He'd yearned for Edinburgh *with* Belle. So many times, he'd daydreamed about showing her round the flat, hearing her exclaim over the superlative views from the front windows, the lofty ceilings (even higher than the ones at Ashers), the fine woodwork, the locked communal gardens close by, the smart shops just around the corner. How very quickly 'us' had become more of a reality than either of them on their own. Half of 'us' didn't work. Had she felt the same way about Roddy? He'd never asked her. He'd behaved as selfishly as any other man.

He'd given in far too easily. He should have been able to persuade her to come with him; for God's sake, he, Fergus Learmonth, was normally able to persuade people less tractable than Belle to do as he asked.

But he'd caved in at once, telling himself that she didn't want to come, and that was that. He'd calmed down and left her with instructions to make sure every door and window was kept locked at all times, to phone the police and him (in that order) if she had the slightest suspicion anyone was trying to get in. She was to leave the car on the High Street, carry a heavy torch in her bag (she'd protested that it was daylight till well after ten; he had pointed out that a heavy torch is a handy weapon). She wasn't to go out after dark. In the end, she'd yelled at him to stop telling her what to do. He'd set off with a heavy heart, despite the fact that he was blazingly angry with her.

He wandered disconsolately from room to room, cursing himself for every kind of fool. There was a simple answer: he'd let out the flat. Even using an agent, he could hope to pocket a grand a month for it. It'd come in useful, because although he meant to continue to work, he was in no doubt that it'd be more difficult to pick up commissions if he was based in deepest Galloway.

Of one thing he was certain: he couldn't face another Christmas alone here. It was a festival he particularly detested. All her life, his mother had insisted that he spend it with her. As a child, he'd been aware that he wasn't the companion she craved, and he'd grappled with the knowledge that he'd much rather be sharing his grandparents' comfortable home than the chilly forced gaiety of the maternal one. *My little soldier. You're the man of the house, Fergie.* He shied away from the question he'd asked himself too many times: had his mother been there for him, or had he been expected to be there for *her*, even as a toddler? She had despised all his girlfriends, loathed all his wives.

Stop evading the truth, Fergus. You can't face another Christmas without Belle.

Not that he could have tenants in the flat as it stood. All his grandparents' dining and library furniture, and the paintings he'd collected over the years; he couldn't leave those at the mercy of any Tom, Dick or Harriet. But there were plenty of storage options nowadays. Not for the first time, he envisaged his paintings on the walls at Ashers — then gave himself a good talking-to, on the subject of counting chickens before there were even eggs. Perhaps she wouldn't have him back. He'd wounded her pride. He'd spent much of the time since they'd become lovers havering on about his ex-wife, and now he'd as good as told Belle his need for urban kicks meant more to him than being with her. Madness.

He surveyed his bedroom. Nothing there of monetary or sentimental value. He'd made a most beautiful cherry wood bed-frame for himself when he first moved into the flat in Stockbridge, but Serena had hated it on sight, and demanded that it was replaced by a pine one from Martin & Frost that had cost the thick end of a thousand. His handiwork had gone to a young couple from Leith, via a Scotsman ad, though he'd always known his wife would have preferred to see it broken up for firewood. After the divorce, he'd fantasised a good few times about tracking down the people who'd inherited his bed, and offering them whatever it would take to buy it back.

He had remarkably few possessions that he could claim as his, in the end. As each of his marriages had crashed and burned, he'd been in a rush to dispose of any joint material goods that he'd been left with. He'd never wanted reminders.

Gorby emerged from his hidey-hole, having forgiven himself and his master. He perched on the kitchen windowsill, glaring at the trees in the garden below, and swishing his tail. He looked up at Fergus with a knowing air, and headed for the front door, where he set up a full-throated yowl. He'd never previously shown the slightest interest in getting out, having been an indoor cat all his life until his sojourn at Ashers.

'You know you can't go outside here,' said Fergus sternly. 'It's a busy road.'

Gorby ignored him, and continued to mew until he was picked up and shut in the study along with his owner.

Fergus checked his phone, for the tenth time since he'd arrived. One new message: *Hope Gorby has got over the journey.* He wiped his eyes and typed a reply: *He's missing both of you. He'd wet his pants en route, but I managed to hang on till I got here* – then thought better of it and revised it to simply: *Both of us are missing both of you xxx*

Within seconds, he was rewarded by another message. *Poor cat.*

To calm his mind, he began to explore the bookcase in his study. All of his childhood Ladybird books were there. His old rocking-horse was in one of the spare bedrooms. He'd keep that; it was an antique. God alone knew how long it had been in the family. He closed his eyes and remembered sitting on its broad, reassuring back, looking out through the low window of the attic nursery towards where the Esk met the Firth of Forth. He still missed his grandparents dreadfully.

He could have the rocking horse safely stored with the furniture, meantime. The Ladybird books too. 'Fuck's sake, are you turning sentimental in your old age?' he asked himself. He'd been that way since Serena's death: it had eroded his toughness. That's why he'd decided he couldn't do his old job properly any more. She'd been utterly selfish. That was the only word for it. She hadn't wanted him, but no one else was to have him either. She'd unmanned him.

He closed his eyes and conjured up the memory of

Belle's shy, capable hands exploring his body.

Really, he should take all of the children's books to a charity shop. He sat on the floor, reading *The Musicians of Bremen*, which had always been his favourite. And here was *Tiptoes the Mischievous Kitten*: that might even have belonged to his mother when she was a child. He had to keep them. Perhaps one day they'd be worth money. They were all in pristine condition, because Fergus had been brought up to respect books as well as loving them.

Gorby, exhausted from his tantrum, settled on his master's lap and went to sleep.

How stupid to allow the squabble over where to live to reach such a pitch. Fergus knew plenty of couples who'd fight and fidget much of the time, setting the scene for when they could make it up in bed. He and Serena had never been like that. The resentment had been scaled up rather than dissipated when he managed to persuade her to crawl between his sheets. Or when he had – in desperation rather than anticipation – crept shamefully down the steep little stairway to the single bed she preferred to the king-sized one they'd chosen together the week after they married.

But Belle…

He sent another text: *What was your favourite book when you were young?*

The reply was almost immediate: *What are you havering about? You're in EDINBURGH. Wooooooo. Aren't you at the theatre or the opera or a Holyrood garden party yet?*

He punched in her number. It went straight to voicemail. 'I'm sorry. I said a lot of things I didn't mean.

Call me,' he said. 'We need to talk.'

As soon as she came in from the garden on the day Fergus had driven off, Mabel realised that the house was too still and silent without him. It was somehow hollow. Her bed would be cold at night again.

'I'm a pig-headed idiot,' she told herself. 'Why did I tell him I wouldn't even entertain the idea? I could always drive through and see him. It's not far. What shall I wear?'

She rifled through her wardrobe, piling garments on the bed.

Nothing seemed to fit any more. She abandoned the clothes, went downstairs to the kitchen and ate the entire box of cream éclairs she'd bought from Tesco the day before. What the hell? In the last couple of weeks, no matter how hard she'd been trying to watch what she ate, she hadn't lost an ounce. These things are genetic, she'd read somewhere. All down to metabolism. She tried to conjure up a picture of Rose's body; soft and curvaceous like her own, she remembered it.

Latterly, his metabolism had been one of the many things that irked her about Roddy: no matter how he abused his body, regardless of how many calories of alcohol he consumed, in spite of the number of bags of chips he shoved down his throat on his way back from the pub, he'd lost weight as he grew older. The more he drank, the more weight *she* gained, it seemed.

The last time they'd shared a bed – well, the second last

time; she couldn't bear to think of the last time, even now – she'd perched on one side of it, Roddy on the other, and the mattress had sunk so appreciably to her side that Roddy had risen ever so slightly into the air.

'See-saw Marjory Daw,' he'd chanted.

She'd been mortified.

'Roddy,' she said aloud. 'Where *are* you? Why won't you at least send me a text, even if you don't want to speak to me?'

She ate supper alone in the kitchen, not bothering to set the table properly. She doodled on the back of an old receipt, before realising that she'd drawn a stylised heart with an F and an M inside.

'Idiot,' she told herself. It'd be F and B anyway. She'd almost become accustomed to thinking of herself as Belle, to the extent that she experienced a small irritation when anyone addressed her by her given name.

She practised writing it out a couple of times. *Belle Learmonth*. Then she tore the paper into a dozen pieces and tossed it in the bin. Remembering Fergus's expertise in assembling fragments of torn paper, she retrieved her doodle and put it in the fireplace. But of course Fergus wasn't there. Her home was her own again. She could even put the nude portrait back in her bedroom, if she wanted to.

She checked her phone for the tenth time that evening. Two new messages. A text from Briony. She glanced at it. One of those ads for the latest meal deals in her hotel. She deleted it. The voice message from Fergus was short and simple.

'I'm not calling him back immediately,' she told Archie.

'I'll make him wait. He's the one who buggered off, after all.'

She forced herself to wait half an hour before dialling his number.

Fergus closed his eyes and smiled as he heard Belle's voice.

'Sorry I missed your call. I was in the garden.'

'I'm sorry about the things I said, sweetheart. You know I didn't mean that rubbish about you caring more for McCulloch. I was just angry and frustrated.'

'We both said things we regret, I daresay.'

'I've been thinking – how about if I rent out this place? Would you have me back, pro tem at least?'

He could tell from her voice that she had tears in her eyes. 'Suppose so, if you promise to stop moaning about the lack of shops and people who play bridge here. I presume you're meaning to stay in Edinburgh till you find someone?'

'It shouldn't take long to find tenants. It's a lovely house in a popular area.'

'I read somewhere it's more difficult to rent out a place that's got an animal in it – or is that selling? Are you willing to rent to someone with pets?'

'Definitely not.'

'Then you shouldn't have Gorby there.'

'It'd certainly be easier to pack anything that needs packed if he wasn't.'

'There's a lot to pack then?'

'I don't want to leave my grandparents' furniture here if it's let, or my paintings. There's quite a bit, but I can put it in storage meantime.'

'Why don't you use a letting agent?'

'I suppose I could. You'd have me back then?'

'Archie's missing the cat,' she said, making a good job of sounding insouciant.

'I'll have to be away the best part of this week. Are you all right on your own?'

She tutted. That was his Belle!

'Of course I'm all right on my own. I've always been on my own. More or less.'

'You promise to call the cops if you even suspect there's anyone lurking?'

'Much good it'd do me, but yes, I promise.'

'And you'll phone me any time, even in the middle of the night, if you're frightened? Or if you just want to talk.'

'I have no intention of phoning anyone in middle of the night.'

'Gorby keeps asking to get out. Isn't it amazing, how quickly he's got used to having a garden?'

'He's got more sense than you. You should have left him here, instead of heading off in a huff and dragging the poor animal with you.'

'Possibly.'

He grinned to himself.

'Fergus. I'm sorry I yelled at you. I should have thought more about what you'd be giving up if you left Edinburgh for good. All your friends.'

'I was equally selfish, expecting you'd want to leave all

your friends.'

'I don't know that I have many real friends. I've been thinking a lot about that, the past few hours. I have acquaintances. I wouldn't call them close friends.'

'Snap. Just let me finish turfing out all the junk I can't leave here, and getting the rest stashed somewhere.'

'You'll need to bring all the personal stuff with you. Bring photos of you as a child.'

He chortled. 'I'll see if I have any. You need to look out yours as well.'

Mabel sprinted back upstairs and surveyed the pile of clothing. Most of it could be taken to the charity shop, but she had nothing suitable to wear. What she longed for was a new dress, but it was out of the question, after the last couple of bank statements. Since Fergus had been behaving so generously over household expenses, she had been extra-strict with herself: no spending on clothes or shoes. If she was very careful for another few months, she could get her finances back on an even keel.

She began to sort through the items for a second time, being a little less ruthless, putting back a skirt here, a blouse there. It still left at least three large bags of items she'd never wear again, even for gardening.

Fergus was a whirlwind of activity for the next four days,

packing up the bulk of his most personal possessions, and requesting quotes from a removal company to uplift and store the antiques. The estate agent had agreed to look after the importation of the additional items that would be required for tenants. The man's beady little eyes had glittered when he was shown round. 'Great market for those flats at the moment, if you change your mind and decide to sell. I have a client looking for one exactly like this.' He mentioned a figure close to six figures more than Fergus had paid for it.

'I mean to let meantime,' said Fergus.

He called Mabel several times a day, and re-iterated his conviction that he should have brought her with him.

She repeated her assurances that she needed to be at home, for Archie.

Sifting through old photographs, Fergus came across the one he'd taken of Serena on their wedding day. It had won first prize in a *Brides* magazine portrait competition. He'd used the big eight by ten Wista camera, so the detail in the portrait was superb. He still had that camera – he'd take it with him (damn! He'd have to find storage for his full Canon kit too; but no, he'd take the lot with him, even if it meant an extra trip. He'd spend happy hours photographing Belle and Archie with first-rate lenses).

Serena had been standing in front of a stained glass window, and the colours had spilled down the front of her white satin dress in a very pleasing way. Her head was slightly bowed, so that the veil framed her profile, which was in shadow. He remembered the day she'd handed it back to him, at work. 'Max and I were clearing out the shed,' she'd said dreamily. 'There was so much rubbish! I had to load the car and take some to the dump, because there wasn't enough space between our bin and Ursula's.'

Rubbish. She and the Russian had been clearing rubbish.

Fergus gazed at the photo for a long time, then ripped it into a hundred pieces, and dropped them into the black bag destined for the communal wheelie bin outside. He was overwhelmed by waves of mingled relief and regret. He'd promised Belle he'd never again mention Serena in her presence. He'd never think about her again either, if he could help it. He'd wean himself off the self-indulgent memories.

Mabel had asked if he had pictures of himself when he was young. He added two ancient photo albums, plus his doctoral graduation portrait to the pile of chattels to be transported. He also added the architectural photos he'd taken with the Wista when he was writing his PhD.

Just as well he'd come on his own. The Volvo would be packed to the gunnels with all the clobber he'd brought with him, plus a couple of his favourite paintings.

He'd kept the only one of Serena's paintings that wasn't a print, while he had the keys to her flat, after she'd decamped with the Irish doctor; a small watercolour of cottages. At the time, it had been enough to break his heart. Now he saw it for what it was. Worthless kitsch. He placed it in the bin bag destined for landfill, then changed his mind and added it to the charity shop pile. He'd take the lot to the Cats Protection shop.

❖

Although she'd only met Angela Cuthbertson a handful of times, always at one of Briony's soirees, Mabel recognised her as soon as she hove into view. Since Angela was heading into the bank, and Mabel was waiting to be served, she could hardly avoid a meeting.

Angela smiled brightly. 'Mabel! You're looking well. Positively radiant. Now, I know I've been hoping to meet you to ask something, but I can't for the life of me remember what it was.' She struck her forehead with the back of her hand. 'Honestly, ageing is no fun. I remember – that man who'd set up the service to trace missing people. Briony said you'd been looking for someone to do that. Did you ever get in touch with him?'

Mabel felt the blush spreading. She tugged at the collar of her blouse. 'God, it's hot today. Fergus Learmonth? Yes, I got in touch.'

Angela grinned at her. 'That's his name! I'd forgotten. And didn't Briony mention that someone called Fergus is staying with you?'

'He was renting my cottage for a month or two. He's gone back to Edinburgh.'

She was saved from further explanation as the teller summoned her forward.

'Are you in a hurry?' asked Angela. 'Fancy a coffee? I'll only be a mo. Wait for me.'

Unable to think of a convincing excuse quickly enough, a quarter of an hour later, Mabel found herself sitting awkwardly in Blaeberries.

Angela watched her shrewdly. 'So no word of your friend who disappeared? Is that the man who used to live with you in the big house?'

Mabel swallowed a mouthful of scalding coffee. If Fergus had been there, he'd have been rolling his eyes and citing nosey neighbours as a prime example of why small-town living was claustrophobic.

'Briony mentioned it,' added Angela. 'You were together a long time, I think?'

'Not "together" in that way for years now. He was just living in my cottage. The police don't seem to be doing anything about finding him. That's why I brought in someone to help.'

'Fergus Learmonth was married to my pal's niece, you know,' purred Angela.

'The dreaded Serena!'

Briony's friend threw back her head and laughed heartily. 'Wait till I tell Gordon that! Gordon's my husband – can't remember if you've met him? Dreaded indeed. I never met the girl. Seen photos; she was certainly striking. But I always thought she must be a prize vixen. The dance she led my friend! I mean, she was her *niece*, it's not as if it was a daughter. But Peigi felt responsible for her. Very protective. We were at teacher training college together, Peig and I, and even in those days, she was obsessed with Serena's welfare. She wasted her life worrying about it. But for the grace of God, she'd have gone to her grave worrying about Serena's kids. My opinion is that the girl was unbalanced. Either that or singularly cold and manipulative. So Fergus still talks about her, obviously?'

'He maybe mentioned her a few times in passing.'

'Sounds as if he's over it then. Peigi said he made the

most awful fuss at the funeral. All for throwing himself into the grave, until a couple of people grabbed him and led him away.'

Mabel studied her coffee cup. 'Really? I wouldn't have put him down as the type for histrionics.'

Angela was watching her shrewdly. 'Peigi loathed the chap, but I've always thought he deserved the benefit of the doubt. Anyone married to Serena has my sympathy. Narrow escape, if you ask me. So, he's moved back to Edinburgh you say?'

'He has.'

'He didn't invite you to go with him?'

'I hardly know the man!'

'Men! When do we ever know them? They're like icebergs: seven-eighths concealed below the surface. We women are much more straightforward.'

Mabel smiled to herself.

Angela pushed aside her cup. 'He'll surely be back though?'

'I have no idea. He seems to have moved around a good deal.'

'You'd have him as a lodger again, if he comes back?'

Mabel finally mastered her expression, and looked up. 'I can't see why you think he'd come back.'

'But you wouldn't mind if he did?'

Bugger! She felt the blood rush to her neck and face once more, and Angela giggled like a schoolgirl.

'My goodness! Is there a love affair on the cards?'

Mabel attempted a sardonic smile, but the result was a rictus. 'I'm well on the way to fifty, and Fergus Learmonth is even older. I think we're a bit long in the tooth for romance.'

'Don't you believe it! Serena's aunt found the love of her life when she was well over sixty, and the pair of them can't keep their hands off each other – as bad as teenagers. You're never too old. Why didn't Fergus want you to go to Edinburgh with him?'

'He did as a matter of fact. But my home's here, and my business.'

Angela pulled a face.

'I suppose he might come back for a longer visit,' added Mabel. It was the first time she'd allowed herself to voice that fact aloud. 'I believe he means to rent out his flat.'

'I love to hear about people getting together. Tell me when I need to buy a hat.'

'Don't hold your breath.'

'Must fly. Gordon's collecting me five minutes ago. I hope we see each other again, Mabel. I'll ask Briony to keep me in the loop anyway. Best of luck!'

And she was off.

Mabel wanted to look especially good when he got back. Although he mentioned Serena less often now, she was still conscious of being in competition with a slender, exceptionally good-looking girl of thirty.

Perhaps she needed to climb off her high horse. She knew women who had grabbed mind-boggling bargains in charity shops in the past: Prada, a Mulberry handbag, even a Dior dress with a price tag of something like twenty pounds. You could still make such finds, presumably, if you travelled to the well-heeled areas of Edinburgh or Glasgow. She pondered whether she should drive to Lockerbie and take the train to the capital that very day? The *smell* of these shops though, even the ones in upmarket districts. She was sure she'd never be able to get it out of anything she bought. She wouldn't dare go to Edinburgh while Fergus was there anyway. Imagine if she bumped into him as she was coming out of a charity shop, clutching a carrier bag? How mortifying that would be.

Now the wardrobe was almost cleared she noticed, for the first time in years, the plastic carrying-case at the back of the right-hand end: her ancient Bernina sewing machine. She'd been a competent dressmaker in her thirties, but it must be easily ten years since the contraption had seen the light of day. In any case, she'd need material, and a decent pattern, and where would she find these locally? Then she remembered what was in the cupboard in the second spare bedroom, neatly packed in moth-proof plastic boxes: her stash.

Half an hour later, the spare room floor was covered in a rainbow of material - dress-lengths, remnants that might make a sleeveless blouse. Woollen cloth, silks, cottons. She selected a slinky deep peacock-blue jersey with a tiny pattern of acorns in deep russet. She held it against herself. There was more than enough for a dress, and the colours were perfect. The cloth draped beautifully too. She'd bought it in Glasgow at least a decade before.

Absentmindedly, she pulled out the John Lewis carrier bag that held all the dress patterns. She found a Butterick one, which she'd probably purchased at the same time as the material: three-quarter sleeves, a tulip skirt, with a flattering drape across the front from bust to hem. It was a classic style. If she made the skirt the right length, skimming the knee, it wouldn't look dated. She knew there would be a spool of thread somewhere in exactly the correct shade, because she'd always been meticulous about that type of detail in the past.

By bedtime, she had cleaned and oiled the Bernina, and cut out the pattern pieces, ready to pin and tack the next day.

On an impulse, Fergus had marched into the Royal Bank's head office and demanded access to his safe deposit box.

He removed two of the old-fashioned jewellery cases. His mother's engagement ring! Even in the dull light of the barren room beside the vault, it sparkled like a Highland waterfall in sunlight. A lovely stone. Around two carats, he'd been told when he had it valued, of superb colour and clarity.

He opened the second box and drew out his grandmother's ruby necklace. He held it up to the light, visualising the dark fire of the stones lying against the creamy skin of Belle's graceful neck. He contemplated how the colour would bring out the highlights in her hair.

Thank God his mother had outlived his last marriage,

because Serena would never have appreciated such lovely items. She'd have complained that the ring's platinum setting was out-dated, and that no one wore rubies nowadays. She'd have pestered him until he agreed to sell them, so that she could buy some modern rubbish. Damn! He'd promised himself even the thoughts of her had to end. *Quit it, you fool.*

He took the ring out of its box once more and slipped it onto the end of his pinkie. Maybe it *was* old-fashioned? But it was also elegant, to his eye. It was Belle's style, he was sure of it. He placed both jewel cases in his pockets, locked the box, and informed the bank that it was ready for stowing again. He made a mental note to notify his insurers.

Mabel stood back and admired herself in the full-length bedroom mirror. The drape on the front of the dress made her seem taller and slimmer.

'Not bad, old thing,' she told her reflection. 'Not bad at all.'

She looked out her best high heels; they were tan, but the colour didn't clash. That was the best of a man with a bit of height, like Fergus. She could wear her favourite shoes without feeling like an Amazon.

Without meaning to be there, Fergus found himself in Dunstaffnage Place, loitering outside the small artisan's house he used to share with Serena.

It was still a pleasant street, though more enclosed and car-crowded than he remembered. He'd bought the house, an upper flat, in 1989, after his second divorce settlement had meant having to part with a rather lovely semi in the Grange.

He tried to picture himself there with Serena. It was the house he'd brought her back to the evening they met, and whose threshold he'd carried her over a few months later as the third Mrs Learmonth. Within less than a year they were sleeping apart. Within another six months, he'd moved out and they'd filed the divorce papers.

He'd sold Serena her half of the house at fifty per cent of what he'd originally paid for it. He'd also helped organise the sale of it, once she'd taken up with the Irishman, and announced her new marriage plans; she made a tidy profit. If he'd not been so naively generous, he'd have an even larger nest egg to share with Belle. He sighed.

'I wonder if Ursula still lives in the downstairs flat?' he asked himself aloud.

He pushed open the garden gate, and approached his former neighbour's door. She looked surprised to see him, but not hostile. He'd been afraid she'd perceive him as the villain, as so many of Serena's friends had done.

'Fergus Learmonth, as I live and breathe!' said Ursula.

'You're looking well. Not a day older.'

She gave a deprecating laugh. 'You always were a flanneler. Come in. What brings you to this neck of the woods?'

'Packing up my possessions. I'm leaving town for a

while. I mean to let my flat meantime.'

'I thought you lived in London these days?'

'I came back to Edinburgh a couple of years ago. I was restless down south after Serena…'

He let the sentence tail off.

Ursula cooed sympathetically. 'That was a sad occurrence. Very unexpected.' She motioned him towards one of her comfortable armchairs.

'You weren't at the funeral?'

Of course she hadn't been. He'd have remembered.

'I wasn't. I lost touch with her, after she left Edinburgh. You were there?'

He nodded. He still couldn't speak about it.

'Sad,' Ursula repeated. 'But how are *you*, Fergus? You're looking well.'

He grinned. 'I'm in good form.'

'And having come back to town you're not staying?'

'I'm going to live on the west coast for a while.'

Ursula blinked rapidly. 'Not on the Isle of Soma?'

'No! In the South-West. Kirkcudbright.'

'A strange choice – what on earth will you do there? Surely there are no TV stations?'

'I've more or less bowed out from television work. I'm going to do some writing. I've a book due out soon, and I'm working on another.'

His hostess rose and produced a bottle of malt. 'Still a whisky man?'

Fergus glanced at the label. Knockando. That would do nicely. 'Indeed I am.'

She poured two generous measures into satisfyingly

hefty crystal tumblers.

'You've bought a house in Kirkcudbright?'

'I'm sharing with someone meantime.'

Ursula smiled broadly. 'A woman?'

Fergus blushed. Was he so predictable?

'A very pleasant woman. I think you'd like her. She listens to Bach rather than pop music. Her name's Belle. She owns a gallery, and what she doesn't know about modern Scottish art could be written on a very tiny postcard. Interested in architecture too, and a passionate plantswoman. I'm sure we'll be visiting Edinburgh in the near future. The three of us could meet for a meal and then a concert or the theatre?'

Ursula gave him a level look. 'That would be delightful. She sounds like a suitable companion for you, Fergus.'

'Which Serena wasn't. I know. I've accepted that, at last.'

'Everyone who knew you wondered what on earth had possessed you. Well, I understand, I think; she was exceptionally good-looking. But not at all your type, surely? So strange and fey.'

'Bonkers,' he said.

Ursula chortled. 'You could be right. Surely you must have noticed, before you married her?'

Fergus knew the deadening between the floors in these old buildings wasn't great, so Ursula would have overheard the screaming arguments, as often as not followed by the sound of shattering crockery or glass. And whatever went on once he'd gone and Serena had shipped in the Russian lad, Max. She must have realised Max was a menace in his own right too. Drinking to excess almost every night, and not even thirty years old.

'I thought she was play-acting,' he said. 'I thought she'd grow up, once she was married.'

Ursula rose again. She laid her hand gently on Fergus's shoulder as she passed him.

'I have something that belongs to you. I've been hanging onto it, just in case. I'll give it to you, and you can decide what to do with it.'

She produced a supermarket carrier bag, and handed it to him. It contained a scarlet plush-covered album, the cover inscribed *Our Wedding* in over-ornate gold lettering. A ghastly, garish object: not at all the sort of thing he'd have chosen. Not what Belle would choose either, he was certain. His mother-in-law had chosen it.

He laid it open across his knee, willing himself not to become emotional. He found that surprisingly easy to achieve. A handful of the photographs had been removed, but most were still in place. He flicked the pages, looking at the images of the bride and groom as if they were strangers. He studied his own face. Had he looked happy on his wedding day? From the distance of years, Fergus could see – at last – how sad his eyes had been. Downcast. Serena looked as if she were in a trance. It had been a disaster from start to finish.

'Where did you find this?'

'The new people upstairs found it, in the shed. They didn't want to throw it away, because they could see it might be important, so they asked me if I knew who the couple were, and of course I did. I said I'd hang onto it. But

I didn't know your address, and I didn't want to send it to Serena's husband.' She blushed. 'I mean the man she'd married. You should have it, if anyone should.'

He replaced it in the bag. 'Thanks, Ursula. Yes, I'll take it away and deal with it.'

Back at Learmonth Terrace, Fergus regretted for the first time that the flat had no open fires left. Fire was the only reliable way to break the spell, once and for all, and kill the ghosts. He went to the nearest B&Q and purchased a small barbecue and lighter fluid. He collected his key to the Dean Gardens, and let himself in. He set up the iron tray, tore every photo out of the album, ripped each into a dozen pieces, doused them in fuel and set light to them. He watched until the last had curled to a heap of flickering, fluttering celluloid ash.

He wondered about taking the barbecue home to Kirkcudbright. It might be fun? Crazy idea. It had only cost a few pounds. Perhaps he was becoming superstitious in his old age, but he didn't ever want to ask Belle to eat meat cooked on the altar on which he'd cleansed himself of the last vestiges of Serena. He'd leave it for the neighbours to use.

On his way back to the flat, he dropped the empty album into the communal bin.

CHAPTER FOURTEEN

As he approached his flat again, Fergus felt preternaturally calm. His last marriage seemed like a bad dream. It couldn't touch him any more. 'You had a lucky escape, old man,' he told himself. He turned his mind to Belle. At last he had a *purpose*.

He had intended to drive back the following morning, but he suddenly sprinted upstairs, packed the cat and his equipment, and as many other personal possessions as would fit in the car, then walked round once more unplugging every single electrical appliance (he laughed at himself: becoming as obsessive about that as the owner of Ashers). As an afterthought, he resolved to find an extra corner to cram in his KitchenAid food mixer. He phoned Belle to say he was on his way, and fled.

On the way home, he remembered that he'd meant to hit Jenner's perfumery department for some of her favourite scent. Never mind. He patted his jacket pocket and smiled.

He drove as fast as he dared all the way. He hummed a pop song from his youth. 'I drove all night to be with you.' Roy Orbison, wasn't it, the one who always wore dark glasses like a blind man? He knew he *would* have driven all night to be with Mabel Mountjoy.

He parked in the High Street, lifting only Gorby's basket and his brief case. He'd unpack later. He almost ran through the close, and up the three steep steps to Ashers' front door.

She was waiting for him impatiently.

'Am I late?' he asked.

'Not at all. I thought I heard the car.'

Fergus hugged her tight and close, while she blushed and giggled like an adolescent. Then she leaned into his body, and sighed deeply. He held her at arm's length and studied her. She was wearing a new dress – at least, he couldn't remember seeing it before. It suited her to perfection, and she'd displayed her usual excellent, under-stated taste in jewellery: plain pearl stud earrings and no necklace. He could smell the delicious aroma that signalled his favourite meal: Moroccan lamb tagine.

Mabel freed herself from the clinch and stood aside to let Fergus pass into the hallway. 'Release your domestic tiger. He sounds as if he's fed up.'

The cat shook himself, and ran into the sitting room, where the pug jumped down from the sofa to greet him. The humans watched them indulgently.

'Shall I help you unpack the car?' asked Mabel.

'It'll be safe enough meantime.'

'Are you hungry? Dinner's almost ready.'

'Starving!'

He laid his bag in the corner, and took her in his arms once more. She snuggled up as willingly as ever. He buried his face against her neck, drinking in the scent of fresh-washed hair, clean, fragrant skin. Essence of Belle.

'I'm so sorry,' he murmured. 'I said a lot of things I didn't mean. I can't do without you. How I've missed you.'

'I've missed you too.' She sounded as coy as a schoolgirl, and blushed rosy pink.

Fergus kissed her again; a long lingering satisfying kiss. 'I won't ever leave you again. Next time I go away, you're coming with me, even if we have to take the animals as well.'

Gorby reappeared from the sitting room, stretched, and began to twine around their ankles, purring. Mabel extracted herself from the embrace. 'The food will burn.'

And away she skipped to the kitchen. Fergus sprinted along the hall to put his briefcase in the study. He glanced into the dining room on his way past. The table was set with flowers and candles. He drank in the delicious aroma of spices and meat drifting from the kitchen. She'd baked a fresh loaf too: thick slices of toast for breakfast. Home. He closed his eyes and let his mind drift. He hadn't thought of any place as 'home' since he was eighteen.

'I have something for you,' he said after they'd eaten. He drew the ruby necklace out of its case and fastened it around her throat. 'Late birthday present.'

Mabel ran to a mirror to admire it. 'This is too generous! It's exquisite. It must be worth a fortune.'

'It's a family heirloom. It looks perfect on you. You don't mind that it's old-fashioned?'

'Mind? You're joking. I've never owned anything so lovely.'

'I like that dress, by the way,' said Fergus. 'New? I haven't seen it before, I think? It complements the auburn in your hair beautifully. Did you find that locally?'

'Very, very locally.'

'Not in Kirkcudbright, surely?'

'Right here, in Ashers.'

'It's one you had already?'

'I made it.'

'You're a talented woman.'

She glanced at him quickly, as if to reassure herself that he wasn't winding her up.

'I don't know what delusion I was under that I could be happy apart from you, but delusion it was. I was so lonely without you,' he said, drawing her close again. 'In any case, you told me that I was the only reason the local deli stays in business. I couldn't have that on my conscience.'

'I couldn't bear to think I'd hardly ever see you,' she said shyly.

'I'm home now. Let's take it as it comes.'

That night all four fell into the type of deep, dreamless sleep none of them had enjoyed for almost a week: the humans wrapped in each other's arms, Gorby lying at Mabel's feet, Archie snoring in his basket.

Mabel wakened first, and lay quietly, trying to analyse her emotions. This was very different from what she'd felt for Roddy in the early days. She'd not call it a *grand passion*. Those don't last anyway. Not hers with Roddy, not Fergus's with Serena, by the sound of it. Too much like trying to light wet logs with kindling that's too dry: a great roar of flame, lots of sparks, and a high risk of setting the chimney alight. But the next time you look, it's gone out. Best to use the small unripe branches that burn slowly rather than brightly, and dry out the logs as they go; a steady flame rather than fireworks. The quiet passions are best, and contented is preferable to consumed.

Who was she kidding? She was head-over-heels in love with Fergus Learmonth. He stirred beside her, and she prepared to indulge in her favourite pastime – lying on her right side, devouring his face with her eyes as if it were a particularly luscious piece of fruit: his honest grey-blue eyes, surrounded by a web of laughter-lines, and a characteristic slightly worried expression in them, a little like Archie's: anxious to please. His healthy, slightly ruddy complexion. His manly beard.

'What?' he'd ask when he caught her gaze.

'Nothing. I like looking at you.'

And he'd blush like an adolescent, and kiss her on the nose, telling her he enjoyed looking at her too. He was in love with her. He *saw* her, in a way Roddy never had. All the artist had ever seen was his own reflection in her eyes.

But why did Fergus believe that breakfast time was ideal for deep conversation? The toast wasn't even ready before he was confessing to being selfish. 'I've never asked you about your life with Roddy. You were together for a long time – longer than I've ever been with any woman,' he said. 'What went wrong?'

'I've told you before. He changed. We grew apart.'

'But twenty years, Belle. That's a long time to love someone.' And he became morose, adding that although he hoped *they*'d have two decades together, even with modern medicine you never knew…

She tried to explain that it hadn't been twenty years of bliss then ker-pow: mutual loathing. It had progressed through exasperation, pity, frustration, fury. There wasn't a line in the sand where love had ended.

He apologised. He confessed that there was a simple explanation: he was burning up with jealousy.

Mabel studied herself in the mirror beside the sink. Angela Cuthbertson had been right. She *was* looking radiant. Her hair was glossy, and her skin had a peachiness it hadn't had since she was in her twenties.

Life was perfect. So why was she so conscious of a small cloud arriving to blot out the sun?

'You're not throwing this out are you?' Fergus lifted the folded scarf from the top of one of the bags she hadn't got round to offloading. 'It's cashmere, surely?' He sounded scandalised.

Mabel took it from him and spread it out, holding the stain up for his inspection. 'It's ruined.'

'What's that – paint?'

'Oil paint.'

'Artist's oil paint?' He gave her a long, level look.

'He didn't do it deliberately,' she said defensively. 'It

was an accident.'

'Don't get rid of it because of that.'

'I asked at the cleaners. They said it'd never come out, since it's cashmere.'

'Nonsense. Have you got any carpet shampoo?'

'*Carpet* shampoo?' It was Mabel's turn to be scandalised.

'Trust me.'

For the next twenty minutes, Fergus patiently dribbled the liquid onto the scarf, before blotting it between two kitchen towels. Finally, he was satisfied. He held it up for Mabel to inspect. 'All this needs now is a good wash in cool water.'

He carefully stretched the clean lacy material flat on top of a folded sheet on the dining room floor.

'That'll be good as new when it's dry.'

'You are the most amazing man.'

'I'm Esmée Fairbairn's grandson. That accounts for a lot,' he said, grinning. 'I'm the ultimate repository of useful household hints. I can even make bramble jelly fit to win prizes at the WRI.'

Mabel experienced a pang of loss; she'd never been taught anything useful by a grandmother, or even a mother. She'd always had to depend on Mrs Dempster and her predecessors.

She wound her arms round Fergus's waist. 'I adore you, Esmée Fairbairn's grandson, as well as being in awe of your accomplishments. Now unpack your car, and show me the photos you promised to bring.'

'I'll show you my second graduation portrait, because

you'd hardly recognise me in the first one.'

The twenty-four-year old Fergus smiled wistfully out at her. Bearded, even then, and not a slender man, but exceptionally handsome.

'My, you were a heart-breaker,' she said casually.

'Would you have fancied me, if we'd met then?'

'Not half.'

'You'd still have been at school.'

'But almost sixteen. Let me see the first one now, to see why I wouldn't have recognised you.' He was right. The clean-shaven version of Fergus looked completely different. 'I prefer you with the face-fuzz, I think,' she added lightly.

'Now you,' he said. 'Where's your graduation photo?'

He gazed at it for a long time, looking sad.

'What's wrong?'

'Nothing.' He shook himself. 'Just thinking about all those wasted years. Do you still fancy me, even now I'm old and fat?'

'You're not fat.'

'Neither are you, although I know you have a complex about it. You're shapely.'

She looked at him sharply, to see if he was being sarcastic. 'More Rubens than Victoria Beckham?'

'I've told you before: women that skinny are hideous. Honestly, they may make look all right fully clothed, but there's not a man in the world wants to go to bed with a bag of bones.'

She twined her arms around his neck. 'What a nice man you are!'

'Let's hang these pictures side by side,' he suggested.

'Not in a public place!'

'In our bedroom then.'

She smiled and nodded. Then she found his photos of Gillespie Graham's most famous buildings. 'Did you take these?'

'I did.'

'You're a skilful photographer then, as well as a writer. You could have made a living at that, if you'd decided not to be a TV personality.'

'My father was a photographer – well, a photo-journalist. He was pretty well-known. Edmund Learmonth.'

She was taken aback. One moment, it felt as if they'd been together forever, the next she discovered that he was a stranger. 'So much about each other we don't know! We have a lot of catching-up to do. I assumed he'd been a soldier, when you said he'd been killed in Korea.'

'He was out there with the troops. What they call "embedded" nowadays, I suppose.'

'You can't have been very old?'

'Around a year.'

'So you don't remember him at all?'

He shook his head. 'Do you remember your mother?'

Mabel lowered her eyes. 'A little. There aren't any joined-up memories. Vignettes. I remember being in the garden with her a lot. It always seemed to be summer. I don't think we went out much, to other places. We didn't go visiting, and I didn't have other children in to play.'

'What was she like?'

'Dark hair and blue eyes. Blue-grey, like yours. I picture her as being pretty, but I suppose every small girl sees her mother as pretty. It must have been especially tough for your mother, left alone with such a young child?'

'She was used to being alone. He'd been away more than he'd been at home, all their married life. I don't know that she coped well with having to raise a child on her own. I was with my grandparents most of my childhood. It was my grandmother who spoiled me.' He looked so wistful that Mabel wanted to hug the small, lonely boy who was still inside there, somewhere. She knew what it was to be raised by a reluctant single parent.

'And taught you to make bramble jelly?' she said, hoping to make him smile.

He smiled. 'I have a couple of books of my father's photos, packed in one of the boxes. I'll fetch them after lunch.'

'Albums?'

'Published books.'

'You have pictures of him?'

'Lots.'

He spread a selection around them on the floor: a fresh-faced Edmund Learmonth with an Edinburgh University scarf wound round his neck; a formal wedding photo (Fergus's mother looked severe, even in her bridal gown); Edmund Learmonth in a rugger shirt – heavily-bearded by now; Edmund Learmonth posing with groups of soldiers. In every one, Belle saw the strong resemblance to his son: the same rugged, handsome, utterly masculine face.

'I'm lucky to have so many,' said Fergus. 'It's not always the case with photographers, you know. Often they leave hardly any images of themselves.'

'You're very like him.'

He grinned. 'I think that's why my mother was so miffed when I decided to stop shaving. Right – where are your family photos?'

'They're for another time.'

Mabel rose to her feet briskly.

By that afternoon, Mabel had reframed both of the graduation photos in tasteful and restrained gilt. Fergus watched her admiringly as she worked.

'That's a real skill,' he said.

'Nonsense. It's a simple matter of being able to cut a perfect mitre joint.'

'And knowing what will look right. Would you frame some of my old architectural shots for me?'

'Of course I will.'

He fetched a hammer and picture hooks, and arranged the two smiling graduates side by side. They made a handsome couple. He grinned to himself. Serena would never have wanted to do that. Never in a million years. She'd been ashamed of him, in some strange way, never proud of him. Had she ever once told him he was handsome? He was sure he'd have remembered. It'd have been stowed in the treasure-house where he'd secreted the Sayings of Serena. Nothing but dust and ashes. She had married him, but he could admit it to himself now: he'd never had any idea *why*. She had never cared to get to know him, and she had never loved anyone but herself.

He asked once more to see photos of Belle when she was a child. He produced snapshots of his parents and grandparents. Mabel only produced one of her father. Fergus studied it for a long time.

'I think you must take after your mother?'

'Perhaps.'

'Don't you have one of her?'

'No. I don't think so.'

Her tone said very clearly that the subject was closed, but he pressed on regardless. She was right: so much they still had to learn about each other's lives.

'What age were you when you lost her?' asked Fergus gently. Over the previous weeks, he'd been pondering the vitriol in her voice when she'd said she'd never want to be called Rose. And it *had* been vitriol, mingled with sadness.

'She went when I was almost four.'

'Ah. Had she been ill for a while beforehand?'

She looked at him with narrowed eyes. 'She'd never been ill a day in her life, as far as I know. When I say she "went", I mean it literally, not that she died.'

'Oh. I'd assumed... '

'She went off with a man.'

'My God. Is she still alive then?'

'I neither know nor care. I'd assume not. She wasn't all that much younger than my father. They'd been married a while before they got me.'

'I'm so sorry, love. You've never heard from her since?'

'Not a word. Father divorced her, end of story.'

'Would you like me to... ?

'No!' she almost spat the word.

'I thought it might give you closure.'

'I have closure, thanks. She wasn't my real mother anyway.'

'I don't understand.'

'I'm adopted.'

She turned away, but not before he saw the first fat tear roll down her cheek.

'Excuse me,' she said. 'I'll only be a moment.'

She fled from the room.

Silly to be so sensitive about it, after all this time. Her parents had always been very honest with her about the fact she wasn't theirs, right from when she first began to understand language. 'We chose you specially,' Rose would say. But Mabel had never felt that made her *special* in any way.

Just after her mother had vanished, the couple at the foot of the close had rehomed a large, cheerful mongrel dog. Then the wife turned ill, and Mabel overheard the neighbour say to her father, 'I can't manage that creature on my own. It scratches the furniture if I turn my back on it for half a second. It's going to have to have to go back to the cat and dog home.' Her father had muttered sympathy and agreement. She'd not seen the mongrel again.

Earlier the same day, Mabel had been smacked for scratching the polished surface of the dining table with a fork (these days, she kept a cloth on it; there was still a faint mark that even the French polisher hadn't been able to get out.) That afternoon, she'd overheard Father say to the young lawyer who was apprenticed in his office: 'I don't know how I'm going to manage Mabel on my own. It was Rose who was so keen to have the child, then she takes off leaving me lumbered. It'd be another matter if she'd brought the girl up to behave well. But that was too much effort for madam, so I'm left to clean up the mess.'

It had all been her fault then. That's why Mother had left: because she was a bad girl.

'Do you not think she'll try for custody?' asked the apprentice.

Mabel had almost slipped from the step where she was hiding. What did custard have to do with it? She was frightened of custard, because it grew a thick, wrinkly skin like a living creature while you watched, so who could tell what it did after you swallowed it?

'I can't see it,' Father had said. 'She and the lounge lizard aren't going to want a brat in tow to spoil their shenanigans.'

Mabel was afraid of lizards too, because everyone knew they grew into crocodiles, with teeth sharp as sabres, unsleeping eyes and bellies that ticked like bombs. A lounge lizard would be terrifying. So many places for it to hide, and leap out to grab you. Mabel made up her mind never to go to live with her mother and the lizard, even if she was invited.

She had run out of the house, taking nothing but her favourite doll, and hidden at the edge of the woodland on Barrhill. She'd been afraid to move more than a little way into the trees, because beyond that the darkness seemed to stretch forever. Who knew what monsters were lurking there, watching her? She'd closed her eyes, and clutched her doll to her chest, waiting to be devoured by a wolf. The search parties found her that night, cold, wet and shivering, but refusing resolutely to be returned to Ashers, because her father was going to hand her back to the orphanage.

She'd got scant sympathy, just a smacking. She became a model child, making no noise or fuss or mess, being seen and not heard, helping out around the house, eating her broccoli without demur. Even at that, she'd lived out the rest of her childhood in fear of being sent away. It had been almost a relief to be despatched to boarding school when she was twelve.

Father had always been impeccably polite to her once she was into her teens, and generous to a fault. But after that day, she had never been convinced that he loved her. However, the adult Mabel remained in awe of the bravery of her not-quite-four-year-old self, because then as now, the one place in the world where she'd felt truly secure was in her home, with its stout doors and high garden walls.

Fergus followed her to the dining room after a few moments. He didn't speak as he drew her into the comfort of his arms.

'I didn't mean to upset you.' He dried her eyes tenderly. 'Did you never meet your biological mother? What age were you when she gave you up?'

'A day or so old.' She pushed him away. 'She just dumped me with them.'

'But that's impossible. Even in the sixties, I'm sure a mother couldn't give her consent to adoption until the baby was several weeks old. Surely there must be a bigger gap between the date of birth and the date of adoption on your certificate?'

Mabel's face began to crumple again, then she pulled herself together. He could see what an effort of will that took, and his heart ached for her.

'Of course there's a gap, because of all the formalities they had to go through. But I know they had me from when I was just a day or two old. It wasn't done through an adoption agency. It was a private arrangement. It was all legal, naturally, with Father being a solicitor.' She looked at Fergus defiantly. 'I think I have a photo somewhere of Rose holding me. You can see I was newly born, more or less.'

'I'd like to see that photo. You'd told me you didn't have one of her?'

She shrugged, and opened a drawer in the sideboard, drawing out a photographer's cardboard folder. She handed it to him without looking at it. Fergus studied the slightly faded image. The face of the woman holding the tiny baby had been cut away, but you could see her neck and shoulders. They were so redolent of *Belle's* neck and shoulders that the thought that had taken root as he listened to her talking about being dumped at two days old blossomed. She *must* have realised the truth herself, if she'd ever actually looked at the photo? She must know in her heart. Rose was Belle's biological mother. It wasn't unknown in the less permissive sixties for an adoption to take place in these circumstances, naming the birth mother and her husband. A way of ensuring respectability.

Mabel handed him another print. A small girl sitting on a rug beside a rose bush, squinting into the sun. It was only half of a photo: the right-hand side had been neatly sliced off.

'Don't you have any photos that show her face?'

She shook her head. 'Father did that to all of them after she left. He was terribly angry.'

Fergus was so choked up he couldn't speak for a moment. 'Och, Belle!' He gave her a quick hug. 'Didn't you ever apply for a copy of your original birth certificate? You have a right to do that in Scotland, you know, as soon as you're sixteen?'

'Of course I know. I never wanted to. I am who I am. I don't want to suddenly find I'm someone else. I don't give a damn about her, any more than she did about me.'

That struck a raw nerve with him. His own mother, married young to a glamorous and exciting man, then plunged into life-long disappointment, had never exactly been close to him.

'It's OK darling. It's just that most people want to know.'

'I'm not "most people".'

The jut of Mabel's chin, as well as the tremor in it, warned him not to pursue the topic. What he couldn't understand was why old man Mountjoy hadn't just accepted his wife's child as his own from the get-go. There was clearly another story there. He knew Mabel wasn't ready to hear it yet. She'd either have become even more distressed, or laughed and said it was the same principle as people growing to resemble their pets. He'd wait until the time when he was more adroit at reading her moods. He'd need to approach it gently, as if creeping up on a wild deer. But it might be, in the end, more bearable than the thought that she'd been given away casually, like an unwanted kitten.

He knew from his own work with adopted children trying to find their birth parents that those were the records where there was never a data leak. Each one was individually sealed, and even if the child exercised her right to see the file, it was sealed up once more in her presence. There was no way he could unearth the truth on the quiet and break it gently to Mabel.

'We won't mention it again. I'm too nosey. Occupational hazard. You're taught to get people's life-story out of them in the first ten minutes.'

'You've known me a little longer than that.'

'I have.' *Moments like this, I feel I've known you forever.* He led her back to the sitting room and the sofa. 'Your father clearly loved you anyway,' he added, when they were both seated.

'He wasn't an affectionate man. Not demonstrative.'

'Yet you spent your whole life looking after him?'

'He looked after me too.'

Such a brave woman, his bonnie, bonnie Belle.

Fergus marched into the gallery at lunchtime next day.

'We didn't do anything special for your birthday. We're going on a little holiday from Saturday night until Monday, as a belated celebration.'

'Birthday treats are for people under forty.'

'Nonsense. I've picked a delightful place, and it's not too long a drive.'

'What about the animals?'

'Isla will manage,' he said. 'We need to trust her on her own some time with Gorby. We can take Archie with us. It's dog-friendly.'

'Where are we going?'

'It's a surprise. I have an ulterior motive. I want us to be on neutral territory. There are things we need to discuss.'

Mabel turned a little pale. 'That sounds ominous.'

'Not at all. We're going to have a delightful break in a top-class hotel, where someone else is responsible for all the housekeeping and cooking, and we can concentrate on each other.'

They arrived in time to appreciate the sunset. Mabel was glad Fergus had had the tact to book the room in both names. She couldn't have borne any false attempt to disguise that they were what they were: lovers, nothing more. Nothing wrong with that either. She couldn't remember having enjoyed any meal more than dinner that evening.

'It's such a relief to be at an age where food is at least as important as sex, isn't it?' she said, dabbing traces of

Cointreau and chocolate mousse from her lips.

'Speak for yourself! I have plans for you, later.'

'Other than the hot tub?'

They'd both been amused (in truth, Mabel had been slightly horrified) to find that their room had French doors opening onto decking complete with a cedar hot tub and a stonking view down Ullswater.

'So what are these things we need to discuss on neutral territory?' she asked, as they walked Archie in the lushly-planted grounds.

'I've changed my mind. We'll discuss them at home. This is your treat, not a time for serious conversations. Except – I love you. You know that, don't you? I love you *seriously* much.'

Next day, they sampled the local spa, and giggled their way through the preparation for a 'couples massage' in a sumptuously cosy room with a real log fire. Unfortunately, it also featured New Age musak, and the floor was strewn with fresh rose petals. Mabel laughed even more, thinking about the sweary words that'd be fermenting in Fergus's mind as he peeled petals from his feet.

'Have you ever done anything like this before?' she whispered.

'Never. Have you?'

'Of course not.'

'It's quite intimate, isn't it?'

'Shhh. She can hear everything we say.'

'So?'

'Just shhhh.'

When they'd entered the room, rather tentatively,

they'd been shown the adjacent bathroom for their post-massage ablutions. It had an enormous, double-ended bath. Fergus had assumed his 'horrified of Tunbridge Wells' expression, and asked Mabel if she reckoned they were supposed to soap up together with someone else watching.

'I assume not. It's hardly boarding school. I'd say they probably leave us to it, once the touchy-feely part's done.'

By the time they were lying side by side on matching massage tables, they were both sniggering helplessly; as bad as schoolchildren.

The bath was a success. Mabel was reluctant at first. She'd never dreamt of taking a bath with someone else. But they were both so relaxed and helpless with mirth by then, she flung off her robe and climbed in: the spa staff had run the water for them, and laced it with lavender oil, judging by the smell. Fergus rolled his eyes, but climbed in beside her, rather gingerly. By the time they'd been immersed for five minutes, they were chattering excitedly about whether or not they could fit a bath that size into the main bathroom at Ashers. They had already decided to pass on the idea of a hot tub on the patio outside the back door – although they'd resolved to experiment with the hotel's one the following morning.

Tom Ellis watched from his office window as two squad cars headed off into the night, sirens blaring. The local guys out west had called for urgent assistance. He still felt the numbness in the pit of his stomach that had struck as soon as he'd received the phone call from the sergeant in Castle Douglas. He hadn't been prepared for this outcome. He had a very bad feeling about it.

'How about we go to Spain this autumn?' said Fergus, suddenly nervous, because he had already bought the tickets. He and Mabel were walking Archie in the hotel grounds before turning in for the night.

'Spain?'

'Granada, to be more precise. The roses in the Generalife will still be in bloom. Lorca said autumn was the best time to visit, because everything's golden.'

It was his favourite city, besides Edinburgh. He'd often dreamed of buying a small house in the Albaicín, simply for the pleasure of being able to sit at a window or on a terrace, sipping chilled Amontillado, as the floodlights of the Alhambra came on at night, so that the palace seemed to float above its gardens in the darkness, a mirage, a vision from a better place and a more civilised era. Belle would adore the area, because it was like a small town in its own right, ensconced on a hillside, its labyrinth of narrow lanes engulfed by flowers scrambling over garden walls: roses, honeysuckle, jasmine, bougainvillea. He ached with the desire to show it off to her, so that he could grow to love it anew himself, seeing it through fresh eyes.

'You fancy Granada then?'

'We should go for your birthday.'

'August's too hot. In any case, that's hardly a fair

equivalence when all you got was a rainy balcony in Cumbria. Tell you what – we'll come back to this hotel for my birthday. If we book right away, we can possibly get the same room. We'll come here every year, for your birthday and for mine.'

Mabel giggled. 'And have a couples massage?'

'We'll go to Spain towards the end of September.'

'That'd be lovely. We'd better book soon though.'

His brow cleared. 'I'll see to that.' He'd already confirmed the booking for Room 304 in the Parador de San Francisco. Having done some research on the Internet, he had been most specific in his demand for that room. Not because he'd stayed there before. The opposite, in fact; he wanted to experience something totally new and special with Belle. 'You'll love it. Now we can plan where we'll go for the next holiday afterwards. Where would you like best?'

'Florence.'

'Thought you hated it?'

'We could go out of season, when it's not so crowded. The early spring's probably best. I've heard you can rent the house the Brownings stayed in.' Her brow creased. 'But I suppose it's very expensive.'

'Hush. Florence it is then. We'll check it out on the Internet the minute we're home. Isn't this fun? We can go on holiday whenever we want, no one to please but ourselves.'

Mabel frowned again. 'Hang on though, I have a business to run.'

'We'll get someone in to mind it while you're away.'

'Between that and the cat-sitter, I'll almost pull the local employment level back up to what it was before I started to run out of cash.'

'Let's go to Edinburgh next weekend, see what's on at the theatre,' he added

He'd done precisely nothing further about letting out his flat. He still hoped to persuade her.

'Maybe.'

'I want you to give the place a chance, Belle. Check it out, see if there's no way you could live there, even part-time.'

The hotel receptionist waved to them as they headed towards their room.

'An urgent message for you Mrs Mountjoy: can you phone home?'

Fergus grew pale as he read the proffered piece of paper.

'That's Isla's mobile. There must be a problem with Gorby. Let's phone from upstairs.'

CHAPTER FIFTEEN

'I'll speak to her,' Mabel said, taking charge. If Isla was about to announce that Gorby had died in his sleep, she wanted to be able to break it to Fergus gently. But it wasn't the cat there was a problem with.

'He's fine,' said Isla. 'The police were here looking for you. They said it's important that you get in touch as soon as possible. They asked if I had your address there, so they could send local cops, but I told them I didn't know. I wanted to speak to you first.'

'What on earth do the police want with me – is it about the break-in?'

The girl sounded dubious. 'I shouldn't think so. Of course, you won't have heard the local news today. A body's been found near the town. That nosey woman in the close said it was probably the guy who used to live with you, because he'd vanished a few months back.'

Mabel sat down heavily on the side of the bed. Fergus took the phone from her. He listened for a few moments, making non-committal sounds, then groped for a pen on the bedside table, and wrote on the pad before ending the call.

'I'm sorry, darling,' he said. 'I think perhaps we'd better head home right away.'

'Why do they want *me*?'

'I assume they have a good idea it's Roddy, and you're the one who reported him missing. I don't imagine there's anything sinister about it. They'll want to get it tied up as quickly as possible. Presumably you can help them identify him.'

Her lip trembled. 'Surely Ali should do that? I gave them a photo. What more can I tell them?'

Fergus shrugged. 'I'll phone now. Probably tomorrow morning's time enough, if we leave here at a decent hour. Never mind; we have our next holiday to look forward to.'

He looked sombre when he'd spoken to the police. 'All they'll tell me is that human remains have been found on the east side of Barrhill – where's that?'

'Just outside town.' Mabel gave an involuntary shudder. 'It's the hill that you see when you drive across the bridge.'

They switched on the TV set. The story had made it to the late news bulletin for Cumbria. Mabel was very quiet as they watched the grainy footage of masked, white-suited figures among the trees. It reminded her of films about the aftermath of a nuclear accident.

'Fergus, when they say that – "remains" rather than "a body" – they usually mean it's… decomposed, don't they?' she said.

'Could mean it's a skeleton.'

'It can't be Roddy then.' She surreptitiously nipped the inside of her left arm. 'If it was him, it wouldn't be a skeleton. He can't have been there for long. I saw him in the house. He's only been missing for a few weeks.'

'A body gets eaten, pet, specially if it hasn't been buried.'

'Eaten by what?'

'Maggots. Rats. Foxes. Dogs. Cats. Birds.'

She began to shiver uncontrollably. Running in her head was an old ballad they'd learned at primary school: 'The Twa Corbies'.

> Ye'll sit on his white hause bane,
> And I'll peck oot his bonnie blue een...

Sobs overwhelmed her.

'Whoever it is wouldn't have known anything about it by then, darling,' murmured Fergus drawing her onto his lap. 'Some cultures think it's a kinder fate than being burned or buried.'

'Don't!'

He lifted her legs onto the bed and lay down at her back, his arm tight around her waist. 'Rest now.'

'I can't.'

> Oer his white banes, whan they are bare,
> The wind sall blaw for evermair...

'Stop thinking about it. Suppose it turns out to be him right enough, at least you'll be able to stop worrying about what happened to him. You'll get some closure.'

'Who else could it be?'

'You know how many people are reported missing in Britain? It works out at near enough a thousand a day.'

'Not *at home* though.'

'You'd be surprised. I bet it runs into the hundreds

every year, even for Dumfries and Galloway. The whole of
Strathclyde's a hot-spot for it, and that's not so far away.'

She stared at him, dabbing her eyes.

'How do you know about that?'

He shrugged. 'I was involved in a documentary not so
long ago.'

'You never hear about people going missing in
Kirkcudbright – well, hardly ever. They'd have found him
long before this.'

'Depends on how hard they looked. It's rare for
unidentified bodies to turn up; incredibly rare, outside
London. Even rarer for them not to find who the person is,
eventually.'

Mabel twisted round and looked him in the eye.

'Surely they must know something – whether it's a man,
height and age and so on? You see that on crime dramas.'

'It takes them a while to figure out.'

'It couldn't *really* be nothing more than bones?'

His lady's ta'en anither mate,
So we may mak oor dinner swate…

'It's possible there might still be a bit of the more
robust tissue like tendons and ligaments,' said Fergus. 'But
we had a warm, wet spring; that makes a difference.'

'Don't tell me these things.'

'You asked.' He sighed and climbed off the bed. 'Get
undressed and settle down. I'll do the packing, so we can
make an early start.'

'I don't want to speak to the police.'

'You have to. If you don't show up, they'll send the local guys.'

'Why *me* though?'

'Possibly you were the last person to see him.'

Mabel sat up and shuddered. 'Why would he have gone to the wood?'

'I have no idea. Maybe if he'd been drinking, he didn't know where he was going.'

'He rarely went walking further than the pub. He wasn't very *strong*, Fergus. Suppose someone put him there, thinking he was dead, and he woke up in the cold and the wet and the dark, and was too badly injured to crawl to some place he might have found help? Suppose he died of hypothermia.' She was remembering the time she'd run away from home; how cold it had been in the wood once darkness fell.

Fergus sighed, and laced his hands behind his head. 'They say it isn't the cruellest death. You just fall asleep. Anyway, the weather's been warm since March.'

'No one's positive they've seen him since February. I mean, I believed it was him in the house, but I think now I must have been wrong. I'm sure you can get hypothermia from exposure even at this time of year. There must be *something* on him to show who he is? He'd taken his wallet with him when he left the house.'

'He may have been robbed. You told them in detail what he was wearing the last time you saw him?'

'The same as he always wore. Yes. I told them.'

'That's the sort of information they'll want to double-check then.'

'There'll still be clothes, even if there's nothing left of *him*?'

'Could be. Man-made materials don't rot quickly.'

Even though man does.

Fergus produced a miniature bottle of brandy from the mini-bar. 'Drink up. Then sleep. I'll walk Archie again before I join you.'

They bought the *Herald* at a filling station on the outskirts of Dumfries. It reported that the remains found in deep woodland outside Kirkcudbright were of a Caucasian male, possibly aged between forty and sixty-five, around five foot seven in height.

'It's him,' said Mabel. 'He'd never have gone up on the hill voluntarily. "Deep woodland". I'm assuming that means he wasn't found beside the road?'

'I can't see a body that was beside the road being undiscovered for so long.'

'How can they get an age range from bones?'

'Changes in the ribs, I believe. The fourth rib in particular.'

Mabel shuddered. Fergus became perturbed by her pallor. He pulled into a lay-by and subjected her to a searching look. 'Do you know more about the disappearance than you're letting on?'

She glared at him, but her lip trembled. 'You think I bumped him off and buried him on Barrhill?'

'Of course I don't. But I believe there's something

you're not telling me.'

'I hit him. He was very unsteady on his feet. I've been wondering if he fell, after I left. Maybe he died on the floor, alone. But he *couldn't* have because he wasn't there when I came home.'

Fergus unfastened his seat belt and turned to face her fully.

'What did you hit him with?'

'I slapped him, quite hard. He'd lunged at me with a paintbrush and ruined some clothes I'd newly bought. That's what made me hit him. Such a trivial thing!'

She dissolved into loud sobs.

'Why did you think he might have fallen?'

'Because there was a bit of blood, I think. Not lots, just a trace. It was as if someone had tried to clean it up. I decided he must have sobered up enough to do that, then left. But maybe he was ill or injured, and he wandered off by himself.'

Fergus swore under his breath. 'Several miles up a hill, in the dark? I don't think so. Where was this blood?'

'On the corner of the stone fender round the log stove. There wasn't a pool of it or anything. There was a small amount of hair too. It wasn't until I wiped it off I realised what it probably was.'

'You cleaned it up? What on earth for?'

'I wasn't thinking straight. I wanted all his mess out of there, blood, puke, piss… '

'Did you dispose of any other evidence?'

'Fergus, don't sound so cold! I didn't "dispose of evidence". I cleaned up a tiny smear of what I'd assumed was red paint, and I chucked out an old carpet.'

'Chucked out how – you took it to the dump?'

'I got the Council to collect it. I had to throw out the mattress from his bed too. It was disgusting. There'll be a record of exactly when they picked them up.'

'They'll have gone to landfill months ago.'

He looked steadily into her eyes. 'Belle, I'll stick by you and get you out of this no matter what.'

'Get me out of what? I haven't *done* anything.'

'Then there isn't an issue. Tell me exactly where on the fireplace you found this.'

'The left-hand corner. Why?'

He started the engine. 'I'm going to drop you with the cops and take Archie home.'

'Can't you come with me?'

'Don't be daft. They won't allow me to. I'll be back for you in no time at all.'

'I've been thinking, if it's Roddy and someone took him to Barrhill, surely they'd have CCTV of all the cars that could have made that journey?'

'There won't be any cameras on the back roads in the village. I want you to rack your brains before we reach the cop-shop. Is there anything else at all that you noticed when you cleaned up, anything odd?'

'No. I should have told them about the blood at the time, shouldn't I?'

He sighed. 'Probably. Too late now, I think. What did you clean it with?'

'White spirit and rags. Then I burned the rags. Why – will they still find some?'

'It's possible. Don't mention it to anyone else, and try to forget you ever saw it. It'll take them a while to be sure it's Roddy, even longer to get round to doing more forensic checks.'

He walked with her as far as the entrance. 'Calm down, or you'll look as if you have something to hide. This is a routine procedure, to help them make sure they get an ID and close the case.'

'How will they be sure it's him, if there's only bones?'

'Dental records, I suppose.'

His teeth; his lovely, expensive white teeth, grinning in a skeleton. Such a ghastly end, so sordid and mundane and needless. The death of an artist should be filled with drama. Comets should zip across the sky. There should be darkness at noon. Poor, poor Roddy.

Fergus drew her aside. 'If they start to ask you anything more than the bare facts, don't answer. I'm going to call a solicitor called Arthur Cross. Wait until he's here.'

'I don't need a solicitor. I haven't done anything wrong.'

'Better safe than sorry. And this is important: don't mention to him, even in private, that you cleaned up that mark.'

Mabel squared her shoulders and pushed open the glass door.

Tom Ellis glowered at the file in front of him. What bloody use was a pathologist's report like this? 'Probable cause of death: Peri-mortem blunt trauma to the left posterior temporal area, causing depressed fracture. Manner of death: undetermined.'

Though to be fair, he knew that the forensic anthropologist who'd had the task of dealing with the remains was a very different animal from a pathologist, and had much less to get his teeth into, so to speak... He hadn't been terribly keen to attend the mortuary to see a rickle of bones anyway; it was a mystery to him that you could tell anything much from that.

He picked up the phone, to try to get more sense out of them. He was in a worse mood than ever when the call ended. All they were willing to commit to was that the injury was 'around the area of the hatline', and the latest peer-reviewed statistical study confirmed the view that skull injuries 'above the hatline' and on the left side were more likely to be caused by a blow than a fall. Where the injury fell on or below the hatline, the jury was still out.

'So what you're telling me is that we haven't the faintest idea how he got his skull bashed in?'

'It's not possible to be conclusive, no. It could have been caused by a fall.'

'You're saying the injury's on the side of the head, right? Surely if you fall sideways you manage to put out an arm and save yourself? No one falls over sideways hard enough to split their skull open.'

'It depends. He may not have been conscious when he fell.'

That made sense, all the same. The local guys had said the man was a notorious boozer. Damn. He'd dealt with enough pathology reports to know that drunks are pretty fragile, even when they look strong.

'He may have lost consciousness, fallen and choked on his own vomit,' added the pathologist.

'But the other forensic guys have told me it's ninety per cent certain that he didn't die where he was found – could the skull injury have happened post mortem?'

'Absolutely impossible to say. You can only tell when a bone injury has taken place an appreciable time before death, and started to heal.'

'I know that! But surely you can give me more idea of whether his skull was fractured after he was dumped?'

'It's feasible. I understand there were no rocks or stones where the body was lying that could account for the size and shape of the fracture. Since the remains had been disturbed by animals, there is no way of telling the position at death.'

'So what you're saying is that the guy could have fallen or been pushed or been coshed and you won't commit to which?'

'The fact that the place where the remains were found is unlikely to be the place of death makes a fall less likely.'

'Fuck,' Ellis muttered under his breath. 'And the timing – are you able to give me anything above and beyond what the forensic entomologist said?'

The SOCOs had collected samples of insect cases and sent them off to the Natural History Museum.

'Why – what did he say?'

'Late winter into early spring. He was confident we're talking some time around early February. He said it's more difficult when the body's been exposed to the elements, as well as being disturbed.'

'Can't do any better than that.'

A SOCO with too much time on his hands had discovered human hair in a redstart's nest in the oak tree above where the body had been placed. Ellis was still waiting for the DNA results on the hair. He'd rung the RSPB, but all they could tell him was that these birds don't nest until May. The same officer had found three hairs on what remained of Roddy's clothing; they were deep auburn. Tom tried to sweep that fact from his mind.

He had asked Monica Torrance, his brightest DS, to lead the questioning. Rachel Field was in the interview room too. He watched from the darkened observation space behind the one-way mirror. He hadn't got over the way seeing Mabs again made him feel. She was still an exceptionally handsome woman. And here she was, arrived at middle age with no husband, just one unsuitable man after another. What a waste. What a couple they could have made! And now this stramash. It was impossible to perceive Mabel Mountjoy as a killer, even if a crime of passion was on the cards. But he'd been a detective for long enough to know it can be the people you least expect who commit the worst of crimes – if indeed Roddy McCulloch had been the victim of foul play. And Mabs had always had a temper on her like a blast furnace being tapped. Inevitable, in a redhead. But no, not this, surely?

He'd instructed Monica to focus on the last time Mabel admitted to having seen Roddy. As he watched, Tom Ellis tried to see the interviewee's feet. He'd read a book about that recently: the feet and legs are the parts of the body to watch for clues, because you don't have full conscious control of body language there. The feet never lie. Annoyingly, he couldn't see anything of Mabel below the table edge, because she'd pulled her chair close in. It crossed his mind that maybe she'd read the same book.

'What was Mr McCulloch wearing when you last saw him?' asked DS Torrance.

Mabel shrugged. 'I can't tell you any more than I told you at the time I reported him missing. A navy blue jersey and jeans, I think; that's what he'd usually wear. Both quite old, and probably in need of a wash. Oh, and trainers, green ones. I remember distinctly, because I thought they looked quite wrong for the time of year, but then I realised he probably didn't mean to go out that day, except to the pub.'

The officers exchanged glances. Monica produced a photograph. Fragments of clothing, laid out on a white surface. The denim trousers and the green trainers, faded and mouldy now, were the only items more or less intact.

'Would you say these are the clothes he was wearing when you last saw him?'

'Could be. As I say, I can't recall anything distinctive, except the shoes. The ones in the photo look the same. What happened to him? *Is* it him? How on earth did he get there?'

The DS looked at her shrewdly. 'I'd hoped you might be able to help us with that?'

'Well, I can't.' Mabel suddenly moved her hands to her lap. Ellis visualised her digging her nails into her palms as hard as she could. He winced and leaned forward.

'I don't understand why you're asking me all this,' she added. 'Is that whose body it is?'

'We're waiting for confirmation, but we have strong reasons to believe that the remains found on Barrhill belong to Roderick McCulloch.'

Mabel cleared her throat. 'Who found him – I hope it wasn't a child?'

'A man conducting a survey of badger setts. Had Mr McCulloch ever had any broken bones, that you know of?'

'Broken bones?' Tom saw how Mabel blanched. 'How do you mean?'

'It can often help with identification if we know about any fractures that had healed, or any that might have required the insertion of a metal plate, or pins.'

'As far as I know, Roddy had never broken any bones. His sister would know much more about it than I do. Can't she identify him? I don't know what more I can tell you.'

'We have reason to believe that you may have been the last person to see Roderick McCulloch alive.'

'The last person? Why?'

'If the remains are confirmed as those of Mr McCulloch, then they were deposited at around the time you reported him missing.'

'*Deposited?*'

'Can you run through for me again the afternoon when you last saw Mr McCulloch?'

'I told your colleagues all this back in February.'

'It would be useful if you told me.'

'I've been advised to ask for a solicitor to be present.'

'You're only helping us with our enquiries. You're not

under caution.'

'I would still like a solicitor.'

'Do you want the duty solicitor?'

'I'll wait for my own one. He's on his way.'

They switched off the recorder, after muttering the usual 'terminating the interview at eleven thirty a.m.'

Mabel half-expected to be put in a cell, but she was left sitting in the interview room, and even given a cup of tea; it wasn't Lapsang Souchong.

Within slightly over an hour, a tall, silver-haired man in a blindingly smart suit strode briskly in, and shook her hand.

'Miss Mountjoy? I'm Arthur Cross. Fergus has filled me in with most of the details.'

'I've no idea why they think I can help with this.'

'I've spoken to them briefly. I understand McCulloch's sister has been interviewed. I gather she may be trying to implicate you in his death.'

'Implicate *me*?'

Cross shrugged. 'If there's anything further you can tell me, tell me now.'

'There's nothing more. They say I was probably the last person to see him alive. Do they think I dumped him in the wood?'

The solicitor looked at her shrewdly.

'They think I killed him?'

He shrugged again. 'They're not saying that. Yet.'

Then the police were back in the room. Mabel knew that she was probably being watched through a one-way mirror, as well as recorded. She stared at the glass, wondering if Tom Ellis was sitting there, calmly watching her being made to jump through all their hoops. Suddenly, she didn't give a damn who had killed Roddy. She wanted out of the claustrophobic space. She could feel the sweat building on her neck and throat. She resisted the temptation to stick out her tongue at the mirror.

There was a new person taking a lead in the questioning. This one introduced himself as Detective Sergeant Cousland. Amazing. They were always bleating about lack of funding for the police, yet they could spare two DSs, plus Tom – and Tom wasn't even the senior investigating officer on this one. Cross had told her that was a DCI Mainwaring. DS Cousland consulted print-outs in a folder.

'I understand that on the fourth of February, you informed uniformed officers in Castle Douglas that you and Mr McCulloch had quarrelled, and that you had asked him to leave your premises?'

'That's what I told them. It's what happened.'

'And you stated on that date that January thirty-first was the last occasion on which you had seen or spoken to him?'

She nodded, then added a subdued 'Yes'.

'Why had you quarrelled?'

'He'd been living rent-free in my property for a long time. I provided him with free fuel, and fed him most days. I asked him to leave because I couldn't afford to keep him any longer, and because I was sick of having a drunk around the place.'

'Mr McCulloch was a heavy drinker?'

'Ask the local police. They know the score.'

'Had he been drinking on the occasion when you quarrelled?'

'When had he not! Yes, he was drunk, even though it was mid-afternoon.'

'This quarrel – talk me through it.'

'He shouted and swore at me, I shouted and swore at him. I told him to clear out of my property at once, then I left. I went to Newton Stewart for the rest of the afternoon and evening. I can give you the name of the person I was meeting there.'

'And during this quarrel, did Mr McCulloch strike you?'

'No.'

'Did you strike him?'

Arthur Cross laid a hand on Mabel's arm.

'My client prefers not to answer that.'

She looked at him in alarm. 'I don't mind answering. I slapped his face.'

Cross sighed and scribbled on his notes.

'He didn't *hit* me,' continued Mabel. 'He lunged at me; well, he staggered against me, holding a paint-brush, and it marked my clothes. That's why I slapped him.'

'You say "slapped". Was this with an open hand?'

'That's what I mean by "slapped".'

'Are you right-handed?'

'I am.'

'So you struck him with your right hand.'

She didn't answer for a moment, trying to rekindle the kinetic sensation of hitting Roddy.

'I slapped him with my right hand, yes.'

'Were you wearing any heavy jewellery on that hand – a large ring for example?'

Mabel spread her fingers on the table top. 'Do I look the type to wear a knuckle-duster?'

Cross pursed his lips and touched her arm again.

She sat back in the uncomfortable chair. 'No, I wasn't wearing any rings.'

'And what was Mr McCulloch's reaction when you slapped him?'

'I think he put his hand up to his face. He looked surprised. I left.'

Cousland leaned forward, and his tone became reassuring, almost confidential. 'How long after striking him did you leave?'

'At once. I was extremely upset and angry.'

'And you went immediately to Newton Stewart. How long after leaving Mr McCulloch would that have been?'

'Perhaps ten minutes, no longer. I fed my dog, because I wasn't taking him with me, I made a very quick phone call, then I put on my coat and left.'

'To drive to Newton Stewart?'

'Yes.'

'The access to your garage from the house is via a door at the rear of the garden?'

'Yes.'

'So you left by the back door of your house, and passed the cottage again on your way out?'

'No, because I didn't have my car in the garage at that point. I often park on the High Street; it's more convenient.'

The officers exchanged a glance.

'You drove away at what time, roughly, from the High Street?'

'I'm not sure. Around half past four.'

There was CCTV on the High Street. There had been a tremendous hoo-ha in the *Standard* when it was installed, because many of the locals claimed it was redolent of Big Brother.

'You could check the CCTV tapes,' Mabel said, 'if they're kept that long. I'd like to think you checked them at the time I reported Mr McCulloch missing, to check for any sign of him.'

She imagined she saw a faint expression of satisfaction flicker around Cross's mouth.

'Was the private surveillance camera at the front of your house operational at that time?'

'No. That was put there much more recently, after the attempted break-ins which the police appeared to think were of little significance.'

'How long did you remain in Newton Stewart?'

'Until after eleven. I had dinner out with a friend.'

Rachel Field took a note of Nancy's name and address, and of the hotel's.

'I'm sure they'll remember. I go there often, so they know me,' said Mabel. 'In fact, I probably have the credit card receipt at home.'

'That would be useful, to establish times.'

'Times of what?'

'The time when Mr McCulloch was last seen alive.'

'He was very much alive when I left him, I can assure you. Alive and as foul-mouthed as ever.'

She bit her lip. *Shouldn't speak ill of the dead, Mabel.*

'And what time did you return to Kirkcudbright?'

'Just before midnight. I dropped off my friend first. Again, you can check with the hotel when we left. They were hanging around waiting to close.'

'When you returned home, where did you park your vehicle?'

'On the High Street. There's usually a space directly in front of the close.'

'So you entered your house by the front door. Did you go out again?'

'I let the dog into the garden. I didn't go further than the back door.'

'You didn't go towards the cottage?'

She shook her head. 'Sorry, I forgot about the tape. No.'

'Were there lights on in the cottage?'

'None. I remember noticing that. I thought Roddy must have gone to bed.'

'Was he normally in bed by midnight?'

'Yes. Specially if he'd been on a drinking binge.'

'Which you said he had?'

'He was on a more or less constant drinking binge for the previous year.'

'I believe Mr McCulloch used to lodge with you in your own house? Why did he move to the cottage?'

'He was often incontinent when he was drunk. I couldn't deal with that in my home.'

They walked her through her actions the following morning.

'And there was no sign of him?'

'None. The cottage was unlocked, so I went in and discovered he'd gone. I checked to see if he seemed to have taken things like his wallet, and it wasn't where he kept it.'

'You knew where he kept his wallet?'

'I'd had to find it for him more than once before. That morning, it wasn't in the usual place in his bedside drawer, but I could see that he seemed to have left all of his clothes.'

'In February and March of this year, did you own or hire or have access to any vehicle other than... ,' Cousland consulted a sheet of paper, 'a Land Rover Defender, registration number T104NSU?'

'No, I did not. I haven't driven any other vehicle since I bought that in 2000. Well, not until much more recently, when I've driven a friend's car.'

Cousland looked up sharply. 'When was that?'

'The first time would have been in late April.'

The DS's shoulders relaxed. 'Have you any objection if we examine your Land Rover?'

'None whatsoever. If you're looking for Roddy McCulloch's finger-prints or DNA in it, you'll probably find them, because he treated me like his chauffeur.'

'I understand you also plan to re-examine Miss Mountjoy's house and cottage?' said Cross.

Mabel started, and gazed at him. He shook his head at

her, imperceptibly.

'We have a warrant to do so,' said Cousland.

'When will this happen?' asked Mabel.

'I imagine officers are there now.'

'That's totally unacceptable. You need to let me make arrangements for my animals. The cat mustn't get out.'

The DS smiled grimly. 'I understand that your partner has already seen to that.'

'Quite,' said Cross. 'I think we've come to the end of what my client can usefully tell you. I assume she is now free to go?'

The officers exchanged glances.

'Please let us know if you are planning to leave the area, Miss Mountjoy,' said Cousland.

'I'm going on holiday in September.'

'Hopefully that won't be a problem.'

She felt like a mole, emerging into bright sunshine outside. The first sunny day for weeks, and she'd been stuck in *that* place.

'I'll give you a lift,' said Arthur Cross. 'We can discuss tactics.'

'Fergus is meeting me.'

'He asked me to take you to him.'

'Are the police at my house then?'

'I should think so.'

'Poor Fergus. I don't suppose you know where he is while that palaver's going on?'

'I know exactly where he is. He's meeting us at... ' He consulted his notebook. 'Knock Bay Hotel. I understand he's booked a room there until they've finished with your house.'

'What has he done with the animals?'

'He tells me he has put the cat into a cattery. Dogs are apparently welcome at the Knock Bay Hotel. By the way, he asked me to tell you he has registered you as Belle Learmonth. He felt it was wiser, in the event that the local media get hold of your name.'

Archie leapt on Mabel as soon as she entered the hotel room. She picked him up and hugged him while she watched Fergus and Cross stroll up and down the gravel sweep outside, talking and smoking. They shook hands, and the solicitor headed towards his car.

Fergus was with her a moment later. 'From what Arthur's been able to find out, McCulloch's skull had been bashed in. But it doesn't sound as if they have any clear idea of what could have been used as a weapon. It could also be consistent with a fall. There's not a lot they can tell when there's no tissue damage to go on. The one thing they seem certain about is that he didn't die where he was found.'

Mabel started to sob. 'Poor, poor Roddy.'

Fergus exhaled noisily. 'I hoped I'd have the chance to give the stonework in the cottage a going-over with neat bleach; that's the one thing that can fool luminol. But I didn't have time. We'll wait and see what happens next.'

'I want to see the place.'

'What place?'

'Where he was found.'

'Ridiculous idea. It would be inadvisable for you to visit it just now.'

'I need to.' Her chin started to wobble

'Later, I promise, I'll take you,' said Fergus quickly.

'Once all the fuss has d... been sorted out. We'll be able to go home tomorrow.'

There was a further phone call. Mabel was invited to call at the local police station next morning, to help further with their enquiries. Fergus wanted to call Cross, but she told him that was crazy; it merely made her look as if she had something to hide. He didn't demur. He'd had to call in a few favours to get Arthur to drop everything at short notice; no point in crying wolf, in case they needed him in a hurry again.

Just Castle Douglas this time, and DS Torrance once more, plus a young PC who sat silently at the back of the room.

'You asked the Council's Environmental Health Department to dispose of some large waste items on the fourth of February. Can you tell me what these were?'

Mabel thought Monica Torrance seemed less hostile and formal in the less forbidding surroundings. Perhaps Tom Ellis was a hard task-master?

'An old Persian rug and a mattress from the cottage.'

'They had been used by Mr McCulloch? And why did you dispose of them?'

'Because both of them had been soaked in urine. More than once.'

The DS frowned. 'You threw out a perfectly good rug, a valuable rug, because it had a few stains?'

'It was old. It had more than a few stains. It was still wet with fresh urine and vomit when I threw it out. It stank to high heaven.'

'You disposed of these articles before you reported Mr McCulloch missing? Before officers searched the property?'

'They were there, propped against the back wall of my garden, in the lane. The Council doesn't exactly prioritise collecting rubbish.'

'But you didn't draw this to the attention of the officers who attended?'

'What – that D&G Council's a bit lackadaisical? No, that didn't occur to me.'

Monica's eyes were unsmiling. Mabel noticed how she glanced at the camera on the wall of the interview room. Was Tom sitting at a monitor somewhere, calmly watching her being made to jump through yet more hoops?

'You didn't draw it to their attention that you had removed these items from the building?'

Mabel cleared her throat. 'They were looking for a man, not the places where he'd wet himself.'

Damn! Misjudged that, Mabel old girl. Stop sounding sarcastic.

'How did you move the items? A mattress is a heavy object.'

'I dragged it. We're talking about a distance of less then ten metres. I'm stronger than I look.'

Stupid thing to say, Mabel.

'I put it to you that you were willing to go to extreme lengths to get Mr McCulloch out of your property, so that you could re-let it.'

'Re-let it? I may have told him that's why I wanted him to move, but I think you'll find I have taken no action to re-let the cottage.'

'Why is that? You stated that you asked Mr McCulloch to move for that very reason.'

'Circumstances have changed. I decided to leave it empty meantime, so that at least I get a small rebate on the Council Tax.'

'Have you found yourself short of money recently?'

Mabel felt her cheeks grow hot. 'I have not.'

'I believe you are facing a substantial bill to have the roof of your house repaired?'

'That's none of your business.'

'We are investigating a suspicious death, Miss Mountjoy. Money can be a powerful motive.'

Mabel laughed aloud, but the sound of her own voice in her ears wasn't a joyful one. 'You think I killed Roddy McCulloch for his money? The man *had* no money!' She recalled the bank statements and bit her tongue.

DS Torrance was watching her carefully. 'You are admitting to killing Mr McCulloch?'

'I am doing nothing of the sort. I was using irony. Are you saying you've got proof he *was* killed?'

'It's a suspicious death. Did you kill Roderick McCulloch?'

Bugger. Where's Arthur Cross when I need him? 'I did *not.*'

She was allowed to leave again. The Volvo was parked outside, the pug's eager face pressed against the side window.

Fergus hugged her briefly. 'Home, my love. We've got our house back.' Loud, furious mews emanated from the cat basket on the back seat.

'They more or less accused me of killing him this time.'

He swore, and dialled Arthur's number.

CHAPTER SIXTEEN

Tom Ellis watched from the observation room as Rachel Field and DS Torrance prepared to question Roddy McCulloch's sister. Alison had told his colleagues defiantly that she didn't want a solicitor present. He took in her weird outfit: baggy dark brown corduroy trousers, topped by an ill-fitting navy blue sweater. He'd read her file very carefully. He didn't know any transgender individuals personally, but he'd been through the same diversity training as his colleagues. It seemed logical to Tom that if Alistair McCulloch had opted to be a woman, she'd try to look more like one? He was convinced that Alison knew a lot more about her brother's disappearance and demise than she'd admitted thus far.

Mabel's friend Nancy McGillivray had confirmed her time frame for the evening when Roddy McCulloch disappeared – and had presumably been killed. Indeed, her defence of Mabel had become quite heated. As for Briony Hall! When he'd asked her on the quiet if she had ever heard Mabel utter threats against McCulloch, he'd feared she'd scratch his eyes out. 'Mabel?' she'd yelled. 'Mabel Mountjoy is the person least likely to hurt anyone, specially that wee nyaff.' Then she'd coloured up a bit, and muttered that she didn't wish to speak ill of the dead, but that Mabel had been devoted to Roddy, given him the best years of her life, in fact, ingrate that he was. Tom was glad she had loyal friends.

The DNA analysis of the hair found in the bird's nest and on the deceased's clothing had also come in: it had been confirmed that the former belonged to Roddy McCulloch. The hair on the clothing belonged to a fox. Even thinking about it still brought him out in a cold sweat – suppose it *had* been Mabel's hair?

He leaned forward attentively as Alison McCulloch started to speak. He noted the way she kept her eyes lowered, and fiddled with a loose thread in her jumper. Yes! She stretched her legs to the side of her chair, where he could see her feet clearly.

'I have already told you, that woman killed him,' announced Alison.

'Can you talk us through this from the start, Miss McCulloch? You say you went to visit your brother on January thirty-first because you were concerned for his welfare – what time was this?'

'Och, some time in the evening. It had been dark for a few hours.'

'Was Mabel Mountjoy there?'

'What do *you* think? She'd done away with poor Roddy, dumped him and scarpered.'

'Why would you assume that?'

Alison's left knee was trembling so that her boot-heel drummed on the floor. She pressed her hand on it, casually, to stop the movement. Tom noted how her nails were bitten down to the quick. A complete contrast to Mabel's neatly manicured hands.

'You seem worried. Why are you nervous, Alison?' asked Moira Torrance.

'Me? I'm not worried. Well, only because my brother's been murdered, and you people are doing nothing about it. Can't I have a more comfortable chair?'

'Sorry, these are the only ones we have. Why did you assume that Mabel Mountjoy was connected with your brother's disappearance?'

'Because he'd never have gone without telling me. I knew she'd done something to him.'

'But you didn't report your concerns to the police. Why not?'

Silence and suspicion hung in the stale air of the room.

'I wanted to give that hard-hearted cow enough rope to hang herself, prancing around pretending to be worried about him.'

The officers glanced at each other.

'Had you heard Mabel Mountjoy utter threats against your brother?'

'She was forever complaining he was a millstone round her neck.'

'Did Roddy ever tell you she'd threatened him, or been violent towards him?'

Tom Ellis held his breath. Alison shrugged.

'Could you answer the question, Alison?'

'He never told me that specifically.'

Rachel Field opened a file. 'How many mobile phones do you have, Miss McCulloch?'

Alison looked startled. Her left heel started drumming

again. 'Just the one.'

'Can you explain to me why recent calls from your brother's phone have been traced to your address?'

'Recent? You mean he phoned me?' Her voice rose to a squawk. 'He couldn't have. You're telling me the poor man's been dead for months.'

'On February fourth, March first, April tenth, May nineteenth, June twenty-second and July sixth, calls were made from the mobile phone registered to Roderick McCulloch to your phone. Both appeared to be at the same address. How do you explain that?'

Alison shrugged and pressed her palm to her knee once more. 'No idea. You must have got it wrong.'

'We have obtained a warrant to search your home, Miss McCulloch.'

'*My* home? Well, that's a bloody disgrace. You're just picking on me because of who I am. Right. That's it. Not another word am I saying till I get a lawyer.'

'You said you didn't require a lawyer.'

'I've changed my mind.'

Tom Ellis rose abruptly and returned to his office. Once there, he lifted the document he had been studying earlier, and frowned. The SOCOs had found not one shred of evidence to implicate Mabel Mountjoy in Roddy McCulloch's death. It was all purely circumstantial: they'd had a noisy and very public fight on the afternoon he'd last been seen alive. Neither in her Land Rover, nor in her house was there an iota of forensics to link her positively to the death. Not that it signified much these days; with all the crime series on TV, people were getting fly about cleaning up. Too many tricks of the trade on public view. He didn't believe for a minute that Mabel would have been so devious. And in any case, even after all the time that had passed, they should have been able to find *something* if she'd been guilty. It had proved impossible to trace the mattress and rug that she'd thrown out.

The real bugger was the blood they'd found on the granite kerb round the fireplace in her cottage. It had been confirmed as Roddy McCulloch's. They'd taken impressions of the sharp stone corner, and apparently it fitted his skull injury perfectly. Since it was clear that no one had lifted the fender and hit him with it, the only feasible explanation was that he'd fallen onto it – or been thrown onto it – with great force.

Now he had a very angry woman, in the shape of the deceased's sister, demanding that the cops got the finger out and arrested the woman who'd murdered her brother, rather than wasting their time searching *her* house. He sensed that the McCulloch woman was lying through her teeth, but DCI Mainwaring had convinced himself that there were grounds for questioning Mabel Mountjoy under caution, since there was a possibility they could still be talking culpable homicide. In fact, on his desk lay the instruction from the SIO to send uniforms round to pick her up again.

Reluctantly, he lifted the phone. He'd have preferred to be able to fetch her himself.

❖

Mabel wasn't in a mood to co-operate when the police arrived at the door of Ashers once more. She reiterated that she had already told them everything she knew. She raised her voice; she was cautioned. The female officer took her firmly by the arm. Fergus was in the hallway, already on the phone to Arthur Cross. Archie had somehow got out of the sitting room, and was taking exception to someone laying hands on his mistress.

As they led her through the close, the little dog ran ahead, excited and afraid in equal measure. He lunged straight past the parked police car. Mabel yelled at him. There was a screech of brakes, and the last thing she was aware of was her beloved pet disappearing beneath the wheels of a transit van.

A small, sandpaper tongue was licking her face. *All the times I've pooh-poohed the idea of an afterlife!* She'd clearly dropped stone dead at the sight of Archie being killed, and here they were, reunited on the other side. Then she realised that Fergus was beside her too. He was kneeling on the pavement, laying something soft under her head (it was his jacket), while people in uniforms milled around, muttering into their radios.

'Archie?' she whispered to Fergus.

'He's OK. Look – he's here.' He grabbed the pug by the collar.

'But I saw him... ?'

'I know. It's nothing short of a miracle. He seems to have got through between the wheels. I doubt he even has a bruise.'

'He must be checked over.'

'I'll see to that the minute we sort all this out. It's *you*

I'm worried about.'

'There's nothing wrong with me. Help me up.'

Fergus struggled to rise without letting go of the dog. 'Hey, you! Give me a hand here.' He handed Archie to a young constable.

The female officer pressed firmly on Mabel's shoulders. 'You should stay still. We've called an ambulance.'

'That's the last thing we want. We need a *vet*.' Mabel sat up and sprachled to stand.

Fergus took both her hands and pulled her to her feet. He slid his arm round her waist. 'Are you still feeling light-headed?'

'Of course not. It was shock at seeing Archie run over. Take him to the vet at once. He must be X-rayed.' She glared at the officers. 'I need to see to my dog.'

'We should wait for the medics, miss.'

'Don't you dare fetch an ambulance here,' hissed Mabel. 'All right, I'll come with you now. Fergus – the vet's number is programmed into the phone in the hall.'

'Shut up,' he whispered in her ear. 'Let them check you out. Buy some time.'

'Nonsense. I want to get this over with. I have done nothing wrong.'

'I'll follow you into Dumfries.'

'You will not. Archie needs to go to the vet immediately.'

'Well, I'll collect you then.'

'I'll take a cab. You mustn't leave him, Fergus.'

He agreed, reluctantly.

❖

Fergus filled the kettle and switched it on. An X-ray had confirmed that the pug had no broken bones, and the vet could find no sign of internal injuries. 'All I can detect is some bruising to his left hind leg. He'll be a bit stiff for a day or two, then right as rain,' he added. Archie was diagnosed as having a charmed life, and allowed to go home.

Once back in Ashers, Fergus settled the dog on a pile of soft blankets in his basket, and ordered him not to try to jump up on furniture. He sighed, mostly with relief. 'Bugger it, dog, I wish I could go home too.'

But that was nonsense. He liked to believe he was, at heart, the decent chap his grandmother had brought him up to be. He'd never leave a woman to face this sort of stramash alone. Besides, he was deeply in love. He'd never leave Belle, no matter what.

'Don't tell her I said that,' he instructed the pug. 'You know I didn't mean it. Wherever your mistress is must be home, for both of us.'

He opened the fridge to see what he could make for dinner, because Belle would surely be back by then. She was well able to handle a bunch of parochial cops. When she recovered from her fainting episode, he'd noticed at once that she seemed lost in thought for a few moments – indeed, he worried that she'd banged her head. Then she was wide awake, and filled with the calm and confidence and forcefulness that signalled a return to the old Belle.

He jumped in alarm when he heard the door-knocker applied forcefully. Surely not more cops? But it was Briony Hall. She glanced at Archie, cosy in his basket. 'I heard what happened. Doesn't seem to be much wrong with him? I'll take over here. You go into Dumfries and collect Mabs.'

Fergus stared at her. 'Has she phoned you?'

'No, of course not, but they can't possibly keep her there for long. She's done nothing wrong. You know that and I know that. Surely even someone as dim as Tom Ellis must know it by now. There needs to be someone waiting for her. She'll be in a very vulnerable state, after everything that's gone on.'

'Tell you what – she'd never forgive me if I leave the dog alone. Would you be willing to go and collect her?'

Briony rubbed her hands together briskly. 'Right. I'll go now.'

'It could be hours yet.'

'I'll go anyway. I'll sit and wait, if I'm there all night.'

Fergus experienced a pang of regret. He should be the one waiting for Belle. He was about to say that this would be the better solution after all, if Briony didn't mind dog-sitting, but she was already halfway out of the door.

'You're a pal,' he said. 'She'll need a friend to talk to. Another woman, after spending all those hours being harangued by men. Thanks, Briony.'

Tom Ellis noted that once they were seated opposite each other in the interview room, Mabel met DS Cousland's eye defiantly. Tom wished he was sitting beside her, rather than that Edinburgh solicitor. He'd have liked to be able to stroke her hand. He suddenly felt self-conscious about watching her this way; able to study her face without being seen. He wiped his brow with the back of his hand.

Arthur Cross had been on his way to the nick even before they brought Mabel in. He'd taken his time too, holding everything up while he insisted on further disclosure of whatever fresh evidence they had. Arrogant bastard. He'd actually smirked when they laid it before him. 'Hearsay,' he said, dismissively.

And indeed it was – but Sylvia Clearthorn had come forward voluntarily with details of the conversation she and Mabel had had, just days before McCulloch had disappeared.

Cousland went over and over the fact that Mabel had admitted being with Roddy that afternoon, and to striking him. There were witnesses to the fact they had quarrelled, and traces of blood had been found on the fire surround.

'I put it to you that you either struck or pushed McCulloch with the result that he fell. You panicked when you realised he was severely injured or dead, and removed the body from your premises.'

Mabel stuck to her guns. She had slapped McCulloch, but when she left he had been on his feet and still shouting abuse at her.

Tom Ellis tried to hang onto an impassive face. DCI Mainwaring had joined him in the observation room, taking a renewed interest in the case.

'There had clearly been attempts to remove traces of the bloodstain found on the hearth,' said Cousland. 'Did you make such attempts?'

Mabel looked him steadily in the eye. 'I cleaned the

entire cottage a couple of days after he disappeared. I disposed of a rug that was soaked with urine and vomit. I already told your officers that. I was not aware of any traces of blood.'

'We have a statement from a witness to the effect that you had issued threats in public about wanting to kill Mr McCulloch.'

'That's nonsense.'

Tom Ellis held his breath; DS Cousland consulted his notes.

'You didn't say: "I've thought about hitting him over the head, or putting arsenic in his whisky, if I knew where to get it"?'

'I never said anything of the sort. Well, I remember now. I was talking to a woman in the town about the fact Roddy's paintings weren't selling, and she said artists' work only appreciates once they're dead. It was a joke. She's the one who raised the subject.'

Cross had been silent throughout most of the interview, merely taking notes. He had rehearsed her well. But now he laid his hand on her wrist. Ellis wriggled in his seat.

Finally, the solicitor ran out of patience.

'There appears to be no substantive evidence whatsoever against my client. As far as I have been made aware, the forensic evidence is inconclusive as to the exact manner of Mr McCulloch having sustained a fatal injury. Indeed, it seems likely he sustained it as the result of a fall while he was under the influence of alcohol. There is nothing to place my client at the scene when he had this fall, nor is there anything to link her to the post-mortem removal of the body. I can find no justification whatsoever for holding my client further, since you clearly do not have any grounds to charge her.'

Ellis was already on his feet, turning to the DCI. Mainwaring had to agree. Mabel was free to go, once more.

Tom Ellis sat alone in his office, mulling over the scene he'd witnessed from his window a few moments before. Briony Hall, who had apparently been sitting in the waiting area for the past hour, embracing Mabs warmly, before settling her in the passenger seat of her Jaguar. Once into the car, Mabel appeared to be weeping on her friend's shoulder. Briony, rather than the Fergus creature? Now *that* was interesting. He nearly jumped out of his skin when Rachel Field popped her head round the door.

'Boss? I thought this might be of interest.'

She laid a printout on his desk.

'Fergus Learmonth,' she said, brows raised. 'The Mountjoy woman's bidie-in?'

Tom flinched, and turned his attention to the sheet.

'He's known to us?'

'Only because he helped identify a misper in Edinburgh a few years back. Another case where not much more than skeletal remains were found, in woodland.'

He handed back the paper. 'Tell me. I can't be bothered reading it. He helped identify – how?'

'He was apparently able to tell them what the guy had

been wearing, and also explain the significance of an address in the pocket of the deceased's coat.'

'Was he questioned at the time?'

'Only about the deceased's ID, and how he knew him.'

'No suspicion attached? How *did* he know him?'

'Seems the guy was a friend of his wife's.'

Tom sat up straight, abruptly. 'His *wife*?'

Rachel studied the sheet again. 'Well, ex-wife. Learmonth had apparently seen this Russian not long before he vanished, and given him quite a lot of cash.'

'What Russian?'

'The deceased was a Russian. Maxim Grigoriev. Illegal immigrant.'

Tom smiled to himself. This girl was good. She'd go far. 'Let's get the Learmonth guy in. I'm not a big fan of coincidences.'

After Rachel left his office, he sighed with relief, and buried his head in his hands for a moment. He'd known all along that Mabel couldn't possibly have had any part in a violent death. But Fergus Learmonth, there was a much better suspect. A big brute of a man, and one who clearly thought he was above the law, because it sounded as if he'd already got away with it once, and because he considered himself a celebrity. He'd deal with this one personally. He'd give him celebrity!

Fergus regarded Tom Ellis coolly across the table between them.

'How long have you known Mabel Mountjoy?' asked the DI.

'Since mid-February this year.'

'How did you meet?'

'She called on my services to help find her former lodger.'

'How do you earn your living these days, Mr Learmonth? I understand you no longer work for Albion television or its parent company?'

'What does that have to do with anything related to Miss Mountjoy's lodger?'

'I'm merely curious.'

'I think you're well aware of what work I do now. Getting tired of the police, are you? Can't say I blame you. I'm sure my consultancy work pays a damn sight better, per day. I also write. I'm one of the lucky few to have received a very healthy advance from my publisher.'

'Congratulations. What is the subject of your book?'

Rolling drunks and stealing their wallets. Can it, Fergus.

'Along the same lines as my TV series: how to avoid being conned by unscrupulous tradesmen. The publisher's predicting high sales, since the police do nothing to combat fraud these days.'

Ellis cleared his throat.

'So Mabel Mountjoy contracted you in February to find her partner, and now you live with her?'

Fergus looked him steadily in the eye. 'What business is that of yours?'

'I am trying to establish whether you lived with her at the time Mr McCulloch was reported missing.'

'I'd have thought the answer was blindingly obvious, since we've already established that she called on me to help find him.'

'And you had never had any contact with her prior to that?'

'Never, unfortunately. I'm very glad to have met her now.'

'Why is that, Mr Learmonth?'

'I'm hoping she'll agree to marry me.'

Tom Ellis developed a severe tickle in his throat, and gestured to Rachel to pour him a glass of water.

'Indeed. Moving to your role in the identification of human remains found on Corstorphine Hill in 2001. I'd like you to run through for me how you knew the deceased on that occasion.'

'He was a friend of my ex-wife's, or a protégé, to be more exact. I had seen him shortly before he disappeared, so I was able to give your colleagues in Lothian a good description of his general height and build, and of the clothing he'd been wearing. I was also able to provide them with a name and place of residence. From that, they were able to obtain dental records from Russia, and get a positive ID.'

'This person disappeared when, exactly?'

Could you have called the Russian a 'person'? A conman, that's all he was. Just the type *he* had the measure of. Another drunk into the bargain. And a lecher. More than once, Fergus had kept Max under surveillance at the pub he frequented in Leith. More than once he'd seen him vanish into the unlit alley behind the building with a woman who was no better than a streetwalker. How could he have let such a filthy creature continue going home to Serena – perhaps even (God forbid) to her bed? In any case, *his* hands were clean. He'd anticipated that the two petty thugs might rough Max up a little (after all, everyone knows it's not always easy to handle an obstreperous drunk gently), before delivering him to the Murmansk-bound ship along with the generous hand-out Fergus had provided. He'd never expected them to go too far... the adrenalin kick had got the better of them, presumably. But after all, it could have happened to Max in Russia at any point, no questions asked.

'This Russian disappeared when, Mr Learmonth?' repeated Ellis.

'November 1997.'

'Why didn't your wife offer to help identify him? You mentioned that he was her friend?'

'Ex-wife. We were divorced in June 1997. By the time he was found, she was remarried and in the final stages of a difficult pregnancy. Everyone agreed it was best not to distress her.'

'She would have been distressed?'

'My wife was the type to throw hysterics over a dead seagull in the street, Inspector. Yes, she would have been distressed.'

'Can you tell me her current address?'

'The Elysian Fields, I hope. I'd hate to think she went to the other place.'

'I beg your pardon?'

'My ex-wife passed away in 2002. Of natural causes,

before you ask.'

'In your statement to Lothian and Borders Police in 2001, you stated that you had given Maxim Grigoriev a substantial sum of money before he disappeared?'

'Indeed I had. More than twelve hundred pounds.'

'For what reason?'

Fergus strove to relax the tension in his jaw. 'To buy him off. I thought he was an extremely bad influence on my ex-wife. I was also worried that he'd get her into difficulties with the authorities, since she'd helped him enter the country illegally. I handed over enough cash to give him a start once he got home. Damn it, I even arranged safe passage on a Russian cargo ship, only he never showed up to board it. We only discovered that a long time later.'

Ellis consulted the sheet once more. 'But no money was found on his person, I understand?'

'So I was told. I've always understood that was the probable motive for killing him, if he *was* killed?' He hadn't made a fuss about the missing cash at the time. Safer to forget about it. 'That's what your colleagues in Lothian surmised. It was another case where the forensics guys couldn't determine the cause of death with any precision.'

'Quite a coincidence, Mr Learmonth?'

'That's all it is.'

'And the paper found in the pocket of his clothing?'

'My ex-wife's home address. Her family home, that is. She hadn't lived there for many years. I always assumed she'd been unwise enough to give him that address for correspondence, so that he could let her know when he got back to St Petersburg.'

Ellis was silent for a moment, studying his notes.

'Has Mabel Mountjoy given you an account of the circumstances in which Mr McCulloch disappeared?'

'Indeed she has. The same account which she has given to you, on more than one occasion.'

'Do you believe she had anything to do with his disappearance?'

'Yes. She'd told him to get out of her property; vamoose.'

'I mean – do you believe she had anything to do with his death?'

'Not in the least. Neither do you, I would hope, since I understand you know her very well indeed. Belle tells me you proposed to her in the 1980s, and she turned you down. That must have left a very bitter taste, Inspector?'

Fergus sat back, pleased with himself, watching the expressions that flitted across DC Rachel Field's face. He'd played his trump card. He was well aware that other officers would be listening in. He was well aware that Tom Ellis had put himself in a sticky position by keeping shtum about his relationship with Mabel.

Reaching into his brief case, he drew out a slim file and laid it before Ellis. 'You may find this interesting.'

Ellis flicked through the pages. 'McCulloch's bank statements?'

'Don't you want to know where I found these? I retrieved them from Miss Alison McCulloch's dustbin. Note the address on them. I took the precaution of wearing gloves to handle them. I assume you're aware that Alison used to be Alistair?'

Ellis nodded, reluctantly.

'So I'm sure you're also aware of the GBH conviction? Nasty temper, by the sound of it. I wouldn't be at all surprised if you find her brother's bank card in her possession, when you get round to searching her house properly. Unless she's disposed of it recently.'

Fergus drew another package from his briefcase. It contained a crystal tumbler. 'Your guys already told me this couldn't be used as any sort of evidence, because you hadn't retrieved it yourselves, so there was no chain of custody. But you might want to check it for finger marks. I'll be most surprised if you don't find Alison McCulloch's prints on it. You could have saved yourselves a good deal of time and effort if you'd taken prints off it when you had the chance.'

'Where did you find this?'

'In Mabel Mountjoy's sitting room, some time ago. I'm certain that the "burglar" was none other than Ms McCulloch. She was trying to frighten Belle out of her home.'

'When was this?'

'Weeks ago. The first time one of your guys turned up.'

'We wouldn't have had Alison McCulloch's prints on the database at that point anyway.'

'Of course you did. You had Alistair McCulloch's anyway.'

Tom blushed. 'As my officer told you, this doesn't constitute any sort of evidence.'

Sighing, Fergus snapped his bag shut and made to stand up. 'I assume I can go now?'

Fergus strolled up the steep, winding road leading out of Kirkcudbright towards Barrhill. The lower part was heavily built up. Just before the houses petered out, he finally spotted what he was looking for. He strode confidently into the driveway, and knocked at the front door.

Tom Ellis was angrier than ever. The local guys had referred to the owner of the private surveillance cameras on the Barrhill road as 'a nutter', but that was no fucking excuse for not eyeballing them. He appeared to be a very organised type of nutter anyway. He'd been burgled in 1999, and was determined to do everything possible to keep his insurance premiums down. He had one camera trained on the approach to his front door, the other trained on the road. He never over-wrote tapes. He had two large bookcases in his house full of them.

Ellis had officers going through the footage starting with the day Mabel Mountjoy said she'd last seen McCulloch. He'd asked them to concentrate on watching for her Land Rover. But within forty minutes an eagle-eyed rookie had noticed a Volkswagen Golf going up the road at 9.56 pm on the night in question, then returning around ninety minutes later. He'd checked the number: it was registered to Alison McCulloch. Within less than two hours, they had her in the interview room once more. She'd changed her tune yet again; she insisted that she didn't want a solicitor present.

Tom Ellis took his seat in the observation room, leaning forward eagerly. Alison's demeanour was quite different this time, even if her dress sense wasn't. Instead of remaining defiant, she bowed her head and sobbed. Ellis was transfixed by a mixture of horror and fascination and fury.

'I found Roddy's body,' Alison said at last. 'I found him lying there dead, in the middle of the floor. It was so *cold*.'

DS Torrance calmly spread a scale drawing of the cottage interior on the table, and slid it across.

'Can you show us where exactly you found him lying?' She watched Ali produce something that looked like a child's drawing of a crime scene. 'What was he lying on?'

'I told you. The floor.'

'Was there a carpet?'

Ali's tone reverted to hostility. 'There was a rug. A tatty old thing that bitch had thrown out of her own house.'

'So your brother was lying on this rug?'

'I can't remember. He might have been.'

'It's extremely important that you tell us whether he was lying on the rug or not.'

'Partly. Yes – he was lying with his legs on it.'

'Was there blood?'

'I don't remember. I was very upset. There may have been a little.'

'Why didn't you summon the emergency services?'

'I knew he was dead.'

'How did you know that?'

'He was stone cold.'

'Was there anything else you noticed?'

'I could see he'd been hit on the head.'

'You say he was cold – did you touch his hands?'

Alison nodded.

'Were they stiff?'

'No. Just cold.'

The officers looked at each other. Indoors in winter, in an unheated room, it takes around four hours after death for rigor mortis to reach the hands.

'It's very important that you remember what time this was.'

Ali huffed and rolled her eyes ceilingward. 'I suppose it might have been about nine. It wasn't earlier than that, certainly.'

That would put the time of death at roughly five. Tom smiled. He knew that Mabel's file contained a receipt from Sainsbury's in Newton Stewart, charged to her credit card, for 5.10 pm on the night in question.

'Why did you not contact the police at once?'

'Because I didn't want to get blamed. I wanted that bitch to take the consequences of what she'd done.'

'What time did you leave the cottage?'

'About ten minutes after I found Roddy. You think I wanted to stay alone with a dead man? My *brother*.'

She buried her face in her hands, but Tom noticed that when she raised it again, her eyes and cheeks were dry.

They asked in even greater detail about her time at the cottage. Since she said it was in darkness when she arrived, at which point had she switched the light on, and had she switched it off again when she left? Did she close the door behind her? And *exactly* what time was that?'

DS Torrance sat back in her chair. 'Your car was seen in the vicinity of the area where your brother's body was found, just before ten p.m. on the evening in question, and later, at around eleven thirty. Can you explain why you were there?'

Ali became flustered. Just as suddenly as she'd become aggressive with her interlocutors, she broke down again, and confessed that Roddy seemed to have fallen onto the hearth. She had not called the police, or an ambulance, but had carried his body out to her car. She was horrified by their suggestion that she'd put him in the boot. No, she had strapped him into the front passenger seat. He was her *brother*, for God's sake. She had driven to Barrhill, turned onto the road to the wildlife centre, then parked and walked as far as she could into the woodland, carrying Roddy in her arms. It hadn't been difficult. He was so thin and frail, since the callous Mountjoy woman had tried to starve him out, he weighed less than a healthy child.

Tom leaned back in his chair and exhaled noisily. He felt light-headed with relief. The guy had simply taken a tumble when he was intoxicated. The fiscal would hardly be likely to want an FAI? The death certificate could be signed off now, surely. An accident. The case might be revisited in years to come, if more evidence became available, but it looked as if Mabs was off the hook.

'Why did you move the body?' Monica Torrance was asking Ali.

'Told you. I wanted that bitch to get what was coming to her.'

'But you knew you had a duty to report the death? The witness is shrugging.' Torrance slid an evidence bag across the table. 'I am showing Miss McCulloch a set of keys. Do you recognise these?'

'Never seen them before.'

'They were found in your house.'

She shrugged. 'They're Roddy's keys, maybe.'

'Which you had removed from the body, or from Miss Mountjoy's cottage?'

'He'd probably left them in my house at some point.'

'And which you have used to gain access to Mabel Mountjoy's house on more than one occasion?'

'No comment.'

The DS laid her finger on one of the keys. 'Miss Mountjoy has identified this as the key to her back gate, which went missing more than a year ago. Can you tell me how it came to be in your possession?'

'No comment.'

'What were you looking for, Alison?'

'No comment.'

'I put it to you that you intended to rob Miss Mountjoy.'

'Bollocks. I was looking for Roddy's notebook, if you must know. The bitch had moved all his stuff out of the hell-hole she kept him in, before he was cold.'

'Why did you want his notebook?'

'No comment.'

'You had also removed your brother's wallet from his pocket?'

'For safe keeping.'

Rachel Field suddenly leaned forward. 'You wanted his notebook because you thought he'd noted his bank pin number in there?'

Alison clutched the edge of the table and almost growled. 'Why should that woman get all his money? She'd never lifted a finger to do anything for Roddy, and she'd had the best of him, all these years. She doesn't need cash anyway, there in her big fancy house.'

The two officers sat back, looking satisfied. Tom Ellis left the room abruptly. He went into the gents' toilet, and shut himself in a cubicle. He wept, for the first time he could remember in his adult life.

Arthur Cross had called to visit Fergus and Mabel. He'd managed to find out the gist of what Alison had said. Mabel couldn't decide whether she felt relieved, or simply depressed.

Fergus sighed. 'You'll be called as a witness when she comes to trial, Belle.'

'What will she be tried for?'

'Moving a body, amazingly, is not a crime,' said Cross. 'I'm not certain what they'll do about the fact she failed to report a death. She'd be guilty of fraud if she'd used his bank card to draw money, but it doesn't sound as if she ever managed that. Then, of course, there's the matter of breaking into your house. Sounds to me as if she's unbalanced.' He turned to Mabel and added more gently, 'For what it's worth, I'd say Roddy would have died very quickly, and in no pain. That's some comfort, I hope.'

'How did she get him into the wood? You'd never get a car in there.'

'I understand she carried him.'

'*Carried* him? Poor Ali! That must have been awful.' Mabel burst into tears again.

'Poor Ali be damned,' said Fergus. 'She tried to lay the blame on you. Nothing poor about her.'

'Why is Roddy's phone still working?' she asked. 'Listen.' She selected a number from speed-dial, and held it to Fergus's ear. *Are you calling me-hee-hee-hee-hee-he-hee? It's Rod on his tod. Leave me a message.* 'I've tried it every week, though he never got back to me.'

She didn't want Fergus to know that she'd found an element of consolation in hearing Roddy's voice.

'I understand that his sister had been paying the bill, so that it wouldn't be cut off,' said Cross.

'So she has a soft side to her after all!'

Both men stared at her in amazement.

'So that no one would know he was dead, and his bank account wouldn't be closed before she'd managed to get into it,' said Fergus.

'Sorry, I'm not thinking straight. Did they find out where he'd got all that money from in the first place?'

Cross shrugged. 'I don't think we want to know anything about that.'

'It's over now,' said Fergus. 'You can come to terms with it, and grieve for the man, and move on.'

'Who'll pay for his funeral?'

'That's not for you to worry about.'

'I wouldn't like him to be buried like a pauper.'

'They don't have pauper's funerals these days.'

"You know what I mean. I want him to have some dignity.'

'Not our problem,' said Fergus.

'It would be unwise to concern yourself overly with that,' added Cross. 'Makes you sound as if you feel guilty.'

'She does,' said Fergus fondly. 'Too soft-hearted by half. In any case, Belle, the man was hardly short of funds. There'll be more than enough assets to take care of that.'

'I suppose Ali will be allowed to decide the details anyway. Maybe she'll want to have him cremated. I don't think he'd have wanted that.'

'I suspect permission wouldn't be granted for cremation in a case like this,' began Cross.

Fergus laid his hand on the solicitor's arm. 'Arthur!'

Too late.

'Why?' asked Mabel.

Cross cleared his throat. 'In case there is any need to reopen the case in the future.'

Fergus looked furious, but Mabel had stopped listening anyway. Her mind was full of a picture she'd seen in magazines when she was young. An open doorway, with a blue sky beyond: could it have been an advert for Dignitas? Probably Dignitas didn't exist in those days. She'd thought of it often after Father died, in the days when she'd believed that any dignity about her own latter days would be purely her own concern.

She made a conscious effort to calm herself. It was over now. She could reach what Fergus kept referring to as 'closure'. What *he* hadn't been able to reach, even though it was ten years since he and Serena had divorced.

But by the next day, it became clear that it was far from over. Under further questioning, Alison McCulloch had become positively voluble. Her brother had made a will. She'd seen a copy, and she knew which solicitor held the original. Under its terms, Roddy had left everything he owned to Mabel Mountjoy.

When she was informed of this, Mabel's reaction was to rush to the nearest bathroom and throw up. Grief had never had that effect on her before. She put it down to stress.

Fergus accompanied her to the solicitor's office to sign the form of renunciation. Apparently Roddy had nominated a residual beneficiary: the Royal National Mission to Deep Sea Fishermen. She told the solicitor she intended to sell Roddy's remaining completed canvases for what she could get, and add the proceeds to his cash bequest.

As they stepped into the street, Mabel suddenly felt twenty years younger. A huge weight had been lifted from her heart.

'Thank you for sticking with me through all this,' she told Fergus.

'You think I'd have left you to face it on your own? Even if you hadn't taken me back after I made that stupid gesture of decamping to Edinburgh, I'd have made sure I was here for you.'

'I'm sorry you got mixed up in it.'

'It's all over now, thank God. After this, what can possibly go wrong for us? By the way, don't forget you already have a buyer for two of those paintings. Sell them to me, and you can still see them every day. I don't blame you for having wanted to hang onto them. I know what he must have meant to you, over the years. I'm trying not to be jealous.'

'You wouldn't mind seeing them, knowing who painted them?'

'I see his portrait of you every day, and I'd never want you to get rid of that.'

'Then I should be content to let you have a photo of Serena on your desk. But I wouldn't be. I'd hate it.'

'So would I. I've realised I never loved her, Belle. I was obsessed with her. There's a world of difference. I *love* you.'

'You can have the paintings you wanted, as a gift.'

'I'll buy them. I promised to.'

'In that case, you have to let me buy the ruby necklace.'

'That was a present.'

'Then so are the paintings. Or else you have to let me pay for the roof repair.'

He slapped her bottom. 'You promised to stop being a stubborn bisom, didn't you? Go and start looking out your glad rags for our trip to the capital.'

Fergus's book was being launched at a fancy do in London later that week.

Mabel's light mood didn't last. By that evening, she was almost ready to admit defeat. Every last person in Kirkcudbright would know about what had happened:

Mabel Mountjoy carted off more than once in a police car. Mabel Mountjoy waltzing off to eat steak, and giggle with her pal, while a man was lying dead on the floor of her house.

'No smoke without fire', the town gossips would be saying. 'Poor Roddy McCulloch, such a shilpit wee creature. What chance would he have against a big woman like that if she attacked him? You should hear the tales Mrs Alexander can tell! If they weren't fornicating in the garden – the *garden*, mark my words, it's true – they were yelling abuse at each other. The foul mouth that one has on her! Her father must be spinning in his grave.'

And Sylvia Clearthorn! Pretending to be a friend, when she'd obviously been the one to go running to the police with chapter and verse of that silly conversation about putting arsenic in Roddy's drink.

Bugger it! No way she was being chased out of her home. She had done nothing wrong. Running away would only prove them right. In any case, Sylvia was just one person. Her other friends had stood by her – the real friends like Briony and Nancy and Angela. She could still hold her head up and look everyone in the eye.

She needed to find a way to thank them. A fancy meal, that was it. A girly night out. She racked her brains. Briony had an excellent chef, so presumably taking her to another restaurant in the area wasn't the answer. She'd give them a slap-up dinner with all the trimmings, at Ashers. With Fergus to help with the cooking, surely she could manage a memorable evening? She'd start planning menus as soon as they were back from London. She should really think of a special present for Briony too. A large framed photo of her cat! Fergus had all those cameras, and he had such a way with animals. It would be the perfect gift.

Mabel had been chary of accompanying Fergus to London for the official launch party for 'Cowboys'.

'It'll be end to end luvvies who know you,' she protested. 'I'll only be in the way.'

'There'll be a lot of people I used to work beside. I want them to meet you. I want everyone to know we're a couple. We'll go down a day or so early, and you can hit the posh shops, get yourself a new frock.'

'We can't leave the animals.'

'Of course we can. Isla's happy to house-sit.'

'Only so she can bewitch the locals with stories of "I lived in a murderess's house".'

'Bollocks. The biggest risk is that Gorby and Archie will be spoilt rotten.'

She agreed, with an ill grace, and was more bad-tempered than ever after her shopping spree. Nothing seemed to fit. Fergus assured her that the plain black dress she eventually chose looked stunning. She knew the truth: it made her look fat. She had more success with putting her foot down over staying in the hotel where the launch was to be held. 'I want to feel I can get right away from it,' she said. Fergus gave in, although she knew he loved official 'dos' like this. Redolent of the wee boy showing off, in the hope that someone important would praise him. She felt a wave of affection for him, and resolved to put on the best act of her life as the confident consort.

As they entered the Marriott's function room a wave of heat and sound washed over them. Fergus glanced anxiously at Mabel. She was very pale. He was having qualms about insisting she came despite the fact she claimed to have a headache.

'Fergus!'

Anita Forrest's throaty voice was too familiar for comfort. Bugger! He'd never got round to dropping her that detailed explanatory note. Before he could take pre-emptive action, Anita had launched herself on him and kissed him on the mouth. Out of the corner of his eye, he could see Belle's expression. Somewhere between shock and awe. She looked as if she were about to flee.

But Anita hadn't lost her touch. Without missing a beat, she disentangled herself from Fergus, and embraced a startled Mabel.

'You must be Belle! I'm so delighted to meet you at last.'

'This is Anita Forrest,' said Fergus. 'We used to work together.'

'For eons. Best not remember how long. I was his boss at one stage – can you imagine?' warbled Anita.

A tall, grey-haired man appeared from the crowd, and made to whisk her away.

'Hang on a mo, Rog. I'm getting to know Fergus's

partner. Belle, this is Roger Braithwaite, another old colleague of Learmonth's. Roger, Belle Mountjoy.'

'Trust Anita to have memorised the guest list,' thought Fergus. He felt a rush of fondness for his friend.

Roger air-kissed Mabel, and thumped Fergus on the shoulder. 'Great to see you, old chap. You're looking younger than ever. Wish I had the gumption to get out before I'm carried off in a mahogany box. Nita – you will make sure I get mahogany? Sustainably sourced.'

Anita rolled her eyes and took Mabel's arm. 'Come with me and meet some of Fergus's other fans.'

In the melee, Fergus lost sight of them immediately. Once he'd managed to extricate himself from PR leeches, he scanned the crowd anxiously.

Anita tugged at his elbow. 'Fergus – can you spare a moment? I don't think Belle's feeling very well.'

She led the way into the corridor. Mabel was sitting on a low windowsill, her head bowed. He rushed to her side.

'What's wrong, darling?'

She looked up at him, teary-eyed. She was very flushed. Almost more worrying than her earlier pallor.

'I'm feeling the heat a little. I must have eaten something that doesn't agree with me,' she said apologetically.

'I'll leave you to look after her,' said Anita, making a tactful withdrawal.

'Shall we go back to the hotel?'

'Fergus, this is your big moment. You can't possibly leave. Just let me sit here for a little by myself.'

'Not if you're feeling unwell.'

'All these people are here to see *you*.'

'Here to see one another, most of them, and guzzle the free booze.'

'You're supposed to be signing books and glad-handing reviewers. I hadn't realised how famous you are.'

'It's all puffery, and terribly transient. You'll see, in a couple of years the book will be remaindered, and everyone will have forgotten I exist.'

He kissed the top of her head, and sat down beside her.

'I'll wait with you until you feel up to it. I need you by my side, my bonnie Belle.'

She smiled at him. She was looking more like her old self.

She squared her shoulders. 'I'll be OK now.'

'Do you want a brandy? I'm sure they can rustle one up.'

'That's the last thing I want. I won't have anything more to drink.'

'Let's sit quietly for a few more minutes then.'

He was relieved to have a little space to think in peace. Roger had been bending his ear almost since they'd arrived, trying to persuade him to come back to Albion and resuscitate *Learmonth on the Lookout*. He had dangled the prospect of eye-watering sums as potential fees. Fergus had insisted he wasn't interested. He'd had his fill of flying the flag for disgruntled home-owners. He told Roger that. He expounded on the fact that although he felt sorry for people who'd been parted from their life savings and left without a roof over their heads, in the greater scheme of things, these incidents were trivial. Think of the true scandals: corruption on the grand scale. Roger's eyes had merely grown brighter. 'Super idea, Fergus! Just name your price. We need people with your flair and experience.'

Not that Roger had been the first to ask in any case. Over the past year, he'd had overtures from three of the production companies based in the South-East.

He'd had to tell Rog he'd think about it, to get the man off his back for long enough to muster his thoughts. He stood up, drew Mabel to her feet and slid his arm round her waist.

'You're looking more like yourself. We'll go in and say our goodbyes.'

The heat of the room seemed to hit her like a sledgehammer, but she struggled to give no sign of discomfort. She took deep breaths, and stayed close to Fergus's side. The ones who'd been fawning on him earlier crowded in again.

Anita appeared again from nowhere and took Mabel's arm. 'You're still flushed. I've found a place at the back where there's a window open. Fergus, go and entertain your adoring public.'

When Fergus came to find them half an hour later, they were trying on each other's shoes. It turned out that Anita shared Mabel's passion.

'Piss off, Fergus, there's a love,' said Anita. 'We're talking girly talk.'

'I was thinking we should head off soon?' he said, standing his ground.

Mabel rolled her eyes at him. 'Shouldn't you stay until the bitter end?'

'People are starting to leave anyway. I'm tired out. I've got writer's cramp in my wrist and my jaw's sore from smiling.'

'Just a moment then.' Mabel rose swiftly and walked as fast as she could in the direction of the hallway.

'Is she all right?' said Anita.

'It's not like her to be off-colour. I'm a wee bit concerned right enough.'

'She's perfect for you, Fergus.' Anita was grinning broadly. 'You sly dog. She's charming. You've found a suitable companion, at last. A sensible woman. If I could have drawn up a spec for your ideal partner, it'd be her, in every detail. She's warm and pretty and funny and clever and civilised. She seems to like all the same things you do. Very similar backgrounds, I'd say?'

'Very. Anita – I meant to write to you at greater length.'

'It doesn't matter. You and I have been useful to each other over the years. We were never cut out for anything longer-term, whereas you and Belle! Is it serious? Don't even answer. I can see it is. You're positively starry-eyed.' She kissed him on the cheek. 'I'm delighted for you. Better late than never, Fergus. I hope you'll be very happy. I assume you're going to make it official, since you're the marrying kind?'

He pulled a face. 'I've tried to broach it with her, but I don't think she wants to. She says relationships are like Galloway drystane dykes – all the stronger because they're held together by skilful design rather than mortar.'

'But you *do* want to?'

He nodded.

'Oh, here she is.'

He leapt to his feet. Mabel was looking much better. Quite back to normal, in fact, a spring in her step.

She smiled at him expectantly. 'Goodbye, Anita. It's been a real pleasure to meet you, because you've known Fergus such a long time. You must visit, when you have a spare day or two. We're not so far from Edinburgh. In fact, we'll maybe be there a bit more often in the future.'

'Love to,' said Anita.

They kissed each other; air-kisses.

Fergus drew Mabel's arm through his. 'Are you up to walking back to the hotel?'

'Not half. I'm craving fresh air. I don't feel sick any more. It's OK – I've rinsed my mouth thoroughly, and I had some mints in my bag.'

'Poor darling. Let's get you back to a warm bath and bed.'

He stopped and tipped her face up to his to kiss her.

'Don't! I want to brush my teeth.'

'Wheesht, woman. I was worried about you.'

'No need.'

'Bloody restaurants. They never pay enough attention to hygiene.'

'I think it was the crowd, as much as anything. I hope I didn't spoil it for you?'

'Not in the least. A very successful evening, or so everyone seemed to think. I've got to do a radio interview tomorrow forenoon, but you can stay in bed if you're still not a hundred per cent.'

She hugged his arm to her side. 'I feel like a groupie.'

'Well, you look about eighteen right enough. You're getting more lovely by the day. Married life suits you.'

She looked at him with raised eyebrows.

'We're as good as, aren't we?' he added.

She smiled, and he couldn't read that smile.

'I like Anita, by the way,' Mabel said. 'Sincere, I'd say. She's not one of the sort who's always looking over your shoulder to see if there's someone more important to speak to.'

'She's OK. Poor darling. You've had so much stress over the past few weeks. Never mind – it'll soon be time for our holiday.'

They left town immediately after breakfast, and the journey home was uneventful. As soon as they stepped into the hallway of Ashers, the cat twining around their ankles and Archie snorting hysterically, Fergus pulled Mabel into his arms. 'It's good to be home, isn't it?'

She pushed him away. 'You taste of tobacco smoke. It's disgusting.' She burped. 'Let go of me. I think I'm going to be sick.'

She rushed to the cloakroom. When she emerged, and joined him in the sitting room, Fergus was as white-faced as she was.

'I'm sorry, darling. I didn't think you minded.' He was

about to add that Serena had complained, every single day they were together, about the smell of smoke on his hair and clothes. He stopped himself in time, on the 'S'. 'S... still not quite over whatever you'd eaten at that damn hotel, do you think? To make you sick, I mean.'

'It's your bloody cigars. You stink of them. Your clothes, your hair, your beard, your breath.'

'I had no idea you felt so strongly, darling. I thought you were happy enough as long as I didn't smoke too much in the house. The last thing in the world I want is for you to find me distasteful.'

'I can't stand the smell.'

'All right, you've made your point. I'll give up.'

He tutted and left the room. Once upstairs, he tore off all his clothes, showered, shampooed his hair and beard over and over, dressed in clean clothes, brushed his teeth three times, gargled with mouthwash, bundled every item of discarded clothing that was remotely washable under his arm and headed for the utility room. He'd never in his life offered to make such a sacrifice for anyone, or even for his own health.

As he passed the sitting room, he could hear sobbing. He dropped the clothing on the hall floor and went in.

'What's wrong, my love?'

She clung to him. 'I'm sorry. I didn't mean to be vile to you. I'm terribly tired.'

He helped her up to bed.

'I'm calling the doctor. You're clearly far from well.'

'I don't want a doctor anywhere near me. It's some stomach bug I've picked up in London. That's big cities for you. I'll be fine if I don't eat any more today.'

But by eleven she was ravenous.

Fergus watched with growing concern as she wolfed down three slices of toasted cheese topped by pickled gherkins. She said she was feeling completely recovered, and indeed she had a healthy glow he hadn't seen about her for days, when he came to think of it.

'Looks as if you managed to get it all out of your system,' he said happily.

'I think so. Fergus, would you really give up smoking for my sake?'

'Of course. I hadn't realised you disliked it so much. I can't think of anything I wouldn't give up for you, Belle. It's just that this dislike seems so *sudden.*'

'I'm relieved. It's bad for you anyway. I must get to bed.'

By the following morning, Mabel seemed to have recovered completely. She thought she knew what was wrong with her. It had been creeping up on her for months, in all probability. The way she found herself blushing for no reason at all, and was unable to prevent the heat and the scarlet flush spreading over her entire neck and face. Sylvia had hit The Change at forty-two, so she was lucky to have had a few years' grace before facing the full-on palaver of hot flushes and night sweats and bad temper. *The idea that menopause reaches women in their fifties is a very broad brush.* Not something she wanted to discuss with Fergus, all the same.

Perhaps she *should* visit the doctor, to ask if he'd prescribe HRT? She'd read that the benefits were reckoned to outweigh the risks, as long as you didn't stay on it for too long... Not that she'd visited the local surgery for years. She loathed having to sit in the waiting room among sick people who glared at her accusingly; people she'd never consciously seen around the town.

Fergus was there at that very moment, getting a pep-talk from the practice nurse on what he needed to do to give up tobacco in short order. She felt vaguely guilty, depriving him of one of his life's pleasures, but it was for his own good, in the end. She'd have to make sure she provided alternative delights. She blushed, even though she was alone, and revelled in the warm glow she felt when she thought about Fergus and bed.

CHAPTER SEVENTEEN

A few days later, Mabel sat on the comfortingly warm and solid mahogany seat of the lavatory in her en-suite bathroom, gazing at the plastic wand in her hand. This was the third time running she'd done the test. She'd gone into three separate chemists in Dumfries, buying one kit of a different brand in each, on the basis that what she feared was impossible, and it was inconceivable that they'd all give the same result. '99.9% accurate' said the blurb on the latest packaging. Even after the first two tests, she'd still clung to the hope of that zero-point-one per cent.

Best out of three, that was always a good rule, wasn't it? Only there was no best. They'd all given the same damning verdict. Guilty as charged, Mabel Mountjoy. A silly, vapid, careless woman.

She hadn't thought too much about it over the preceding few weeks. After all, she'd never been one of those women who was regular as clockwork. She simply couldn't remember the last time she'd bled. There had been so many other things to think about, she hadn't been paying attention.

She peered again at the plastic wand. The 'plus' symbol was unmistakable.

This couldn't be happening to her. It was like one of

those trashy soap operas, or an article in the sort of women's magazine she'd never buy. 'My miracle baby.' Utter tosh.

How could she have a child? She knew nothing about how to raise them, how to talk to them. She positively disliked them. She'd much rather have a new puppy. In any case, to be a successful mother, you needed to have had one, however indifferent. A role model was required

'Fuck!' she muttered. She couldn't recall ever saying the word out loud before. Roddy had peppered almost every sentence of his conversation with it.

Oh well, nature would always have her little joke. Thirty-three years since her first period, and now the jolly japester, her fickle, treacherous body, had sprung this on her. The same body that had let her down by wanting Roddy, in the early days. The same one that was ageing faster than she could cope with. The same one that had melted in Fergus Learmonth's arms at the first invitation.

That same Fergus who was even now driving happily back from Castle Douglas (the Kirkcudbright Tesco didn't stock Gorby's preferred food, and had proved less accommodating than the deli), unaware of the ghastly cataclysm awaiting him. Nothing for it but to share the news at once, since – at this point she began to giggle hysterically – he'd be bound to notice, sooner or later. Because there was no way she could ever contemplate... never, even if she'd had the remotest idea about how you start the process of finding someone to do it. She knew you could have it on the NHS nowadays, no questions asked, but *imagine*! Imagine trekking in to see one of the doctors at the local health centre, asking about *that*. At least two of the senior partners had known her since she was a teenager. It was only a couple of years since the one who'd treated her for measles at age three had retired, for God's sake.

She wouldn't expect Fergus to help financially, or any other way. After all, he'd never hidden the fact, since the days when they first had a business arrangement: he had never wanted children. He certainly wouldn't want his first at fifty-four. She chortled again at the mental image of Fergus Learmonth pushing a pram.

She'd be almost forty-six by the time it arrived. The age at which a lot of women became grandmothers. The age at which... Oh, God. That meant there was a high risk... and she was sufficiently self-aware to know how badly she'd cope with that. All her life, she'd crossed the road if she saw a parent with a Down's Syndrome child approaching, because she'd never known what to say, or how to speak to anyone who was different in that way.

She stood up, tossed the wand into the bin and gave herself a mental prod. She would most definitely have to go to the doctor, not to ask for some unspeakable operation, but to make sure everything was proceeding as it should.

First things first. She needed to compose a script for breaking it to Fergus. She'd be severe with him. She'd order him to go home to Edinburgh at once, so that he didn't have time to think about it, or imagine he had to 'do the right thing'. This was her dilemma, hers alone. She supposed he'd pack up and leave quite soon afterwards. Just as well he'd dragged his feet about letting the flat. Poor Gorby, uprooted again.

Fergus started to laugh. He'd never suspected that there was anything at all wrong with his hearing, but once you're over fifty, it can creep up on you, he'd read. You didn't appreciate how much you'd lost until you began to have difficulties in following a conversation or making sense of the TV news – not that it made much sense these days anyhow; standards hadn't half dropped since he was a young journalist. Nowadays, it was all about soap operas, and film stars' babies, and that sort of dumbed-down tosh. Babies. Fucking hell, that was what he'd thought Mabel had said.

'*What* did you say?'

'I'm pregnant.'

'You can't be. For God's sake, at our age, I thought that was the last thing we had to worry about.'

'I'm a little younger than you, Fergus.'

'I know. I'm sorry. I'm not thinking straight. Surely it's impossible?'

'It's what I thought too. Apparently, I was wrong.'

'Has the doctor confirmed this?'

'I haven't been yet. I wanted to tell you first. I've done three pregnancy tests in a row. They're supposed to be ninety-nine per cent accurate. I don't expect you to be overjoyed, by the way.'

She rocked back and forth on her chair, tugging distractedly at her hair.

Fergus pulled her hand aside, gently. 'Don't do that to your hair,' he said.

She wrapped her arms around herself instead.

'How pregnant – I mean, how many months?'

She shrugged miserably. 'I'm not sure; two at least. It could actually be nearer four.'

'Holy fuck!' he muttered. 'But listen – you've just newly got morning sickness. Surely that means it's less time than that?'

'I haven't had morning sickness, you idiot. I had a touch of food poisoning.'

Fergus felt his face work with conflicting emotions. Damn it, he'd been married three times, and it had never happened. He'd not thought twice about going in bareback, because he'd thought both he and Belle were past all that. He'd always married women who didn't want sprogs, so assumed they preferred to see to their side of it.

'Fuck's sake, Belle – how the hell did you manage to let that happen?'

'I didn't *let* it happen. You think I used a turkey baster? It just happened. I think you'll find you played a part. How did *you* let it happen?'

'OK, OK.' He strode to the window and stood looking down the garden, fists clenched in his pockets. 'I knew you'd been sleeping with the artist for years. I assumed you had all that in hand, if there was still a chance you could get pregnant.'

'Roddy was infertile. He'd had mumps in his teens.'

Fergus sighed. He'd never spoken this thought aloud. 'To tell you the truth, I'd assumed I wasn't particularly fertile. None of my wives ever got pregnant.'

'Well I haven't had a visitation from the angel Gabriel.'

'You must have realised *I* wasn't being careful?'

'As you've already pointed out, it's all my fault.'

'I need a moment by myself.' He fled to the bottom of the garden.

Of course, when he was younger, he'd contemplated this eventuality from time to time. Neither of his first two wives had seemed all that bothered one way or another, and he'd certainly never given much thought to either taking precautions against it or trying to make it happen. With Serena, he'd been sure from the start: she wasn't cut out to be a mother, and she had never expressed the slightest desire to have a child.

What a naive idiot he was. How could it have happened now, when he was approaching his mid-fifties? Maybe it was because you needed love, and all he'd had before was lust? But that was nonsense. What about the children born as a result of rapes? What about all the teenage pregnancies among kids who were too young to know what love is?

He sat on the Lutyens bench, distractedly pulling apart an overblown rose and trying to steady his thoughts. One thing was clear: he couldn't – wouldn't – leave Belle alone to face the situation. She needed his support. And she wasn't cut out to be one of those modern brides who waddled up the aisle looking as if the midwife should be walking two paces behind, ready to call for clean towels and a supply of boiling water. They must get married without delay.

In any case, ever since he'd taken his mother's ring out of the safe deposit box, he'd known that's what he wanted. He should have got around to asking her sooner, but it couldn't be helped.

They were so right for each other. Even Anita had noticed. Meeting Belle had been like getting his first pair of reading glasses: suddenly, the small print was so distinct it threw him off balance. The clarity made his head spin. He'd never before had a relationship with a woman who loved him for who he was, rather than his job or his money or his status, such as it was. No woman had ever loved him that way.

He walked purposefully back into the house. 'Will you marry me, Mabel Mountjoy?'

She glared at him from red-rimmed eyes. 'No, I will not.'

That set him back on his heels. Not the response you expect when you're trying to do the right thing. He started to stammer platitudes about it being for the best, that they were both old-fashioned people, with traditional values.

He knelt on the floor in front of her. God knows, he'd not be able to get up again with any semblance of elegance, but at times like this, form had to go out the window. He tried to put his arms around her, and felt her tears soak into his shirt-front.

'There are no circumstances under which I'd ever want to get married because I had to. Why are you even asking? You've been married three times and divorced three times. You're clearly not cut out for it.'

'I want to marry *you*.'

'I wouldn't marry you if you were the last man on earth,' she sobbed. 'You swore at me and blamed *me* for all this mess.'

'I wasn't swearing at you, dearest. And of course I don't blame you. I was just taken aback.'

'You asked me how I'd let it happen. Seems it's nothing to do with you. So we'll keep it that way. It *is* nothing to do with you. Bugger off.'

'You know that's not what I meant.'

'It's exactly what you meant. Your first reaction was to make it all my fault. I want you to go. Now.'

'I was shocked. It all came out wrong.'

'You're telling me.'

'You can't send me away. I want to look after you. It's my duty, and it's what I long to do, more than anything in this world. You need someone to be with you – why not me? Let's go on our holiday as we planned. You'll still be able to fly, won't you? We'll get married very quietly first, and have our trip as a honeymoon. We should take a break now, because God knows how we'll get away once the baby's born. It'll be a while before we can take him abroad. I can't be doing with those folk who take tiny babies to just anywhere. It's far too risky.'

'Take *him* abroad?'

'Sorry, her. Is it a girl then?'

'How the hell would I know? The pregnancy test doesn't tell you that. You imagine it's a pink line for a girl and a blue one for a boy?'

'Whichever it is, we'll give it the best childhood we can. Let's get married next week.'

'Stop jabbering, Fergus.'

'I know you've always said you don't like children, but it'll be different when it's your own. *Our* own.'

She started sobbing loudly again.

'Belle, if you feel so desperately unhappy about it, we could always... I'll go along with whatever you want to do.'

'That's a big help. You want me to murder it?'

'I don't want you to be so unhappy.'

'You're the one who raised the subject.'

He bit his lip. It was surely the hormones, making her irrational? 'It's you this'll have the bigger impact on. You seemed to be saying you didn't think you could go through with it on your own – only, you won't be on your own.'

'So you're claiming you suddenly love kids and know how to deal with them?'

'We can learn together. Imagine the giggle the rest of the people at the antenatal classes will get.'

'Antenatal classes! You must be joking.'

'We can read some books then. We must know people who've had kids.' He wasted a moment in trying to visualise asking Susie, his second wife, for advice. After all, she'd had three in a row after she remarried. Not a good idea. 'We'll handle this situation exactly as you want to. You're the boss. I'll go along with whatever you decide.'

'I don't want you to go along with anything. I just want you to *go*.'

Mabel raised her head, and wiped her nose on her sleeve. Fergus tutted gently, and gave her his hankie. She looked into his eyes.

'That's better,' he said. 'You don't really want me to leave?'

'I don't mean to try to make you take any responsibility. This is entirely my affair. I have known almost from the first day we spoke that you want a child the way you want a pet crocodile.'

'That's because I'd never had one. I want *this* one.'

'So do I.' She clasped her hands protectively over her stomach. 'I want it, but that doesn't mean you have to.'

'We made this baby together,' said Fergus. 'Surely you didn't think I'd abandon you?'

'It's not abandonment. You have never made any sort of commitment to stay.'

His brain was whirling. He stood up and began to pace the room.

'Would you please not do that?' said Mabel after a few minutes. 'Father used to do it, and it nearly drove me mad.'

'Sorry. I was thinking – I'll be over seventy by the time it's going to university. But we Learmonths are a long-lived family. I'll give up smoking completely this moment. I'm half way there, in any case. And I'll cut down on the booze too, try to lose a bit of weight. If I'm lucky, I can still be here and in sound mind by the time it's in its twenties. Might even see my grandchildren. You never know. Another Learmonth generation!'

'Mountjoy.'

'We can give him – her – both names. He can have a trendy double-barrelled handle. We'll give him – her – the perfect childhood you and I didn't have.'

'What kind of parents would we be? Me growing up without a mother, you without a father. I'll make less of a hash of it on my own.'

'We'll be exemplary parents. It'll balance out. We're a matching set, like bookends.' He spread his hands and looked helpless. 'I'll make sure we have a proper pre-nup contract, so that I've no call on what's yours if anything *did* go wrong.'

'See? You're preparing for divorce in the same sentence you're asking me to marry you.'

'I was trying to reassure you, dear.'

'You think that's reassuring? I may never have wanted to get married; I certainly don't ever want to get divorced. You admit yourself, you're a quitter not a stayer. I'd rather you went now, rather than walk out on me in a couple of years.'

'It's different this time. I'll never walk out on you.'

'Baloney. You already did, once, because Edinburgh was more important to you than I was. What happens when I'm the size of an elephant with your child and some fruity twenty-something with black hair happens along?'

'Belle, you know you're being ridiculous.'

'I will *not* put a child through the experience of a parent walking out on her. Pack up your clobber and your cat, and leave. I need peace to figure out what to do.'

Fergus hauled himself to his feet. 'Hang on a minute.'

He sprinted upstairs and fetched the ring box.

'I brought this to give to you. If this one's not to your taste, I'll buy you another.'

He held it out to her. She kept her hands folded in her lap.

'Won't you at least try it on?'

He took her hand and slid the diamond onto her finger. 'It fits! You have the same slim fingers as my mother.'

She removed the ring calmly, and handed it back to

him. 'Fergus, I am not your mother.' He realised he'd picked the wrong script. She'd needed him to tell her he couldn't live without her.

She rose heavily and fetched a box from the bureau drawer. 'Here's your necklace.'

'It was a present. It's yours.'

'I don't want it.'

'Don't want this, don't want that. Too fucking bad. You've got it.'

He stood up and left the room.

He banged the door as he was leaving, with a heavy heart. Part misery, part cold fury. How dare she treat him like an anonymous sperm donor? As if he had no say in matters, as if he'd had no part at all in the conception of this child. He'd been racking his brains to figure out when it could have happened. He'd been convinced at first that it must be the outcome of his return from Edinburgh; they'd celebrated their reconciliation with a level of passion that had made him feel young again. But if Belle was right about dates, it could have happened almost as soon as they'd begun sleeping together. This idea brought him a moment of instinctive pride, until he remembered: he'd blown it. He'd never see his child grow up.

His child! A cold sweat broke out on his forehead. It was a matter of minutes rather than hours to cram most of his possessions into the car – his suitcases, the yowling wicker basket that was Gorby.

❖

Mabel sat where she'd been when he left, while it grew dark. Lights out, Mabs old thing. The blackest night, the deepest darkness. *All your own fault, and you're in it alone.*

The most important woman in Kirkcudbright? Hah! What an ambition. Not a chance now anyway. It might be the twenty-first century, but an unmarried mother in her forties was not eligible for that role. Her plight wouldn't even arouse pity, merely derision.

She might have steeled herself to tough it out after all the trauma of Roddy's death, but there was not the slightest chance she could stay put now, hearing the sniggers behind her as she walked up the street. *Waddled.* Oh God.

She watched Archie sniff disconsolately around Gorby's favourite spot on the hearth rug.

She'd have to sell Ashers of course. It'd fetch a good price; such an elegant house with almost all of its original features intact was unusual. It'd break her heart, but there was no alternative. The gallery could go too. She'd buy a modest cottage in a place where no one knew her. Just two bedrooms – one for her, one for the child – and a tiny garden. She gazed out of the window at her existing plot, in its full summer glory despite the rain they'd had.

The worst thing of all was losing Fergus. Already she missed him so much it hurt; a dull ache in her chest. She'd been so sure that sending him away had been the right thing to do. It *had* been; he'd hardly stayed to argue. And really, she had no patience with precipitate declarations of love.

Her little dog gazed anxiously into her face, then

started to paw at her knee. She lifted him onto her lap.

'We're going to have a baby, Archie. That'll be fun won't it?'

She began to sob again.

Within a few moments, Fergus was on the outskirts of the town, about to cross the ugly concrete bridge over the Dee. Bugger! He hadn't meant to come this way; force of habit. He reached a decision. He stood on the brakes and wheeled round in the road before he reached the bridge, triggering an angry blast on the horn from the white van behind him.

He parked opposite the harbour. This was madness. The first chance of real happiness he'd run into in his entire life, and he'd chucked it away, as like as not. He'd spent so long wrapped up in the idea that there could never be anyone after Serena. And yet Belle had put her finger on the problem, precisely and calmly, after only knowing him for a few weeks. Serena had been a very bad choice. Every bit as bad as the women he'd married precipitately when he was still in his twenties. He'd spent thirty years pursuing chimeras, and now when the truth was staring him in the face, he'd almost overlooked it. Almost. Belle was the most suitable woman in the world for him. She was what he'd craved all his life: someone to spoil and cherish the way his grandmother had spoiled and cherished him. Someone who saw love as a cosy refuge, not a trap. Someone who was her own woman, but not so aggressively independent as Anita Forrest (who'd as soon be cosseted as garrotted), nor so needy that it was impossible to please her. It was Anita herself who'd teased him about always wanting to be someone's husband. Suddenly, that seemed like all he longed to be.

But he'd blown it. The only woman in the world he loved didn't seem to want him around.

All the plans they'd had. Off to wherever they pleased in Europe at the drop of a hat, the two of them: Fergus and Belle – and perhaps occasionally, Gorby and the pug. Everything lay in ruins. He'd always believed he couldn't abide the palaver and fuss of a child. The noise, the upheaval, the messy business of nappies.

'Shush,' he told the wailing cat. He knew it was pointless. Gorby would keep it up until they reached journey's end.

He sighed, wiped his eyes, and headed once more for Edinburgh. This time, he made it as far as Dumfries. Lousy bloody roads! We'd all believed we'd be living on Mars by now, and what did we have? The A75. Driving across southern Scotland was a nightmare.

He stopped at the red light on a pedestrian crossing at Heathhall, on the northern outskirts of the town. A middle-aged woman was crossing, pushing a pram. He sat watching her, fascinated. Perhaps the child's grandmother. That's what Belle would have said. His eyes filled with tears again. The light had changed to green, but still he sat. The drivers behind hooted. He wakened from his dwam, and pulled away.

Once into the countryside, he watched a scene play out in a lay-by. A man bundled a small boy out of a car-seat and carried him swiftly to the grass verge, pulling the child's trousers down as he did so. The man had grey hair. Possibly the child's grandfather. Possibly not. What did it matter? Fergus's mind spun back to his own childhood. The truth stung him like a wasp, and he pulled into the first available turning-place. He laughed aloud. Who had tucked him in at night, and cajoled him out of food fads, and taught him to give sufficient warning of his need to pee when they went for a run in the car? The person who'd seen him through teething and the terrible twos and childhood ailments wasn't his mother but his grandmother, and she'd been many years older than Belle.

And a child was every bit as portable as a cat – even more so, with all the gadgets you could buy nowadays. They could still live the peripatetic life they'd dreamed of, only with a small person in tow. They'd only need to settle in one place when it was time for him to go to school. Him? Fergus chuckled. He must stop thinking of the child as 'him' until they knew for certain.

One thing was very clear: this was *meant*. When you thought of all the years both he and Belle had been with other people, then this had happened out of the blue, at their age, and so *effortlessly*. Fate had intervened, no mistake. Perhaps the child she was carrying would be the next Einstein or Niels Bohr or Glenn Gould.

He wasn't going to take no for an answer. She'd *need* him, more and more as the weeks passed. For purely practical reasons she'd need him. Things like carrying the laundry basket outside, and drying properly between her toes after her shower (a ritual much valued by his grandmother; one he'd observed life-long).

They could call the child Edmund, after his father. Eddie. Or perhaps Belle would want to use her father's name? He realised he didn't even know what that was. There was so much ground to make up in getting to know each other. No more time to waste.

School would mean settling in Edinburgh as their principal home, but Ashers would still be there for weekends and holidays. It wasn't much over a hundred miles by road, for God's sake. There would be an eighth generation to inherit Ashers after all.

No, damn it. He couldn't expect her to live in the flat. Not even pro tem. He took out his phone and dialled the Edinburgh estate agent.

'That client of yours still interested in Learmonth Terrace at the figure you mentioned?'

The reaction was eager.

'Tell him I'm selling. I'll email you the contact details for my solicitor.'

They'd buy a new house together, with a garden full of roses and camellias. He'd take up Roger's offer and go back to Albion for a couple of years, grow the nest-egg now that he had a nest, so that they could afford to give the child the best of everything. He'd name his price right enough, and it'd be a high one.

He'd build a cradle (once they knew that everything was as it should be); a proper, old-fashioned one, so that Belle could relax in her armchair and rock it with her foot. He smiled at the memory of what pretty feet she had.

He listened to Gorby's plangent cries. It was mildly

irritating, but the noise didn't unduly distress him, because he loved the cat. How much more would he love his own child? Damn it, if the price of having his own true love was a sprog… They'd cross each bridge as they came to it, together. In his heart, all he'd ever wanted to be was the sort of man his grannie would have admired: a family man. His entire collection of cameras could be put to good use. He and Belle would have the best baby photo albums in the western hemisphere.

He turned the car carefully. 'Change of plan, Gorby old chap. Unless I've lost my touch entirely, we'll have you out of there in short order.'

And he headed back towards the A75, westwards towards Kirkcudbright, driving as fast as he could without breaking the speed limit.

When Mabel heard the door-knocker, she ignored it. She couldn't face anyone just now, not even Briony or any other of her friends. Then she heard a fumbling at the keyhole. She'd locked up after Fergus left, so that no one would disturb her, and left her key on the inside. Damn! He must have forgotten something. Maybe he'd only come to hand his keys back. He must have realised he still had them when he'd travelled a good bit of the road to Edinburgh. Then she heard the yowl of an angry, basket-bound cat. Archie, suddenly awake, shot from her lap and ran eagerly into the hall.

Mabel smiled in spite of herself, dabbed her eyes, and went through to let the rest of the family in.

ABOUT THE AUTHOR

Fiona Cameron was born in Glasgow, and has worked as a lecturer, journalist and PR consultant. She now lives in South West Scotland.

Her previous novels, all published by Flying Swan Press, are:

WHITE CRANES DANCING
CONTAINMENT
THE SWAN WIDOW
BY HEART

If you enjoyed A SENSIBLE WOMAN, and want to read more about Serena and Fergus's story, you'll find this in WHITE CRANES DANCING and THE SWAN WIDOW

All are available as e-books (Amazon Kindle plus other platforms) and paperbacks.

www.fionacameronwriter.com

Follow Fiona on Twitter @fionacamwriter

And on Facebook – Fionacameronwriter